11/02

HE KILLS
COPPERS

Also by Jake Arnott

The Long Firm

HE KILLS COPPERS

JAKE ARNOTT

First published in Great Britain by Hodder and Stoughton in 2001

Copyright © 2001 by Jake Arnott

First published in the United States in 2002 by
Soho Press, Inc.
853 Broadway
New York, NY 10003

Library of Congress Cataloging-in-Publication Data

Arnott, Jake.
He kills coppers / Jake Arnott.
p. cm.
ISBN 1-56947-271-8 (alk. paper)
1. Police—England—London—Fiction. 2. London (England)—Fiction.
3. Criminals—Fiction. I. Title.

PR6051.R6235 H4 2001
823'.914—dc21   2001020559

10   9   8   7   6   5   4   3   2   1

'For I ain't, you must know,' said Betty, 'much of a hand at reading writing-hand, though I can read my Bible and most print. And I do love a newspaper. You mightn't think it, but Sloppy is a beautiful reader of a newspaper. He do the Police in different voices.'

Charles Dickens, *Our Mutual Friend*

1956

Immediate Action Drill

1

Billy's hand rested against the trunk of a tree.

The tree was damp.

He felt along the ridges of bark.

Damp. Warm.

He sniffed his fingers. They smelt of piss.

Human piss.

He looked down. At the base of the tree wet moss bubbled.

He turned to the men behind him. A four-man Reconnaissance Patrol. Tony Wardell, Ronnie Allen, Chin Ho, their SEP tracker, and himself. Billy Porter, Service Number 32265587. Acting Corporal, Section Leader. Lance Jack. Not bad for a conscript. Drafted into National Service straight from Youth Detention. 1st Battalion of the Queen's Own Royal West Kent Regiment. Basic Training at Mill Hill and Canterbury. He found the discipline easy compared to borstal.

He caught the eyes of the rest of the patrol. Everybody froze.

He sniffed again. The sharp tang of urine cut through the funk of jungle humidity and he caught something else in his nostrils. A whiff of exhaled smoke. The unmistakable smell of Chinese cigarettes.

After Basic Training they were shipped out. Malaya. The Emergency. Anti-terrorist operations. Jungle bashing. Stationed at Kuala Kubu Bharu. Taken up-country in Whirlwind helicopters. Fighting Patrols secured rubber plantations and cut into the jungle to set up ambushes against Communist Terrorists. CT. The Charlie Toms.

Bandits. Seek out and destroy. They were on a four-day op in the Selangor valley. The Assault Group had sent out Reconnaissance Patrols to track down a CT camp in the area, fanning out into the jungle like the fingers of a hand. A Recce Patrol was supposed to avoid contact with the enemy, seek information and report back to the main patrol. But they had to be ready for anything. Billy was Patrol Leader. He had to decide what to do.

He leaned up against the piss-stained tree and gently pulled a vine to one side to look beyond. Three bandits were sat in a clearing, sharing a cigarette. Their rifles in their laps, they talked in singsong voices. He turned to the rest of the patrol and gave hand signals. A thumbs-down sign meant CT. He then held up three fingers.

If they withdrew now their movement might alert the bandits. They were so bloody close. If they started firing they could disclose the presence of the whole Assault Force. He only had seconds to decide what to do.

He gave the sign for Immediate Ambush. A hand placed over his face.

Immediate Ambush. This drill is designed to deal with an ideal situation, when there is no problem in gaining the initiative but rather one of making the best use of such an initiative. It is a drill which depends on a very high standard of discipline and training – and the ideal circumstances. Given these factors the killing potential is extremely high.

He pointed to where the bandits were. Tony and Ronnie moved slowly and silently into position. Tony crouched low and brought his .303 up to his shoulder. The clearing where the bandits were resting gave them a good killing ground. Ronnie found a standing position, his Owen gun held against his hip. Billy unslung his Sten and slowly and quietly cocked it.

This method demands high standards of jungle craft and self-reliance which can only be achieved and maintained by training and rehearsal.

It was Chin Ho, the SEP, he was most worried about. He had stayed crouched behind the rest of the group, staring ahead. SEP meant Surrendered Enemy Personnel. Chin Ho had spent nearly fifteen years in the jungle and it had taken its toll. He'd fought the Japanese with the MPAJA until '45, then the British with the Min Yuen until '55, when he had taken amnesty and had been used to hunt down his former comrades. He was a broken man. SEPs often reacted badly during an encounter. There were even cases of them leading troops into ambushes.

An Immediate Ambush should be sited only on one side of the CT line of advance to avoid confusion.

Billy motioned for Chin Ho to lie flat and got into position himself.

The automatic and split-second reaction to a chance encounter must continually be practised again and again under different conditions of terrain and varying circumstances.

All three of them had acquired targets and were ready for Billy's signal.

The Ambush should have depth.

They fired in concentrated bursts, spraying the whole clearing. The CT fell back in spasms as the bullets tore into them. Basic Jungle Warfare Course. Weapons Training. Classification Course Instructional. Shooting on the Classification Range, the Malayan Range, the Jungle Lane Range.

Good instruction and practice – the constant need for shooting practice cannot be overemphasised. If properly taught and coached on the Classification Range, a man will have learned to align quickly and to release the trigger steadily without dwelling on the aim.

They ceased firing. Gunshots echoed down the valley towards the Selangor river. The jungle clattered into startled life above them. They moved forward to check the bodies.

Brass everywhere. All the Patrol officers. The bodies were being searched. Identified. Recovered weapons and equipment lined up on display like a hunting bag. Chin Ho was jabbering away with the JCLO interpreter trying to keep up with him. Not sure if he could actually recognise any of the dead CT. Lots of pointing and crying hysterically. Jungle happy. A Special Branch Liaison Officer was supervising the identification of the dead CT. Everything would need to be collated for police records. The army, after all, were only assisting the civil authorities in their fight against insurgency. The ambush had occurred too far away from a landing zone for it to be feasible to evacuate the bodies by helicopter. So fingerprint kits were issued and an army photographer was on hand. Soldiers were detailed to clean the hands of the dead for fingerprinting. Others washed the faces of the bodies and brushed back their hair so that clear shots could be taken.

The rest stood about in groups talking. The officers in a huddle, assessing the situation. The commanders of the Assault Group and the Support Group in deep conversation. Billy stood near by. He'd already given the brass a short account of the engagement. He could hear the officers chattering away.

'They really should have reported back, sir. I mean, this action's rather given away our whole presence and position to the enemy.'

'That is if there are any other bandits in the area.'

'Well, we won't know that now, will we, sir? They'll be miles away by now.'

'Look . . .' It was the Company commander speaking. 'We can't afford to be dogmatic about operational conduct. We rely on junior leaders to make snap decisions. It's what they're trained for, for Christ's sake. It's what this whole bloody campaign depends on.'

'I'm just concerned about discipline, sir.'

'Well, morale is as important as discipline. They've bagged three bandits, for goodness' sake. We don't want the men to think that they've done something wrong, do we?'

The officers moved on. The Company commander patted Billy gently on the shoulder as he passed by.

'Good hunting, Corporal,' he said. 'We'll have a proper debriefing when we're back at base.'

The whole unit was buzzing with the dull euphoria that comes after a kill. Billy stood on his own, looking up at the canopy of the rainforest. The jungle too chattered away. Throbbing with life. Every living thing fighting for the light above. He lit a cigarette. His hand was shaking but his head was calm. Wonderfully calm.

1966

Breaking the Queen's Peace

Before the soccer thousands arrive . . .
'CLEAN UP' FOR WORLD CUP

Drive on London 'clip joints'

An intensive police 'clean-up' is being made of London's West End ready for the thousands of World Cup visitors who will begin pouring in this month.

A special 12-strong squad of detectives working at night with their own radio cars has been visiting 'clip joints' and coffee bars in Soho and Mayfair for the past two weeks.

Scotland Yard CID chiefs have approved the plan of Det.-Supt Ferguson Walker, West End CID chief, to organise a drive against confidence tricksters waiting to fleece the thousands of foreigners looking for a good time in the West End between World Cup matches.

Fruit juice

The 12 detectives, led by Detective Chief Inspector Leonard Read, one of the West End's two deputy CID chiefs, are to be reinforced as visitors begin to arrive for the first World Cup match between England and Uruguay at Wembley on 11 July.

The squad, operating between 9 p.m. and the early hours of the morning, has visited more than 20 one-room 'clip joints' where visitors are lured in – sometimes to one drink, usually a harmless concoction or a glass of fruit juice – and then asked for money on the false promise that they will be introduced to a girl.

The detectives have taken lists of names and addresses of girls working in these one-room 'clubs' and made inquiries to establish their ownership. At least one has closed following police inquiries, but detectives have learned of others planning to open.

Powerless

Frequent complaints from people who have paid sums of money, usually £5 to £20, or handed over 'tips' on the promise that the girls will meet them after the club closes, have generally left detectives at West End Central police station powerless to prosecute for obtaining money with false pretences.

The complainant usually is not prepared to lay a formal complaint or give evidence in court, and many of those who have gone to the police for help after handing over money are usually leaving London within a short time and cannot stay to give evidence.

11

2

A verbal.

It's always good to start with a verbal.

When giving evidence in court, that is.

A verbal isn't just subtly incriminating. It primes the jury. Sets the scene. Lets those twelve people know that there's been a wrongdoing. It sets the scene, all right. The scene of the crime.

A verbal is just a little bit of dialogue that you put in the mouth of the accused. Something he was heard to say just before, or just after, he was cautioned. Something tasty.

Who grassed this time? That's a good one. Read that out of your notebook in court and it places your man for them. It's about language, see? That's why it's called a verbal. The right words, well, they can place someone. You know what I mean? *Yeah, I done it but you'll never prove it.* Hasn't that one got a ring to it? You see, you're not allowed to mention previous during the trial so the jury isn't to know that the defendant is a villain. That would be prejudicial. But how else are they supposed to know that he's been at it in the past? Do a verbal and it puts them straight. Gives a bit of atmosphere to the proceedings.

It's not as hookey as planting actual evidence on a suspect. You ain't fiddling with the forensics as such. You're just planting the odd word or two.

That's a verbal.

So if this was evidence I was reading out and you wanted a good verbal, how about: 'On the evening of the second of July, Detective Sergeant Frank Taylor was heard to say to Detective Constable Dave Thomas: *Here comes trouble.*'

There. That sets the scene for you. Except it doesn't really count. Not as a verbal, I mean. You see, I actually did say it. I just didn't have any idea how fucking true it would turn out to be. But let's start at the beginning, shall we? Or at least the start of that day.

West End Central, Savile Row. C Division. Crowded Crime Room briefing. Nipper Read out front giving the spiel. Clampdown on vice in Soho. Reinforcements drafted in to swamp the patch. Subtle hints: West End Central needs a bit of a clean-out itself. The area has a reputation – nasty rumours abound about officers on the take. Newly appointed DCI Nipper wants to change all that, apparently. Wants to make his mark. Well known as an absolutely straight-down-the-line copper. Well liked by those who work under him. Short he may be, but tough and tenacious. A fighter. Lightweight boxing champion for the Met in 1950. Story has it that he did stretching exercises to beat the height regulations to get into the force. Transferred from the East End, still smarting after having his case against the Kray twins thrown out of court in the spring.

I'm there as part of the extra officers drafted in from all over the Met, crowded together at the back of the Crime Room. I'd just come out of the one-year Special Course at Bramshill College, waiting to go up to the Flying Squad. Part of the new Rapid Promotion Scheme. Eyed with suspicion by old-school coppers who'd been around longer and hadn't got as far. Not that I gave a fuck what they thought. Time-servers, most of them. I was a bloody good thief-taker. And I was ambitious. I knew where I was going and I didn't mind cutting a few corners to get there. I thought I was fucking clever, I really did.

Right next to me at the briefing was Dave Thomas. We went back. We were aides to CID together back in '62. F Division, Shepherd's Bush factory. Just out of uniform, temporary secondment to plain clothes. He was my partner. My buck. No closer bond, really, than the person you're teamed up with when you're trying to prove yourself to CID. It's a trial period when you're an aide. If you fuck up in that period you can be back plodding the beat in no time. So who you're partnered with, who your buck is, is dead important. We looked after each other. Watched each other's back. There was a shit-nasty DI in charge of us on Division back them. Three pairs of aides went back to uniform in one month. You had to get results. And we got them. Dave had the makings of a good detective, better than me, I reckoned. But he'd always play it dead straight. He'd never do a verbal or scriptwrite a statement.

I was more, shall we say, flexible. Not bent. Well, not bent for myself anyway. Bent for the job? Well, just a bit. Only when you know that they've been at it. When you know they've been at it a little too much and it's their time to go away for a bit. You know they're guilty but you might have to fit things up a bit to take them off the pavement. No harm in that. After all, they might have some smartarse brief who could get them off on a technicality. But Dave never saw it that way. Always wanted to do it all to rights. Impossible to get around him if it was a job we were working on together. And if he noticed anything the slightest bit hookey that I might be doing he'd have a go. 'What are you?' I used to say. 'My bloody conscience?' But he insisted that it wasn't the morality so much as that he didn't want to get into bad habits. Besides, he'd argue, if they're at it there'll always be another time to nick them properly.

And I'd never be bent in a bad way. I'd never take bribes or anything. Do deals for information or bodies, for sure. But never the bung. If you can turn a villain into a snout, well, that's the crucial part of being a good thief-taker. Knowledge, that's what you need.

And as things turned out, me and Dave made a good team. A good double act. Good cop, bad cop, a tried and tested formula. And we both made it on to CID permanent. But it was me that went up for Rapid Promotion. I was the ambitious one, you see. Dave just loved being a detective and wanted to concentrate on getting the experience. And the Bush was a good patch for that. Busy. But I wanted to get on. Did my Sergeant's and got on to the one-year Special Course at Bramshill. Came out made up to DS and just waiting for appointment to Flying Squad while Dave was still stuck in Divisional CID as a detective constable.

I gave him a nod at the end of the briefing. He smiled back and gave me a wink. He was still my buck – you don't break a bond like that. Nipper Read was dividing Soho up into nine different areas, two detectives to each patrol.

'Let's make sure we're working the same relief,' I suggested.

'Yeah,' he replied, still smiling. 'As long as you promise to behave yourself.'

Morale was good on Nipper Read's Clean-Up Squad. For those of us seconded for a fortnight or so there was a chance of a better arrest and clear-up rate than you'd ever get out on Division. Bound to look good on your record. And definite chances of commendations for those who excelled at nicking. But I was itching to get to the Flying Squad. Always a big ambition to work for the Heavy Mob. An élite team. But as temporary secondments go this wasn't at all bad. A bit of fun maybe. And it gave me a chance to work with Dave again.

The regular West End Central officers had already gone around the clubs and clip joints and given the 'warning formula'. Taking names down and letting the dodgy Soho operators know, in no uncertain terms, that their freedom to fleece the suckers was over. Showing the flag to all those Maltese ponces. But a lot of places clearly didn't get the message. Or else they felt the temptation was far too great. World Cup fever. Tourist season gone mad. The chance to make easy gelt from all the gullible fans that would crowd into the West End. And a lot of the foreigners weren't exactly innocent themselves. The draw of the Jules Rimet Trophy brought in con artists and tricksters from all over the globe. An international event. Fraudsters from Mexico and Venezuela, dipsters from Italy, drug-pushers from Holland and second-storey hotel thieves from

America. And as they preyed upon the crowd, so we preyed upon them. Me and Dave pulled a whole team of pavement artists doing the three-card trick on Tottenham Court Road. Nicked a pair of Argentinian pick-pockets on the whizz, Latin style, with their own particularly nimble little stall-and-hook routine on the tourists that poured out of Oxford Circus Tube. But it was the home crowd that was really at it. Clipping crazy. Just as one near-beer joint would be closed down through pressure from us, another would set itself up for business. And we'd be ready to play at being the punters, the suckers, the mugs.

'Here comes trouble,' I joked to Dave when this clip girl sauntered over to us.

That's when I said it. The verbal, if you like. We were on the corner of Brewer Street, just acting dumb, like we'd just drifted into Soho looking for a good time like all the rest of the tourists. If only I'd known then what trouble that girl would bring. We knew what she was, or at least what she was up to. But she was different. Not your usual dolly-bird type. She had mousey blond hair cut short, Vidal Sassoon style. She wore a low-cut top and miniskirt, but there was something altogether relaxed about her demeanour, something casual about her dress and the way she held herself. With most tarts it's all superficial. I mean, that's the whole point, isn't it? But with her, well, it was like you might not have noticed with your first look. But then the second glance. That was the killer. Yeah, then you'd see how beautiful she was and it was like you'd discovered her. It was *you* who'd seen how good she really looked.

'Looking for a good time, boys?' she drawled.

She had these huge mottled green eyes that looked us up and down. It wasn't hard to appear enthralled by them. And there was such a playful way she had of pretending. It made you enjoy the sense of being taken in. Acting innocent. Dave was always better at this than me, of course. And he was a handsome bastard, with his dark Welsh looks. He gave this bird a bashful smile and they just sort of clicked.

'I know this great club,' she went on. 'You could buy me a drink.'

Me and Dave sort of shrugged at each other, like we didn't know the score, and I said:

'Yeah, all right, darling,' with a lecherous tone to my voice. 'Why don't you take us there.'

Let me explain clipping. It has many variations. Sometimes it ain't exactly subtle. The most common variety is the Corner Game. Promise a punter sex but ask for money up front and arrange to meet them later. Then this silly cunt who's already parted with his cash is left hanging around at this supposed rendezvous with no fucking bird. Sometimes the mug is told to wait 'around the corner' (hence the name of the game) and that the money is a deposit on a hotel room, or whatever. Other times the arrangements are more complicated. Under the clock at Victoria Station is a well-worn favourite. Marble Arch, by Big Ben, outside the Ritz – at any number of tourist sites you'll find a clipped punter waiting in vain for a tom who's stitched him up. Nipper Read, in his briefing, said his favourite was Morden, right on the end of the Northern Line, where a poor Dutch seaman was waiting for a girl. He'd paid her £100 and still seemed completely bemused: 'Well, this is where she tells me she is living,' he had said. And although the clip girls don't have sex with punters, they can still be prosecuted under the 1959 Act, if you can prove that they are loitering for the purpose of selling sex. Soliciting. If they are working the Corner Game it is, of course, bloody hard to track them down. But if they are taking you to a club, a clip joint, well, then you can nick them there and then. And then turn over the club itself. They would've had their warning by now, after all. And anyone we didn't actually nick would be logged and cautioned, for the next time. Nipper was dead serious about closing these places down if they didn't get the message. So there we were with what we thought would be a simple job. Put the pressure on, maybe get a few tasty little arrests. Simple? It bloody wasn't simple.

Her name, she assured us, was Jeannie. And the place she was taking us to was described with as much playful confidence as 'a right kinky scene'. But the Pussycat Bar was a depressing place. A couple of bored-looking heavies on the door, obviously employed to stop people leaving too early rather than to prevent anyone entering its plastic bead curtain entrance. The low lighting in the dive couldn't quite hide the peeling flock wallpaper. Six chipboard tables, all empty, were covered with thin paper tablecloths. On a raised area, supported by what looked like beer crates, two tarts who'd long since seen better days did a listless bump-and-grind routine to chintzy organ music piped out on a crackling sound system.

Jeannie showed us to our table and a waitress sauntered over with the near-beer drinks list. I gave it a quick scan and winked at Dave.

'Let's push the boat out,' I declared, tossing the menu on to the stained table-top. 'Champagne!'

'Oh!' Jeannie gave this mock giggle. 'You certainly know how to have a good time.'

'We certainly do,' I agreed, and we waited, expectantly, for a couple of wineglasses filled to the brim with Tizer or fizzy grape juice.

I picked up the drinks list again and squinted in the gloom at the microscopic small print. 'All drinks are de-alcoholised by law,' read one line. And below it: 'Seated covers with a hostess warrants a hostess fee of £10. Acceptance to buy a drink for the hostess is done with the understanding that the customer is going to pay.'

The waitress returned with our drinks on an aluminium tray. All eyes in the dingy club were now looking sidelong at our table. A thickset little Maltese guy in a cheap suit and slicked-backed hair had come behind the bar to eye up his latest victims.

I picked up one of the dirty glasses of fizzy pop and proposed a toast.

'To Jeannie,' I said. 'Our hostess with the mostest.'

Jeannie half smiled, half frowned as she lifted her glass. I stared at her.

19

'Well, that's what you are, isn't it? Our hostess. That's what it says here.' I picked up the menu and flapped it at her.

If she was at all fazed by this she was bloody good at hiding it. She just smiled. Lovely teeth. Yes, she was good, all right. Too good for this cheap racket.

'Yeah,' she replied. 'I guess. Let's have another drink.'

'Yeah.' I downed the glass in one. Tizer. 'More champagne!' I demanded, clicking my fingers at the bored-looking waitress lighting a fag.

'The thing is, Jeannie,' I went on, 'my friend Dave here is looking for a good time. Aren't you, Dave?'

Dave gave his best nervous nod and grinned.

'Yeah,' he said, all wide-eyed innocent.

'And do you think, Jeannie, as our hostess for the evening, you could arrange something?'

Jeannie leaned across the table and ruffled Dave's thick black hair with another false giggle, her green eyes all wide and limpid. Dave squirmed, part act, part obviously affected by the seediness of the whole charade. I saw his deep brown eyes catch hers for a second. Like he was actually looking into her for something. For a moment it was fucking sad. The whole thing. But it worked. It looked like he was gullible. The waitress, fag in mouth, returned with a fresh tray of Tizer.

'So ...' I pursued my line of questioning. 'Could you sort something out?'

Jeannie straightened up and coughed, taking her hand from Dave's ruffled locks. She shrugged.

'Well,' she said, breezily, 'let's see,'

The Malteser was starting to hover around our table, making eyes at the boys on the door. Jeannie looked up at him and with a nod he came over.

'Well, can you, I mean, arrange something for me and my friend here?'

But Jeannie was looking up at the man with the slicked-back hair, who was by now standing at our table.

'Gentlemen,' he said tersely, 'it's time you settled your bill.'

We both looked up. I grinned. Dave folded his arms and gave a hard stare.

'Really?'

'Yes,' replied the Maltese. 'Concha,' he barked at the waitress. 'Bring these gentlemen their bill.'

The door heavies moved across to our table. Concha appeared with a hastily scribbled addition. It was placed on a saucer in front of me. *Champagne: £10/Hostess Fee: £10/Cover Charge: £5/Service Charge: £5/Total: £30.*

I picked up the bill and laughed. I handed it to Dave.

'You expect us to settle *this*?' I demanded.

The doormen were now on either side of us, looking menacing. The Malt laughed back at us and nodded slowly.

'Oh yes,' he replied. 'We most certainly do.'

I laughed again, and everybody joined in, even the door gorillas. But not Dave. He was looking at Jeannie with a frown.

'OK,' I said with a shrug. 'Let's settle this.'

I pulled out my warrant card.

'We're police officers. And you are fucking nicked.'

The Maltese blanched and backed off a little. I heard one of the doormen mutter *oh fuck* under his breath. Jeannie looked puzzled.

'Now, gentlemen,' said the Malt guy, suddenly all friendly and shit. 'Let's not be too hasty. Maybe you'd like a real drink. You do drink, don't you?'

Drink. Well, we all know what that means. A nice little enveloped bribe. I could see this was winding Dave up. I'd have been willing to say: *Sorry, son, not this time, we're on our best behaviour.* But Dave wouldn't have seen it like that. Then Jeannie really let the cat out of the bag.

'But,' she said, looking towards her boss, 'I thought we'd already paid.'

Dave's ears pricked up at this.

'What?' he barked.

The Maltese glowered at Jeannie. A slight shake of the head, an open-palmed gesture. Showing out to her to keep shtum.

'What?' Dave continued. 'What do you mean you've already paid?'

Dave was staring at Jeannie. The Malt leaned across to block his view.

'She don't mean nothing, Officer. Do you, Jeannie?'

'No. I mean, I meant, you, you know, have already paid.' She was thinking fast, this one.

'No we haven't,' Dave came back.

'Haven't you?' Jeannie's eyes lit up, all innocent. 'I thought you had.'

Dave frowned at her for a second and then stood up.

'You're nicked, darling.'

'What? What for?'

'Soliciting. Come over here.'

He led her away from the table. The Maltese followed. Dave turned on him and pointed a finger at his chest.

'You, you fucking stay where you are.'

Dave started to read Jeannie her rights. I went over.

'Dave,' I muttered sharply out of the side of my mouth. 'I don't want to start pulling rank here but do you mind telling me what the fuck is going on.'

'You hear what she said?'

'Yeah, I heard. So what?'

'I'm sorry, Frank. But I ain't standing for this.'

This was trouble we could do without.

'Come on, Dave. Leave it, for fuck's sake.'

'But you heard what she said. "We've already paid." You know what that means, don't you?'

'Well, I ain't stupid.'

'So?'

'So what?'

'So, what are we going to do about it?'

'I'll tell you what we're going to do. We're going to take their names, caution them, close down this filthy little joint and then call it a day. That's what we're going to fucking do.'

'But if we can get her to make a statement . . .'

'Saying what? The club bungs a bit of cash towards the Old Bill once in a while. So what, Dave? It happens all the time.'

'Yeah, well, I ain't standing for it.'

'And you want to start making a case against fellow officers?'

'Yeah,' he cut in. 'I know, Frank. I know. Turn a blind eye. Don't make any waves, it ain't good for your career.'

That stung.

'That ain't fair, Dave. You know I'm not bent.'

'Yeah, Frank, I know. And I also know you want to get on in the department. But listen. Any other time we'd have no fucking chance clearing up something like this. We'd be back directing traffic within a week. But we've got special circumstances. This operation is supposed to be cleaning up Soho. Top to bottom. If we can't catch these hookey coppers at it now we never can.'

I sighed.

'So what are you suggesting?'

'Take this bird in. Get a statement out of her and follow it up from there. Take it up to Nipper if need be. We know he's clean and wants this sort of thing dealt with.'

Nobody wants to deal with this sort of thing, I thought. But I didn't say anything. I just sighed again and shook my head. Trouble. Any luck it wouldn't lead anywhere.

'All right,' I agreed. 'You take her in and I'll clean up here. I'll see you back at the factory.'

So Dave radioed the area car and I went about taking names and issuing cautions. The Maltese guy gave a moody name. Arthur Springer. Malt ponces would often stick up English-sounding names as cover. I made a mental note to check with CRO for anyone using that alias.

I got back to West End Central and checked with the custody

sergeant. Dave was just finishing questioning Jeannie in an interview room.

'So?' I asked him as he came out into the corridor.

He shrugged and fished in his pocket for a fag.

'She hasn't said much.'

'You charging her?'

'Not yet.'

'You going to?'

Dave sighed and frowned. He took it all so fucking seriously
sometimes.

'I don't know, Frank,' he said. 'I was thinking of using her as
an informant.'

'For fuck's sake, Dave. A tart as a snout. That ain't a very good
idea, you know.'

There's an old copper's rule. The three Ps. Prisoners, Property
and Prostitutes. Any one of them spells trouble. You have to be
bloody careful. Standard procedure and common fucking sense.
Deal with any of these things in the wrong way and it's you that
can be made to look hookey. Especially a tart. She can make all
kinds of accusations as to how you've behaved with them.

'I know, Frank,' Dave went on. 'We've got to tread carefully.
But we're on to something here. Maybe we should take this upstairs.
Like I said, talk to Nipper about it.'

I had to stall all of this. The last thing I wanted was to be caught
up in a full-scale investigation against other officers. That sort of
shit sticks to you for good.

'Wait a minute, Dave,' I said, thinking on my feet. 'There's no
point going anywhere with this without a statement from her. I
mean, we haven't got much so far, have we?'

Dave took a drag of his fag and nodded.

'Yeah, you're right.'

'You want me to have a go?'

'Yeah,' he replied hesitantly. 'All right. But go easy.'

I grinned at him. Just like old times. Nice cop, nasty cop. Good
cop, bad cop. Except back at the Bush it was me that would go

first. Heavy into them. Shake them up, wear them down. Then Dave would appear with a nice cup of tea and a fag and a *tell me all about it before that nasty bastard comes back*. Best way to get them to cough something up. And here we were working it the wrong way around. Arse about front. And I thought, well, maybe this aint such a bad idea since I don't want her to talk. I want her to keep shtum. *Go easy*, yeah, sure, I'll go easy. I'll scare the stupid bitch into staying quiet about all of this nonsense.

I walked in and slammed the door behind me. She looked up. I'd made her jump a little but she soon regained her composure. I strolled in, slowly, staring down at her. She managed to hold my glare for a moment with those terrific green eyes of hers. Kind of flecked, they were. Like flint.

Then she looked away and chewed her lip. Crossed her legs slowly. Uneasy at first but adjusting into a more upright posture. Shaping up the front.

'How long you going to keep me here?' she asked.

'You ain't bad-looking, you know,' I said as I sat down. 'For a tart. Not been on the game for long, have you, love?'

'I'm not on the game.'

'You know what a tom looks like after a few years. The face starts to go first. It ain't a pretty sight.'

'I told you, I'm not a prostitute.'

'That right? Just clipping, is it?'

No response.

'Just a bit of fun, is it? Conning the punters. Bit of a laugh? Thing is, darling, all the clip joints are being closed down. The fun's over. And your boss might have other ideas for you.'

'What are you talking about?'

'He might want to set you up in a nice little flat. Get you working properly. Would you like that? Nice little flat in the cheap end of Mayfair, new punter every quarter of an hour.'

She tapped a finger against the side of her mouth. Nail varnish chipped on incisor enamel. I leaned over the table a little.

'Would you like that?' I said, a little louder.

'Look,' she snapped. 'I'm not a whore. You can't get me on that.'

I leaned back in my chair and gave a little chuckle. I was enjoying this.

'Oh,' I singsonged. 'Know your rights, do you?'

'I don't have to say anything.'

''Course you don't. I could verbal the statement for you. Look, darling, West End Central is coming down hard on vice. There's a permanent queue of tarts and ponces outside Marlborough Street magistrates'. One girl last week, she knew her rights. Decided to go to Inner London Sessions instead. She got three months. Fancy a stretch in Holloway, do you?'

'No, I don't.'

'Then start co-operating.'

'What do you want?'

'That's better. Your boss's name.'

'Arthur Springer.'

'And I'm the Queen of Romania. His real name.'

She shrugged.

'Attilio something. I don't know his second name.'

'And this business about him bribing policemen.'

Jeannie looked up at me. Flinty eyes wide. She looked worried.

'Look, please, I don't know anything about this.'

I nodded slowly at her.

'Good. We'll keep it that way, shall we? What did you tell my friend about that?'

'I didn't say anything.'

'That's right. You see, my friend has got it into his pretty little head that there's been some naughtiness beyond the usual going on. Now you don't know anything about this, do you?'

She shook her head slowly.

'That's good.' I grinned. 'You liked my friend, didn't you?'

She gave a flat little smile.

'He's a lot more nice than you are.'

Nice. For a moment her face was soft. Childlike. Just for that second she looked so serene. Beautiful. A horrible hunger deep inside. Desire. I thought about how much she must hate me. It made me feel empty.

'Maybe you'd give him one for free,' I said with a sneer.

Her face tensed with disgust.

'You're a sick fucker,' she muttered quietly, contemptuously.

I suddenly felt an unaccountable pang of jealousy. Couldn't place it. Then I thought: maybe Dave's fallen for this tart. Maybe this is what this is all about. I wouldn't blame him. I decided to wrap things up as quickly as possible.

'Well, Jeannie,' I announced. 'It's your lucky day. We're just going to caution you.'

I stood up and my chair scraped against the floor. Jeannie looked up at me, frowning.

'Come on, darling. We're letting you go.'

She walked around the table to the door. I blocked her path.

'You're right to keep quiet about your boss. Those fucking Maltese can be brutal. You know, I once saw a tart whose face had been striped with a razor. Right across. She obviously hadn't been behaving herself. Wouldn't testify against her ponce, though. Silly cow was terrified out of her wits.'

And then I let her pass.

'You want to get out of that business, Jeannie,' I called softly after her. 'It ain't healthy.'

Outside I had a quick chat with Dave.

'She ain't saying nothing,' I told him. 'I'm letting her go. That all right with you?'

'Yeah, sure,' he agreed, a little too readily.

I let Dave process her out. They walked down the corridor, chatting to each other. I felt jealous, sure, but also uneasy, there was a nagging feeling in the back of my mind. Something wasn't right or something was about to go wrong.

*

Sid Franks always liked there to be a nice story somewhere. Sid

27

was the news editor on the *Sunday Illustrated*. Human interest. Well, that's what it was all about. And amidst all the exposé and gossip you needed something reassuring, something sentimental. A feature that would make the female readership emit a collective sigh of delight. The 'womb trembler', he called it. 'Get me a nice picture of a baby, Eric,' he said one week to the picture editor. 'I'll find a way of putting it in'.

Elsewhere was titillation and scandal – morality through the keyhole. Some big exposé of contemporary importance (THE GREAT SHRINKING BANGER MYSTERY had been the most recent example of the paper's major investigative journalism). And the nasty stories. Something sordid – sex or crime or, hopefully, sex and crime.

'There you are, Tony,' Sid would say, handing me the TORSO MURDER or whatever. 'You'll like that.'

Sid maintained that I had a nose for a nasty story, and he was right. I have a morbid fascination for such things. There's something primal about them that I find reassuring. An infantile pleasure. It could be said that the whole of the *Sunday Illustrated* was an exercise in infantilism, but it was in this, I always thought, that the nasty stories were crucial. Horror is the most infantile feeling of all. A return to childhood when all stories are dark and sinister.

And maybe that's where it all began for me, right at the beginning. I'd had a traumatic birth. My mother never ceased reminding me what a difficult delivery it had been. When she wasn't saying *I've brought a monster into the world*, that is. But it was her fault. She'd nearly strangled me at birth. I'd nearly died, the umbilical cord tangled about my head as I emerged, a noose around my neck as I was pushed through the trapdoor. My birth a hanging, the long drop. Well, nearly. I got a last-minute reprieve, a stay of execution. A diligent midwife managed to unknot me before I choked. Otherwise my whole existence might have been dispatched there and then without too much fuss. Instead it was commuted to Life.

And maybe that's why I turned out the way I did. Difficult birth, difficult child. My poor stupid mother clinging on to me, always suspecting something sickly about me, something gruesome. I liked to collect things in jam jars. My specimens, I called them. Creepy-crawlies. I found a dead cat and brought it home. I wasn't sure what I was going to do with it – some infantile notion of taxidermy. Of course, Mother wouldn't let me keep it so I buried it in the garden. With full ritual, of course.

I suppose I'd always wanted to write. Ever since I can remember I was making things up, telling tales, nasty stories. But this creativity was never nurtured when I was a child, never understood. *You're a dirty little liar.* My own mother's words. Can you imagine the effect of such an accusation on a young mind? I did well at school but I got into trouble, an unpleasant business that meant that I left earlier than I might have done. I wasn't expelled but the headmaster asked me to leave. Mother was very upset but she never saw my side of the story.

I worked as a clerk in a pickle factory for two years. I did shorthand at night school and got a job as a junior reporter on the *Reading Mercury*. Not terribly exciting, I must say, but at least I was writing. I stuck that for a year or so but as soon as I'd saved enough money I came up to London and got away from Mother, at last. I had some mad idea that it was here that I would become a great writer. I got a cheap bed-sit in West London. Just a few meagre possessions – a Remington typewriter, a battered chest of drawers that I improvised as a desk. I was a loner. I'd always felt different, apart from people, like Colin Wilson's Outsider. I was an existentialist, I decided. As with Barbusse's hero that Wilson refers to, the Man Outside. I had come to the capital with 'no genius, no mission to fulfil, no remarkable feelings to bestow, I have nothing and I deserve nothing. Yet in spite of it, I desire some recompense.' I was meant to be a writer, I felt. This could be my revenge, my way of getting back at them all, my way of articulating my painful solitude. The problem was what to write about? I waited in vain for inspiration. I managed a half-finished first draft of a novel – derivative stuff, purple prose and descriptions of emotions I'd never felt. I couldn't bear to look at it. I kept it in a shoe box under my bed, collecting dust. I had this received notion that a novel should be somehow autobiographical, that fiction should be personal. But the very thought made me feel sick. I didn't want to write about myself, I had no desire to express my inner feelings. On the contrary. I wanted to use ink the way an octopus does, to hide.

The money ran out and I started doing bits of freelance journalism. I had the basic skills for it, after all. The gutter press was teeming with life, with stories. I found what I was looking for, a peephole to look through. I particularly liked crime stories, the more brutal the better.

I worked as a casual on the *Sunday Illustrated* one of the 'Saturday Men'. On the Saturday shift at the *Illustrated* the newsroom was crowded with casuals, extra staff brought in to get the paper to bed. The inside pages had already gone, so most of the permanent staff didn't have to be in. Sid Franks would pace up and down with a fag in his mouth, browbeaten. He always seemed to wear the same brown suit.

For the Saturday Men there was the day shift for ten guineas or you could work until three in the morning to make it twenty. A lot of the casuals worked on local rags during the week or freelanced for other nationals. I sold the odd story here and there but I hadn't had much luck lately and the Saturday shift had become my main source of income. I needed the money, and I also needed some sort of proof that I could write. And I still harboured literary aspirations. Here, perhaps, I could plumb the depths. I had this little thought in the back of my mind: if only I could find a story, a really big one, something that could get me out of Grub Street for good. Truman Capote had just published *In Cold Blood* that spring, the story of an actual murder done in full. The whole case in beautiful detail with no subs to hack it to death. True Crime executed as High Art. It was hailed as a new form – the 'non-fiction novel', they were calling it. Ken Tynan criticised Capote in *The Times* for waiting for the boys to go to the scaffold before finishing the book, but that was the genius of it. The story needed an ending. It was all done so objectively, as ruthless as the murder itself.

The *Sunday Illustrated* suited my purposes, but what I really wanted was a staff job. It was still nominally a Labour paper back then, but it was no secret that its new proprietor, who Sid Franks always referred to, half in derision, half in fear, as 'The Boss', wanted to make it more racy. Ted Howard was kept on as editor-in-chief to maintain a semblance of continuity and Sid Franks was made up as deputy to lower the tone. The old 'mission to educate' values dropped in favour of a more populist approach. But I'd never been interested in politics, just stories.

I'd been working in Soho that day, getting a bit of colour for the 'Clampdown on Vice' feature we were running that week. Alf Isaacs, the *Illustrated*'s 'snatch man', a photographer whose speciality was catching on film *in flagrante* those who were up to no good, had got a nice shot of a clip joint being raided by some of Nipper Read's Clean-Up Squad. A lovely picture of a clip girl being led out of a near-beer joint into a waiting area car. The circulation manager was a happy man – the northern working-class readership always lapped up vice. The Evils of the Capital, the decadent fleshpots of London – they loved that sort of thing.

I managed to catch Sid in his office. He hardly ever used it except for highly confidential meetings or to bawl out one of his minions. The staff always referred to it as the 'bollocking room'. Sid had started as a casual on the Saturday shift himself back when he'd worked on *Tribune* during the week. He'd once been a leftie, CP member and everything, but after '56 he'd torn up his card and had been moving increasingly to the right ever since. Now he constantly railed against the print unions and loved any excuse to do an exposé on 'pinkos, liberals, do-gooders'.

He'd just come from the Saturday conference. The Big Table, they called it. All the editors would hammer out that Sunday's edition with Ted Howard, still nominally editor-in-chief, with his Thermos flask and greaseproof paper packet of sandwiches next to him, nodding silently at the head of the table.

Sid closed the frosted-glass panelled door, sat down behind his desk and stubbed out his cigarette. He gestured at the seat beside me. He picked up a finished page on his desk and gave a pained expression. He sighed and waved it absently at me.

SUMMER SCORCHER, was the headline. *Crowds clamour for the coast as temperatures soar.* There was a picture of a girl in a bikini, caught in midair jumping for a beach ball with her chest thrust out.

'Look at that,' he muttered. 'Another of Franklin's titless wonders.'

Harry Franklin was the paper's main portrait photographer, specialising in the obligatory glamour tit pics. He was good at getting a photo of some near-naked bird in a salacious pose next to a flimsy excuse for a story, but for some reason he always managed to pick flat-chested girls.

'We're never going to get our circulation figures up unless he can get birds with bigger tits. I mean, what do you think of that?'

He thrust the picture in my face. I recoiled slightly. I never quite knew what to say about girls.

Sid shrugged and dropped the sheet on to his desk. There was a white crust around the corners of his mouth. He took sodium bicarbonate to combat nervous indigestion and his lips were regularly flaked with it. He squinted at me across the desk. I handed over my copy and Alf Isaacs' snatch of the clip girl being arrested.

'That's more like it,' he said, picking up the glossy. 'Now she's really got something. Good work, son.'

'Sid . . .' I began.

He looked up at me with a suspicious frown.

'What do you want?'

'Well, I was wondering if there was any chance of a staff job.'

He sighed and rolled his eyes.

'I'm a good reporter. You said so yourself.'

'Yeah, yeah. Well, you've got a nose for it, I'll give you that.'

'So?'

'Well, I thought being casual suited you. Gave you time to work on your masterpiece.'

When word got around the paper that I'd been trying to write a book it had become a running joke. I gave a thin smile.

'Look, son,' he went on, 'I'm running a tight ship here. I can't really afford to give out too many permanent contracts.'

He was right. It made better sense to employ a lot of casuals for the Saturday shift than to take people on a weekly basis.

'I think I'm worth it, Sid.'

'Oh, you do, do you?'

'Yeah, I do.'

'Well, if something comes up, I'll bear you in mind.'

'You'll think about it?'

'Look, if you come up with something really tasty' – he licked his powdery lips – 'if you can prove you're worth it, well, you never know.'

*

A mystery. That's what they called them. A girl come down South to escape God knows what drudgery. A runaway. No past, no history. A mystery. Looking for somewhere to stay. Easy to pick up. Easy to impress.

Billy noticed her first. He was sitting in a booth of the Ace all-night café on Goldhawk Road with Jimmy and Stan. They'd done a job that day and were flush with cash and still buzzing from the excitement of it all. She was at the back peering gloomily over a long-nursed cappuccino. Froth turned to scum on the glazed rim of the cup. Duffle bag on the seat next to her and a worn-out look on her young face. Telltale signs.

A couple of mod kids were showing off at the pinball table. Thrusting away with their hips as they tickled the flippers, like they were giving it one. Stealing glances over at the mystery girl to see if she was watching. She ignored them and lit another cigarette.

'We want to do something proper next time,' Jimmy was talking animatedly in a low voice. 'A bank. We want to do a bank. Need to nick a good motor for the getaway.'

Jimmy was always talking big. Stupid Glaswegian thinks he's

hard, thought Billy. Thinks he's the leader because he's the oldest. Hair scraped over his stupid balding head like Bobby Charlton. Billy had met Jimmy in the Scrubs. Always talking big plans in association or as they plodded around the exercise yard. They'd met up again earlier in the year and Jimmy had introduced him to Stan one night in the Hop Garden Poker Club in Notting Dale, and they'd all kind of teamed up.

Stan just sat there nodding. Docile. Some fucking gang, thought Billy. He was bored already. Sure, they'd screwed a bookie's that very afternoon. And he'd been the one waving the shooter around. He was the one that knew how to handle guns. Jimmy and Stan were hardly more than gas-meter bandits.

'Uh,' croaked Jimmy, nodding towards Billy. 'What you reckon, Bill?'

Jimmy sounded nervous. He was a bit scared of Billy but anxious not to sound like he was deferring to him too much.

'Yeah, sure,' replied Billy, looking over at the mystery girl.

They hadn't got much from the bookie's. Just over three hundred quid. Not many in the shop. Everyone watching the football. The England–Mexico game. Not many punters about, which made it easy, but also meant that there wasn't much in the way of takings. Bit of a thrill, holding the place up. Stocking masks, American Tan. Made the face look yellow and flat. Like a bloody Chinese. Bandits. Weird feeling, the head squashed into something that should be around a bird's thigh. The mesh wet about the mouth and nostrils. A bit kinky. The mystery girl was stubbing out the cigarette, picking up the packet of Park Drive. Empty. She let the hollow cardboard drop on to the Formica.

Billy got up to go over, picking up his fags from the table. The mod boys had their backs to him, in a huddle over the pinball machine. Bill saw a bag of purple hearts on the glass surface.

'This face I know works for Roche out at Welwyn Garden City. He's nicking 'em and selling 'em six quid a thousand down Wardour Street.'

The mod doing the talking was wearing a fishtail parka. *The Who* stencilled on the back. *Maximum R&B*. The Who? Who the fuck are the Who? thought Billy. An arrow coming out of the O. No fucking sense. The parka like a uniform. Jungle green. Army surplus. Like Billy. Surplus to requirements. They didn't want him. Tried to get into the SAS after National Service. He had a good record. Corporal stripes and plenty of commendations. He'd seen a lot of action. But his borstal form counted against him. He was offered a place in Two Para in the Territorial Army Regiment at White City. Territorials. Fuck that for a game of toy soldiers, he'd thought.

'Excuse me, boys.'

The parka mod scooped up the pills and turned around. Speed-nervous, jaw chewing away. Billy gave them a grin that brought out the scar below his right eye. Intimidate the little hooligans. The cold stare that says *I've killed people, you cunts*. They moved back. Gave Billy a wide berth. The mystery girl looked up.

She saw Billy, suddenly woken from her runaway reverie to clock his arrogant swagger. A hard man with a boyish face. Late twenties, she reckoned.

'You seem to be out of cigarettes,' he said.

'I was trying to give up anyway.'

He offered her one from his packet. She shrugged.

'Oh, go on, then,' she said with a tired smile. She pulled the cigarette out of the packet. Grubby fingers. Chipped nail polish, bitten cuticle.

'Mind if I join you?' he asked.

'Suit yourself.'

He sat down and lit her fag, lit one for himself. Tried to place her accent. Northern.

'Where you from, darling?'

'What's it to you?'

She was acting all tough. Like a kitten that puffs itself up for protection.

'Only asking,' he said.

'Leeds.'

'So, what, you've run away?'

'You're full of questions, aren't you?'

Billy smiled and took a drag from his cigarette.

'Give us another cup of tea, mate!' he called out over his shoulder. 'And what do you want?'

'Cappuccino.'

He grinned.

'Yeah. And one of those frothy coffees for my friend here. What's your name, love?'

'Persistent, aren't you?'

'Yeah, that's right.'

He knew all he had to do was keep chatting. Chatting her up. She was all alone in the big city. Nowhere to stay. In the end she wouldn't really have any choice but to come home with him. The café owner came over and put two steaming cups down on the Formica table between them. She stirred her cup thoughtfully and looked up at him.

'Sandra,' she said. 'My name's Sandra.'

'Pleased to meet you, Sandra. I'm Billy.'

She scooped a spoonful of froth into her mouth. A dab of foam stuck to her upper lip.

Billy watched her sleeping. Sandra was curled up with her thumb in her gob like a little kid. She'd hitch-hiked down from Leeds the day before. A lorry driver had dropped her off on Shepherd's Bush Green. 'What you come down to London for?' he'd asked her, and she'd just shrugged. He'd lit the gas fire and they'd undressed under the gloomy forty-watt bulb that hung unshaded from the ceiling of the bed-sit. She'd gone through it all without any fuss. Like she knew what was expected of her. A blank look on her face like that Chinese whore in KL. Afterwards they lay together on the bed for a bit. She traced the tiger tattoo on his right shoulder.

'That's nice,' she'd said. 'Never seen one like that before.'

'Had it done in Malaya,' said Billy.

Sunlight streaming through the dirty cutains. Picking out motes of dust in the air. He lit a fag. It was Sunday morning. He'd have to get going soon. He gave her a nudge.

'I got to go out.'

'Where you going?'

'Going to see me mum.'

'Oh.'

He didn't have time to get rid of her. Couldn't really take her to see Mum. Couldn't just kick her out.

'You can stay here if you want.'

'Can I?'

'Yeah. Just don't touch anything.'

Billy would always try to visit his mother on Sunday. It took him back to when it had just been the two of them. Little Billy. Mummy's little soldier. Mummy's little man.

He'd been born in the Red Lion Hotel in Wanstead. Just a big pub, really. Mum always wanted things to be better. She was always trying to make it work as a hotel. Dad just drank away the profits, bringing in all sorts of dodgy clientèle. Making it just a big pub again. Dad was supposed to be the manager. All he could manage was to get drunk by lunch-time. All sorts of things went on in the public bar. Dad used to fence stuff.

Rows, shouting matches. Little Billy at the top of the stairs listening.

Then Dad left. Came into Billy's room to say goodbye.

'I tell you what your mother is, son,' he muttered boozily. 'She's a whore.'

Billy didn't even know what a whore was. When he found out, he wanted to kill his father for saying it.

Business picked up a bit after Dad left. Mum had never realised how much of the takings he was drinking or spending on horses. Or dogs. Or tarts. But the brewery said that they couldn't stay.

They moved to Paddington. Mum got a job in a restaurant. Manageress. Put enough money aside to send Billy to a private school in South London. But he didn't fit in. The other kids laughed at his accent. They called him 'Southend Sid'.

He started getting into trouble. At fifteen he was on probation for receiving. Two years later he was done for assault with intent to rob. Eighteen months' borstal. Gaign's Hall, Huntingdonshire. A strict regime. Plenty of exercise and hard labour. He went straight from there into National Service.

After demob he got a job driving a van in North London. It bored him shitless. He got the sack when he was caught nicking from the warehouse. He met this girl who worked as a stripper in the Cabaret Club in Praed Street. Trixie. She had strung him along, let him spend his money on her. He'd drifted back into trouble again. House-breaking. He did a tie-up one night in a house on the Burma Road and the stupid old fucker wouldn't tell where he'd stashed away his savings. Billy had cracked a cut-glass decanter over his head. The old bugger had nearly croaked. Trixie got picked up on a soliciting charge and she'd grassed him up, the rotten bitch. He ended up in the Old Bailey. Robbery with violence. He got seven years. Wormwood Scrubs. He served four years eight months.

Sunday roast. Billy bought a bottle of Mackeson's for her and a large bottle of light ale for himself. Best linen tablecloth laid out. Napkins in silver rings he'd nicked in a house-breaking and given to her as a present. He'd carve.

'How's business?' she'd ask.

She'd saved up a grand while he'd been inside. Given it to him to start a business. He'd learned a trade in the Scrubs. Bricklaying. He'd also done art classes. This bloke had come in once a week to teach painting. Billy had loved that. The teacher had said that he had a 'real feel for it'. This had brought sniggers from the other cons and sneers from the screws. Billy didn't care. He found himself absorbed by it. Form and colour. The classes had lasted only a couple of months, though. Prison was all right. Eat your porridge every day, do your time the easy way. Discipline. He was used to that in the army. Coming out, he was supposed to just go straight. Mum was always worried about him. Gave him the hard-earned money to set up a little building firm. And he'd gone along with it. But it bored him rigid. He hated laying bricks. He hated walls.

He'd started to lose jobs and end up in all the pubs and clubs he'd frequented before he'd gone inside. He'd bumped into Jimmy in the Cabinate Club in Gerrard Street, and before he knew it he was at it again.

'Going through a lean patch, Ma. Bloody Harold Wilson's bad for trade.'

'Billy,' she said chidingly. 'You staying out of trouble?'

'Oh, don't go on, Ma.'

He got back to the flat at about four in the afternoon. She'd found the gun. Silly cow had found the .38 revolver. Billy had left it under the bed. The bloody thing was still loaded. He'd lost all his training discipline, he thought. Post-operational procedure. Zero your weapons. Armourer's inspection. He'd become fucking sloppy.

'Put it down.'

She held it up in front of him.

'Is this real?' she said, with a stupid grin on her face.

'Put that fucking thing down!' he barked at her.

She let it drop on to the dresser.

'How was your mother?' she asked.

He picked the gun off the chest of drawers and pulled out the cylinder. Bullets clattered over the floor.

'You ever shot anyone?'

He sighed.

'No,' he replied. 'Not as a civilian.'

A civilian. That was a joke. Demobbed and chucked out on to the street. Borstal training. National Service. Prison. He'd had no time to be a civilian. He felt the weight of the gun in his hand. It was reassuring. He could trust it. He couldn't trust Jimmy or Stan with their stupid plans for blags and capers. And he couldn't trust this northern girl.

He slapped her across the face and she fell on to the bed.

'I thought I told you not to touch anything,' he said coldly.

She started crying into the pillow like a child. He felt a bit bad about that. After a while he sat on the edge of the bed and stroked her shoulder. He put the revolver down carefully on the bedside table. He'd get another one soon. Maybe an automatic. Sandra was still sobbing. He ran his fingers through her hair.

'There, there,' he murmured.

The sobbing subsided. She was just a little kid, really.

'Shh,' he shushed, soothing his own mind with the white noise of it as he stroked her hair. 'Shh.'

3

I didn't have this Maltese ponce Attilio's second name so I couldn't request a file search from CRO. I had to go down myself. Scotland Yard. Central Office. Coco, we always called it. Looking for a body with only a first name to go on. I thought of going through the Method Index but I didn't have any particular MO for my man. Then I figured on cross-checking alphabetically. A lot of the Maltese would use English-sounding moody names but keep their first initials. For example, Alfredo Messina called himself Alfred Martin. Not exactly subtle. But then most detective work is looking for the bleeding obvious. You'd think that they'd be a bit more clever. Maybe they've got bad memories or they're scared of losing their identity or something.

So I went through foreign-sounding names starting with S. It took a bit of time but there he was: Attilio Spiteri, known to use the alias Arthur Springer. Checked the file. Blurred photo of him. On the form: convicted of Living Off Immoral Earnings in 1962. Malicious Wounding in 1956. Known associate of the Messina gang. Suspected of being active in prostitution rackets in Soho and Mayfair.

On my way out I nearly bumped into Vic Sayles. Flying Squad DI. Tall, dark-haired, charismatic man in a well-tailored suit. A reputation for cultivating snouts. Known as the best-informed police officer in the Met. My future Guvnor, I hoped. We'd worked together when I was in F Division and his team were plotting up an armed blag on our patch. It was him that recommended me for the Flying Squad.

'Sir,' I said, giving him a nod.

A squint, then a smile. Recognition.

'It's Frank Taylor, isn't it?'

'Yes, sir.'

'I thought you were coming to join us. There's a gap in my team. My best DS has just got promotion, the bastard.'

'Yes, well, sir, I've kind of been drafted into West End Central. They needed extra officers.'

'Nipper Read's Clean-Up Squad, is it?'

'Yeah. It's just for a couple of weeks. I'd much rather be on your squad, sir.'

'Well, I'll see if I can't hurry things along. Been at Bramshill, haven't you?'

'Yes, sir.'

'Could do with a college boy. Hope you're good at paperwork. I need a good scriptwriter. If you know what I mean.'

He gave me a sly wink. I smiled back.

'Thank you, sir.'

'Well, I'll be seeing you.'

He started to walk off. I had a sudden hunch. Sayles's encyclopedic knowledge of villains.

'Sir?'

He stopped and turned.

'What is it, son?'

'You don't know anything about a certain Attilio Spiteri, do you?'

'Spiteri. Let me think. Yeah. One of the Messinas' old gang, ain't he?'

'Yes.'

'Well, look, son, vice ain't exactly my manor. But I tell you what. You want to ask George Mooney. He's the expert. He knows all the Maltese.'

Tracking down George Mooney wasn't difficult. The Premier Club on Little Compton Street. Known for its mixed clientèle on both sides of the law. A bit seedy. A good place to get information, though. George Mooney, new DI at OPS. Obscene Publications, the Dirty Squad. West End Central used to be his patch. Known for heavying into the Maltese. Commendation for breaking the Ricardo Pedrini racket back in '61. A bit of a reputation for over-the-top fit-up tactics here and there. Rumours of him planting bricks in leftie demonstrators' pockets. A bit of bother with the National Council for Civil Liberties but nothing proved. A stocky man with cropped hair and beady little eyes. I introduced myself and bought him a drink.

'You at West End Central?' he asked.

'Well, temporary secondment. I just finished the Special Course at Bramshill.'

His little eyes lit up.

'Ah!' he exhaled. 'On the Rapid Promotion Scheme, are we?'

'Yeah, and I was going to Flying Squad but they needed extra officers on this West End operation.'

He nodded and pursed his lips.

'Nipper Read's Clean-Up Squad,' he announced with contempt. 'Yeah.'

'Shortarse Read. The new broom sweeps clean.' He grinned. 'But the old broom knows all the corners.'

Mooney tapped his nose.

'I used to work West End Central,' he said.

'Well, it was that I wanted to talk to you about,' I began.

'I tell you what you need to do,' he cut in. 'You have to contain it. Filth, vice, lustfulness. The sins of the world. You can't clean them all away. That's what that little cunt Read fails to understand. Nick them and they just start to fester again. You need to keep a lid on it. You have to deal with the temptations of the outside world but remain above them. One has to look within.'

'Sorry?'

He was starting to lose me.

'To keep oneself clean. There's none more pure than the purified.'

He sipped his Scotch thoughtfully.

'Anyway, it was your knowledge I was after,' I said.

'Really?' He smiled. 'What do you want to know?'

'I wanted some information on a certain Soho face.'

'Who?'

'Attilio Spiteri.'

Mooney's little eyes flickered for a moment but otherwise he remained impassive. He put his drink down.

'Oh yeah?' he murmured. There was a soft caution in his voice.

'You know him?'

'Yeah,' he replied. 'He was an informant of mine. What's the matter? Has he been at it?'

'Well . . .'

'Can't trust the spicks,' he spat with sudden venom. 'What's the little Maltese toerag been up to? Maybe it's time he went away for a bit.'

'Well, it's a delicate matter.'

'Really?' he asked with a prurient smile. 'What?'

'I've heard a little rumour that he's on the bung.'

Mooney picked up his glass and held it in front of his face.

'He tell you that, did he?' he asked flatly.

'No. Not exactly.'

'Because they do, you know. Always trying to implicate others in their sordid little ways. What did he say?'

His beady eyes narrowed into a piercing stare.

'Well, it wasn't him so much, just this tart we picked up who clips for him.'

Mooney looked thoughtful. He took a sip of Scotch. He swallowed and let out a sharp sigh.

'A woman?' he declared disdainfully. 'Well, you can't trust them, can you? Irrational creatures. She's probably lying.'

'You think so?'

'Second nature to them. Look, people are always trying to implicate police officers. It's an old trick.'

'So you wouldn't know about anything like this?'

'Certainly not.'

Mooney held up his empty glass. I bought him another drink. As I sat down next to him his little eyes darted around the room then settled on mine. He leaned closer.

'Are you on the level?' he whispered.

'Sorry?' I retorted, a bit indignant.

'I mean' – he smiled – 'are you on the square?'

Then I twigged. This was freemason talk. One of their codes.

'Er,' I replied hesistantly, 'no.'

'You know, West End Central, Vine Street, Bow Street, all of C Division. The Manor of St James, if you like. It's a forcing house, that's what it is, son, a forcing house. A hotbed of vice, wealth, deviousness of all kinds. A fetid place. It's so easy for a young officer to go astray. Temptation. You know what I mean, don't you? I mean the spirit is willing but the flesh . . .'

Mooney sniffed and gave a little shrug. I started to say something but he held up a hand and went on.

'You know what they say, don't you, son? If you're off the track, get on the square. You know?'

I nodded indulgently.

'You know what profane means, don't you?'

I frowned.

'Well, um, swearing and that, isn't it?'

'Blasphemy, yes, son, certainly. But it literally means "outside the temple". You get my meaning?'

'Well . . .'

'The profane world can drag you down. Through the Mysteries of the Craft you can keep yourself clean. The All-Seeing Eye of the Great Architect. *Lux e tenebris.*'

'Sorry?'

'Light through darkness. That's your actual Latin.'

'Really?'

'Ancient arcane knowledge. Oh, yes. There is a world within the world. And it can bring much comfort. I mean, the work that I do – all the filth, the sinful and beastly degradation I have to be witness to.

45

I couldn't do that without my lodge. It's a purifying thing. A column of mutual aid and support. Think about it.'

I nodded.

'A young officer like you amidst the fleshpots exposed to desires and temptations. You need guidance. Society has given up on moral standards. You know what I had to do this week? Investigate a so-called art exhibition. Pure filth. A group of dirty long-haired hippies have filled a gallery full of obscenities and called it art. Full-frontal nudity. We take them to court and they make a joke out of the whole thing. *Regina versus Vagina* one of these hippy rags call it. Charming. The thing is some of the so-called respectable papers take their side. Standards are falling. No respect for authority. Society has lost its way. One has to give up any arbitrary social notion of morality. The Craft teaches you to look to the restraining standards of morality that reside in one's own soul.'

'Really?'

'Oh, yes. You know what I do?'

'No.'

'I ask inside. This is the Path of Honesty.'

'Yeah, well . . .' I started, trying to change the subject, but he went on.

'More than you'll ever learn from college, you know. And it offers its own promotion scheme, if you know what I mean.' Mooney emitted a dark little chuckle. 'The Winding Stair. Believe me, if you really want to get on, get on the square.'

'I'm sure you're right,' I agreed. 'But about Attilio Spiteri.'

'What?' Mooney frowned. 'Oh yeah, that little slag. Want me to have a word?'

'Um . . .' I hadn't really thought. 'Yeah, all right,' I agreed.

'I'll find out what he's been up to. Now, listen.' Mooney leaned close to me, bad breath sweetened with Scotch. 'You could join my lodge if you wanted to. I could propose you as an Entered Apprentice. A rough ashlar. The stone that must be hewn and shaped. What do you say?'

His tiny eyes twinkled. I coughed.

'Well,' I replied hesitantly, 'I'll certainly give it some thought.'

'Good lad. Now, let me buy *you* a drink.'

*

'When they got rid of hanging it was an end of an era in crime reporting,' Sid Franks once told me. 'You just don't get the sense of drama any more. The place of execution. The wait for the last-minute reprieve which hopefully never comes. The long drop. There was this one freelancer, I knew, Harry Tibbs. Bit of a con man really. He used to get in to see the condemned. Not as hard as it sounds. He'd usually pose as a clergyman. I used to see him wearing a dog-collar in the Feathers on Tudor Street. He'd get all these letters off people waiting to hang and sell them to us and other papers. Good stuff, it was. Funny thing was he was an abolitionist. "I'm against it in principle," he said, "but when they get rid of it it's the end of my profession."'

The sense of completed narrative was all gone. A conclusion, that's what gives it all some sort of shape, makes it a story. Can't have a story without an ending. The climax, if you like (speaking of which, Sid also told me that he'd heard that a certain High Court judge would have an orgasm when he passed the death sentence. The Clerk of the Court would be instructed to have a spare pair of trousers ready whenever he was to put on the black cap, but that's beside the point), the End, that's the point. Life, well, it just doesn't have the same ring to it. That's why Truman Capote had to wait for the boys to swing and did nothing to help save them.

With particularly brutal murders the *Illustrated* would often call for a return to capital punishment. 'Bring Back the Rope' was one of Sid's routine editorial comments. And if not then Life should mean Life. A life sentence, it should mean something. Life should mean Life.

And he was calling for the noose that spring. The Moors Murderers were rich pickings, dark tales unfolding in what Jack

Appleyard, the *Illustrated's* northern correspondent, described as the 'sunless assize court of Chester'.

I got a week's freelance work with the paper. We were trying to buy up witnesses or family members connected to the killings, knocking on doors and leaving calling cards with a fiver tucked underneath. The *News of the World* beat us to it with David Smith, the main prosecution witness, who'd actually been there when Edward Evans was hacked to death by Brady. Promised him £1,000, after the trial, if the terrible two were convicted. So we ran a spoiler instead, denouncing these deplorable journalistic practices, discrediting witnesses and so on. An inside source said the police had found a diary of Smith's with the entry *people are like maggots, small, blind & worthless.* I liked that.

I managed to get a couple of days in the press gallery during the trial but it was Jack Appleyard's story. His style was flat and sombre. He did nothing with the extraordinary forensic evidence, the dog hairs found on Evans's anus, the photographs and the tape recordings. This was all rather played down. Instead he seemed obsessed with Myra Hindley's hair. 'Blue-rinsed and ash-blond, piled up in a sort of semi-bouffant' at the beginning of the trial and 'fresh-yellowed in a peroxide perm' at the end. The copy in double-page half-columns on pages ten and eleven squeezed between the advertisements for underwear and constipation cures.

Nylon Corselet at pre-Budget prices! A delightful corselet in Nylon Taffeta. Absolute comfort is assured with full length Elastic side panels.

In the dock they 'showed no emotion' as the sentence was passed.

RUPTURED But 'On-Top-of-The-World' Thanks to the NEW 'Autocrat' AIRMATIC RUPTURE APPLIANCE.

Life should mean Life.

I wanted to write something about the motivation behind the killings. I saw a twisted romantic angle, a classic *folie à deux*.

'*Folie à deux?*' Sid Franks had retorted. 'What the fuck's that, some French dance act with birds with their tits hanging out?'

'No, Sid,' I replied patiently. 'It's madness shared by two people. An obsessional relationship that leads to crime.'

'Well, we ain't having none of that. No explanations please. No "A Doctor Writes" with these two bastards. They're evil, pure and simple,' he declared, licking his crusted lips.

Pure and simple. Given the nature of my entrance into the world it seemed hardly surprising that I became obsessed with strangulation. My own nostalgia for the noose, my own lonely call to bring back the rope. I experimented from an early age with asphyxiation, on myself and on others. Just childhood playfulness at first, making each other faint on the playing fields, stuff like that. But with the onset of puberty I found that the pleasure of masturbation could be greatly enhanced with something tight around my neck, and with the thought of myself strangling somebody else. The mass murderer Carl Panzram enjoyed pain so much that he imagined that he was endowing it on his own victims, that he was bringing them joy as he killed them. The fact that I had similar thoughts frightened me. I began to want desperately to repress them, but I couldn't – there were too many things that gave rise to lustful visions in my mind.

Then one day, in the school library, leafing through Roget's Thesaurus looking for long words to show off with, I came across 'Punishment': *bodily chastisement, smacking, trouncing, hiding, dusting, beating, thrashing, t. of a lifetime, kicking, caning; whipping, flogging, birching; scourging, flagellation, running the gauntlet; ducking, keel-hauling; slap, smack, rap, rap over the knuckles, box on the ear; drubbing, blow, buffet, cuff, clout, stroke, stripe; third degree, torture, peine forte et dure, racking, strapado, breaking on the wheel, death by a thousand cuts.* And so it went on: *rack, thumbscrew, pilliwinks, Iron Maiden, triangle, wheel, treadmill, torture chamber, scaffold, block, gallows, gibbet, Tyburn tree, cross, stake, Tarpeian rock, hemlock.* I became more and more excited as I read all these awful things. The very words themselves caused a dreadful tumescence. But, I reasoned, if words could stimulate such feelings in me, then might not I be able to use their own power to articulate

49

and control my desires? I suppose it was then that I felt the lonely impulse to be a writer. It could be a salvation of sorts – I could write out my awful wishes, create word-hoards of my secret longings.

So if my imagination could be given a free rein in artifice I might be spared its degradation in reality. My nickname at school was 'weirdo'. Not a particularly cruel example of playground nomenclature. Being perceived as strange was a fairly good defence policy. I had crushes on other boys but I resolved to resist enacting any of my urges. But I gave in to what I thought might be a harmless fascination and it proved my downfall.

In a locked wooden cabinet in the biology lab was a stillborn baby in a jar, curled up in a cylindrical womb of fluid. I was transfixed by it. It reminded me of the 'specimens' I'd collected as a child and I wanted it. It seemed to glow from within when held against the light, wreathed in silvery bubbles, glistening with augury. Translucent skin, tiny hands clutching at the broken cord that was wrapped around it like a fouled anchor, lizard lidded eyes bulging with sleep. It looked so peaceful, so perfect. I felt a kind of jealousy of one dispatched at birth as I should have been. Can there be any worse fate than to be sentenced to Life? Existence is a cruel trick. Life should mean Life. The dead baby looked so calm, so much at peace, not like me, tormented and cursed. So I stole it.

The headmaster made a big fuss when they found out it was missing. It was a terrible crime, he announced in assembly the next morning. The culprit would be punished severely, he promised. Somebody blabbed and I was accused of it. But I denied it. The head said if I'd only admit to it, there and then, they could deal with the problem. Something was wrong with me to do something as sick as that. If only I'd come clean. Then I could be sent to the school psychiatrist or whatever, they could straighten me out. But I wasn't admitting to anything. They couldn't prove it, you see. They'd never find the baby. I'd buried it by the edge of a field, in the damp warm earth beneath an electricity pylon that hummed with power.

So I was asked to leave the school and it broke my poor mother's heart.

Another Saturday shift. The rest of the newsroom was buzzing with the World Cup game. Bloody football everywhere. England v. Argentina. It was a dirty game, though, that was some consolation at least. Argentina's captain sent off, police on the pitch as he'd refused to leave, the referee exiting the field with a uniformed escort at the end of the match.

'Dirty fucking dagos,' was Sid Franks' unofficial leader comment.

Alf Ramsey, the England manager, was himself outspoken about the game. The splash-sub led on the front page with: *'ANIMALS!' says Alf. Foul Play as Latin Lunacy plunges game into chaos.* A nice touch, we all agreed. But otherwise it was a slow news day and Sid only needed me for the one shift so I knocked off at ten. I arranged to meet Julian after work. The *Illustrated* was on Shoe Lane. I wandered down through Holborn into the West End.

Julian was another Saturday Man, though less of a regular than me. His real speciality was gossip. He'd wasted his youth by being kept by various rich queens, one of whom had said to him, 'Jules, what will you do for money once your looks start inevitably to fade?' And so he'd decided to write. He'd become quite well connected. He'd feed tidbits of scandal to Sid Franks and any other editor who was keen. What he really wanted was his own column, but he was too lazy and prone to drunkenness to get ahead. Always a slothful eye on the lookout for the easy way.

We usually met in the Casbah Lounge coffee bar but it had been closed down for the duration. The big Clean-Up had taken hold of Soho. Most of the clip joints and tacky dives closed up, hardly any girls on the streets. Or boys. We ended up meeting in a dingy drinking club in Piccadilly.

I'd first got to know Julian when I went back to his bed-sit on Portobello Road after we'd both done a second shift. We drank Nescafé and I talked earnestly about existentialism while he sat nodding at me languidly. In the early hours, his patience gone, he leaned over and patted me on the knee. I tried not to flinch. The sudden contact made me feel a bit sick.

'So tell me,' he'd said. 'Are you so?'

'So?'

'Yes.' He'd rubbed my leg. 'You know.'

I'd pulled back. So?

'I . . .' I coughed. 'I don't think so.'

'Then' – he'd smiled mischievously – 'are you TBH?'

'TBH?'

'You know. To Be Had.'

To Be Had. Was I to be had? I felt an awful tightening around my throat as we fumbled about on the sofa. Bad thoughts in my head. Horrible urges. Julian grabbed at my crotch. I was hard. I suddenly stood up.

'What's the matter?' he'd asked softly.

In proper crime journalist style I made my excuses and left.

I remained friends with Julian, though. He could be horribly bitchy and scathing, but when he wasn't too drunk he was quite entertaining.

That evening the talk was about Teddy Thursby, who'd just started to do an opinion column for the *Illustrated*. I told Julian how he'd made a pass at me. I'd been helping him get his copy filed and I'd noticed his intent, knowing gaze. 'You shouldn't be on a paper like this,' he said to me furtively. 'Let me take you to the south of France to meet Somerset Maugham. If he places his hand on your knee, do not recoil as you do with me.'

'Mmm, I know a thing or two about that one,' said Julian.

He noticed a man earwigging our conversation.

'*Vada the homi marconi*,' he hissed.

Julian still used this archaic homo slang. *Look at the man listening in*, he meant. *Marconi* being used to indicate a gesture of eavesdropping, hands to the ears like radio headphones. He glared over at the man, who shuffled away sheepishly.

Later on he chatted up a swarthy-looking man with lank greasy hair. They planned to go to a party somewhere.

'Want to come?' he asked. 'We might find somebody for you.'

'No thanks,' I replied.

'Go on,' he tried to insist. 'Live a little.'

Live a little. Life should mean Life. I walked out into the night. Piccadilly very quiet, the Meat Rack nearly empty. A few sad junkies huddled around Eros, loitering outside Boot's 24-hour chemist's, keeping their heads down. Tourists drifting in happy groups up through theatreland. Above, the flashing advertising hoardings, coloured lights pulsing, constellations spiralling over my head. My temples throbbed in drunken melancholia.

A young man in a denim jacket leaned by the doorway to an amusement arcade, a mop of blond hair, blue eyes that clicked with mine as I walked past. Pinprick pupils, voice hoarse and languid.

'Got a light?'

I struck a match. The boy's face underlit with phosphor flare, his pinched little face marvellously demonic. He was trying to look tough, a rough-trade act that might work on a timid old queen. The 'I'm-not-bent-I'm-rent' demeanour. Murderous thoughts in my head as he sucked at the damp pith of the filter tip and glared at me, his throat pulsing as he inhaled.

I hurried off to find a cab to take me home. Life should mean Life.

*

Billy had heard about this Greek guy who was selling. He arranged to meet him. The Dionysus Restaurant. Finsbury Park. Run by this big guy Tony. Rumoured to be part of Harry Stark's firm. A private room out the back. A bottle of Metaxas on the table. Costas, the seller, sat with a small glass in front of him. He stared at Billy intently. He nodded at the chair opposite. Billy sat down.

'Costas,' he announced, and offered his hand.

Billy took it and shook it.

'Billy,' he replied.

Costas poured Billy a drink.

'Tony says you are looking for something.'

He spoke slowly, with a heavy Cypriot accent.

'Yeah, that's right.'

'Well, I got something.'

'You got it here?'

'Yeah.'

'Well, let's have a look, then.'

Costas reached under the table into a toolbag on the floor. He brought out something heavy wrapped in a grease stained cloth. He rolled it out on the table. A pistol. Billy picked it up. The angled butt fitted into his palm pleasingly. He slid the magazine out and clicked it back in again. He worked the action on it. Brought it up to his eye to look along the barrel.

'Luger,' Billy named it. 'Nine-millimetre. Very nice.'

He weighed it in his palm. Held it up in front of Costas.

'Now, this wouldn't be the gun that shot George Cornell, would it?' he asked with a smile.

Costas grinned back. He had a blackened front tooth.

'No,' he said, shaking his head. 'No. It has been in my family for years. My uncle took it off a German officer before the partisans hanged him from an olive tree.'

Costas grinned again. Billy put the gun back down on the rolled-out cloth on the table. Costas looked down at it, then up at Billy.

'You know how to use a thing like that?' he asked.

'Sure,' replied Billy. 'I was in the army.'

Costas leaned back in his chair. He frowned across the table.

'Where you serve?' he demanded.

'Malaya.'

Costas leaned forward and picked up the gun.

'I was in EOKA,' he said, quietly. 'If you had served in Cyprus, I might have shot you.' He held up the gun. 'With this.'

'Yeah,' Billy agreed, smiling. 'And I might have shot you and all.'

They both laughed. Billy picked up his glass and held it up. Costas took his and knocked it against Billy's. They drank.

'So,' Billy went on, 'how much you want for it?'

4

Late relief with Dave. We had a fairly dull evening of it. All quiet on the patch. I didn't mention my little meeting with DI Mooney. I hoped he'd forgotten all about that girl. I couldn't quite get her out of my mind, though. Dave seemed quiet, pensive. But that's the way he is.

This German fan comes into the station with a complaint. Seems he's picked up this tart on Old Compton Street. They've gone back to his hotel room and she's whizzed his wallet. Familiar story.

'I do not understand,' he said. 'She seemed such a nice girl. And so good is the sex we were having.'

He gave us a description. She wasn't hard to find. There she was plying her trade in the same place. She was Indian or half-caste or something. Petite with delicate features. Very pretty. She didn't make any fuss when we nicked her.

But there was something odd about her. Something I couldn't quite put my finger on. She had this mannered way of talking. Exaggerated gestures. Play-acting flirtatious. There was no sign of the wallet. Dave was doing the reasonable approach and I was supplying a bit of threat as per usual.

'You're very sweet,' she said to Dave. 'But I like your friend better. He's *so* tough.'

She was taking the piss.

'Look,' I cut in, with an edge to my voice. 'This is getting us nowhere. Let's go and get a WPC to search her.'

Well, she just rolled those big brown eyes of hers.

'I think you better do that yourself, big boy,' she drawled, her voice just a little bit too husky.

Then I twigged. I started to laugh.

'What's up?' Dave asked.

'Well, for a start,' I said, 'we're going to have to charge our friend here with importuning, not soliciting.'

'You mean . . .' Dave was wide-eyed. Slow on the uptake, but he'd been a bit vague all evening.

'That's right honey.' She-who-was-really-a-he fluttered his eyelashes. 'I'm a talented girl.'

The German tourist was shocked when we told him.

'This, this cannot be so,' he spluttered. 'I am not believing this.'

I did a quick frisk which gave the little tranny an excuse for more camp nonsense. But we didn't find the wallet. Understandably, our foreign visitor didn't want to press any charges. So we just did the fairy for importuning for an immoral purpose.

'You're very convincing,' I told him. 'On the face of it.'

'So are you, darling,' he replied with a wink. 'So are you.'

We came off duty at about three in the morning. I asked Dave if he wanted to go somewhere for a drink.

'Nah,' he replied. 'I'm going to get off.'

I wanted to have a bit of a chat. We hadn't really talked much that relief. That business with Jeannie kind of hung in the air between us. Unfinished. I found myself brooding about the situation. About her. I wanted her off my mind. And I relied on Dave. I could trust him. I could trust his judgment. Usually. But with this thing, well, I wasn't so sure. I wanted to tell what I'd found out about the ponce, Spiteri. That maybe we should go up against him. He was the real villain, after all.

'Come on, Dave,' I pressed him. 'Come for a quick one. We could do with it.'

'Not tonight, Frank,' he replied wearily. 'I'll see you tomorrow night.'

I don't know what it was that made me follow him that night. Dave kept himself to himself, for sure, but we were pretty sociable with each other. I just felt there was something edgy about him. It made me worried. And suspicious.

I watched him leave the station. He walked in the opposite direction from where he'd parked his car that evening. Something was up and I was on his tail.

Now, it ain't easy tailing somebody on foot at the best of times. It makes me laugh when you see it done in films or on the telly when they are, what, fifteen yards behind the person they are following. I mean, that's a fucking joke. And with an experienced detective like Dave was, I had to be bloody careful. But the West End is a maze of little streets so I let Dave get to the end of the road he was on and hoped that I could judge which way he was turning, catch up and watch him again from the next corner. I felt like a fucking rubber-heeler. Checking up on him like that. A fellow officer. A friend.

He went along Clifford Street and crossed over Bond Street into Mayfair. Curzon Street. Shepherd Market. A row of prostitute flats. Dave rang the buzzer of one of them. I saw him talk into the intercom. Another buzz and Dave pushed the door open. He went in. I watched all of this with incredulity. Dave was the straightest copper I ever knew. What the fuck was going on?

A light went on in a third-storey window. I could make her out. The short-cropped hair. Jeannie. It was her. She had ended up just where I said she would. She was opening the door of the room for Dave. For a minute I could see the both of them in profile. I felt sick. Dave gone over the side with this tart. Good cop gone bad. That's what this was all about. And I was jealous. I wanted her. I wanted her even more seeing her with him.

Jeannie went to the window and pulled down the blind. I'd seen enough anyway. I had a horrible sinking feeling. Like I wasn't sure of the ground beneath my feet. I mean, Dave, for Christ's sake. Mooney was right, I thought, the West End had a bad atmosphere about it. Vice duty could drag you down. Take you over the side.

I went up to the flats. A row of buttons by the door. Third floor was marked NEW YOUNG MODEL. I pressed second floor: FRENCH LESSONS. The door buzzed to let me in.

I flashed my warrant card at the tart on the second floor and ushered her back into her flat.

'Close the door and keep your mouth shut,' I told her.

I crept up to the next landing. Ear to the door. I could hear them.

'There's nothing much I can do unless you make a statement.'

'But I'm scared. Your friend's right. Attilio's a real nasty bastard.'

'How did you get involved with someone like him?'

'I was working as a go-go dancer in this club in Paddington. He took me out. We had a really good time together. Then he got me clipping. It was a laugh, at first, then, when the clip joint got closed down, he made me work here.'

'Made you?'

'He beats me. Threatens me with worse if I don't do what he says.'

'Look, Jeannie, you've got to get away from all of this.'

'Help me,' she pleaded.

'I will. But you've got to be prepared to testify against him. Look, think about it. Keep in touch. You know how to get hold of me.'

I could hear Dave walking towards the door.

'Stay for a while.'

Her voice soft, plaintive. Touching him, holding him.

'No, Jeannie.' Dave's voice clear, definite. 'That ain't what I'm here for.'

'Please.'

Dave at the door. I crept up the next flight of stairs and flattened myself against the wall. The door opened.

'Don't go yet,' she said. 'I'm frightened.'

He patted her shoulder tenderly. Gentle, innocent.

'Look, Jeannie, we can work this one out. Call me.'

And he was gone. I waited until I heard the front door slam and then went down and rapped on her door. She opened it. She was wearing a silk red kimono thing.

'Hello, darling,' I said.

A gasp of shock. Flinty eyes flashed. Pinprick pupils. Probably doped.

'You,' she said. 'But Dave said . . .'

'Dave doesn't know I'm here. I followed him. I thought he was up to something.'

'What do you want?'

'Aren't you going to let me in?'

She stared at me with a slight sneer. Then a little smile opened up on her mouth.

'Yeah,' she drawled. 'Sure.'

We went inside. The room was bare-bulb bright. A cheap Formica sideboard with a bottle of Johnny Walker's on it. A mirror screwed to the wall by the bed.

'So, what did Dave say?' I asked.

'What?'

'You were about to say. "Dave said", you said.'

'Oh yeah.' She sounded vague. Acting dumb or just stoned. Or both.

'Well?'

'He tracked me down. Wanted to ask me some questions. I said what about that bastard partner of yours and he said it didn't involve you.'

So Dave didn't trust me on this one.

'Want a drink?' asked Jeannie, picking up the bottle.

'Yeah,' I replied. 'Why not? He tracked you down?'

She gave a bitter little laugh.

'Yeah. It wasn't difficult. You said yourself that this is where I was headed. He wants to help me get out of here. Isn't that sweet?'

I stared at her. A head full of ugly thoughts. She handed me a glass.

'But you,' she went on, 'you're not like that, are you?'

She pulled at her gown, showing a shoulder and part of a breast.

Creamy white skin brought out by a purple bruise on the top of her arm. 'You want this. Don't you?' she taunted. 'You want a free one.'

She smiled, her mouth slashed with lipstick. I drank down the Scotch in one.

'Come here,' she said. 'You'll do just as well. Better.'

'What are you playing at?'

'Come.'

She grabbed my lapel and pulled me over to the bed.

'Look.'

She nodded at the mirror, loosening the sash of her gown. The kimono thing came open, exposing her naked figure. I watched her and me staring out from the glass.

'Me, you, me, you.' She pointed and chanted like a child doing dibs. 'All four of us. Quite a party.'

'Whatever you're on, darling, you ought to go easy.'

'Oh yeah. I go easy. Come.'

She pulled me down on the bed and ran a hand down my front to the fly of my trousers. Unzipping me with an ugly little laugh. I was hard.

'C'mon, honey,' she whispered, huskily. 'I'm supposed to be nice to you.'

I tried to kiss her on the mouth and she pushed me away.

'Uh, uh.' She grabbed my head and turned it to the mirror. 'Keep watching the show.'

I knelt over her as she scissored her legs around me. She arched her back and, lifting her hips, guided me into her.

'This is what you want, isn't it?' she taunted.

She went through the motions. Talking dirty to make me come quickly. Coarse oaths, pretend ecstasy. Easily learned. Me panting and thrusting blindly. Full of need. Part of my brain hating it all. Hating her. Hating me. The rest of my head sick with desire. Hungry. Eating up all of the hatred, lustily. I looked down at her. She pushed my face towards the mirror again.

'Keep watching,' she said.

I saw my face in the glass. All clenched up. Blood thumped around my head in a steady rhythm. Beating it into blackness. Calm oblivion for a second then a sharp dawn of the senses. Red haze then white light, bare-bulb sharp.

All over. I felt all choked up. She sighed and pulled away from me. Lit a cigarette. I stood and did up my trousers.

'Well,' she said, mouth wreathed with smoke. 'That was easy enough. Got what you wanted?'

I raised a hand to slap her then let it drop and ran it across my face. My mind dull. Her face tightened then straightened out to stare back at me. Flint eyes. Cold, hateful.

I got out of there. As I went I noticed a silver-grey Ford Consul parked up with somebody in it. Someone else was plotted up. Watching.

Dawn. Birdsong in Soho Square. The sun coming up over the grimy city. I got a Sunday paper and found an all-night caff open in Tottenham Court Road. Breakfast. I barely had the stomach for it. Match report from the England–Argentina match on the front page. A dirty game.

*

Julian became my only confidant and a pretty unreliable one at that. He wasn't exactly known for his discretion. I tried to explain to him that I was more than just queer. But he didn't really understand. I'd allude to my actual proclivities and he'd just giggle and make some fatuous remark. He thought I was just 'kinky', as he'd put it. But at least there was some fellow feeling between us, a kind of *esprit de corps* against normal people. 'The norms,' Julian would call them dismissively. 'Look at them all, norming about.'

The *Illustrated* ran a feature, HOW TO SPOT A HOMO, a while back. There'd been another spy scandal and a lot of talk about the danger of queers in security-sensitive postitions. The article had expert advice from a 'psychiatrist' who was actually Dr Kenneth Forbes, the *Illustrated*'s resident drunken quack, who'd narrowly avoided being struck off by the BMA back in the fifties and was usually responsible for the 'A Doctor Writes' column in the paper. Various 'types' were identified and all sorts of clues offered as to how to 'pinpoint a pervert'.

THE MIDDLE-AGED MAN, unmarried, who has an unnaturally strong affection for his mother. THE CRAWLER. THE TOUCHER. The man who has a consuming interest in youth and is ready to give ALL his spare time to working and talking with boys or youths. THE FUSSY DRESSER. THE OVER-CLEAN MAN. The man who is ADORED BY OLDER WOMEN. The man in the bar WHO DRINKS ALONE and is forever looking at other customers over the top of his glass.

Julian found the whole thing hilarious and sent it up terribly. He could somehow get away with being camp and flamboyant. I think the rest of the shift were a bit scared of him. And Sid Franks tolerated him because he always felt he could verify scandal and gossip. 'Say what you like about these poofters,' he once confided to me after a few drinks in the Three Feathers, 'when you're checking those kinds of facts they're rarely wrong.'

'Anybody with a grain of sense can *smell* the homos among these men,' the booze-ridden Forbes assured the readership. But I made sure nobody sniffed me out. I could not have chosen a profession in which being queer was more of a handicap than it was in Fleet Street. Its morality was that of the saloon bar. Every sexual excess was spoken of and usually bragged about just as long as it was 'normal'. I managed to passably imitate this demeanour. It wasn't difficult, going along with the comments about 'crumpet', the jokes about queers and pansies. They wouldn't find me out – I was to be nobody's 'type', nobody's specimen.

*

She began to notice how badly he slept some nights. Twisting about in the bed. He'd tense up and mutter hoarse oaths. His face clenched up in fear and aggression. He was back in the jungle. She knew that much about him now. He'd said something about it once when he'd woken up in a cold sweat, screaming. But he didn't like to talk about it much.

It wasn't easy living with him. The bed-sit was small and only half furnished. But it was better than the back-to-back in Hunslet where she'd come from. Her bedridden father drunk half the time. Invalided from an industrial injury in a cardboard box factory in Kirkstall. Sickness benefit didn't go far. Dad crippled and full of hate. Banging his stick on the floor of the bedroom when he wanted something. Swearing at Mum, leering at her. Finding any excuse to touch her. Calling her his *little princess*. She hated him and she hated Mum for putting up with it all. But Mum couldn't help it, poor cow. Trapped, she was. I'll never be trapped like that, she promised herself. She got a job on the broken biscuits counter in Woolworths in the town centre. She'd go out with her girlfriends on a Saturday night. Get chatted up by lads who might splash out on a brandy and Babycham and try to impress her with some tired old patter in the hope of a knee-trembler in one of the shop doorways on Briggate. There's got to be more to life than this, she thought. She dreamed of escape.

And one morning she simply upped and left with just a holdall and the little bit of money she'd saved. She had no idea of what she would do, of what would happen when she got to London. But at least her life had some sort of story to it.

Billy had called her a 'mystery'. She got to know that this was what guys in London called runaways. Strays. No past. Easy to prey on. Easy to get rid of. Cheap. But she liked the word. It was romantic to her.

Billy wasn't easy to live with. Moody. Always liable to fly off the handle. She learned quickly not to ask too many questions, not to touch any of his stuff. Especially his guns. He'd regularly take them out, strip them down and oil them lovingly. She knew that she should have been more frightened of all of that than she actually was. She understood it somehow. How he loved these little mechanisms of power. The way their parts clicked together was so satisfying, so reassuring. And Billy would show her their differing principles. Automatic. Revolver. Spring-loaded magazine. Rotating cylinder. An automatic was faster, Billy explained, but if it jammed your whole magazine was fucked. A revolver was slower but more reliable. And it left less forensic. No cartridge cases all over the place. But it took longer to reload. Have one of each. Billy insisted, and you're sweet. She was determined not to be scared by all of this. Billy had been in trouble before and would probably be in trouble again. She didn't care. In fact, for the moment, she found it all quite exciting.

It was a hot summer. She had thought about looking for work but Billy always insisted that they wouldn't have to worry about money. She'd get a job when the weather turned colder, she decided. In the meantime she could enjoy the sunshine. She felt carefree for the first time in her life. She knew that it couldn't last. She'd spend whole days with Billy. Going into the West End. The city was full of people showing off the latest fashions. She got Billy to take her to Carnaby Street. He bought her a multicoloured minidress. They spent the afternoon lazing about by the Serpentine Lido. Watching people in the hazy sunlight. She liked the childish sense of freedom in the air. The Swinging City. The Beautiful People. Of course, Billy had no truck with these types. 'They ought to bring back National Service,' he'd mutter resentfully. But Sandra felt that he was a lot more exotic than any of these so-called rebels. On the inside, at least.

In the evening they went to Shepherd's Bush Odeon to see *The Glass Bottom Boat* with Doris Day and Rod Taylor. In the cool darkness Billy held on to her hand. A stupid Hollywood film. Technicolor. People don't fall in love like that, she thought. Love isn't like that. Love is – she squeezed Billy's hand as she thought this – desperate. She felt cleverer than the brightly coloured images up on the screen. And more romantic.

5

I went to see Nipper the next day. I thought hard about what I was going to say to him. I didn't want to drop Dave in the shit, just get him away from the West End. I figured Nipper would simply want it nipped in the bud and just transfer him back to Division, sharpish. I wanted a transfer of my own, too. I wanted to get to Flying Squad sooner rather than later. And I wanted to get out of West End Central. Away from her. Jeannie kept nagging at my mind. It was me that had gone over the side. And someone had been watching that night. Someone plotted up in a motor.

'I'd like a word, sir.'

I towered over him. He smiled and nodded at a chair.

'Well, sit down, son.'

Nipper sat on the edge of his desk.

'So, what's this about?' he asked.

'Well, it's the DC I'm working with, sir. He's kind of got a bit friendly with one of the girls.'

It was an easy lie. Nipper sighed and shook his head.

'Oh dear,' he said.

'He's a good officer, sir. And a good detective. It isn't like him. It's just . . .'

'He's given in to temptation. Well, it happens.'

'I don't think there should be a disciplinary or anything, sir.'

Nipper nodded slowly then looked straight at me.

'So, what do you think I should do?'

'Send him back to his own factory.'

'Out of harm's way?'

'Yes, sir.'

'Right. Well, that's probably the best course of action. Thanks for bringing this to me swiftly, son. I can't afford to jeopardise the operation. I'll deal with it.'

He stood up.

'Another thing, sir.'

'Yes, son.'

'I wondered if I might be taken off this particular duty too, sir.'

Nipper frowned at me.

'Why's that, son?'

'Well, with respect, sir, the operation hardly needs so many officers any more. Soho's never been so clean.'

'Yeah,' Nipper nodded, thoughtfully. 'But for how long? I guess I could spare you too. Where are you?'

'Well, I was about to go to Flying Squad when I was seconded to you.'

'Oh, yeah. You're the Bramshill boy, aren't you?'

'That's right, sir.'

'Keen to get on?'

'Yes, sir.'

'Ambitious?'

'Well, I guess so, sir.'

'Not too ambitious, I hope.'

'I love the job, sir.'

'Well, that's the main thing.'

Late relief. Orders had come through transferring us from the operation. We went for a drink. Now Dave did want to talk.

'I don't understand it,' he said as I brought a couple of pints over to our table. 'What the fuck's going on?'

I sat down and took a sip of beer. I let out a sigh.

'Well,' I said, 'they don't need so many bodies on this job any more. It's all quiet on the West End front.'

I smiled. Dave didn't see the joke. He supped away, brooding.

'Look, it's nearly all over. It's the final on Saturday. Most of the tourists are on their way home. The whole of West One is as clean as a whistle. We ain't needed. I'm glad to be out of it, if you ask me. If anything they'll need extra Old Bill to protect the referee, if that Argentina game's anything to go by.'

'But they haven't transferred any other officers. Just me and you.'

'Well, Nipper's probably reducing the squad gradually, you know? Anyway, if we beat Portugal Tuesday we'll be in the final. Do you reckon Ramsey will play Greavesie?'

Dave frowned at me.

'I didn't come for a drink to talk about the football, Frank.'

'Right,' I said flatly.

I traced a finger around a circle of liquid that my pint glass had made on the table.

'So,' I went on, 'what's on your mind, Dave?'

'Did you know about this?'

'About what?'

'About us getting transferred.'

'Look, Dave, if you must know, I had a word with Nipper.'

'You did what?'

'Certain things were getting out of hand.'

'You can say that again.'

'Look, mate, I know you've been to see that tart Jeannie.'

Dave stared at me. Fierce.

'I told you I wanted to find out what was going on with that clip joint,' he said.

'And you didn't think to tell me that you were actually going to do anything about it?'

'No.'

'You didn't trust me?'

'No. To be honest, Frank, I didn't.'

'Thanks a lot, mate.'

'Well, let's face it, you weren't exactly keen to do anything about this, were you?'

'Do anything? Do anything? What the fuck have you been doing? Visiting whores off duty? You're well over the side on this one.'

'What do you mean?'

'Well, it just looks like you've got a thing for this bird. The way you've been going at it. It looks well dodgy.'

Dave looked at me pityingly.

'You really think I'm like that?'

'It don't matter what I think, Dave. If anyone else found out what you'd been doing, what would they think, eh?'

Dave shook his head.

'You're such a cunt, Frank.'

'Look, even supposing anything was up, do you think anyone's going to believe the word of some cheap tart? Allegations against serving officers? Do me a favour.'

'So it was you, wasn't it?'

'What?'

'That asked for this transfer.'

'I was protecting you, Dave.'

'You were what?'

'How do you know that this girl wasn't trying to set you up? She's a clever bitch, that Jeannie.'

'You bastard,' said Dave quietly, and stood up.

'Look, Dave, stay and have another drink. I didn't mean it to turn out like this. But it's for the best, mate. Really it is.'

He started to walk out.

'Dave!' I called out after him.

'Goodbye, Frank,' he said, without looking around.

*

The 'rich and rare' is another of Sid Franks' favourites. Strange but true, believe it or not stuff that was always a staple of the *Illustrated* which the splash-sub would have fun with. LAWN ORDER – a man sells his house but takes all the turf from his garden when he moves;

THUGS BUNNY – a public house's pet rabbit, brought up with dogs and imagining itself to be one, savages an after-hours intruder. Sid would often think that the particular eccentricity of some of these stories was wasted on the great unwashed. 'This story is too good for our readers,' he'd say. 'They just won't appreciate its rich and rare quality.'

And summer, of course, was traditionally the silly season. It was also, that World Cup summer, when people started talking about 'Swinging London'. There had been that *Time* magazine article in the spring and suddenly even the yellow press had terms like 'groovy' and 'with-it' turning up in its copy. Julian was allowed the occasional fashion spread for the *Illustrated*. He decided to investigate the 'Beautiful People'.

Of course, with the West End Clean-Up clampdown, Soho wasn't actually that swinging. So he ended up dragging me along to the homo haunts on the King's Road instead – Le Gigolo coffee bar and the Hustler, with that ridiculous motorbike hanging from its ceiling.

And our own area had become fashionable now. I was living in a crumbling rooming house in Walmer Street. West Eleven, the Bed-Sit Jungle. Half the street had been demolished to make way for the new Westway flyover. To the west was Notting Dale, a white working-class enclave; White City, dog track and dodgy council estate. To the east was the black ghetto between the Groves, Westbourne and Ladbroke, West Indians everywhere. The Polish woman in the flat below complained that things had gone bad ever since *Rachman got the schwartzes on the de-stat*. White long-hairs into jazz and bluebeat; hippies, attempting to look cool as they nervously hung out in the shebeens and record stalls around the Grove and the Gate, trying furtively to score a 'quid deal' of grass. Squats and communes sprouted up here and there, multicoloured graffiti on the crumbling stucco of the half-derelict mansions along Elgin Avenue. Protest, that's what they were all talking about. And Letting It All Hang Out. I didn't like the sound of that. Keeping It All In, that was my slogan. I lived there because it was cheap. Julian loved the atmosphere. I think he hoped that these long-haired bell-bottomed types might be TBH.

There were other expeditions. We went to the El Rio on Westbourne Grove. We sat awkwardly amidst the lively atmosphere of the place, West Indians grouped noisily around tables eating chicken with rice and peas, drinking Cockspur rum they'd brought in themselves. There was the sound of dominoes being noisily slammed on a table at the back. We were the only white men in the place. A peroxide blonde and a ginger-haired girl were being chatted up enthusiastically in the corner. We were eyed up suspiciously. Julian began to put on his coquettish act. I kicked him under the table.

We were harassed by this young dealer and ended up purchasing a quid deal. Julian was very keen to try it. We went back to his flat and he clumsily assembled a joint.

'Come on,' he said with a smile, 'let's "turn on".'

I wasn't so sure. I didn't want to mess about with my mind. But we both ended up smoking this horrible, reeking stuff, coughing and spluttering.

Nothing seemed to happen at first.

'Think I'd prefer a pink gin,' Jules declared, and then collapsed into a fit of giggles.

I just felt a bit nauseous and a nasty paranoid state descended upon me. Julian talked of a new magazine he was getting involved with, an 'underground' publication. He was their token queen, it seemed. In his heightened state he was burbling on about colours, offset litho printing. Why didn't I get involved? he was asking. They needed writers, they were having a meeting next week. Why didn't I come along? There was a party afterwards. A Happening.

The room went into a lurching spin. I went out to the bathroom and retched into the sink. My head throbbed with horrible demons.

*

He took her to see Mum. Sunday dinner. Billy seemed more nervous about it than Sandra was. He made such a fuss. He wanted her to look as smart as possible. It was a special occasion. He bought wine and put on his best suit.

'Has Billy been behaving himself?' Billy's mum asked Sandra.

'Oh, Ma, please,' Billy interjected.

'Well, he's fallen in with a bad lot in the past. He needs someone to look after him. Someone to keep him on the straight and narrow.'

'I can take care of him, Mrs Porter,' said Sandra.

Billy's mother smiled.

'Call me Lily, dear,' she said. 'Everybody does.'

Lily asked Sandra all sorts of questions. She lied about her age and the fact that she'd run away from home. Lily asked Billy how the business was going.

'It's looking up, Ma,' he said with a smile. 'We got a big job coming up.'

After the meal Billy took a cup of tea over to the armchair in the corner and read the Sunday paper. Sandra went to help Lily wash up in the kitchen.

'He's a good boy really,' Billy's mum explained. 'It nearly broke my heart when he went inside. He's always been up to something, has that one. I tried to do right by him. Sent him to a good school but he got thrown out of there. He treating you right, dear?'

'Yeah.'

'All I ever wanted was for him to do well for himself. To better himself. I never had the chance. I just wanted him . . .'

Lily's voice broke into a sob. Sandra saw that she was crying. Her hands were covered in suds and so she was dabbing at her eyes with her wrists. Sandra went up to her and, wiping her hands on the dishcloth, patted her on the back.

'It's all right, Mrs Porter,' she said softly.

'Lily, please.' Lily snorted up tear phlegm. 'I'm just a silly old woman.'

'No you're not, Lily,' Sandra lied.

'Come on,' Billy's mum announced, pulling herself together. 'I got something to show you.'

She led Sandra into the front room. Billy was slouched in the chair reading the sports page. He glanced up. His eyes were dull, cold.

'Been having a natter, have we?' he asked, and slurped at his tea.

'Look,' said Lily, taking a photograph album down from the shelf. 'You can see what he was like when he was a kid.'

'Oh, Ma,' Billy complained. 'For Pete's sake.'

The two women sat on the settee, poring over the pages, cooing at the images of infant Billy. Billy sighed and looked sheepish. Sandra thought about how his mother had spoiled him. Doted on him. *Silly old woman.* It hadn't done him any good. One of the pictures showed Billy, aged six, dressed up in a little army uniform.

'Look at that,' said Lily. 'Mummy's little soldier.'

A hot, muggy night. It brought the jungle back. Tangled up in other memories. Playing in the woods when he was a kid. The tension of being on patrol merged with the dark excitement of childhood games. Insurgency, counter-insurgency. Hide and Seek. Seek Out and Destroy. *If you go down to the woods today, you're in for a big surprise.* Count to a hundred. Moving slowly and silently through dense rainforest. Always alert. Always ready. *Remember Track Discipline. DO NOT signpost the route with litter, such as cigarette packets, sweet papers, cigarette ends and waste food. All these should be kept and burned. DO NOT while away the time by plucking leaves and breaking twigs – this blazes a trail.* Boys playing at war in the forest. *If you go down to the woods today you'd better go in disguise.* Count to ten. Identification of Dead CT. The bodies of the dead bandits they had killed being prepared for photographing and fingerprinting. *It must be borne in mind by Security Forces at all times that while the killing of individual CT is in itself a worthwhile object, the identification of the body may be of even greater value.* 'Smile, please,' somebody joked. The bodies being searched. Sometimes men took some sort of trophy off a dead enemy when the officers weren't looking. For good luck. *Picnic time for teddy bears.*

Landing Zone. A Whirlwind helicopter clattering above like

a huge insect. Rapid Eye Movement. Flickering into life. Billy was semiconscious. Coming to the surface. Trying to debrief his thoughts. After the ambush in the Selangor valley he'd given a full report to his CO. All the details of the engagement. Then on to the range. Whenever troops had fired their weapons in contact with the enemy, they were sent out on to the range when they were back at base. It was an opportunity to correct any mistakes made in an ambush. There was a tendency to aim high, at the light face of a bandit, rather than at the body. A tendency for each member of the patrol to select the same target. There were misfires and stoppages through failure to clean, inspect and test weapons and magazines. It was never said, but Billy suspected, that being ordered on to the Jungle Range after a kill was a way of depersonalising the whole process of killing. Making it routine and systematic again.

The sun streamed in through the dirty curtains. Billy blinked at the light. Sandra snored softly beside him. He rubbed his face; his mind felt drained from his dreaming. Everything was so vivid there, so alive. Intense. Malaya was still more real than the dull grey city that he awoke to.

6

Last day at West End Central. Paperwork to finish off. I tried to find Dave but he wasn't about. Or else he was avoiding me. Instead there was a message for me from George Mooney. He wanted to meet me in the Connaught Rooms in Great Queen Street. I suddenly remembered the business about Attilio Spiteri. I'd forgotten about him. Maybe Mooney had found something out. He said he was going to have a word.

At first I figured, well, that's all done with now. But then I thought about that greasy little ponce and all of my anger and frustration kind of got fixed on to him. It was all his fault. This whole business had soured things between me and Dave. It had got out of hand and I was fuming about it. Someone, as sure as fuck, was going to pay for all this aggravation. Too late to nick him since I was no longer on the patch. Officially, that is. But I wanted to get him. It had all started with him. And her, of course.

Jeannie. I couldn't stop thinking about her. The purple bruise on her china-white skin. He'd done that. Spiteri. His hands on her flesh. Anger mixed with the sickening feeling of lust I had for her. And something else. An empty feeling. The look of contempt on her face as I did up my trousers. Humiliation. A sad longing that I couldn't throw off.

She gave me so much grief.

Horrible confusion. I'm not a complicated person. I'm a police-man, for fuck's sake. College didn't prepare me for anything like this. All I wanted to do was get the bloody job done. To get on. But everything seemed skewed. I couldn't fathom it. Dave was the one person who I could talk to about shit like this and I'd gone and blown it with him. He'd always been so solid for me. Kept me on the straight and narrow. Well, tried to, anyway.

I was glad to be getting out of the West End detail. Flying Squad would make sense after this, I thought. Going after the heavy villains, not dealing with ponces and tarts. But this was unfinished business. I wanted to get that bastard.

I cleared out my locker and chucked all my stuff in the boot of my motor. I went off for this meet with Mooney.

Covent Garden. Found a parking space on Drury Lane and walked down. The huge, dirty-white Masonic Temple looming over Great Queen Street. Of course. Mooney had been fannying on all the time about me joining his lodge. My first thought was: we'll soon put him straight there. Then I chewed it over in my mind.

As I walked down the street the Temple got bigger. The great ugly power of it bearing down on me. And I thought: why not? I wanted to get on and no copper had ever done his career any harm by being on the square. Far from it. And maybe there was something to all that mumbo-jumbo after all. Maybe I needed something that could make sense of things.

I got to the Connaught Rooms and ordered a double Scotch. A group of business types were filing through the hall, all carrying little briefcases. Mooney was at a corner table. He gave me the nod and I went over.

'Good news,' he declared. 'I've got a seconder.'

'Sorry?'

'A seconder. To initiate an Entered Apprentice to the lodge you need a proposer and a seconder. Well, I've put your name forward and got somebody to second the proposal. They're always keen to have serving police officers among the Brotherhood.'

'Look, sir . . .' I began.

His little eyes blinked intently.

'You said you'd think about it.'

'Yeah, but . . .'

'I've arranged it all. I'm a Worshipful Master of the lodge, so I've been able to make it all really simple. We can do it today. What do you say?'

'Well . . .'

'You given it some thought?'

'Yes.'

'So what do you say?'

'I'm not so sure.'

'I'm disappointed, son. I thought you were a bright lad. Think what you could gain by learning the mysteries of the Craft. Think what you could lose by missing this opportunity.'

'What do you mean?'

'Well, you're off to Flying Squad soon. You want to get on, don't you? Want to make sure that you make the right friends? There are lots of brothers in the old Sweeney Todd, you know. Half the Squad's on the square.'

He leaned across the table.

'You're lost, son,' he whispered intensely. 'I can tell. You need guidance. A true path.'

'I just need time to think, sir.'

'Well, I rather think it's time you made up your mind, son.'

There was a gentle hint of threat to his voice.

'What do you mean?'

'This Spiteri business. There's been a rather disturbing development.'

I didn't like the sound of this. Mooney pulled out a large bluff envelope. He handed it to me.

'Have a look at that, son.'

I reached in and felt a glossy surface. A photograph. I suddenly felt queasy.

'Go on,' he insisted. 'Take it out.'

It was a black-and-white print. A man and a woman having sex. Bodies. Faces. My face clenched with need staring into the mirror. Staring out of the photograph.

'Oh, fuck,' I blurted out.

'You really are off the track, aren't you, son?' Mooney muttered furtively. 'You need to be cleansed of these iniquities.'

A two-way mirror. I thought these things only existed in cheap thrillers and scandal sheets.

'I was set up.'

'Indeed you were. Spiteri and his whore were trying to entrap your colleague. It seems they got you instead.'

'What does he want?'

'Well, he wants you and your jumped-up little DC to leave a few things alone. Luckily he approached me. It would be terrible for something like this to fall into the wrong hands.'

Mooney glared implicatingly. I felt sick. I tried to reason my way out.

'It's all sorted. I got me and Dave transferred off Nipper's squad.'

'That's all straightened, then. And I'm sure that I can persuade our Maltese friend to see sense. Of course, as a serving officer in the Obscene Publications Squad, I should really be holding on to this as evidence.'

His thin lips twisted into a nasty smile.

'You wouldn't . . .' I began.

'Wouldn't what? It certainly counts as material that would tend to corrupt or deprave persons exposed to it. I have to do my duty.'

'What do you want?'

'Want? What do I want, son? I want to help you. And you are in sore need of help. A lost soul. I see it as my duty to help my brother officers that have fallen by the wayside. You need the purification offered by the sanctity of the lodge. Say you'll join and I'll have no more said about this filthy business.'

Mooney stared right into me. Beady eyes, hypnotic. Offering me a way out. A way in.

'You've got promise, son. I can see that. Ambition. The Craft will nurture that. You'll go farther than me in the job, I know that.

One day you might even be my guvnor. But I'll always be a higher degree in the Craft.'

Mooney's implication was clear: I'd always owe him for getting me out of this mess.

'So what do you say?'

'OK.'

'Good lad.'

'Just one condition.'

He frowned.

'Name it.'

'I want the negative.'

Mooney nodded thoughtfully.

'Yes, well, we should be able to get that from Spiteri. Let's go and see him now. Then we can be back in time for the ceremony.'

We took Mooney's car and drove over to Soho. Spiteri's flat was on Greek Street. Arthur Springer on the name-plate. Mooney buzzed and gave his name. We were let in and we went upstairs.

Spiteri looked edgy. Wary of looking me in the eye.

'Hello, son.' Mooney's voice all fat-copper jovial, nodding over at me. 'I believe you've already met Detective Sergeant Taylor.'

Spiteri grunted an affirmative. I stared him down.

'Well, my colleague has agreed to deal with this business off the record. He's had that DC that was snooping around transferred off the patch.'

'That's good,' said Spiteri, managing a weak smile in my direction. 'No hard feelings, eh?'

I glowered at him.

'The thing is,' Mooney went on, 'my friend here wants the negative.'

'Hang on a bloody minute,' Spiteri replied. 'That wasn't part of the deal.'

'What do you mean?' I demanded.

'I keep the bloody negative. It's my insurance.'

'Now that's not very friendly,' said Mooney. 'Don't you trust us?'

'I don't understand, Mr Mooney. This wasn't part of the plan.'

Mooney suddenly punched him hard in the stomach. Spiteri doubled over, wheezing.

'You have the right to remain silent,' Mooney intoned softly. He nodded over at me. 'Go on, son,' he implored.

I kicked Spiteri's legs from under him and he collapsed into a sprawling heap on the floor.

'Please, no,' he groaned.

'Don't get above yourself, son,' Mooney told him. 'You're my informant. I run you. You understand?'

'That's not true,' Spiteri sobbed.

'Oh yes, my little darling. Oh yes. A nasty little grass. Uncle Georgie's snout. Wouldn't be very nice for you if that got around, would it?'

Mooney turned to me, his face glowing.

'Discipline,' he hissed. 'That's what these people need. Discipline.'

He pulled out his truncheon. He bent over and prodded at the prone figure beneath him.

'Maybe Mr Wood wants a word, eh?'

He swung the club against both sides of Spiteri's lower back. Aiming at the kidneys. There were nasty retching sounds.

'And you can tell your bosses,' Mooney panted, a little out of breath from his exertions, 'they're finished. The Messinas are finished. Understand? I might have moved to OPS but this is still my patch. I say what goes. You got me?'

Spiteri whimpered in compliance. He vomited. I caught a whiff of bile. Mooney wrinkled his face in disgust.

'Fucking spicks,' he muttered. 'Only way to deal with them. Now, the negative.'

Spiteri crawled across the floor and pulled himself up on the arm of the chair. He pulled open a drawer and took out an envelope. I snatched it off him. A small brown negative was inside. Mine and Jeannie's ghostly figures just visible as the afternoon light caught it. I fumbled in my pocket for my cigarette lighter. I touched the flame against the edge of the film and it soon caught. I dropped it and it zigzagged down to the floor, smouldering. We left Spiteri groaning and muttering in the chair with a smell of sick and burned celluloid in the air.

Out on the street Mooney seemed in a good mood. Whistling merrily as he got his car keys out. I got into his silver-grey Ford Consul and we drove back to the Connaught Rooms.

I wasn't feeling quite so jolly. I felt a bit jittery from the violence. Adrenaline. *Well, that's what you wanted, wasn't it?* I said to myself. But it just made me feel anxious. I thought about betrayal. Myself betrayed by Jeannie. No, that wasn't right. It wasn't as if there was anything between us except my own obsession with her. No, I had betrayed. I'd betrayed Dave and my own instincts as a copper. We'd never found out who Spiteri had been paying off. Not that any of that mattered any more.

And I wasn't looking forward to this ceremony thing. My mind started to race. Mooney was jabbering away as we sped along Shaftesbury Avenue.

'Some lead, others grovel,' he was saying. 'You'll learn that in the lodge. The Brotherhood respects all social distinctions. Some must rule, others must obey and cheerfully accept their inferior positions. You're ambitious. You know what it takes to get on. Not like that goody-two-shoes DC of yours. He ain't going nowhere.'

There was a connecting passage from the Connaught Rooms to the Grand Temple. We went down this corridor into a little vestibule. There was a bloke in full regalia waiting for us.

'This is the Tyler,' Mooney told me. 'He will prepare you.'

I was told to take off my jacket and tie and my right shoe. Mooney unbuttoned my shirt while the other man rolled up my left trouser leg and my right sleeve. Some sort of slipper was put on my left foot. Mooney slipped a noose over my head and pulled the knot snugly at the back of my neck. I shuddered.

'Don't worry,' he whispered. 'It's the cord of life. New life. New birth. Now the hoodwink.'

I was blindfolded.

'I must go and prepare myself,' he added.

Darkness. I was being led. *This wasn't part of the plan*, Spiteri had said. What did that mean? Mooney had laid into him after he'd said that.

The man who led me knocked on a door in front of us. I could hear muffled voices in the room beyond. The door finally opened.

'Whom have you there?' a voice droned.

'Mr Frank Taylor,' another voice responded. 'A poor Candidate in a state of darkness who has been well and worthily recommended, regularly proposed and approved in open lodge, and now comes of his own free will and accord, properly prepared, humbly soliciting to be admitted to the mysteries and privileges of freemasonry.'

There was a murmuring of voices throughout the room. Someone put the point of a blade against my chest, just above the heart. Cold metal against bare flesh. I took a sharp gulp of air.

'Do you feel anything?' someone asked.

'Yes,' I replied.

The blade was taken away and I was led by my right hand until my knees touched a chair or a stool.

'Mr Frank Taylor, as no person can be made a mason unless he is free and of a mature age, I demand of you, are you a free man and of the full age of twenty-one years?'

It was Mooney's voice.

'I am,' I replied.

'Thus assured,' he went on, 'I will thank you to kneel, while the blessing of Heaven is invoked on our proceedings.'

I knelt on the seat in front of me. I could hear shuffling around me, feel myself being surrounded by the people in the room.

'Vouchsafe Thine aid, Almighty Father and Supreme Governor of the Universe . . .' Mooney droned, chanting a litany of words.

My mind drifted again. Spiteri denying that he was Mooney's grass. Mooney wanting him to keep quiet. Going on about the West End still being his patch.

'. . . and grant that this Candidate for freemasonry may so dedicate and devote his life to Thy service . . .'

Mooney standing over Attilio Spiteri, his face beaming. Whistling a little tune and jangling his car keys after we'd kicked a man half senseless.

'. . . by the secrets of our masonic art, he may be better enabled to unfold the beauties of true godliness, to the honour and glory of Thy holy name.'

'So mote it be,' came another voice.

The car. Fuck, the car. The silver-grey Ford Consul. The one I'd seen that night I'd followed Dave. It hadn't been Spiteri's. It had been *his*. Mooney's.

'Mr Taylor.' Mooney spoke directly to me. 'In all cases of difficulty and danger, in whom do you put your trust?'

It had been him. Of course. How could I have been so stupid? He was the copper that the Maltese were paying off. He must have set the whole thing up. The photograph, everything. He'd even beaten up his own man to cover his tracks and fool me. Set me up with Jeannie. They'd wanted Dave to fall for it but they got me instead. *I'm supposed to be nice to you*, she had said in that awful drugged-up voice. I had been such a mug.

I pulled the blindfold off and stood up. Mooney was standing in front of me in full masonic fancy dress.

'It was you,' I said to him. 'You set me up.'

'Put your blindfold back on at once!' Mooney ordered.

'Fuck you,' I muttered.

A hand grabbed my arm. I wrenched myself free. I pushed my way through the crowd of weirdos around me. There were gasps of outrage and muttered comments. Mooney called out after me.

'You have violated the sanctity of the Temple! The wrath of the Great Architect will come down upon you!'

*

I had too much time on my hands, time to kill. I couldn't seem to concentrate on work. I didn't have enough of a routine. I found the days drifting by and my mind wandering, dwelling on my own story rather than seeking out others. Bad brooding thoughts again. If I had a staff job I'd have something to distract me from distraction, I reasoned, a calm occupation.

I spoke to Sid Franks about doing a big exposé on organised crime in London. The Richardson gang had all been arrested and were due in court at the end of the week. *Sub judice* rumours of torture and beatings that piqued my interest, a reign of terror. There were hints that the Krays might be arrested for the Blind Beggar shooting in March. I talked up the story as a call to SMASH THE GANGS, to come down heavily on the racketeers and mobsters. Sid liked the idea but I couldn't seem to get down to it.

I found myself lurking in the underground public toilets off the Portobello Road, the afternoon sunlight streaming through the glass tiles above. Cool shadows, a low hiss of plumbing punctuated by a rhythmic, echoed dripping, like submarine sonar, created a tranquil ambience. Even the smell of piss and disinfectant was somehow reassuring. I stood, balanced on the tiled ridge in front of the cracked and stained porcelain, and waited.

The wall was covered with inscriptions. Hastily sketched figures and crude outlines of penises illuminated the text here and there. Childish scrawl described innocent depravity. Dates were given, chronicled entries. 4/3/66 I'M 35 SLIM 7″ – WANT FUCKING BY 3 COCKS ONE AFTER THE OTHER, 5/6/66 SLAVE SEEKS MASTER MAKE DATE. Often GENUINE, or even 100% GENUINE, were added, as if to insist upon the authenticity of the records. MAKE DATE, many implored, and indeed there was some haphazard correspondence, entries in an endless logbook of want. The wall was cleaned intermittently but one could make out traces of older writings, a palimpsest of desire.

Like splash subheadlines, self-declared scandals. There were also subtitles of invective. I HATE QUEERS and I WOULD LIKE TO HANG A POOF UNTIL I HEAR HIS NECK SNAP. Little haikus of hatred, articulating the lonely impulse of murderous longings. Words – I'd always tried to use words to give vent to my frustrations, but here the words were calling out to me, leading me astray. The poetry of psychopaths. The mass murderer William

Hierens had left a message on the wall by one of his victims, written in her lipstick:

FOR HEAVENS
SAKE CATCH ME
BEFORE I KILL MORE
I CANNOT CONTROL MYSELF

I knew this feeling so well: self-loathing, fear of what I am. And yet here I was, waiting. I hardly dared think what for, hardly remembered what brought me to these lower depths.

There were echoing footfalls on the stairs and I was suddenly alert. A middle-aged businessman, on his lunch break no doubt. He caught my eye with a horribly implicating gaze. *He knows*, I thought. He came closer, opening his mouth to say something. I couldn't bear to hear what nasty accusation might pass his ugly thin lips. I was in a sudden rage, grabbing at his throat.

'No,' he squealed. 'Oh God, no.'

His voice was small and choked, real terror in his eyes. He didn't even try to struggle he was so paralysed with fear. He knew that he was guilty, that he deserved this. I felt my hand tighten around his cheap school tie.

Then I regained control, and pushed him against one of the lock-ups. The door banged against the tiled wall and I ran up the stairs out of there.

Back at my bed-sit I tried to calm myself down. I attempted masturbation but felt the hateful thoughts flood through me. I collapsed on to my unmade bed sobbing.

Against my better judgment I went in the evening to this meeting that Julian had spoken of. It was in the basement of a bookshop on Kensington Park Road. A motley crew assembled – beards, beads, multicoloured clothes, peace sign badges. Everyone talking about Utopia, Peace, Liberation, Revolution, Love. God, did they go on about Love. Julian and I both stood out as being the only people in the room with short hair and ordinary clothes. I guessed they must have thought us real squares. Normal. But when I saw the way that one of the women talked, looking in our direction, trying to include us as she rambled on about 'sexual liberation', I figured that the beatniks were trying to include us. Julian suppressed giggles as this silly cow wittered on. This bunch of well-spoken hippies liked to call themselves 'freaks', as if it were something glamorous and bohemian. As if they had any idea what horror it was to be a real freak.

Somebody talked about offset litho printing and the magazine having really bright groovy colours. He showed the group some of his designs – art nouveau lettering, strange fluorescent figures and rainbow skies. There was a discussion as to whether this was affordable yet. Then a long, inconclusive debate about the title. Nobody was sure what to call it.

We went for a drink afterwards. Henekey's on Portobello Road. It was full of 'freaks'.

'Not very beautiful, are they,' I commented. 'The Beautiful People.'

'No.' Julian sniffed. 'They're all unwashed and hairy too. Not my favourite combination. What is it about the English character that is so averse to soap and water? You really notice it in the summer. That tang. And look at that dolly bird with no bra on. Shocking.'

Julian sniffed again.

'And you smell that?'

A pungent scent hung in the air. I recognised it from the other night. Cannabis. A joint was being passed around in the beer garden, a couple of West Indians, obviously dealing. Julian wanted to know if I was interested in the magazine. My mind was elsewhere. I suddenly realised the potential for a story. An exposé – long-haired decadence, the drugs angle. Sid Franks would love it. And I hated this hippie crowd with their Free Love, thinking themselves so exotic and wild. I could have some revenge. There was muck here to be raked.

We went along to this party later. A Happening, they called it. It was in a disused warehouse in Camden Town. Naked figures on a stage doing some sort of performance art, a light show, oily blotches projected on to a whitewashed wall. Music, a heavily amplified electric dirge, a tray of sugar lumps passed around, supposedly laced with hallucinogens. I demurred, but Julian grabbed one like a greedy child. Surprisingly, I quite enjoyed the atmosphere. But although it was all supposed to be so beautiful, in fact the scene was quite grotesque and ugly. Like a Hieronymus Bosch vision of Hell. A Garden of Earthly Delights. Julian pointed out one of the Rolling Stones lurking in a corner, smoking a joint. I thought about what a great scoop it would be, a snatch shot of a pop star taking drugs.

*

They met at Stan's flat in a tower block off Ladbroke Grove. Stan's missus made no attempt to conceal her disapproval of Jimmy and Billy. Their talk of big money, easy money, made her sick. She knew what they were. Petty villains acting tough. She worried that they would lead her Stanley astray. He had held down a job for over a year now. She wanted him to keep going straight. She wanted him to be respectable.

She frowned at Stan as his friends shuffled into the flat and made themselves comfortable on the settee. They had come around to watch the football. England–Portugal. But they were up to something, she could tell.

'I'm off to bingo,' she announced, grabbing her handbag and going to the door.

Stan followed her out.

'See you later, love,' he said, leaning towards her to kiss her cheek.

She pulled her face away.

'Just you make sure those two are gone before I come back!' she hissed.

'Don't be like that, love,' he muttered quietly. 'They're my friends.'

She slammed the door. As Stan came back through to the living room, Jimmy and Billy were laughing.

'Fuck me,' said Billy. 'Your old lady's in a bad mood.'

Stan grinned uneasily. He turned on the telly. *World Cup Grandstand* had just started.

'She still think you're working?' asked Jimmy.

'Yeah.' Stan nodded sheepishly.

Jimmy and Billy erupted into laughter again. Stan hadn't worked for over a month. But he hadn't told his wife. So every weekday morning he got up at eight and kissed her goodbye. She thought he was off to an engineering works in Northolt. He'd drive off in his blue Standard Vanguard to a café to have breakfast and study the day's racing form. He might be meeting up with Billy and Jimmy during the day. Otherwise it would be the pub at lunch-time and the betting shop in the afternoon. He'd get back to the flat at about half past five. The wife suspected nothing. So he hoped.

'You're fucking henpecked, that's what you are,' said Billy.

Jimmy got a bottle of Scotch out of a carrier bag. Stan got them some glasses.

'Right,' Jimmy announced when they'd settled down. 'The thing is, we need to get a proper motor.'

'Yeah, well, that old banger of Stan's not much cop, is it?'

Stan smiled. Jimmy cleared his throat.

'Yes, well, as I've said, we need a proper getaway vehicle. I've got an idea.'

'Oh yeah?' Billy remarked with a grin. 'What's that, then?'

'There's a blue Ford Executive parked on my road. We get some plates made up the same as this motor and nick one the same. Then if we get spotted the Old Bill will track down this other car. It'll put them on a wild-goose chase.'

Billy nodded slowly. Stan frowned. He didn't understand why they should do something so complicated. Why not just nick the original Ford? He didn't say anything.

'Yeah,' Billy said, continuing to nod. 'That's a good plan. We just need to sort out where we're going to hit.'

'We should do a jug,' Jimmy declared.

Billy laughed.

'A jug?'

'Yeah,' Jimmy went on. 'You know, a bank.'

'I know what a fucking jug is.'

'Well, what's so funny?'

'You're talking like you've been at the heavy all your life. "We should do a jug." What do you fucking know about it?'

'Listen, son . . .' started Jimmy.

'Fellahs, please!' Stan came in. 'Take it easy. Let's all have a drink, eh?'

He poured out the whisky. The TV flickered. The teams were lined up on the pitch. The Royal Marines Band playing the Portuguese national anthem.

'If we want to do a bank,' said Billy, 'we need to be properly tooled.'

Billy reached into the holdall by his feet. He pulled out the Luger and held it up in front of the group.

'I've got us another shooter. Here you are, Jimmy,' he said, handing it to him.

Jimmy examined the pistol with pretend expertise. Stan smiled nervously and chewed at a hangnail.

'Want me to get you one?' Billy asked him.

'Nah,' he said. 'I'm the driver, ain't I. I don't need no gun.'

7

It was the day of the final when it all came tumbling down. The end of my first week with the Flying Squad. C8. I'd got where I wanted to be. The new boy on Vic Sayles' team.

The squad's plainclothes style was a bit more flash than Divisional. Tailor-made suits rather than off-the-peg Burtons. Leather or sheepskin topcoats so that you could dress down to be less conspicuous when you were plotted up somewhere on surveillance. The job of the squad was to go after the top villains. It was expected that you'd get close to them. Dress like them. Think like them.

I was wary of my fellow officers' attitude to me. One of the Bramshill lot. A Special Course college boy. Very careful to act humble, not say anything that might sound know-it-all. I was also worried about the freemason business. Mooney's comment about Brothers in the the Flying Squad. Word must have got around about what had happened at the Temple. I just thought I'd keep my head down. Get on with the job. Get on with my career.

I felt all right about what had happened with Dave. I kidded myself that I had done him a favour. Got him out of the West End. Out of danger. He'd be better off back at the Bush. I figured he'd thank me for it in the long run.

I'd spent the first day getting used to procedure. I was worried that I'd be kicking my heels all week. I was keen to get my teeth into something after all that palaver at West End Central. It had left a bad taste in my mouth. Well, vice is a dirty job. You're bound to get tainted by it sooner or later. Here I'd be up against serious villainy. I wanted to prove myself. Then the second day Vic Sayles came up to me.

'Frank,' he said.

'Yes, guvnor?'

'Fancy a job, son?'

Stupid question. Stupid grin on my face.

'You busy?' he asked.

'Nothing special, guvnor.'

'Right. Get an operational unit together. Something's come in off a snout of mine. A whole lorry-load of phosphor bronze was had away last week. Expensive stuff. Use it to make aeroplanes and that. He reckons he knows where it's being slaughtered. I got the address. A scrapyard in Harlesden. Get a brief and go and check it out.'

So I got the brief – the search warrant, that is. Got together a couple of DCs and three drivers. One for each car and an extra one to drive the truck if we got a result. Turns out that this phosphor bronze is very valuable. The lorry-load was meant to be worth a hundred grand.

The scrapyard looked deserted when we arrived. Just a fat little geezer on his tod in a trailer that was used as an office. He was just sitting there picking his nose and reading an *Exchange & Mart*. When I flashed my warrant card and the brief he looked up and rolled his eyes.

'Fuck,' he said. 'Someone must have grassed.'

Now I nearly laughed out loud at this. That was a verbal if I ever heard one. Straight out of the notebook. I'd never actually heard a villain utter anything so pat. I should have been suspicious, but I just figured that this little toerag had been watching too much *Dixon of Dock Green* or he was taking the piss.

We found the lorry and nicked the bloke for receiving. A good day's work. Lovely little job. First week in the squad and I'd got a result. But I had a nagging little feeling that it had all been too easy.

World Cup Final day. A bit of a buzz about that in Coco. That and events in South London very early that morning. Charlie Richardson had been nicked in a dawn raid. Now we had the whole gang in the frame.

I was finishing off the paperwork for the recovered lorry-load in Harlesden and the receiving charge against the bloke in the scrapyard. We'd been working on a tip-off so the informant would be entitled to payment from the Information Fund. If the stuff had been properly covered the insurers could pay ten per cent of the recovered value into the fund. A tidy little sum. But it was Vic Sayles' informant and he would have to authorise the application to the fund anyway, so I went to see him about it.

'Nice little job, Frank,' he said.

I mentioned the Information Fund and he nodded slowly and lit a cigarette.

'Sit down, son.'

'What is it, guvnor?'

'You're new to my team and I want you to get to know how things are done here. That's why I gave you that job.'

'I don't understand.'

'Yes, well, it ain't exactly covered in the one-year Special Course. Information, that's what it's all about, isn't it? I mean, without that we can't be expected to solve crime, can we?'

'Of course not, guvnor.'

'That's why I put so much emphasis in the way I work on cultivating informants. And they do need cultivating. It's give and take. Sometimes you need to keep your boot on their neck, other times you need to sweeten them up. Do you get me?'

'I'm not sure, guvnor.'

I didn't like the way this was going.

'This little job, for instance. Your initiation into my team, if you like. Talking of initiation, I heard about that fiasco at George Mooney's lodge, but don't worry, you won't have to roll your trousers up to be part of my firm. No, you just have to remember that things get divvied up properly.'

'Guvnor?'

'The insurance reward. Ten per cent of the recovered value. Tidy little sum. Well, some of it will go to the team that blagged it. With the understanding we'll want bodies handed up from time to time in the future. The bloke you nicked for receiving, well, he'll have his share. He's some mug with no form and he'll be happy to do six months' bird. And the rest of it goes to us. Some of it goes upstairs, the rest is divvied up among ourselves. I'm giving you your share in advance.'

He pulled out a brown envelope and tossed it on to the desk in front of me.

'There you are, son. Welcome to the firm.'

I felt such a fucking mug. That's why it had been so easy. I should have spotted that. Dave would have noticed something like that. I was always in such a fucking hurry. Now what was I going to do?

'Look, sir . . .'

'Pick it up, Taylor. Don't be a cunt. Nobody got hurt. Everything weighed off nicely with a little sweetener. It'll buy us information for the next time, you mark my words.'

I stared at the envelope.

'Go on. Pick it up. You know how long it took me to get to DI? No fucking Rapid Promotion Scheme, I can tell you. It was a fucking hard slog. Look, college boy, we keep the peace. Take a few heavy villains off the pavement now and then. We get to know where everybody is so that when it's their turn to go away for a while, by Christ we make sure that they do. The great British public sleeps soundly in its beds and lets us get on with it. We deserve a little extra every now and then for that, don't we?'

I looked up at Sayles. He caught my stare without flinching.

'Pick it up, son.'

I lifted the envelope and put it in my pocket. That was that. Either that or transfer back to Division. I walked out of his office, bad money in my pocket. I had to get out. Think about what to do. A voice says:

'We're setting up a telly in the briefing room, Frank. To watch the match.'

The final. I'd been looking forward to it up until now. Didn't have the stomach for it any more.

'Got to go out,' I replied. 'Got a job.'

Out. Need to think. Talk. Dave. I need to talk to Dave about this. He was right all along. Need to talk to him. Ask him: *What the fuck do I do now?*

Motor over to West London. Shepherd's Bush factory. Desk Sergeant Reg Wilson with a big smile as I come in. He was skipper when I first started here.

'Hello, stranger,' he said.

Radio on in the background. The match.

'The Krauts have just equalised. I hear you're on the Flying Squad now. A bit more glamorous than Division, I'll bet.'

'Yeah.' I nodded vaguely. 'Dave Thomas about, skip?'

'He's out on Q-car duty.'

Q-car – an unmarked CID car on constant patrol. So named after the Q-ships which hunted U-boats disguised as merchant vessels.

'Right.'

'I could radio him for you.'

'Nah. It's all right.'

Leave the station. Walk along Shepherd's Bush Green. Feel in my pocket. Thick wad of notes in the envelope. Think: What am I going to do with this bent cash? See a bookie's and go in. I decide to punt the whole lot on a horse. Hardly anyone in the place. A big West Indian with yellowy teeth scribbling out a Yankee. Turns to me and asks:

'How's your luck, man?'

Put the whole lot on Horned Moon in the 3.30 at Thirsk. The fucking nag comes in at 5–1. Collect my winnings. Four hundred-odd quid. Try to put the whole lot on again but they won't take the bet. It's too much and they haven't got time to lay it off.

Manage to lose three races in a row. But I put forty quid on

King's Bounty in the four o'clock at Newmarket and it fucking wins.

No use. Walk out of the bookie's. Yellow betting slips all over the floor like trampled party decorations.

Get out of there and walk over to the White Horse. Crowded with punters watching the game. England are winning, 2–1 up. A lot of shouting and cheering. I stand at the bar. A double Scotch. Then another. It's nearly full time and we're still ahead. Everyone in the pub rared up, shouting at the little figures on the screen.

I feel sick of all this. Stupid national pride. Queen and Country. Showing the Flag. Can't believe in any of that any more. Can't believe in the job.

From the telly I can just hear the strains of 'Rule Britannia' coming from the terraces. *Come on, England!* somebody shouts in the bar. *Never, never, never shall be slaves*, groans the crowd from the terraces. I feel suddenly traitorous. I want them to lose. Want us to lose.

Four minutes left, comes the commentary. *The clouds have parted, the sun is now streaming down on Wembley.*

People are already celebrating. Then two minutes to go and Jack Charlton gives away a foul. Groans from the pub. Nobby Stiles arguing with the referee. Free kick outside England's penalty area. The wall lines up. The ref gets them to move back. Pacing out the ten yards.

The pub is almost hushed. Just a few votive mutterings. One minute to go. And I want the Krauts to score. The free kick is taken. It beats the wall. It's free in the penalty area. Everyone in the pub is shouting. Urging it clear. Goalmouth scramble. The commentator is flustered. Unable to make out the confusion.

And it's . . . he splutters. *Oh yes, they must. They have done.*

It's in the net. Mournful keening all over the saloon bar. They've equalised.

'Yes!' I hiss to myself through gritted teeth.

England have just enough time to kick off when the referee blows his whistle.

Full time. Wander about the Bush. Find another pub without a telly and drink my way through five doubles. It's quiet and I try to think things through. Bad money in my pocket. Have to find a way of getting rid of it. I'm part of a bent team. I'm the sort of copper that Dave despises.

*

Extra time. Crowded around the telly in Stan's flat. Jimmy, Billy and Sandra round to watch the football. Even Stan's missus going along with the spirit of the thing. Putting on a spread. A few sandwiches, cocktail sausages, slices of veal-and-ham pie. Beer. Jimmy joking that he's supporting the Krauts because he's Scottish. Extra time and Billy's feeling bored by the whole spectacle. The whole nation going crazy over a poxy game of football.

A clock comes up on the screen. Ten minutes of extra time gone.

Just twenty minutes of the match left, intones Kenneth Wolstenholme calmly. Of the old school. His commentary avuncular, unintrusive.

Nobby Stiles in possession in the centre circle. Alan Ball finds an opening on the right wing. Stiles passes quickly, scarcely looking up. An instinctive long ball. Thirty yards through the air, dropping, let's say, five yards in front of its intended receiver. Ball races towards it on tired legs, Schnellinger chasing. For a second Ball thinks he's finished. All run out. Extra time has taken its toll. Socks rolled down to his ankles, calves aching with the onset of cramp. Then, maybe in desperation itself, he finds energy, acceleration. Schnellinger beaten, he has space.

Here's Ball, running himself daft.

Wolstenholme enunciates *daft* with a shortened vowel sound. Northern rather than BBC. The excitement betraying a long-tamed native accent.

First touch. Ball hooks a low curling cross square. Geoff Hurst in the penalty area. Just outside the six-yard box. He traps the pass with his right foot and turns. Tilkowski, the German goalkeeper, stays on his line, crouching down, ready for a low shot.

Now here's Hurst. Can he do it?

But Hurst is not over the ball as he swivels to make the shot. He's leaning away from it, falling back as he drives. So it goes high. Right over the keeper. It hits the crossbar. The net shudders slightly as if anticipating a catch. A deafening exhalation from the crowd as its line of flight skims the surface of the goalmouth. The ball cannons down on to the goal line. The noise echoing around the stadium into a crescendo. A heightened sigh of relief. Then an in-breath of doubt as the ball bounces back out. The triangular path of the ball. The rectangle of the goal. The two shapes join but do they bisect? The odds of a shot hitting either solid line of woodwork or painted line on turf are long enough. To hit both, in close sequence, in the same trajectory, is a miraculous trigonometry. The ball flies back into play. Weber heads it away. Roger Hunt turns and appeals. Did the ball cross the line? The crowd roar comes again, more in belief than in certainty. Consumed by the sacred geometry of the moment.

Yes, yes, Wolstenholme enthuses. Then suddenly: *No. No. The linesman says no.*

Again, emphatic:

The linesman says no.

The players make signals of appeal. The Germans waving arms or shaking hands. Dismissive gestures. The English indicate certainty by holding their upper limbs aloft, rigid.

The referee is running up to meet the linesman. Close-up of Hurst on the screen. He has dropped his hands to his knees. For a moment despondent. Then he leans forward, looking intently towards the meeting of officials. Eyes plaintive.

The crowd roar subsides into a low ululation. Then the whistling starts up. Demanding judgment rather than mere arbitration. Meaning triangulated. Hurst's shot, the impact on the crossbar, the ball finding the limit of the playing area. Surely this is enough? But there are other meanings beyond these tangents. The referee, Gottfried Dienst, is Swiss. Supposedly neutral. The linesman, Tofik Bahkramov, is Russian. Much is made, in the recounting of this incident, of the fact that Bahkramov had served in the Red Army in the Great Patriotic War against the Third Reich. There are reports that there were shouts of *Remember Stalingrad!* that came provocatively from the terraces as they conferred.

But the fact was, at any angle, it was a hard one to call. Within the rules of Association Football, for a goal to be allowed, the whole of the ball must be over the line; if any part of it does not cross it must be disallowed. No one, least of all Bahkramov, was in a position to accurately judge the physics of it.

The officials had no shared language. Bahkramov could, as Wolstenholme had already commented, *only speak Russian or Turkish.* Only the English can be so dismissive of bilingualism. But the semantics of the situation are simple. Binary. Yes or no.

The officials are face to face now. Bahkramov nods his grey head. Dienst turns and blows his whistle. He starts walking back down the pitch, pointing at the centre spot.

It's a goal. It's a goal. Wolstenholme deadpan. The crowd ecstatic.

The German players continue to protest. The English are jubilant. Martin Peters runs up to his West Ham team-mate Hurst, arms outstretched. He hugs him about the waist, lifts him off the ground.

The action replay comes up on the screen, silently. No commentary as there had been with the other goals. Slow motion reveals how dubious the decision was.

Stan has risen from the settee, a beer bottle held aloft, cheering.

'That was never in,' Jimmy mutters.

'It does look a bit dodgy,' agrees Billy.

'Yeah, but it doesn't matter now, does it?' Stan with a stupid grin on his face. 'The ref's given it, hasn't he?'

*

Suddenly there's noise out on the street. The match is over. People are singing and chanting. I go outside.

We won the Cup, we won the Cup, ee-ay-addio, we won the Cup!
Cars driving past hooting their horns, some with Union Jacks

fluttering from them. People dancing, actually dancing with each other on the street. Strangers hugging each other. Calling up to people hanging out of their windows. Flags flying everywhere. It's like fucking VJ day.

Find myself in a crowded pub propping up the bar. Some bloke looks at me and frowns.

'What's the matter, mate? We won, didn't we?'

I turn away. We won. Everyone fucking won. I won. Got a result the bad way. Got what I wanted.

I stagger out of the pub. The street party in full swing.

We won the Cup, we won the Cup, ee-ay-addio, we won the Cup!

I want to lose. Lose all of this bad cash in my pocket. Think about throwing it in the air around me. But that would add to the party atmosphere. And I hate all these happy bastards. Lose it, that's what I need to do. Gamble it. Tried that on the horses. I'll have to go to the dogs. I head over to White City.

*

Final whistle in Stan's flat. Everybody getting carried away. Shouting and cheering. Except Billy. He watches the screen morosely.

Bobby Moore goes up to the Royal Box to collect the trophy. Bobby Charlton is weeping openly.

'Look at that silly cunt,' Billy mutters to himself.

And they want Alf Ramsey, Wolstenholme announces. *And Alf Ramsey doesn't want to come.*

Why don't they leave the poor fucker alone, thinks Billy.

The Band of the Royal Marines strikes up 'God Save the Queen'. The crowd sing along, dirgelike. Stan is on his feet.

'Send 'er victorious,' he chants.

'Leave it out, Stan,' snaps Billy.

The band breaks into 'When the Saints Go Marching In'. A lap of honour. Moore hands the trophy to Nobby Stiles. Stiles does a funny little victory dance. A pixilated hornpipe, gapped teeth showing in his demented grin. Jimmy laughs.

'Will yer look at the mad wee fellow,' he says.

And throughout it all, comes the commentary, *Alf Ramsey walks quietly off the pitch.*

'Right, then,' says Stan, switching off the telly. 'Let's get down the pub. It'll be heaving.'

They all go out on to the street. It's crowded with people. Flags everywhere. Clapping, chanting, spontaneous choruses of 'Rule Britannia'. Victory. Billy felt so fucking lonely. He couldn't understand it. He couldn't join in. Didn't feel any part of it. He'd fought for this fucking country. Killed for it. No fucking thanks at all. Demobbed and forgotten about. No fucking parade.

We won the Cup, we won the Cup, ee-ay-addio, we won the Cup!

'Let's go home,' he said to Sandra.

'But we've won, Billy. We ought to celebrate.'

'Why?' he asked, flatly.

Sandra put her arm around him.

'What's the matter, love?'

'Nothing,' he replied. 'I just don't like crowds. Let's go home.'

She looked at him. He seemed distant. Alone. She'd never quite understand him. A car raced by blaring its horn, a Union Jack fluttering from the back window. She kissed him on the cheek.

'All right,' she whispered in his ear. 'Let's go home.'

The noise on the streets went on all night. *They think it's all over*, thought Billy, lying on his back in bed. He tried to sleep. He'd drift off for a while but the sounds outside disturbed him. And the memories inside. Back in the jungle. Always alive with something. Crickets, cicadas, tree frogs. A bloody racket. They'd build temporary shelters with groundsheets and ponchos. *Bashas*, they call them. Make a frame with branches to support a hammock. British Nylon Pattern. Spare set of clothes for sleeping dry. Then in the morning it's back in your filthy half-sodden combat fatigues.

One night there was a firefight in the darkness. Tracer bullets lighting up the forest like Guy Fawkes Night. One of the officers grabbed a Very pistol. A flare gun, used to signal or dislodge air-drop canisters from high trees by burning off the parachute canopy. They held fire as this beautiful orange light fell slowly through the trees.

Picking out shadows. But there was nobody there. The CT must have slipped away into the night. Maybe they'd never been there at all and they'd been firing at ghosts.

He woke up in a cold sweat. Sandra was snoring next to him. He got up and went to the window. Lit a cigarette. *Everybody's happy*, he thought. *What's the matter with me?* Victory celebrations. *They think it's all over.* The intermittent sounds reminded him of a street riot one night in Kuala Lumpur. Anger and joy indistinguishable. *Stupid bastards*, he whispered to himself with strange and vague thoughts of revenge. *They think it's all over.* It ain't over.

*

The Saturday shift was as hectic as ever. It was a 'World Cup Final Special', of course, so more pages than usual had to be kept back until we knew the result. Even Teddy Thursby came in to finish his copy, saying that his comments depended on whether England won or lost. Not that he seemed particularly impressed by the event.

'Bread and circuses, dear boy,' he muttered to me. 'A post-Empire consolation prize. It's all downhill from now on.'

Sid Franks' ears pricked up.

'Don't worry, Sidney,' Thursby continued. 'I won't be sharing these gloomy thoughts with our esteemed readership.'

Extra time played havoc with the deadlines. Sid was pacing up and down with a glass of bicarb in one hand and a fag in the other, looking like he was going to have a coronary any moment. Loudly cursing the print unions.

'Those cunts want extra for working on World Cup Final day.'

Jubilation when the final result came in. A mad rush to get all the match reports and photos composed. Then Sid got any spare staff men and casuals to go over to the big reception for the team at the Royal Garden Hotel, Kensington. The main brief was to get a comment from Alf Ramsey. Apart from the rather choice declaration after the Argentina game, Ramsey had been far from loquacious with the gentlemen of the press. 'Tight-lipped,' was how the *Illustrated* had described his reticence earlier in the tournament.

'Tight-arsed, more like,' Sid had said. 'Get that cunt on the record with something, for fuck's sake.'

So a load of us went over to the Royal Garden. A stag do, no wives or girlfriends present. Jimmy Greaves, left out of the team for the last three crucial games, was also conspicuous by his absence. Jack Charlton, in preparation for the heavy drinking ahead, wrote on a card: 'This body is to be returned to room 508, Royal Garden Hotel,' and put it in his top pocket.

Outside, a huge crowd had assembled, singing 'You'll Never Walk Alone'. And the familiar chant striking up at any opportunity.

We won the Cup, we won the Cup, ee-ay-addio, we won the Cup!

Players took turns to walk out on to the balcony to receive the ovation. Calls for Ramsey to appear, and he wandered out briefly, looking reserved, slightly bemused by the whole thing.

Harold Wilson was swanning about, making the most of the happy occasion. There were gloomy forecasts for the economy, a wages freeze announced to deal with the crisis, the boom time officially over. A couple of members of his cabinet there, Jim Callaghan with a big friendly grin on his face, George Brown staggering around, already three sheets to the wind.

No comment from Ramsey. One prominent sportswriter went up to him, offering congratulations and thanking him, on behalf of all the press, for his co-operation. Ramsey frowned, beetle-browed and disbelieving, and said:

'Are you taking the piss?'

I phoned in what I had to Sid and he ordered me over to the West End to cover the crowd celebrations there.

'Get out there and get a bit of colour,' he said. 'You know, the people of England celebrate. It's a fucking national womb-trembler, son.'

The West End was afire, motor horns blaring, flags fluttering amidst passing traffic. World Cup Willie mascots hanging from car aerials, Trafalgar Square packed with people. A circle of girls was doing a knees-up in one of the fountains.

Piccadilly teeming with revellers, a mad charivari. A young man on top of Eros waved the red, white and blue. The mob struck up 'Rule Britannia'. I had to push my way through the crowd. The horrible squirming intimacy of all these bodies made me quite sick. Back at the *Illustrated* we had plenty of copy. Everyone was half pissed as the paper was put to bed in high spirits.

*

White City Stadium. Putting as much as I can on trap number three. Think about how easy it is to fix the dogs. Jumbo Edwards, a trainer who ran ringers and did the odd bit of doping, used to phone up the Bush with tips for the night's racing. All a bit of fun. It's all fucking fixed. Geoff Hurst's shot never crossed the bloody line.

Punt away a load of cash but I've still got some left at the end of the meeting. Feel I've got to keep gambling. Gamblers are losers. Loners. No loyalty. No side. Only odds. The longer the better. Got to get rid of the bad money.

The Hop Garden Poker Club in Notting Dale. One of the hundreds of little casinos that sprang up after the '59 Betting and Gaming Act. Roulette table in the front. A real mug's game. *Faîtes vos jeux*, says some tatty-looking croupier with a Black Country accent. I buy a load of chips and start making silly bets. Big piles on single numbers. Lose a lot then one of the bastards comes up. Big gasps around the table as a whole load of chips gets shovelled back at me. More than I fucking started with.

The wankers running the place think something's up and come over.

'Everything all right here?' asks some cunt in a monkey suit.

I push the chips back on the same number.

'Excuse me, sir,' he continues. 'I don't think the house can cover that bet.'

'You don't understand. I want to fucking lose.'

'Maybe you've had enough, sir.'

Go up West. Piccadilly Circus heaving with bodies. Someone's climbed on top of the statue of Eros and is waving a flag. *You'll never walk alone*, sings the crowd. Want to bet? I think to myself. Want to bet? Waste of fucking time. The money should go to its rightful owner. Whoever the fuck that is. I'm living off immoral earnings. We're all living off immoral earnings.

Suddenly think: Jeannie. Yeah, why not? I'm just another sucker in the West End ready to waste all my money on a whore. Immoral earnings, ought to share them about. And I want her. I don't care if she's been involved in blackmailing me. How much she despises me. I don't care if I have to pay. I want her. I push my way through the crowd. Head up towards Shepherd Market.

Get to the flat and press her buzzer. No reply. Kick the door in and stumble inside. Shrieks come from the ground-floor flat. Geezer buttoning himself up hurriedly. Looking frightened, trying to avoid my mad-eyed stare.

'It's all right, son,' I tell him. 'We won, didn't we?'

'What the fuck do you think you're doing?' the ground-floor-flat tart screeches. 'Get out of here before I call the police.'

'I am the fucking police, darling.'

I pull out a load of notes and hand them over to her.

'What do you want?' she demands, her voice a little less harsh.

'I want to see Jeannie.'

'Well, she's not here.'

I stumble up to the first-floor landing. Knock on the door. Another tart opens up. Not Jeannie.

'Where is she?' I demand.

'It's all right, Joan.'

Jeannie. Her voice coming from the landing.

'What do *you* want?' she demands.

'I've got something for you.'

I start up the stairs. Jeannie has a bottle in her hand. She's holding it by the neck.

'It's all right,' I croak. 'I don't want to hurt you. I got something for you.'

'What?'

I pull all the cash out of my pocket and hold it up for her to see.

'It's dirty money, Jeannie.'

I sniff at the pile of cash. Used banknotes have a horrible smell. Of all the sweaty palms they've rubbed by. All the filthy palms they've greased.

'I want you to have it,' I mutter, pushing all the notes at her. She starts laughing.

Everything starts to spin. I stagger on to the landing.

'I got to lie down. Let me lie down for a bit.'

'Oh, Christ,' she groans. 'In here.'

She leads me into a room.

'We won the Cup,' I start singing.

'Yeah, yeah.' She guides me across to the bed.

Everything spinning, falling.

'Ee-ay-addio.'

Falling. Mattress springs squeaking. Blacking out.

8

I woke up, fully clothed, laid out on top of the bed. Didn't know where the fuck I was at first. Hung over, my mouth dry, my head throbbing in dull agony as it struggled to think. Then it all fell painfully into place. Jeannie was gone. So was the money. All the bad money.

I staggered into the bathroom and splashed some cold water on my face. The sound of an argument out on the stairs. A man and a woman. Voices high and low like some bloody duet. Female protestations making shrill stabs at my bleary mind. I dried my face on a threadbare towel and went to the door.

I pushed it open and looked down. Attilio Spiteri and one of the tarts framed by the stairwell.

'I told you,' the girl was saying, 'I don't know where she went.'

Spiteri caught sight of me.

'All right,' he muttered to her sharply. 'Go on. Get downstairs.'

Spiteri mounted the stairs, eyeing me warily. He moved awkwardly, probably still smarting from the beating he'd taken the other day.

'Well,' he said with a flat grin, 'the little bird has flown.'

'Don't you . . .' I blurted out, grabbing the front of his jacket.

He winced painfully.

'Take it easy, for fuck's sake,' he protested. 'I ain't going to do nothing. She's more trouble than she's worth. I'm surprised that you care after what she put you through.'

I let go of him.

'Mooney set the whole thing up, didn't he?' I asked.

'Yeah,' he replied, leaning forward to whisper, as if we could be overheard. 'You want to be careful of him.'

I pushed past Spiteri and went down the stairs and out into the street. The bright morning hurt my eyes. I looked a mess but then the whole of London seemed to be recovering from the hangover of last night's victory celebrations. I crossed the street and a car pulled out and kerb-crawled me. It was a silver-grey Ford Consul. Mooney.

'Get in, son,' he called out, and I tried to ignore him.

'Well, well,' he continued, chidingly. 'You can't keep away, can you? You really are off the track, brother.'

'What do you want?'

I stopped and he put on the brake. He opened the passenger door and I climbed in reluctantly.

'Just to get a few things straight,' he said. 'That girl of yours has gone missing. Oh yes, Uncle George sees everything.' His peephole eyes twinkled with pride. 'The All-Seeing Eye of the Great Architect guides me. And a few very good connections. You know the motto of the Temple? *Aude, vide, tace*. Hear, see and be silent. Now we want to be sure that certain people remain silent, don't we? If that little tart has run off to that DC friend of yours there could be trouble all round.'

'So?'

'So, I want you to warn him off. And her.'

'You set me up.'

'Yeah, well.' He sniffed. 'That was meant for your friend. It wasn't my fault that he wouldn't play ball and you were all too keen. Look, Taylor, it's best for all concerned if you make sure that this little unpleasantness goes no farther. And I'm prepared to overlook the disrespect that you have shown towards the Brotherhood. You have shunned the protection of the Temple, that is your lookout. I am taught to view the errors of the profane with compassion and show the superior excellence of my faith by the purity of my conduct. Now fuck off.'

I got out of the car.

'My regards to Vic,' he called out after me. 'Remember, both me and him have your best interests at heart.'

I felt completely burned out. Everything had moved so fast. I'd known so much and understood so little. That's the problem with rapid promotion. There's so much to learn in the job. It takes time. There's no substitute for that. So easy to get into bad habits. To get led astray.

And I was tainted now. On the bung, like the rest of Vic Sayles' team. Not just bent for the job. Bent for myself. And the thing was, I really liked Vic. He was a good guvnor in so many ways. He got results and he treated those that worked for him well. He was just very, very hookey. I started to see how easy it was to go along with it all. A close-knit team, good morale and plenty of perks. Pretty soon it would all become second nature. I felt like I was falling into it. But deep down I knew that it was just all wrong. And that ate away at me.

Booze helped, or rather helped to numb all the doubts I had. For a while anyway. Then a maudlin sense of self-loathing would come to the surface. I tried to think about what I could do. I could always ask for a transfer, but that wouldn't do my precious career any good at all. I had no one to turn to. To talk to. Except Dave. And I'd really fucked up there. But I did need to talk to him. I needed to warn him. Mooney was diabolical, he seemed capable of anything. If Jeannie had gone to him and spilled the beans he'd have to be very careful. Being right wouldn't be enough. He'd have to be devious about it. Maybe I could help him out there. And maybe with Dave I could muster enough courage to do the right thing. He was my conscience, my better half. But I was on my own now. Lost.

I tried getting in touch with him but he was hard to track down. He was on Q-car duty so he was hardly ever at the Bush. I left messages but he never got back to me. To be honest there was something else I wanted. Jeannie. I wanted to see her again. It was a sad, stupid obsession. Another reason to hit the bottle.

I finally managed to get through to Dave after a skinful one night.

'Detective Constable Thomas,' came his voice down the blower.

'Dave?'

A pause then a weary sigh.

'What do you want, Frank?'

'I've been trying to call you.'

'Yeah. I know. What is it?'

'I'm sorry, Dave.'

'Bit late for that now, Frank.'

'Look, can't we talk? Go for a drink or something. For old times' sake.'

'Oh, please.'

'Everything's turned to shit, Dave.' My voice broke, almost sobbing with booze melancholia. 'I need you, mate.'

'Take it easy, Frank. For fuck's sake.'

'I mean it, Dave. I need to talk to you. There's things I need to tell you.'

Another pause. Another sigh.

'Yeah, all right,' he agreed, not nearly as grudging as he should have been. 'Look, I'm off Q-car duty next week. Why don't you come around then?'

*

On the Monday after the final, in Austin, Texas, Charles Joseph Whitman, an ex-Marine, climbed a tower in the campus of the University of Texas and shot fourteen people dead with a high-powered rifle. He had already killed his wife. And his mother. 'I didn't want,' he explained, 'her to be embarrassed by this.' A noble enough sentiment, I thought.

Later that week Julian said that he could arrange a meeting with the Kray twins. I was still trying to shape up this story on London gangs for the *Illustrated*. Julian knew one of Ronnie's ex-boyfriends.

He took us to a small pub in Bethnal Green. The place was crowded; a celebration was in progress. Ronnie had been in another identity parade for the Cornell shooting that day at Commercial Street police station. The Flying Squad had once again failed to get anybody to finger him and he'd been released that afternoon.

We sat in the corner as the ex-boyfriend gingerly approached Ronnie Kray. Ronnie patted him on the shoulder gently and squinted his heavy-lidded eyes in our direction. The saloon bar was filled with all kinds of characters – heavy-looking men, tarty-looking women and some curious types. A huge African with a shiny bald head called Cha-Cha seemed to be some sort of master of ceremonies, referring to Ronnie Kray loudly as 'Mr Ronald'. A pair of dwarfs play-acted fighting moves with the largest of the heavies present, to much laughter. There was a strange circus-like atmosphere in the pub.

Ronnie finally came over and offered us both a drink. We stood up as he approached, but he motioned for us to be seated and joined us at the table.

'So, you're journalists, are you?' he demanded. His voice was soft and slightly sibilant.

'Yes, Mr Kray,' I replied.

'Well, there's been loads of rubbish written about me and my brother by you lot.'

'Maybe it's time you told your side of the story,' I suggested.

'Yeah,' he agreed. 'That would be a good idea. It'd be a good story, you know? I've met loads of famous people. I've got loads of – what d'you call them? – antidotes.'

'Anecdotes?' I corrected him stupidly.

He glared at me with those toadlike eyes.

'Yeah,' he declared. 'That's what I said.'

'Maybe you need a biographer.'

'A what?'

'Someone to write your life story, you know, like Truman Capote did with *In Cold Blood*.'

Suddenly the idea of writing a book came back to me.

'Who's he?' Ronnie asked brusquely.

'You know, *Breakfast at Tiffany's?*'

'Oo!' Kray announced. 'I liked that. Saw the film with Audrey Hepburn. Lovely. You reckon you could get him to do it?'

'Well, I didn't mean him actually. I was just using him as an example.'

'What do you mean? You think we're not good enough for him or something?'

'No, I didn't mean . . .'

'Because we want a proper writer to do our story. Not some twopenny-halfpenny hack.'

'Of course.'

'Well, you get on to this Truman geezer. I'm sure he'd be interested.'

'Er, right,' I agreed, not quite knowing what to say.

'Well, if you'll excuse me.'

He stood up and was gone. So that was that. We left the pub empty-handed. At least I did have a story for Sid Franks that week. I'd set up a drugs bust at Henekey's on Saturday afternoon with a police contact I had at Notting Hill nick.

9

Fucking gas-meter bandits, thought Billy. Some fucking gang. I'm stuck with a couple of gas-meter bandits.

Stan and his nagging missus. His non-existent job that he's never late for. He's never knocking off early from. Clocks in and out of this gap in the middle of the day to keep the missus happy. Makes her think he's on the straight. Evil little looks from her every time him and Jimmy go around to Stan's poxy flat. Mean little expression trying to warn them off. Too fucking late.

So's there's Stanley with what must be the best work attendance record in West London and she goes and says that he needs to take Friday morning off to take her to St Mary's Hospital. An appointment at out-patients. The very morning that they were planning to do the blag.

'I'm sorry, chaps,' he says, all sheepish. 'She's got to see this doctor.'

'Nothing trivial, I hope,' Billy replies.

Stan is all red-faced. Embarrassed.

'It's, you know, women's trouble.'

Yeah, yeah, thinks Billy. Women's trouble. That's Stan for you.

'Well, we'll have to do it next week.'

'Bugger next week,' says Billy. 'I'm fucking skint. We'll do it tomorrow.'

'Tomorrow?'

'Yeah.'

'But tomorrow's a Saturday.'

'I know tomorrow's a fucking Saturday.'

'Well, Billy, the banks don't open on Saturday.'

'I fucking know! We'll do a bookie's again. We've got to do fucking something. I'm sick of all this wanking about.'

Jimmy flustered. Trying to look calm. Act calm. In control.

'Aye,' he agrees, nodding sagely. 'We'll do it tomorrow.'

Jimmy. Thinks he's so fucking clever. At least Stan knows he's useless. Jimmy thinks he's some sort of tasty villain. Big plans. Big talk. *Right, well here's the MO* and all that pony. Big talk in the exercise yard in the Scrubs. He acted like a criminal genius in association. Outside he's just another gas-meter bandit.

His big plan. The moody number plates, duplicate of a Ford Executive parked in the area. Nick one like that and if we're clocked they'll trace it back to that motor. Complicated. It always has to be complicated with Jimmy. He doesn't know how useless he is. Thinks he's the brains behind it all.

So, on Saturday morning they were driving around in Stan's beaten-up old Standard Vanguard van looking for a particular motor to steal. They drove up to Regent's Park and cruised around the Outer Circle, because a lot of commuters parked there all day and there'd usually be plenty of motors to choose from. But they'd forgotten that on a Saturday there weren't many cars around.

They ended up motoring out of London. Up north towards Harrow. There were more people about, it being the weekend, so it was more risky. They finally found a blue Ford Executive parked in a side street by Park Royal Tube station.

Billy and Jimmy got out of the van and sidled up to the motor. Jimmy crouched down and pushed a small piece of wire into the lock on the driver's side. He jiggled it about as Billy kept watch. The wire broke in the lock.

'Fuck!' Jimmy hissed.

'What's the matter?' Billy asked, impatiently.

'It's broke.'

'What?'

'It's broke. The fucking wire's broke.'

'Oh, for fuck's sake!' Billy snapped, and stomped back to the van.

They drove down through Northolt, along Western Avenue. They found a pub and parked the van. Billy was still fuming. Impatient. They had some lunch and a pint and Billy calmed down a bit. He even had a game of darts with Stan.

'Shall we have another?' suggested Jimmy.

'Nah,' replied Billy. 'Let's get back to work.'

They headed back down towards the Bush. There was some talk about doing the bookie's anyway, nicked getaway car or no nicked getaway car. Coming down Scrubs Lane the prison came into view. Bad memories. *Wormwood Scrubs*, thought Billy. The devil himself couldn't have come up with a more evil-sounding name.

Stan noticed a car behind them in his rear-view mirror. A Triumph 2000.

'I tell you what we could do,' Jimmy said. 'We could do the rent collector.'

'You what?' said Billy.

'The rent collector. The bloke from the council who comes around to collect rent.'

'I know what a fucking rent collector is.'

'Hang on a minute,' said Stan.

'You see, I've watched him. I know the route he takes. We could jump him.'

'Hold up,' said Stan.

'So when does he do his rounds?' asked Billy.

'Look at that car behind us,' said Stan.

Billy turned around.

'Friday,' said Jimmy.

'Great,' muttered Billy.

'Looks like it's following us. What do you reckon, Bill?' Stan asked.

'Nah. Slow down. Let it pass.'

Stan did what he said. The car accelerated and overtook the

van. A hand came out of the passenger side and flagged them down.

'Oh, fuck,' said Jimmy. 'The Old Bill. That's all we need.'

Stan pulled the van up by the kerb. Two men got out of the car and walked slowly towards them.

'Just stay calm,' muttered Billy.

'But we've got the fucking guns with us!' Jimmy hissed.

'I know we've got the fucking guns,' replied Billy.

On the back seat of the van was a shopping bag with a pair of overalls in it. Underneath the overalls were the revolver and the Luger. One of the men was tapping on the window. Plainclothes. CID. Billy grabbed the bag. Stan wound the window down.

'We're police officers,' the man by the window announced.

'Really?' Stan all fake cheery. 'What seems to be the trouble, Officer?'

'Mind telling me what you're all doing, running about three-handed this time of day?'

The copper nodded at Billy and Jimmy.

'We just been to the pub. For a game of darts.'

The copper laughed and said to his partner:

'We've got a darts team here, Dave.'

The other copper smiled knowingly and peered into the van.

'Yeah, well, they're some kind of team. That's for sure.'

'This your vehicle, is it, sir?'

Stan nodded.

'Yeah.'

'Your tax disc is out of date.'

'Yeah, well, I've applied for a new one. It's in the post.'

'Let's see your driving licence and insurance.'

One copper asking all these questions, the other snooping around the van, looking in at them. Billy felt the shape of the pistols in the shopping bag. Staring gloomily out of the passenger window, careful not to meet the eyes of the coppers, he caught sight of the walls and parapets beyond. Wormwood Scrubs. The prison loomed down at him.

'Your insurance is out of date too.'

'Give us a break, guv,' Stan pleaded.

'Let's have a look inside.'

One of the coppers looked in at Billy.

'What's in the bag, sir?'

Billy pulled out the overalls and held them out.

'Yeah, and the rest.'

Billy reached in again. He found the butt of the Luger. He clicked off the safety. This was it. This was the drill. Immediate Action Drill.

'Come on, you cunt. Empty the fucking bag.'

Billy pulled out the gun and shot the copper by Stan's window in the face. The other office froze for a second and then started to run back to the car. Billy got out of the van. He fired at the back of the fleeing man. The first shot missed.

The third policeman put the car in reverse. Jimmy grabbed the revolver and was in the road shooting at the police car. Billy fired again at the running man, who was now level with the car. He got him this time and the copper collapsed on to the tarmac, in front of the Triumph.

Kids playing on a patch of grass across the road. They hear the dry crack of gunfire. The delay of the sound of the shots from the movement makes it all look surreal. 'It's the telly,' one of them says. BBC down the road at White City. Often using local streets for filming exteriors. The man on the ground is twitching, one foot fluttering. Sudden knowledge. Horror. There are no cameras. This is really happening.

Jimmy was shooting out the windows of the police car. The driver, in a blind panic, crunched the gearbox into first and the Triumph shot forward, its front wheels running right over the body before it, jamming it beneath its chassis. Jimmy shot the driver through the windscreen. He slumped against the steering column. His weight was still on the accelerator but the body wedged under the car had lifted the back wheels a fraction off the ground. They spun wildy, free of any traction.

Billy and Jimmy ran back to the van. Stan was wide-eyed, muttering:

'Fuck, fuck, fuck.'

'Right, get us out of here,' ordered Billy as they got back in.

'What the fuck have you done?' whined Stan.

'Just fucking drive!'

*

All Flying Squad units are to telephone in immediately.

It came over the radio. Something big, I thought. Maybe I had a funny feeling around then. I don't know. Looking back it's hard to tell.

I was with an operational unit plotted up by a breaker's yard in Harlesden. Two cars. Me, DC Micky Parkes and a driver in one. C11 surveillance boys in the other. We had some information about a team at the jump-up. Lorry hijacking. This breaker's yard was supposed to be their slaughter. Maybe another of Vic Sayles' set-ups. I wasn't sure. I'd begun to lose track of what was to rights and what was hookey. Micky went to use the phone.

He came running back to the car.

'What is it?' I asked.

There was a puzzled look on his face.

'A Q-car's been ambushed in Shepherd's Bush.'

A Q-car in F Division. Dave.

'What do you mean, ambushed?'

'There's been a shooting.'

'A Q-car from the Bush?'

'Yeah.'

Foxtrot Eleven. Dave.

'What should we do?' Micky was asking. 'Hang on here?'

Dave Dave Dave Dave.

'Let's go!' I shouted at the driver.

Everything mobile was going west. The air alive with alarm bells. We got to Scrubs Lane. The whole street heaving with Old Bill. Uniform, plainclothes, motorbike coppers wandering about with their helmets still on, dog handler vans. Chaos. Officers trying to seal off the area as more bodies and vehicles came and went. Facts coming through the blur. Shocking stories running around. A shooting incident. Rumours of policemen dead.

The crime scene. Q-car with its windows shot out in the middle of the street. Foxtrot Eleven. A body lying in the gutter being covered with a bit of tarp by two officers. Blood on the tarmac. A figure in the driver's seat slumped over the wheel. Under the car a horribly twisted corpse. I wander up, flashing my warrant card at nobody in particular. Dazed, like everybody else on the scene. I crouch down and peer at the mangled body beneath the chassis.

Dave. It's Dave. I can see his face, twisted in shock and agony. Still recognisable. Dave. I'm on my hands and knees crawling towards him. Someone's pulling me back. I want to pull him out of there. I can't believe he's dead.

'Take it easy, Frank,' someone says, leading me away.

Sirens wailing in lamentation. Two-note keening into the summer sky. Dropping in pitch as they pass. Doppler shift. A semitone more mournful.

The sun in my eyes. Blinking at tears, red blotches swimming across my pupils. My mind racing. I'd done Dave a favour. Got him out of the West End. Out of danger. Back to the Bush. To this.

Guilt and anger. Guilt that it had been me that had put Dave here. Anger at Dave. Hard to account for. I just felt: *You stupid bastard, what did you want to go and get yourself killed for?*

Disbelief. He can't be dead. Dave, you can't be dead. I need to talk to you.

*

I was in Henekey's on Portobello Road with Alf Isaacs when it happened. I was there for the drugs bust I'd set up. I'd pitched the story to Sid and he let me have Alf for a couple of hours to supply the pictures for a nice little story. THE MENACE OF THE DRUGS RACKETS, that sort of thing. I was wearing a big canvas money-bag full of pennies in case I had to call into the news desk.

Chances were, on this story, I wouldn't have to phone anything in. We'd have time to get back to the *Illustrated*. But, I thought, you never know.

Alf Isaacs told me that there was this American press photographer who got the nickname Weegee, from Ouija board, because it was like he had a sixth sense. He'd always be first on the scene of the crime, sometimes even before the police had got there. Now Alf's a good snatch man, meaning that his speciality is getting a photo of someone who'd rather not have their face splashed all over the papers. Scandal, exposé, someone seen coming out of a club they shouldn't have been at with someone they shouldn't have been with. A con man or racketeer's likeness revealed to the public he'd cheated. He had good instincts but hardly the clairvoyance of this Yank. But this time, well, we were charmed.

It was a hot afternoon and Henekey's beer garden was full of long-hairs, their dirgelike music blaring out of the juke-box. A couple of West Indian guys, who'd clearly been dealing, now looking worried by the presence of a pair of rather obvious plainclothes who were trying to mingle with the crowd. Alf kept his camera hidden but we didn't exactly blend in with the surroundings. The black guys knew the game was up and were trying to ditch their gear. The Drugs Squad boys made their move and Alf got ready for the snatch. Then a whole squad of uniformed officers came trooping in. There were half-hearted protests from the freaks; some hippy girl tried to give a flower to an inspector. Sniffer dogs were panting in the heat. A couple of arrests were made, the rest of the crowd were searched. Alf Isaacs snapped away merrily.

Then suddenly there was a strange lull in the police activity. One of the uniforms spoke intently to his inspector. Something was up, I could tell; so could Alf. He lowered his camera and we glanced at each other in anticipation. Then the inspector started barking orders. The operation was aborted and they all started trooping out of the pub. The two black guys were laughing with relief. Something was happening, something serious was up. I looked at Alf and he frowned back.

'Come on,' I said. 'Let's go.'

We followed the convoy of police vehicles as it crossed Ladbroke Grove, going westwards towards Wormword Scrubs. The air was filled with bells ringing. It seemed that the whole of the Met was racing towards something on Scrubs Lane. Wormwood Scrubs loomed before us.

'Maybe there's been a jail-break,' Alf suggested.

We got there before the scene of crime had been cordoned off. We were the first press there – we even beat the BBC television crews who were just around the corner at White City. Alf got some extraordinary snatches before the whole area was sealed off, some that we'd never be able to use. The dead policeman slumped at the wheel, looking like he was just having a nap, a grotesquely mangled body beneath the car. The third policeman lay sprawled in the gutter. It was a bloody massacre.

I felt quite exhilarated, thrilled to be amid such slaughter. It was hard not to smile at all the shocked faces. I had a sense of being complicit in the brutality. This was my story. Soon the whole scene was screened off.

'Move back now,' a traffic cop commanded gruffly.

Kids had been playing in the street when it had happened. I got quotes from them. One of the killers looked like Bobby Charlton, they said. Somebody else was driving past when it happened. They got the number plate of the killer's car. I made a note of it as it was being taken down by a police officer. It was all happening so quickly I hardly realised how big it was.

I found a phone box and called Sid, piles of pennies laid out in front of me.

'I've got a big one, Sid,' I told him. 'Front-page stuff.'

'What is it, Tony?'

'Well,' I said, thinking that now was the time to bargain, 'you know you said if I got a real corker of a story there'd be a staff job for me?'

'Stop fucking about. What's going on?'

'I could go somewhere else with this. Just being a casual.'

They'd have Alf's pictures, of course. But I'd got lucky and I knew that I could push it a bit.

'You cunt,' he hissed down the phone. 'You better not be having me on.'

'On my life, Sid,' I said. 'Something really big is just breaking.'

'Well, tell me what it is.'

'And I'll get the job?'

Sid Franks sighed heavily.

'Yeah, yeah, whatever. This better be good.'

So I told him. He sent down all the Saturday Men he had spare and a staff man to co-ordinate it all. I ended up running it all, though. I knew more of what was going on than anyone else. The word was out and all the other Sundays were soon scrambling over it. But we had the drop on them. We got the story out in time for the first trains for the provincial editions while the enemies were struggling to meet the late deadlines. MASSACRED IN THE LINE OF DUTY was how the splash sub told it. Alf had got the best pictures, shocking images that emerged from the darkroom. The lead story had 'The *Sunday Illustrated*'s Crime Team' as its byline but I had my own piece on page three: 'First Man on the Scene, Tony Meehan'.

Sid himself grandstanded the whole edition with a Page Two Opinion: *TOUGH ACTION MUST BE TAKEN: In a quiet West London street where children played in the August sunshine an answer was given, a final sickening answer to the theorists, to the namby-pambies, to the misguided do-gooders. To those who have given crime and brutality a far too easy run in this country; who have removed the fear of death from even the most callous murderers.* And so on. Sid started the *Illustrated*'s campaign to bring back hanging. He wheeled out Lord Thursby, for a bit of punditry. A 'Why We Should Bring Back the Rope' column.

We put the paper to bed very happy men. The circulation manager was delirious, wandering about with bottles of champagne, declaring: 'It's a coup, gentlemen, it's a fucking coup.'

10

They headed south. Over Hammersmith Bridge and east towards Vauxhall. Stan had a lock-up there. On Battersea Bridge roundabout the van's engine started to pink and they slowed down.

'What the fuck's the matter now?' groaned Billy.

'The tank's empty,' muttered Stan. He slapped the steering wheel in frustration. 'Jesus Christ, we're out of petrol.'

He kept his finger on the starter motor button and the van lurched along the road.

'There's a garage up ahead,' Jimmy observed.

They made it to the petrol station and pulled up behind a Morris Minor. A little old lady in a tweed suit was having the full works and there was only one attendant.

'Could you check my oil?' she was saying.

Police bells ringing in the distance. Panic in the city. Stan drummed his fingers on the wheel nervously. Jimmy looked wild-eyed. Billy's head was numb, calm. Just as it was after a jungle killing.

At last they got some petrol and sped off through Nine Elms to Vauxhall. The lock-up was in a railway arch by the river. Stan crunched a wing of the van as he backed it in. They walked down to the Embankment. The tide was low. A pram skeleton washed up on the muddy banks of the river.

'What the fuck are we going to do?' Stan asked nobody in particular.

'We got to get some money,' Billy answered. 'We'll have to screw somewhere.'

'Leave it out,' said Stan. 'Fuck this. I'm off.'

And he ran off down the road. Billy and Jimmy watched him disappear. Jimmy was very edgy now, sweating like a pig. Never killed anyone before, thought Billy. They saw a bus coming and they ran for it. A number 68. They travelled on it to Euston, went into the station café and had a cup of tea. Jimmy's cup rattling against the saucer as he picked it up with a shaking hand.

'You look as white as a sheet,' Billy told him. 'What's the matter?'

'What do you fucking think?'

'You ain't going to lose your bottle, are you?'

'For Christ's sake, Billy.'

'So what's the plan this time, eh? What's the SP? What's the MO?' he needled Jimmy.

Billy had a mad grin on his face. Shock. Jimmy sucked noisily at the hot tea.

'I'm getting out,' said Jimmy.

'Oh yeah? Where you going to go?'

'Back to Glasgow. Lie low until all of this calms down.'

Billy laughed contemptuously.

'This ain't never going to calm down. Never.'

They split up after that. Billy felt safer on his own. The other two, well, they were a fucking liability. He still had the guns.

He went back to the bed-sit. A smell of fried fish in the hallway. Sandra came out of the kitchen to greet him.

'What's the matter, love?' she asked. 'You look terrible.'

'I feel terrible.'

'I got a nice bit of rock salmon for tea.'

'I'm not hungry. I feel sick.'

He pointed at his throat.

'Sick up to here.'

'Did you hear the news?' she asked. 'About the policemen being shot?'

He stared at her.

'Oh no, Billy.'

'Shut up!' he snapped. 'Keep quiet about it.'

*

I badly wanted to be in on the investigation. Things were moving very fast. Detective Superintendent Tommy Fairburn had been appointed to take charge of the case. He was 'in the frame'. Quite literally. There was a wooden frame in Coco listing three senior officers on call to take on major murder investigations. It was Tommy's turn. He'd only just got back from Gloucester assizes, where he'd been giving evidence in a murder trial. DCI Jack Walker was his second-in-command and DI Ernie Franklin had been chosen from the Flying Squad. They were putting the operational team together. I managed to get to see Ernie.

'I really want a transfer on to the operation, sir.'

'Yeah, well, a lot of people are keen to get involved. It's understandable.'

'But I know the manor, sir. I've still got informants on the patch.'

'You worked F Division?'

'Yeah. I mean yes, sir. At the Bush.'

'So you know the men who were killed.'

'Dave Thomas, sir. We were bucks together.'

A sharp intake of breath.

'That's tough, son. Look, maybe you're too close to it. Anyway, it ain't up to me who's on the team. You're new on the Flying Squad, aren't you, son?'

'Yes, sir.'

'Well, look, the Heavy Mob is going to have an important role in this operation. We need to put the pressure on the other side to hand up the bastards that did this. Who's your guvnor?'

'Vic Sayles.'

'Well, don't worry, he'll keep you busy.'

And busy we were. Firearms were issued and the squad spent

the night tearing about all over the place. Along with the newly formed Special Patrol Group, the Flying Squad's brief was to check on every possible hiding place in the city. Every dodgy pub, club, spieler or lock-up. Every known team of villains, anybody who had form for being at the heavy. They were all going to get a visit that night. The whole of gangland was going to get the shakedown.

Vic Sayles' role was obvious. He knew all the major-league faces. He'd done deals with all of them in his time, cut them enough slack in order to maintain his who's who knowledge of the underworld. Favours were owed. Now it was payback time.

'We want to start with the big guys,' he told me as we motored over to the West End. 'Well, we can forget about the Krays. The twins aren't going to be much use. They don't stray very far from the East End and they just don't play ball. The Richardsons are all wiped up. That leaves Freddie Foreman and Harry Starks. Frank Williams knows Freddie well so he's going after him. So we're going to have a word with Mr Starks.'

We got to Soho. Harry Starks' nightclub. The Stardust. Starks was a good place to start. He had West London connections. He'd worked for Rachman before he'd set up on his own. And though he wasn't known for being involved with armed blagging himself, he was known to offer protection to those getting their hands dirty. And his club was a regular meeting place for any number of London faces.

At the entrance to the club I whipped out my warrant card but one of the doormen was already nodding in recognition at Vic.

'Evening, Mr Sayles,' he muttered with gruff deference.

'Want a word with your guvnor,' Vic announced.

'Yeah.' The bouncer nodded again. 'Right. You'd better come in, then.'

He led us into the club. On stage some tart in a sequinned evening gown was bawling out 'You'll Never Walk Alone' in front of a mangy backing band. A lot of eyeballing from tables here and there. Dodgy-looking customers shuffling uneasily. Knowing who we were and wondering whether this was a raid, no doubt.

Harry Starks was at the head of a big table in the corner. A young blond kid next to him. A couple of business types being entertained with plenty of booze and a brace of busty tarts. A doorman went ahead and whispered in Starks' ear. Harry looked up at us as we came to the table. He stood up, smiling.

'Vic,' he said, all affable. 'To what do I owe the pleasure?'

'This ain't a social call, Harry,' Sayles replied.

'What's up?'

'I think you know why we're here.'

Starks frowned. Heavy eyebrows knitted.

'There's been a massacre, Harry. A bloody massacre.'

Starks sighed heavily.

'Terrible business,' he said, shaking his head. 'Terrible. Look, gentlemen . . .' He turned to his guests. 'You must excuse me.' Back to us. 'We better go upstairs.'

In his office Harry Starks poured us all a large brandy and we got down to business.

'Surely, Vic,' he said, 'you don't imagine I had anything to do with this, do you?'

'Yeah, but you might know who did.'

'I ain't heard nothing. Honest.'

'Don't fuck me around, Harry. Most of London's villainy come through this gaff at one time or another.'

'Straight up. Don't you think that I want this sorted out as much as you do? It's completely out of order. It fucks everything up. If I knew anything, you'd be the first to know.'

'I'm glad you see it that way, Harry. It's bad enough when you lot are killing each other. But this is something else. Our side is angry, fucking angry, and we want blood. My DS here' – he nodded at me – 'lost a best friend this afternoon.'

I felt an odd kind of shock as Vic said that. It still hadn't sunk in yet, I suppose. Dave dead. Dead. My face darkened as I stared at Starks. He looked a bit shaken.

'I'm sorry, son,' he muttered. 'I'm . . .'

'This is fucking grief, Harry. We want a result soon. A lot of

125

us have played the game with you lot. Straightened things, done deals to keep the peace. Well, we're on the fucking warpath now. If anybody's hiding these bastards they better hand them up now otherwise there'll be hell to pay.'

'Look, Vic . . .' Starks all soft-voiced, reasonable. 'As I said, we all want this business dealt with.'

'Just let everybody know. Every firm, every team. Every fucking villain in every fucking manor. Anyone who so much as gives these cunts the time of day will have their cards marked. And I suggest you don't wait around for the duration. I suggest you lot find the killers and turn them in, pronto. 'Cos in the meantime there's going to be the biggest fucking clampdown you ever did see.'

'Yeah.' Starks nodded, thoughtfully. 'Point taken. I'll see what I can do.'

'Any information, no matter how small, let me or my DS here know. OK?'

We stood up to leave. Starks came around the desk to the door.

'Don't worry,' said Vic. 'We can find our own way out.'

*

Sunday and the story was everywhere. My story. Thanks to me the *Illustrated* had scooped most of it. A nation in shock, Union Jacks half-masted everywhere. There were constant bulletins on the television and the radio, endless angry comment. The bring-back-the-noose brigade was in full throat. That would keep Sid happy, I thought.

The Home Secretary visited Shepherd's Bush police station. Television cameras were there and a large mob, baying for blood. As he was being interviewed, hecklers in the crowd were shouting out to bring back hanging.

'I can well understand the strength of feeling at the present time, of, quite rightly, outrage at this heinous crime, but it would be quite wrong for me to make a major policy decision in the shadow of one event, however horrible that event may be.'

The mayor of Hammersmith launched an appeal for a fund for

the dead policemen's dependants, and all across the country citizens were emptying their piggy-banks to make a donation.

Then came all the theories. What on earth had been the cause of the massacre? Two main notional motives were firming up. It had been a planned jail-break from Wormwood Scrubs or an underworld power struggle. The Q-car had come across two rival gangs and had been caught up in the crossfire of a shoot-out.

I was summoned to lunch at the proprietor's that day. I went with Sid Franks to his huge penthouse on Park Lane.

'You lucky cunt,' Sid muttered to me. 'The Boss hardly ever invites me, let alone a fucking reporter.'

It meant that my staff job was secure and I'd been noticed. I felt pretty pleased with myself.

'Just don't speak unless you're spoken to,' Sid was briefing me as we went up in the lift. 'And if he offers you a drink, decline. The old bastard's teetotal.'

We were ushered in by a butler with bulging eyes and a fishlike mouth.

'How is he, Francis?' Sid asked.

Francis gave a hollow chuckle.

'Oh, you know, tetchy. Very, very tetchy.'

The Boss was pacing up and down his cavernous apartment. He had a small shrewlike secretary who sat in the corner and would occasionally make shorthand notes on her pad when he wanted a comment recorded. Ted Howard, the washed-out-looking editor-in-chief, was already there, perched on the edge of an enormous black leather sofa.

Lunch was extraordinarily bland. Boiled fish in a tasteless parsley sauce, potatoes, carrots and peas, also boiled. Ted Howard had a plate of sandwiches instead and sat there munching at them, looking ghostlike. Francis, the butler, came around with a chilled bottle of Pouilly Fumé and a mischievous look on his face, knowing that we'd all settle for iced water, like the Boss. He fired questions at Sid and Ted and nodded at their answers, occasionally turning to comment to his secretary. The conversation moved on to stories the paper could run.

'I think we could do an investigation into psychic phenomena,' Ted suggested in his slow, gloomy voice.

I caught a glimpse of Sid barely concealing his impatience with this. Ted Howard had increasingly become obsessed with the paranormal; he appeared to have already joined the other side. Sid could often be found fuming in the newsroom, muttering, 'Ted wants another fucking table-tapping article.' There was some discussion that Sid steered back to general aims. They talked of the 'enemies', the *News of the World* and the *People*. Sid offered an obvious opinion.

'We've got to give the readership what it wants,' he declared.

'No, no, Sidney,' the Boss retorted. 'You've got it the wrong way around. We've got to get the readership to want what we give it.'

Eventually the big story of the day came up.

'Terrible business,' said the Boss. 'Terrible. But a great issue. Circulation figures were tremendous.'

He turned to me for the first time.

'And you're the young man that broke it.'

'Yes.'

'How did you manage that?'

'I don't know. I mean, I was in the right place at the right time, I suppose.'

'That's what the paper needs, gentlemen!' the Boss exclaimed. 'People in the right place at the right time. You'll see to that, won't you, Sidney?'

11

They hardly slept at all. They held on to each other in the darkness. When dawn came Billy turned the radio on to listen to the news. The police had the registration number of the van. They'd soon be on to Stan. He'll grass us all up in no time, thought Billy.

And the van. Fuck, the van. There was forensic all over it. They should have burned it. Too late for that now.

Billy started packing a small case. Sandra watched him wandering about the bed-sit like he was in a trance.

'I've got to get away,' he explained.

'I want to come too,' she said.

He stared at her, wondering how far he could trust her. He remembered Trixie, grassing him when she was picked up by the Tom Squad. You couldn't trust a woman. Sandra looked back at him, imploringly.

'Please,' she said, softly.

He smiled.

'Yeah,' he replied, nodding slowly. 'OK.'

So she packed her little duffle bag. The same one she'd packed when she'd run away from home. She was running away again. But anything was better than going back there.

'Where are we going to go?' she asked.

'I don't know yet. But I'll tell you what we'll do first.'

'What?'

'We'll go and see Mum.'

Sandra laughed. She couldn't help herself.

'What's so fucking funny?' Billy demanded.

It was just like the usual Sunday lunch-time ritual except this time they went first to Paddington Station to leave their bags in the left luggage. Lily was full of the news of the shooting.

'I don't know what the world's coming to,' she declared.

Sandra checked Billy's response, and his eyes darted to hers. But they both remained impassive. Giving nothing away, except perhaps in being so subdued. She felt that maybe they should join in the outrage, comment on how terrible things had become, but she knew that neither of them had the stomach for that.

They ate in near-silence. After they had finished eating Billy coughed and looked towards his mother.

'So, Ma,' he began. 'I need to ask a favour.'

'What is it, Billy?'

He sighed.

'It's the business.'

She frowned.

'I thought you said the business was going well.'

'It is, Ma, it is. The thing is, I've got a bit of a cash flow problem.'

'What do you mean? I thought you said you had a big job coming up.'

'Well, that's just it, Ma. I need to invest in some new plant to get this contract done. As I said, it's just a cash flow problem.'

'Cash flow?'

'Yeah, I need a bit to tide me over.'

Lily stared at her son. Sandra saw an awful look of knowing.

'Are you in trouble, son?' she asked.

Billy laughed nervously.

'Of course not, Ma. It's just . . .'

Billy's mother turned to Sandra with a piercing gaze. Sandra dropped her spoon and it clattered on to her plate.

'Oh, Billy.'

His mother's voice was a soft, mournful wail.

'It's all right, Ma,' he tried to placate her. 'Honest.'

But she had already got up from the table and gone over to the tea caddy on the mantelpiece. She knows, thought Sandra. She watched as the older woman stoically counted out the notes. It looked as though there was actual physical effort in her holding herself up. She was pretending not to know. Only this was bearable. Giving in to the knowledge of it would send her crashing to the floor. She sniffed and lifted her head as she closed the lid of the box. As she came back to the table with the money her eyes were glistening. She handed the little bundle to Billy.

'You better go, son,' she said.

'Well,' he said, 'we don't have to go yet, Ma. We can stay a little while longer.'

'No,' she said deliberately, coldly. 'You'd better be off.'

As Billy kissed her on the cheek, Lily's eyes shut tight and a tear squeezed out from each one. As they closed the front door behind them they could just hear a muffled sobbing from inside.

They got their bags and found a hotel near the station. They signed in as Mr and Mrs Crosby. A young married couple on holiday, thought Sandra, almost believing it herself for a moment.

In bed Billy smoked incessantly, staring at the ceiling. She moved up close to him. He put an arm around her and held her against his chest. Suddenly she wanted him. She slid her leg slowly over his groin and moaned softly. He sighed sharply and pushed her away.

'Leave it out,' he hissed. 'For Christ's sake.'

She rolled over and curled up into a ball. She put her thumb in her mouth and rocked gently on the bed. She soon found sleep. There was nowhere else to go. Billy lit another cigarette and stroked her back. His hand was shaking. She was a liability. Sooner or later he'd have to leave her behind.

*

Monday morning and the van's owner had been traced via a car dealer in Kilburn. We had a name, Stanley Mullins, and an address in West Eleven. A whole load of us were issued with arms and sent to surround a block of flats off Ladbroke Grove. The Special Patrol Group was there in force too. Their first big operation, so they wanted to make a good show of it. Two of their guys in position with tear gas pistols. There was a strange feeling on the raid with us all being so tooled up. An expectancy of something we didn't quite know yet. We weren't ready for this. It was like we were playing with new toys. And a kind of rivalry was emerging between the SPG and the Flying Squad. It had been plainclothes officers who had been killed so we wanted to get the bastards before anyone else. And I suppose both teams considered themselves to be the élite of their type. The SPG for uniform branch, Flying Squad for the Department.

So there was a whole mob of us waiting, dogs and dog handlers at the ready. When we knew we had all the angles covered, Ernie Franklin kicked the door in and stormed in with a couple of lads, Webleys at the ready. I clocked this bloke they hauled out but it wasn't anyone I recognised. His wife was bawling away on the access balcony. The estate forecourt was filling up with onlookers; the SPG went into crowd control as he was bundled into a black Maria. I started thinking, maybe he was just small fry. All these theories about a planned jail-break or a gang shoot-out, well, they didn't really add up. Maybe it was just a minor-league team. Time to look farther down the food chain. Maybe I could get a lead from my local informants. I got in touch with Golly, who'd been a snout of mine when I'd been at the Bush.

I figured that maybe I could get the drop on the investigation. Ernie Franklin would already be hard at work on this Mullins bloke, but if I could come up with some other names I'd be ahead of the game. Golly always liked to meet at the cinema. He was paranoid about being seen in daylight. I arranged to meet him at our usual place for a matinée at Shepherd's Bush Odeon. I got there for the second show. One for the circle. A bored usherette tore my ticket and handed me the stub. Upstairs. The place was nearly empty. Just a couple in the back. Boy and girl. Furtive teenage movements. Truant fumbling. I could make out Golly easily enough from his trademark shock of frizzy hair. There he was in his usual place at the front, rattling a little box of chocolate-covered peanuts.

The Pearl & Dean advertising fanfare started to blare out as I sidled along the row to sit next to Golly. Giggles from the back row. *Probably think we're a couple of queers*, I thought.

'You know what this is about, don't you?' I whispered.

Golly rolled a nut around his rotten molars, mashing it thoughtfully.

'Mmm.' He sucked at his teeth and probed cavities with his tongue. 'Long time no see, Mr Taylor. Or should I say Detective Sergeant Taylor.'

'Yeah, yeah.'

'In the Flying Squad now, aren't we?'

'Golly . . .'

'We have come up in the world. I suppose it's kind of a promotion for both of us, isn't it?'

'What the fuck are you on about?'

'Well, now you're a DS. In the Heavy Mob. That makes me . . .'

'Makes you what? You're a grass, Golly. Don't get above yourself.'

'Yeah, but a Flying Squad grass.'

'Look, stop fucking me about, Golly. I need some info.'

'All I'm saying . . .' Golly smacked his lips.

'Golly . . .'

'Congratulations, that's all.'

'Right. Now, you know what this is, don't you?'

'The shooting.'

'Yeah, that.'

'Terrible business. Let me take the opportunity to offer my condolences to . . .'

'Golly, for fuck's sake, let's just get on with it, shall we?'

Golly rattled another nut from his box and popped it into his mouth.

'Stanley Mullins,' I said to him. 'Mean anything to you?'

'Mm.' Golly worked the nut around his mouth. 'Stan, mm, yes.'

'You know him?'

'Mm, yeah. Petty thief. Small-time. Wouldn't expect him to be involved in this.'

'What about associates?'

'Yeah, well, he was knocking around with a couple of geezers.'

'Who?'

'Jimmy something. Scotch. And this bloke Billy. They were kind of teamed up. Nothing big, though.'

'Right. What about second names?'

Golly made a fluid sniff.

'Sorry. Dunno.'

'Well, that'll do for now. See what you can find out and I'll be in touch.'

I got up to leave. Golly grabbed my arm.

'Mr Taylor?'

'Yes?'

'I expect there'll be quite a reward for information leading and so on.'

'I expect so, yes.'

'Well, I was wondering if I couldn't have a bit of a sub, like.'

'You're a fucking parasite,' I told him, and handed him a fiver.

I rushed over to the Bush where Mullins was being held. I got someone to haul Ernie Franklin out of the interrogation. He sighed heavily when he saw me.

'Taylor,' he said impatiently when he saw it was me. 'I thought I told you there's no room for you on this investigation.'

'I know, sir, but I've got something.'

'What is it?'

'Something off a local snout, sir. Known associates of this man you're holding. Ask him about two blokes he knocks about with. Jimmy and Billy.'

'I'm still in the process of checking his alibi, son.'

'Yeah, but just ask him.'

'Listen, son, let's not jump the gun. We've got to be methodical about this.'

'But, sir . . .'

'But nothing. Listen, Taylor, you've got your orders on this operation and I suggest you stick to them. We can't afford to have every officer in the Met conducting his own private investigation.'

'I'm sorry, sir, it's just . . .'

'Yeah, yeah. Look, thanks for the information. And if you'll excuse me I've got an interview to attend to.'

*

My first day as a staff reporter on the *Illustrated* and I was put in charge of the paper's 'Crime Team' covering the Shepherd's Bush shooting. When I asked who else was on the team Sid said:

'You're it, son. We'll use other staff men and casuals whenever we get any breaks. Your job, for the moment, is to stay on top of it. And let me know as soon as anything happens.'

So I put together all we had on the case so far. I called it the Shepherd's Bush Shooting Crime Dossier.

'Yeah, I like that,' said Sid. 'Sounds dead professional.'

He, in the meantime, was working on the public outrage angle. His latest idea was a 'Readers' Poll: Should We Bring Back the Rope?' Some Tory MP had already brought this up in the House. Sid was sure that this aspect of the case would be a winner, no matter what happened before the Saturday deadline.

'And we'll need a bloody good womb-trembler,' he announced to the whole newsroom. 'All this doom and gloom is going to be too much otherwise.'

I felt a sudden sense of confidence in myself. Something had gone right for once in my life, a dream of a story. Sid drew up a contract for me to sign. And there was something about the crime itself that made me feel bold. It had been so ruthless. Someone had taken their revenge – it was reassuring in some way.

Then news came through that a man had been arrested and taken to the Bush. I rushed over there with Alf Isaacs. He got a good snatch of the man being bundled into the nick under a blanket, but there was only a brief comment to the press about a man 'helping with their inquiries'. No name yet. So we decamped, with the rest of the press, to the White Horse.

I realised then that there would be a hell of a lot of waiting around. And a lot of drinking. I'd known that that was part of the routine but I'd never really got into it when I was a Saturday Man. But there just wasn't much else to do. All the press men in huddles, swapping stories and theories, an endless buzz of information and opinion and gossip. We had to be on call around the clock, and that would usually mean holing up somewhere where you could get a drink and maybe a sandwich.

I met up with Julian after work. I bought him dinner at the Gay Hussar.

'Congratulations,' he said. 'Legitimate at last.'

'If you can call the *Illustrated* legitimate.'

'Don't knock it, darling. It's a job. Now if only I could get a gossip column somewhere.'

Julian told me that he was cultivating Teddy Thursby.

'He's a great source. And, you know . . .'

He shrugged and gave this queeny smile. He was up to his old tricks of latching on to an older and richer homo.

We went on to Le Gigolo on the King's Road. I can't really remember very much about the evening as I got very drunk. Woke up fully clothed on my bed with no idea of how I'd got home.

12

Billy lay in the grass in Hyde Park. A sunny day. A red glow on the backs of his eyelids. Killing time. *Here I am*, he thought. *I'm the one you're looking for.* His mind was reeling. Ever present. An animal paranoia. Of being hunted. He couldn't relax for a second. When he was a kid he thought if he closed his eyes and everything disappeared he would disappear too. He would become invisible. But now he felt himself being watched all the time.

He sat up. A group of hippies in a circle near by. Having a picnic. Passing around a joint. He had to wait until five. Then he'd go to see Sam. He'd phoned him that day and made an appointment.

Sam was a forger he'd met in the Scrubs. Maybe he'd be able to get him a bent passport. Then he'd be off. To Ireland, he reckoned. Sandra was wearing the minidress he'd bought her. She sat beside him, eyeing him nervously. They'd run out of things to say to each other. He'd have to get rid of her.

She went and got an *Evening Standard*. They'd found the van in the lock-up. His dabs were all over it. What a fucking mess, he thought. He sent Sandra back to the hotel and got a bus to Camden Town.

Sam had a second-hand bookshop on Chalk Farm Road. A musty smell of old paper in the place. Sam closed the shop and led him out to the back. He lit a fag.

'What can I do you for, Billy?'

'I want a passport.'

Sam took a drag and smiled.

'What's the matter? Petty France closed, is it?'

'You know what I mean.'

'Yeah, sure.'

'So?'

'Well, I'll need a photograph. Should be able to sort something out by tomorrow.'

'How much?'

'A ton.'

'You're joking, ain't you?'

'Take it or leave it, Billy.'

*

Tuesday. Vic Sayles called me into his office.

'Got a message from our friend, Mr Starks. Says he might have something for us.'

'That's great, guvnor.'

'Yeah. Thing is, Frank, I've got to go to a senior officers' briefing. Seems like this bloke they've pulled has coughed. Can you go over and check it out?'

I went over to the Stardust and met Starks in his office.

'Well,' he said, 'I've been checking on all the faces I know who are known to use shooters. Nothing. But then a business associate of mine knows somebody who's been dealing them quite recently.'

'A business associate?'

Starks grinned.

'Yeah. Bubble,' he said. 'He reckons he knows something.'

Tony Stavrakakis, he meant.

'I thought the big Greek had gone straight.'

Starks shrugged.

'Well, he keeps his hand in, you know? Turns out one of his fellow countrymen was looking to sell a Luger. Could be a lead. Anyway, Tony's got a restaurant up in Finsbury Park. I'll give you the address.'

He wrote something on a scrap of paper.

'We want these bastards caught, you know. This whole thing has been a pain in the arse. Your lot breathing down our neck all week.'

He handed me the address.

'Be lucky, son. If you don't get them' – he grinned – 'we will.'

I got up to go. At the door he slipped a wad of notes into my hand.

'Wait a minute,' I said. 'What the fuck is this?'

'No, no,' he said, pushing the money into my palm. 'Don't get me wrong. It's for that benevolent fund thing.'

The Dionysus restaurant, Finsbury Park. Stavrakakis was in the kitchen watching the chef putting these chunks of meat on big skewers. I flashed my warrant card and he nodded. He'd been expecting me.

'Listen,' he said, 'if I tell you what I know, that's it, innit?'

'That depends on what you've got.'

'No, you listen here. Harry said I just tell you what I know and there ain't no trouble for me.'

'OK.'

'It's a deal?'

'Yeah, sure. It's a deal.'

He smiled and shook my hand with a big meaty paw.

'OK. Look, this man Costas. He's political. A troublemaker. He sell a gun to this man.'

'Where? Here?'

'Look, I told you. I tell you what I know and that's it. I no involved in anything else. OK?'

'OK.'

'Well then, I tell you where you can find this man Costas.'

I got my notebook out.

*

There was a press conference at Scotland Yard on Tuesday morning. I went along, bleary-eyed and hung over. The man who had been helping the police with their inquiries was named as Stanley Mullins.

He had now been remanded in custody. Two other men suspected of being involved in the killings were named as Jimmy Drummond and Billy Porter. Descriptions were given. Distinguishing marks: Drummond, tall with balding hair, the man the kids at the scene had remarked 'looked like Bobby Charlton'; Billy Porter, thick brown hair, a tattoo of a tiger on his right shoulder.

The public were warned not to approach these men, they were dangerous, possibly armed. All of this would make the late editions of the evening papers and the six o'clock news bulletins. My deadline seemed miles away. I had a long boozy lunch.

Sid called me into his office in the afternoon, the 'bollocking room'. I knew I'd done something wrong. He waved a handful of pink expense forms at me dismissively.

'This is no good,' he said. 'No bloody good at all. It really won't do.'

'I'm sorry, Sid,' I said. 'I didn't realise it was too much.'

'Too much?' he retorted. 'Too bloody much? It's not too much, you silly cunt. It's too little.'

I frowned and he sighed and sat me down, patted me on the back and whispered in my ear.

'Listen, son. If accounts start noticing that one of our reporters is claiming less than half everybody else is they might start adding a few things together. And we don't want that, do we?'

I felt exhausted so I went home and had a long soak in a hot bath. Julian came around to my flat later. He had a mischievous look on his face.

'Well,' he declared as I let him in, 'didn't we have a good time last night.'

'What are you talking about?'

'You, darling. You were quite on form.'

I couldn't remember a thing. I had an awful sinking sensation. I had made a fool of myself, no doubt.

'Oh, Christ,' I murmured.

'Yes, dear,' Julian continued with an evil smile. 'You were quite the entertainment for the evening.'

'What did I do?'

'Well, you went into this extraordinary . . .' Julian paused to conjure a word. '. . . routine. It was quite wild.'

I felt sick. The thought of making an exhibition of myself was nauseating. But I worried more about losing control.

13

Billy and Sandra went to Paddington Station to the photo-booth there to get a picture for Billy's passport.

'Where are we going to go, Billy?'

'I don't know, love. Over the water somewhere. Dublin, probably.'

He suddenly thought that he was stupid telling her anything. As soon as he'd ditched her she'd blab everything. But he needed to keep her sweet for just a bit longer.

As he was putting the money in the machine she suddenly had a thought.

'Billy?' she said.

'Yeah?'

'You only need one picture, don't you?'

'Yeah.'

'Well, once you've got that, I could come into the booth with you.'

'What?'

'So we could have our picture taken together.'

'Are you fucking mad?'

'I just thought . . .'

'What if somebody found that on you? That would look good, wouldn't it?'

'I just haven't got a picture of us together.'

'A nice little souvenir, is that what you want?'

She started to cry.

'I'm sorry, Billy.'

She looked pale and pathetic. She was just a kid, after all. She could crack up at any time. He had to be careful with her no matter how stupid she could be. He put his arm around her.

'Don't worry, love. We'll get our picture done. One day.'

She went back to the hotel and he went up to Camden for his appointment with Sam. He passed a newspaper stall. YARD NAME TWO 'ARMED MEN' was the headline. Stan had cracked. It was all closing in on him. He hoped to God that Sam hadn't seen the evening paper.

Sam closed up the shop again and they went out the back. Billy handed over the passport photo. Sam took it and sat down at his desk. He had a passport there that had its photograph removed. Sam placed Billy's picture over the original photo, turned them over and picked up a pencil. His hand was trembling. He began to move the pencil to and fro across the back of the photographs.

'Piece of piss, really,' he explained as he worked. 'You see, there's an embossed stamp that goes over the corner of the photo and on to the front page, see?'

He showed Billy the round seal on the front page of the passport, a quarter-circle missing in the box where the photograph had been.

'It's like brass-rubbing. All you've got to do is transfer that impression from one photograph to another.'

He continued to scrawl away with the pencil. He seemed agitated.

'There,' he declared, turning both pictures over again. There was now an impression of the stamp on Billy's likeness. 'Instant new identity.'

He placed the photo on the passport.

'All I got to do now is trim it so it fits flush. And bingo.'

He gave a big nervous smile.

'Bet you're wondering why I need a moody passport, aren't you, Sam?'

'Oh, no, Billy. You know me. No questions asked.'

Billy saw Sam sneak a look at his watch.

'Running late, are they?'

'What do you mean?'

'The people you're expecting. The people you've told I'm going to be here.'

'I haven't told anybody.'

'You fucking liar.'

Billy pulled out the Luger, pointed it at Sam's head.

'You've grassed me up, haven't you?'

Sam was shaking.

'No I ain't, Billy. Honest.'

Billy pressed the gun against his head.

'Tell the truth, Sam.'

'Honest. I haven't. I ain't said a word to the Old Bill.'

There was a rapping against the glass in the door of the shop.

'Then who's that, then?'

'It ain't the Old Bill.'

'What?'

'It's the other side. They want to hand you up, Billy. What you did has caused so much aggravation. No firm's going to get any peace until it's cleared up. Everyone knows I do bent passports so they figured that you might be paying me a visit.'

The rapping came again. Louder, more insistent.

'I wouldn't grass to the Old Bill. But I'm hardly going to say no to that lot, am I?'

Billy shut the door of the back room and pushed the desk against it.

'Where's the back way out of here?'

'You'll have to go through the window.'

'Right. Turn around. I better give you a lump. Don't want to get into trouble with that lot, do yer?'

'No need for that, Billy.'

'Turn around, you silly cunt.'

Billy whacked Sam around the back of the head with the butt of the pistol. He could hear the sound of glass breaking as the shop door was kicked in. He put the gun back into his waistband and opened the window. He turned back to the desk for a second and looked at the passport. That would be no use now. He pocketed his photograph and climbed out.

*

Ernie Franklin called me into his office.

'I just want to thank you, Frank. Those names your snout gave you, well, they jogged a few memories.'

'I didn't want you to think that I was jumping the gun, sir.'

'No, of course not. It's just that everybody's so bloody keen to be in on the sharp end on this one. I just have to make sure that we're allocating resources properly. We don't want officers duplicating each other's investigations.'

'I've got another lead, sir.'

'Christ, you've been busy. What is it?'

'I think I might have found the bloke that supplied the guns to the gang. Greek Cypriot. Ex-EOKA apparently.'

'What have you got?'

'A name and an address. Finsbury Park.'

I jotted it all down for him. Ernie sat there for a while looking at this scrap of paper. Then he peered over it at me.

'Look, Taylor. Since you've been so busy and all maybe you'd like to be in on it when we pull this Greek bloke.'

I grinned.

'Not half. I mean, yes, sir.'

'Well, I'll have a word with Vic Sayles.'

So early the next morning we got an operational team together and plotted up plenty-handed outside the address Tony Stavrakakis had given me. A dawn raid. We sledgehammered his door down and went in, guns drawn. This Costas guy was in bed with a blonde tart. We dragged him out half naked and bundled him into the back of a black Maria. We found a small arsenal of guns and ammunition under the floorboards of his dingy little flat.

After five hours of questioning Costas admitted to selling a Luger to a man fitting the description of Billy Porter but denied knowing of his whereabouts. This didn't get us very far but Ernie was pleased with the result.

'Well, at least it's something,' he said.

'Yeah, but it doesn't get us anywhere closer to Porter, does it, guv?'

'Maybe not. But at least we're seen as doing something. That's good for morale. Look, Frank . . .'

'Yes, sir?'

'I'm going to recommend a commendation for this.'

'Thank you, sir.'

'You've been busy. But more importantly you've been lucky. And that's what we need right now. A bit of luck. So how would you like to be drafted in as part of the main investigation team?'

'I think you know the answer to that one, guvnor.'

'Right. Well, you're in.'

*

The front page of the *Illustrated* that week was a blown-up photo the police had issued. MANHUNT FOR BILLY PORTER, splashed the headline. *Yard warn public: 'He is armed and dangerous, do not approach him.'* Sid Franks was drumming up the lynch mob with his Readers' Poll on Capital Punishment: 'Let The Powers That Be Know What *You* Think'. There were reported sightings of Porter everywhere. My byline was on the 'Profile of a Killer' feature on page five. I collated the sparse details: borstal as a teenager, National Service, a GBH charge in the late fifties. He was shaping up as Public Enemy Number One. Attention was drawn to the intense gaze in the police photograph. Dark, hooded eyes, thick arched eyebrows. 'The Eyes of a Killer,' I wrote, 'the ruthless stare of evil.'

I found myself studying the face. It seemed to be looking out at me, quizzical, goading, the eyebrows joined. That was supposed to mean something, wasn't it? Born to hang. That's what they said. Maybe Porter was as cursed as I was. Everyone was still trying to work out what the motive for the killings was. Maybe this was it.

Physiognomy, the knowledge of outward signs. Stigmata. *It's written all over your face*, my mother used to accuse me when I'd done something wrong and was refusing to admit to it. And could not physiognomy be used as divination as well? Just like the reading of a palm, you could tell by the face the fate of its wearer. I wondered what my own features betrayed. I looked at Porter and thought I recognised a fellow monster.

All of these mad thoughts seemed to possess me, as if they were driving me on to something. Porter's mouth, slightly open as if he were about to say something, to tell me what to do. I was drinking too much. Too many long boozy lunches were taking their toll on my mind and I felt that if I wasn't careful, I'd lose it. I almost yearned for such a release.

Walking back to the office from lunch one day, I caught my reflection in a shop window. Through a glass darkly. It hovered over a display, transparent and ghostly, a hunted, frightened expression. And something else. The eyes of a killer.

14

He sent Sandra out in the morning to get a paper. Jimmy had been picked up in Glasgow. The stupid bastard had been staying at his father's house. Two down, one to go. Now he was on on his own. Well, almost. He'd already decided what to do.

They checked out of the hotel. Billy tried to look relaxed as the manager added up their bill. Every glance, every delay could be significant. The police photo was everywhere. He wasn't safe in the city.

They got a bus over to King's Cross. Billy held hands with Sandra. This would make him look less suspicious, he thought. Part of a young couple. She could give him cover for a while. But it couldn't last.

He led her to a shop on Pentonville Road. CAMPING AND ARMY SURPLUS, it said above the door. He bought a groundsheet, a sleeping bag, a Primus stove, some mess tins, a combat jacket, combat boots, some thick white socks and check shirts, a small radio and a rucksack to put it all in.

Special Operations, he thought. They want a hunt. I'll give them a fucking hunt. He stopped off at a grocer's and got some provisions. A loaf of bread, three tins of beans, Oxo cubes, a packet of tea, dried milk. Rations. He bought a couple of tins of Old Holborn tobacco and some green Rizla papers. They got the 720 Greenline bus to Epping Forest. They got off at a stop at the edge of the forest.

Billy changed into his new boots, lacing them up slowly.

'Are we going to hide in the woods?' asked Sandra.

'I'm going to hide. It's time for me to go it alone.'

Sandra started to cry.

'But I can help you,' she sniffed. 'Please let me come with you.'

'You can't. I got to do this on my own, now.'

'But,' she sobbed, 'I've got nowhere else to go.'

'Get the bus back into town,' said Billy. 'Maybe you should go back home, you know.'

'I ain't going back there,' she replied.

And she meant it. She wouldn't go back. Never.

Billy held her and kissed her hard on the mouth. He pulled away.

'I got to go,' he announced.

He turned and walked away into the forest, without looking back. He started making ground. He had a long way to go but knew where he was headed. Epping Forest was too obvious. And he couldn't be sure that Sandra wouldn't go to the police. Thorley Woods by Bishop's Stortford. That's where he would go. Where he had played as a boy. His mother had taken him there. The thought that she might know where he was was vaguely comforting. *If you go down to the woods today, you'd better go in disguise.* He knew the lie of the land. He would find a hiding place. Some of the bandits he had hunted in Malaya had lived in the jungle for years. He was the bandit now.

The bus took Sandra back through North London. On her own once more. Left behind. She'd have to start all over. Like none of it had ever happened. She was a mystery girl again. And she would keep the mystery. Keep the secret. She knew that she could. She would never tell and that would give her strength. She would never betray him. He was a stupid bastard for what he had done. But she knew why he had done it. It didn't excuse it, didn't even explain it. But she knew she would never speak of it to anyone. Because she knew. He'd never talked about it but she had felt him moving and muttering at night, twisting and turning next to her in bed. The horror he had been through. She knew that.

*

Vic Sayles had organised a stag night for his team. 'Time for some shore leave,' he announced. We had been busy, after all. He hired out a club in Paddington. It was all laid on. A buffet dinner, a couple of strippers and all the booze you could drink. A regular part of his team's 'work hard play hard' ethic. All paid for by DI Sayles' own version of the Police Benevolent Fund. And we did need a morale boost, after all. We'd got some results. Two down, one to go. But the pressure was on. It seemed that this Porter bloke was the real killer – the rest had just gone along with it. If we couldn't catch this bastard there'd be hell to pay. I mean, if the police couldn't protect their own, how the fuck was the general public supposed to feel safe?

And it wasn't just police. It was detectives that had been killed. Plainclothes. Our lot. It almost seemed a point of honour that someone from the Department should bring him in. The unhealthy competition between the Flying Squad and the SPG continued. And with different command structures it could cause confusion when there was a sighting and two different groups of officers would arrive on the scene. Of course, CID always considered themselves superior to uniform, and the SPG resented this arrogance. They had special training, particularly in large-scale operations. Probably saw us as a bunch of wankers swaggering about in sheepskin coats.

For me, of course, it was a lot more personal. Dave. I couldn't get his mangled body under the Q-car out of my mind. His murder had been so senseless. A routine check on a dodgy motor. I mean, you expect to take risks in this job, that's part of the glamour of it, but something as stupid as an out-of-date tax disc. It made you wonder what was the bloody point. And I guess I still felt a little twinge of guilt about it. It was me getting him sent back to Division that put him on Q-car duty that day. I know it's stupid thinking like that but I couldn't help it.

So I sort of concentrated all these thoughts and feelings on to getting this Porter bloke. Now I was with the main investigation team I could really focus on that. I just had to tell Vic that I was being transferred. I hoped he wouldn't take it the wrong way.

I'd already had a skinful when he called me over to a quiet corner in the room.

'I hear you're going over to Ernie's team,' he said.

'Yes, guvnor.'

'You might have told me.'

'I was going to.'

'I suppose you're glad to get away from me.'

'It ain't that. I just want on to the main investigation.'

Vic nodded slowly.

'Yeah, yeah. Makes sense. You're a fucking pushy one, aren't you, Taylor?'

I sighed.

'I need another drink,' I said.

'Ernie does things slightly differently from me, you know?'

'Yeah?'

'Yeah. A bit more, let's say, orthodox. You probably prefer that.'

It was probably the booze but I suddenly had a strange thought. That being on the investigation could get me back on the straight and narrow. That Dave was looking after me even after he was dead. Like some sort of fucking guardian angel. And if we could find his killer then maybe that would be some sort of redemption.

*

Julian wanted to go to some new club just off Leicester Square and he dragged me along. It was all black leather chairs and gleaming chrome, full of fashionable media types.

'What do you think?' he asked.

'It's a bit pretentious.'

'Not for the gutter press, then,' he said with a supercilious sneer.

'I suppose not.'

'We are all of us stars,' Julian announced with the flourish of one hand, as if to signal he had come up with something clever. 'But some of us are looking at the gutter.'

He thought he was so clever. Probably considered me dull and suburban, which was right. London was becoming 'sophisticated', 'swinging'. I loathed the cheap decadence of it all. Julian talked of his new friendship with Teddy Thursby. 'His Lordship,' he insisted on calling him.

'He isn't as rich as he makes out, though,' he said sniffily.

Of course, I ended up paying for both of us. Julian got into a very elaborate conversation with some awful woman from a fashion magazine. He was obviously angling for work and generally showing off. It annoyed me that he always needed to draw attention to himself. I just sat there and brooded. I drank quite heavily. I felt a sense of disgust rise within me.

'Let's get out of here,' I said to him when the woman had left.

'All right. Where do you want to go?'

'Don't care,' I muttered.

I stood up and the whole room swayed. Julian grabbed my arm.

'Oops-a-daisy,' he said, steadying me. 'Are you all right?'

'I'm fine. Let's go.'

We wandered into Soho. The 'Clean-Up' was over and the streets were busy with tarts again. We got to Piccadilly. The Meat Rack thronged with delinquent rent boys, sad-eyed junkies huddled outside the 24-hour chemist's. *People are like maggots, small, blind and worthless.* The Casbah Lounge had reopened.

'Come on,' Julian said.

'No,' I protested. 'I don't want to go in there.'

But he insisted. I tried to sober up with an espresso. Lights were swirling around my head, the shrill voices of the queens in the place reverberating in my mind. Their faces contorted in laughter, betraying their disgusting physiognomy. They were guilty, all of them. I felt the hatred for them burn inside me, hatred for myself. I had to control it all, I reasoned. I wanted to get out, get some air. I turned to Julian but he was chatting somebody up, giggling inanely. They were going through the sordid ritual.

'I'm going for a walk,' he murmured to me. 'I may be some time.'

'Wait a minute,' I mumbled. 'Wait.'

But he was gone.

'All on your own?'

Somebody sat next to me, taking Julian's vacant stool. He had pale skin and a mop of mousey hair, dark-rimmed eyes, sunken cheeks and a tight little mouth. He wore a short-sleeved shirt open at the neck.

'Don't mind if I join you?'

His eyes made contact with mine, like he was trying to beguile me with his evil intent, tempting me. The neck, the throat, his oesophagus bobbing as he talked. As he swallowed. A fleck of spittle on the side of his mouth. He smiled and I smiled back, knowing. I could tell his fortune by the look on his face, his implicating stare. I had to take control.

I remember going outside, the air cold against my face. His hand stroked my leg, warm. We took a taxi back to his place. Streetlights strafed the cab as we drove through the night. A bed-sit in Earl's Court, Dusty Springfield wailing from the flat below, him spooning Nescafé into two mugs, kettle whistling on the Baby Belling. I sat on the edge of the bed.

'You're a quiet one,' he said as he came over with the coffee.

He put the cups on the floor by the bed and sat next to me.

'Here,' he whispered softly.

His lips brushed against mine, a horrible flick of his tongue against my teeth. He pulled back.

'What's the matter?'

'You know,' I said. He frowned.

My mind darkened then came to. Mouth, lips, neck, throat. Fingers and thumbs, itching. His adam's apple, tempting.

I pushed him onto his back and straddled him. We thrashed about on the bed. So much of a struggle, I thought, it's all so much of a struggle. But in the end he gave in and so did I. My mind darkened again and I gave in to all my pent up desires. I rolled off him and felt such a sense of relief flood through me. I had done it, I thought calmly, I had finally done it. As he lay quietly next to me I stroked my fingers along his body gently, touching his flesh with a marvellous sense of possession. He was all mine. I lay there watching over him until the dawn came and then crept out into the morning.

15

The canopy above glowed with light. The sun burned the edges of the leaves a bright emerald. Welded them to the sky. Camouflage patterns in the bracken about his feet. He had walked for hours. Making tracks gave him a sense of purpose. Distance between him and the city. The damp, earthy smell of the forest floor was ancient, primal. He was going to ground. Returning to a more natural state.

And he knew what to do. All his army training could be put to use. Jungle craft. It was simple. All he had to do was survive. And he knew how to do that.

At sundown he began to flag. He was exhausted and maybe ten or fifteen miles from his destination. And he was parched. He needed to find water. He found a secluded coppice and made a makeshift camp, then set off with a water bottle. In a field he found a cattle trough. There was green scum on the surface. He wiped it away and filled his container with murky water.

He boiled it up on the Primus stove and made tea. It tasted dank and fetid but he was so thirsty it didn't matter. He took off his boots. His feet were covered in blisters. He rested his head on his rucksack and soon fell into a deep sleep.

He woke to a cacophony of birdsong. He rubbed at his face. For a couple of seconds he had no idea where he was. There was a light film of dew on him. He blinked and looked around at the shadowy dawn. His whole body ached. He felt the awful sinking realisation of his predicament. The brief respite of sleep was over. He had to be on the move again. He washed himself with the water left over from the night before. He leaned against a tree and pulled on his boots again. His feet were so sore it was almost unbearable but he had to get going. A few yards of tramping through the woods and the pain subsided. He made his way to the edge of the forest.

He had to travel on the roadside now. This would be more dangerous. He just hoped that people would take him for a holiday hiker. After a few miles' walking a car pulled up beside him.

'Want a lift, mate?' the driver called out.

Billy kept on walking, turning his face slightly so he would not be recognised. He was so tired that the prospect of a lift was almost irresistible. But he couldn't risk it.

'Come on, mate,' the driver continued. 'Where are you headed?'

'No thanks,' Billy muttered, his face still turned away from the road.

'Fuck you, then,' the driver said as he pulled away.

It was getting dark again when he reached Thorley Woods. Childhood memories flooded back to him. He knew the lie of the land, that was a comfort. He would have to find an isolated place. Somewhere ramblers and dog walkers wouldn't stumble upon. But he was overcome with fatigue. He found a little hollow and unrolled his sleeping bag. He would set to work making a proper shelter tomorrow.

Billy found an area of thick undergrowth that was isolated from any beaten track in the woods. He tunnelled through the thicket and found a small clearing. He dug a shallow hole with his hands, which he carpeted with the groundsheet. Then he cut a series of short branches and stuck them into the ground as picketing and using the earth that he had excavated made a kind of breastwork around the whole area. He pitched his tent over this and then camouflaged it with bits of bush and bracken.

He set up his stove, his sleeping bag and the radio inside. He felt safe within. The earthworks gave him the sense that he was in a burrow. That he was hidden beneath the ground. They'd never find him here. He set up a tripwire near his camp attached to a string of bottle tops that would rattle if anyone stood on it. He had enough supplies to keep himself going for a week or so, then he'd have to go out foraging.

The radio was his sole company but he only listened to hourly news bulletins because he needed to save the batteries. He'd hear reports of the hunt for him. It was strange listening to his name being repeated again and again over the airwaves. Curiously reassuring as loneliness began to gnaw at him. He was also comforted by all the false sightings and red herrings that had put them off the scent. Epping Forest had been combed by police, as he thought it would be. There was a quiet satisfaction in outwitting them. *Billy Porter, the police murderer, is still at large,* a voice would announce. *At large,* he thought, a stupid way of putting it, made it seem that he was conspicuous. But instead he was hidden from view. Obscure.

Then, on the third or fourth day (he had already started to lose count), he heard a familiar voice on the wireless. At first he thought he must be dreaming or that he had gone mad. It was his mother speaking. He turned up the volume, his heart pounding in his chest.

'Billy, if you're listening,' the voice wavered in maternal lamentation, 'this is your mum speaking. Give yourself up, son. Please, Billy, before there's any more bloodshed. I'll come with you if you want. We'll go to the police together. Please, Billy. This is your mum. Everything will be all right.'

Billy started to sob. Her voice sounded so sad. She was the only person that ever really cared for him. He felt torn apart. She was betraying him. And yet she sounded so gentle. Gently scolding him as she had when he was a child. *We'll go to the police together,* just as they had when he'd been shoplifting as a kid or whatever.

'Sorry, Mum,' he whispered as he choked on tears.

He left the radio on for a while longer, hoping that he might hear her again. But the news report ended and he switched it off.

*

The funeral. At a church opposite the Shepherd's Bush factory where me and Dave were bucks together. The Church of St Stephen and St Thomas. The Martyr and the Doubter. Not hard to tell which was which. A long cortège coming around the corner of Uxbridge Road. The streets lined with crowds. A canopy of umbrellas, like scales on a huge beast. It was a wet, miserable day. The first rain since the World Cup Final. Dave in the back of a hearse. His mangled body in a box. They're burying the better half of me today.

The rain steaming off the hot tar of the roads from the long hot summer. A smell of washed asphalt in the air and the sickly scent of hundreds of cellophane-wrapped floral tributes and gaudy wreaths that were piled up by the church gates. Bells tolled as the coffins were brought up the path. Family mourners out front then pews filled with top brass.

The Commissioner read the eulogy and a passage from Revelation. *And there shall be no more death, neither sorrow, nor crying, neither shall there be any more pain.*

I spotted George Mooney sitting a couple of rows in front of me, nodding along to all this nonsense. The Metropolitan Police Choir sang 'Abide with Me'. Uniformed pall-bearers took the coffins out. Weeping relatives followed behind and we all tramped out into the wet graveyard.

The vicar was saying his piece over the boxes as they were each lowered down in turn.

'Hello, Frank,' came a voice by my shoulder.

Mooney.

Man that is born of woman hath but a short time to live, and is full of misery.

'A terrible loss.' His voice was soft, unctuous. 'But then who can judge the Mysteries of the Craft? He was meddling in matters that did not concern him. The Temple protects its own, you know.'

'What do you want?'

'Want, son? Want? I'm just a fellow mourner. Surely it is incumbent upon brother officers to console each other at a time like this. Of course, for you, it's quite a personal loss, isn't it?'

'Leave me alone.'

'A soul in torment? I wouldn't dream of it. A terrible tragedy. Of course, it's been wonderful for our image. There's been an unhealthy tide of criticism of the force lately. But through sacrifice we are cleansed.'

Earth to earth.

Mooney wouldn't stop talking. I wanted to get away from him.

'This shows the public what risks we take in keeping the Queen's peace.'

Ashes to ashes.

'And it brings us all closer together.'

He was up close. I could feel his steamy breath.

'And though you shun the solace of the Brotherhood, we follow the same path, if you get my meaning.'

Dust to dust.

I shook him off and pushed my way through the throng and out of there. A mob of gawping civilians around the gates. A girl in a cheap raincoat near the front. Soaked through. Holding a sad little bunch of sodden pink carnations against her breast. It was Jeannie. She spotted me seconds after I'd clocked her and she turned to walk quickly through the crowd. I followed. She was impeded by all the bodies standing around in the rain, so I was easily able to catch up with her. I caught her arm. She tried to shake it off.

'Jeannie,' I implored. 'Please. I just want to talk to you.'

We walked along the road, away from the crowds, in silence. The rain subsided into a drizzle.

'Come on,' I said. 'Let me buy you a drink.'

She turned to me with those green eyes of hers. Her face was wet. Maybe she'd been crying. Maybe it was just the rain.

'All right,' she replied.

We found a quiet corner in a pub near by. I didn't really know what to say. It was hardly a time for small talk. Her little bunch of bedraggled carnations on the table. She picked them up. Water dripped from the cellophane wrapper. She stared at them.

'I just wanted,' she said quietly, 'to pay my respects.'

159

'What happened with you and Dave?' I asked.

'Nothing much. He promised he'd help me get away from Spiteri. He found me a flat where they wouldn't reach me.'

'And did you make a statement?'

'Yeah. I told him everything I knew. It wasn't much. He wasn't sure that it would be much use.'

I thought about this for a moment. If I had any kind of bottle I could follow it up, make a case. But I was a coward. And something else was playing on my mind.

'And you and him?' I asked, tentatively.

She stared at me.

'What?'

'You know.'

She looked down.

'Well . . .' she murmured.

'I see.'

'Look, it just happened,' she said, picking at the damp flowers on the table. 'One night. I was scared. He stayed with me. He was very sweet.'

She looked up. Her eyes brimming with tears. I felt sick with jealousy. For the both of them. I fancied her like crazy but I loved Dave. Not in any queer way, you understand. But I felt jealous because she'd been close to him while I'd been far apart. I'd never made it up to him and now he was dead. And buried.

'He liked you, you know? He really did. He was worried that you were getting into bad ways. He was a good person. Not like you. Not like me either.'

'So, how are things, you know, with you?'

'You mean, am I still on the game?'

'I didn't mean . . .'

Jeannie laughed.

'I know what you mean. I understand you better than I did him. We're both of us not very nice people, are we? But no, I'm not on the game any more. I've got a job at a hairdresser's. And that money you gave me. That's tided me over a bit. Thanks for that.'

'It was bad money anyway.'

'Yeah, well. I never want to rely on bad money again. Not ever.'

I looked at her. Her hair was a mess from the rain and make-up streaked down her cheeks. She was still beautiful. I still wanted her.

'Jeannie,' I said, drawing closer to her, 'I'd like to see you again.'

She pulled her face back from mine and frowned.

'I don't think that would be a very good idea.'

'But . . .' I struggled for the words. 'We, you know, understand each other.'

And that's how I felt. This washed-up girl was the only person I could think of that would understand what had happened. All the awful feelings of guilt that I had about Dave. I wanted to talk to her about that. Tell her everything.

She looked at me with a sad smile. Pity in her flint eyes. We ended up getting drunk. It seemed the right thing to do. Our little wake for Dave. There wasn't much to say so we just sat there and knocked back the booze until chucking-out time.

She let me see her home. She had a little flat in Earl's Court.

'I'm sorry about setting you up like that, Frank,' she said at the door. 'I hope you don't hate me for it.'

'No, I . . .' Stumbling over the words, all choked up.

And I started to blubber in the drizzle by her doorstep.

'I'm sorry,' I mumbled, turning away.

'Hey,' she whispered softly, touching my arm. 'Come here.'

She held on to me and I sobbed away. She let me come inside. I wiped at my face with my big stupid hands and she made us a cup of tea. I stayed with her that night. We didn't have sex or anything like that. We just held on to each other through the darkness.

*

There were constant sightings of Billy Porter once his photo had been issued. They were all false leads but the great British public were seeing his face everywhere. In the crowd at Speaker's Corner. Drinking in a pub in Camden Town. Eating breakfast in a café in Euston. Walking out of a flat in Dolphin Square. There was even a story going around that Porter was masquerading as a woman. A girl in a beauty salon swore that she had dyed the hair of a masculine-looking woman who had a deep-set stare and thick eyebrows just like Porter.

People are so open to suggestion – show them something and they start seeing it everywhere. They're vulnerable on a subliminal level. The masses are conditioned – like those dogs that start salivating when they hear a bell ring.

Porter had become an ogre, a bogeyman. A convenient hate figure upon which all of society's ills could be heaped, an embodiment of evil, something other. A specimen. It reassured them that sin existed outside, not in the depths of their own souls. He was a wanted man. All the time, haunted by his photograph, they dreamed of Billy Porter, a creature of their own imaginings.

And it allowed them to vent their own hatred. Sid Franks crowed over the reaction of the *Illustrated*'s readership. Results of the 'Readers' Poll on Capital Punishment': *89% Say: Bring Back the Rope!* There was another tub-thumping leader comment from Sid calling for 'strong action'.

Since that night in Earl's Court I had been possessed with a warm glow of contentment. But it was a fugitive sense of happiness, something that I could not or would not fully comprehend. I'd felt an extraordinary euphoria and a gentle calm had followed it. But what had happened? I had been so drunk and there had been moments of black-out. Flickering images of savage physicality, disjointed flashes of frenzy and violence. It was hard to tell what was real and what was imagined. There was something, well, only just palpable in the memory, something dark and dreadful and exquisite. I should have taken something, I thought, some sort of souvenir, evidence of some kind. I had a fearful longing for some proof.

Then it came through the crime desk. A news item. *Police seeking the killer of 32-year-old Denis Fowler say that his assailant was most probably known to him as there was no sign of forced entry into his flat in Earl's Court. Fowler was a known homosexual and police believe that there may have been a sexual motive to the murder. They are investigating a number of clubs and coffee bars frequented by homosexuals where Fowler may have met his killer.*

There was a photograph with the piece. It was him all right. I had done it, I had really done it. It all came back at once, his face contorted into a grimace as I had throttled him, his body growing cold and stiff as I lay in the bed next to him. I had done it, it was real, the typewritten copy proved it, the flesh made word. I nearly swooned with the sudden knowledge of it all.

'Are you all right?' said the copy boy who had handed me the piece.

I managed to regain my composure and I felt a smile spread across my face.

'Yes,' I replied. 'I feel fine.'

And I did, I really did. It was as if a terrible weight pressing down on me had been taken away. I felt free. I had done it. It gave me a sense of confidence and power, my body relaxed, my head clear for the first time in my life. A peaceful lucidity, as if I had broken the curse, that I had killed my hateful desire, cleansed myself of it. I had put it to rest.

16

I was put in charge of surveillance on Billy Porter's mother. We ran a rota system of WPCs that would shadow her. One or two detectives but mostly seconded from uniform branch. It was mind-numbing work. Plotted up in a van outside her flat, logging the same routine every day. To the shops, from the shops. To the pub, from the pub. Bingo on Tuesdays and Fridays. But observation had to be kept up. There was always a chance that Porter would make contact with his mother. Like most of these supposedly hard villains, he loved his dear old ma. She had co-operated on the investigation, made that radio broadcast appealing for her son to give himself up. But we couldn't trust her to turn him in if she knew where he was.

Nothing glamorous about being on the plot all day. Boring as fuck. But it felt OK putting the hours in. Routine police work. I was glad of it. It felt normal.

And I started seeing Jeannie. It was all very gentle and proper. We'd go out for a meal or catch a film. I'd see her home and we'd have a chaste little kiss on the doorstep. I didn't try anything on. I didn't want to, to be honest. I wanted us to be able to trust each other and, given our past, this wouldn't necessarily be easy. We were wary of each other. But the caution we showed to each other was sort of romantic. Like we were trying to find something that had been lost. I think we both played at being innocent as if it was something we both needed in our lives. Something we'd both missed out on. It was as if we could somehow redeem each other by going through the motions of a courtship. We wanted to be good people, not the bent copper and the ex-whore. We clung on to the idea of it in hope and desperation that we weren't kidding ourselves.

I'd talk to her about Dave. Keeping his memory alive. Reminding myself of what I should be like. I didn't feel that urgent sense of lust that I'd first had for her. Something else took its place. Affection. Us not having sex made it all the more intense. I guess it was a whole mess of confused feelings and hopeless longings.

As the weeks passed the 'sightings' of Billy Porter continued. So many false alarms and frustrated leads. The longer he was at large the more damage it did to public confidence in the police. And it burned away at the confidence we had in ourselves.

*

It had gone quiet on the Porter case. After the arrest of a Cypriot gun dealer in connection with the case a new theory had emerged that he was being sheltered by members of EOKA, the Cypriot guerrilla organisation, but that was about it.

So I had time to work on my own story. I got in touch with the detective in charge of the investigation into the murder of Denis Fowler and I took him for a drink. They didn't have much to go on.

'I'm afraid we've sort of run out of leads,' he said.

I felt a tremendous thrill at talking about a murder I myself had committed. I was almost disappointed that they hadn't got anywhere with the case.

'What about the clubs and bars that you visited?' I asked.

'Yes, well, Fowler was known to frequent one of them. The Casbah Lounge in Piccadilly. But that's about as far as we've got.'

Someone might have seen me there with him, seen us leaving together. But I didn't panic. I felt utterly cold-blooded about the whole thing. No one would suspect me, after all.

'I don't suppose we'll turn anything up,' the detective said. 'Unless the killer strikes again.'

I gulped at my drink, nervously, and nodded. I hadn't thought of this.

'Well,' I said, handing him my card, 'let me know if anything comes up.' I got back to the *Illustrated* and typed it all out. I had to control it. Turning it into a story made perfect sense. Words. I'd always been able to channel my impulses with words, and this would be my souvenir, my memento mori.

Sid Franks came by my desk and looked at the copy. He wrinkled up his face.

'Jesus,' he said. 'Some people really are sick.'

'You going to run it?'

He shrugged.

'Well, it's got a nasty little angle. The "Twilight World of the Homosexual", that sort of thing. Yeah, we might fit it in somewhere.'

I became obsessed with whether the story would stand up at the Big Table of the Saturday conference and how it might be subbed. I was horrified at the prospect of it being spiked. A spike through my heart. As it was it ran and was perfect, a small piece at the bottom of page seven. HOMOSEXUAL HOMICIDE. *Man strangled 'knew his killer', say Police.*

*

Billy would go foraging at night and sometimes risk a journey into town during the day. He found that there was a gypsy caravan farther into the woods from his camp. He figured that this might afford him some cover when he was out in the open. He could avoid suspicion. Town people would take him for a gypsy. And if the gypsies spotted him, they would think he was a townie.

He'd walk down to to the nearest main road and get a bus into town. He still had quite a lot of the cash that his mother had given him but sooner or later he would have to start stealing to buy the provisions he needed. He'd wander around the supermarket, clutching at the wire basket in his hand, trying to look intently at the rows of tins and boxes. His mind would throb as he tried to concentrate on shopping and not let his head dart about too much. He felt a paranoia that was wild, instinctive. Like any animal that is constantly sensitive to being hunted or preyed upon. He kept one of his pistols firmly tucked in his waistband.

Once, in a newsagent's he had entered to buy some tobacco and rolling papers, he found himself standing between the shopkeeper and another customer, caught in the drone of their conversation.

'Well, I'd know him if I saw him,' the customer was saying.

Billy hadn't spoken to anyone for weeks. Except to himself. *Think we need some more wood*, he'd say. *Well, better go and chop some, then.* Little muttered exchanges with his own shadow. The radio provided some sort of company, though he had to ration its use. The Home Service. Calm and soothing. He sometimes wondered forlornly if he'd hear his mother's voice again.

'They reckon you ought not to approach him. Armed and dangerous, they say,' the shopkeeper chipped in.

He realised they were talking about him. His stomach sank and he suddenly felt the hardness of the gun against his gut.

'What do you reckon, mate?' the customer asked.

'What?' Billy muttered.

'About this Porter bloke. Where could he be hiding out?'

'Uh?'

Billy didn't know what to say. He tried to avoid engaging with people in shops at the best of times. Any little pleasantry or comment would be greeted by him with just a grunt or nod of acknowledgment. His heart was racing. He'd grown a beard but surely up close they would recognise something from the police pictures that were everywhere.

'I reckon he's gone abroad. That's what I reckon,' the shopkeeper said, looking at Billy.

Billy flinched a second then looked back.

'I wouldn't know, mate,' he said quickly. 'Can I have an ounce of Old Holborn and some green Rizla papers?'

The shopkeeper looked a bit slighted, as if Billy were cutting him.

'Please?' Billy added, to placate the situation, but in its urgency the word came out terse and demanding.

The shopkeeper shrugged and with a grudging sigh turned and reached for the tobacco and papers on the rack behind him. He rang them up on the till. Billy's hand was shaking as he handed over the money, but the two men had already started chatting about something else and they didn't seem to notice. He picked up the items that the shopkeeper had dropped on the counter and walked briskly through the shop. As the bell on the door chimed someone called after him.

'Oi, mate!'

Billy froze in the doorway. The dull roar of the traffic filled his head. Should he run? Or turn and face them? His hand was in his pocket with the tobacco. He could feel the outline of the gun.

'You forgot your change,' the shopkeeper said.

Billy felt safer not spending too much time outside in the broad daylight. He became intermittently nocturnal. Sleeping securely in his hidden camp during the day and venturing out after dark. Night manoeuvres. He felt a greater sense of freedom in the darkness. At night he was the hunter, not the hunted. He found an allotment within walking distance of his camp. He could supply himself with fresh vegetables from there. There was a poultry farm, though he had to be careful; sometimes the farmer would check the big battery sheds with a torch and a dog. He mapped out his territory. When the money ran out he would have to find places to break into.

He became quite bold. Wandering into the outskirts of the town. There was a small factory that he cased out, finding where the main offices and the safe were. Reconnaissance patrols. He felt a sense of power roaming around fearlessly. He had his guns with him. All those people tucked up in their beds, what would they think if they knew he was so close at hand? He'd climb into the back gardens of houses and peer into the windows. Just for the hell of it. There he was, he thought. Their worst nightmare.

He began to get used to living in the woods and his strange

routine. It was like time was turned on its head. It played tricks with him. Upside down – maybe it was going backwards, too. He sometimes lost track completely. He'd forget why he was hiding out. Maybe they had forgotten about him. It made him reckless.

He went out with the intention of house-breaking one night. He was halfway up the back garden path of this place when he suddenly heard a thumping noise. It sounded like somebody running downstairs. He quickly pressed himself against the wall by the back door and waited. The thumping sound came again. Someone was coming quickly out to the back door to check on it. They must have heard something. Billy made his way slowly and quietly back up the garden path, ready to run if the back door opened. More thumping. What the fuck was going on in that house? Maybe the bloke was rushing around, checking each room. Billy kept moving stealthily up the path. He went past a squat little shed. Thumping again. This time much louder. He suddenly realised that the noise was coming from the shed. It was a rabbit hutch. Rabbits, he remembered from somewhere, thump their back legs when they sense danger.

You little fucker, he thought, and opening the lid of the hutch he reached in and pulled the animal out by its long floppy ears. He shoved it in the sack he had brought and took it back with him. He broke its neck, skinned it and cooked it on a spit over the fire.

He had to be more careful, he reasoned. He had been clever so far. Planned things out. He had survived, against all the odds. One false move could be the end of him.

Just then the string of bottle tops rattled. Someone had trodden on the tripwire. Someone was outside his hideout. He grabbed a gun and crawled out. It was very dark and he could only just make out a figure standing there. He didn't know what to do.

'Hello, mister,' came a young voice.

'What do you want?' asked Billy.

'Just passing. Saw the light from your den. Thought I'd say hello.'

Billy hadn't realised that light could leak out of his camp.

'Hello,' he said to the young man.

This is ridiculous, he thought. Then he realised that this must be one of the gypsies from the caravan in the woods. He'd play it carefully. Be friendly and get rid of him. It would probably mean that he'd have to move on the next day. Or he could kill him. But that would complicate things.

'What are you doing this time of night?' he asked, stalling for time.

'Hunting rabbits,' replied the youth.

Billy burst out laughing.

'What's so funny, mister?'

'Well, I just caught one. Want some?'

And Billy invited him into the camp.

The youth looked around at the cramped but neatly organised interior with wide eyes.

'This is a crafty little place,' he said.

Billy brewed some tea. The youth had raven hair and piercing blue eyes, sparse dark hairs on his top lip.

'You a gypsy, then?' Billy asked him.

'Half and half,' the youth replied. 'Diddicoy, that's what Dad calls me. Mum was a gorgio.'

'Gorgio?'

'You know, outsider. Met her when he worked the fairgrounds. She ran off when I was just a little chavo. He blames me, I reckon.'

'So it's just you and him?'

'Yeah. Miserable old bugger.'

'I suppose you're wondering what I'm doing hiding out here.'

'Ask no questions, mush.'

'But maybe you've got to thinking.'

Billy had to make sure what this youth might know or suspect. Only him and his dad. He could kill them both if he had to. The youth shrugged at him.

'What with all that's been in the papers,' Billy went on.

'Don't have no business with them.'

'Don't you read the papers?' asked Billy.

'Can't read. Dad neither. Welfare people came on to a site once and tried to get us sent to school. Didn't bother with that.'

Billy smiled with relief and started to pour out the tea.

'What's your name, son?' he asked.

'Danny,' replied the youth. 'Yours?'

Billy thought for a moment.

'Joe,' he said. 'The name's Joe.'

17

I'd managed to get a Saturday night off and me and Jeannie went up West. It was a warm autumn evening with plenty of people milling about. We couldn't help but feel in a good mood. Holding hands as we walked through the crowds around Cambridge Circus. Jeannie looked great and I felt pretty pleased with myself. I'd got tickets for the second show at the Palladium. As we walked through Soho she went a bit quiet. I didn't think anything of it at the time.

We passed a pub and I said:

'Let's have a drink.'

She nodded and we went in. There was a bit of a crush at the bar and it took me a while to get served. Whisky and soda for me, gin and tonic for her. As I threaded my way back with glasses aloft I caught sight of her in the far corner. Some bloke was talking to her. My first feeling was distrust, right there in my gut. I thought, yeah, there she is, showing out to the first guy that comes along once my back's turned. Then I saw the look on her face. It was frozen with fear and anxiety. She had turned away from the man and was trying to ignore him but he was up close, leering at her.

I pushed my way through quickly and handed over her drink. She smiled thinly at me.

'Come on, Jeannie,' this bloke was saying with a drunken slur to his voice. 'You remember me.'

'Leave me alone,' she said.

'What's your problem, mate?' I demanded, staring straight at him.

He grinned at me.

'Well, look what my little pussycat's dragged in,' he taunted. 'It's all right, son. Me and little Jeannie here are old friends, aren't we?'

'I think you'd better fuck off,' I told him.

Jeannie saw the look on my face.

'Please, Frank.'

'Oh, she's good, you know. Really good.'

I still had the whisky glass in my hand when I smashed him in the face. He knocked over a table as he went down. There was shouting and a commotion. I looked down at him sprawling on the floor. My hand was cut and bleeding. I sucked at a knuckle. Jeannie had grabbed my arm.

'Frank,' she pleaded. 'Come on, let's get out of here.'

And she started to lead me away. The landlord had come out from behind the bar and was confronting us.

'Oi!' he shouted. 'Just you wait a minute. Someone call the police.'

I took out my warrant card and waved it in his face.

'I am the fucking police!' I shouted back at him.

Jeannie was crying when we got outside. I was so stupid. I only had one way of dealing with things. But I'd felt so protective of her. So clumsy.

'Take me home, Frank,' she croaked.

We drove back to her flat in silence. I figured she despised me for making a horrible scene. I'd wrapped a hankerchief around my bleeding hand and it throbbed as I held tightly to the steering wheel.

'I better find a bandage to put on that,' she said at her door.

'It's all right.'

'Come on,' she insisted, and led me inside.

The sting of the Dettol came almost as a relief. It cut through the awful numbness in my mind. At least I could feel something.

She put a wad of gauze on the cut and wound a length of sticking plaster around it to hold it in place.

'There,' she said.

'Look, Jeannie,' I began. 'About what happened . . .'

I wanted to apologise for how I'd behaved. For making such a scene. It was because of how I felt about her. But I didn't know how to say it.

'Frank, I know,' she cut in. 'I can pretend that it's all in the past. But there'll always be people to remind me of what I was. What I am.'

'What are you talking about?'

'You know.'

'No, I don't.'

'Yes you do!' she suddenly exclaimed. 'You know all about me. That's why you didn't say a word on the way back here. You know as well as that man in the pub what I am. You just can't bear to talk about it.'

'It's not that.'

'Then why didn't you say something?'

'Because I felt like an idiot. Lashing out like that.'

'I thought . . .'

'No. No, it's not that. I don't think about you like that.'

She looked me in the eye.

'So, what do you think of me?'

'I . . .' I swallowed hard. Feelings that felt like a solid lump in my gullet. 'I love you, Jeannie.'

She frowned at me. Like she couldn't quite understand what I was saying. I realised then that no one had ever said that to her. Not properly. She gave a thin nervous laugh.

'Oh, Christ,' she said.

'It's true.'

'Then why don't you want to touch me?'

'Because . . .' I brushed her cheek with my bandaged hand. 'I want more than that. Than this. I want . . .'

'Oh, for God's sake, Frank,' she sighed. 'Touch me.'

174

That night we made love. At least, we tried to.

*

The weather was changing. It was getting colder, wetter. Billy had mended the holes in his tent and make the whole shelter waterproof again. He dug a small drainage trench on the sloping side of the hideout to channel away water during rainstorms. In heavy downpours he'd have to fight against leaks, using cooking utensils to catch the rivulets and cataracts and to bail out the rainwater. But when he had it all under control, he quite liked sitting in his camp in the rain. Its reverberation on the canvas roof was soothing. Like the sound of distant applause. It was then he felt most safe. Safe in his dugout. Beneath his canopy. Buried. Under the ground. It was a sense of being inside. Hidden away. The outside was washed away. It lost any sense of coherence. Sound and vision blurred like interference on the telly. Inside was all that mattered.

The season was changing too. The undergrowth that covered his shelter was losing some of its foliage. The whole area around him was becoming more and more sparse as the leaves began to fall. Billy set to work to recamouflage the camp. Smoke was more visible now, in the damp air, so he had to be careful with fires and did his cooking at night.

There were still news reports about him on the radio, though less and less frequently. He would limit his trips to town as much as possible but he'd always buy a paper. There would be the occasional item about the search for him there too. Lots of mistaken sightings. Red herrings. But interest had started to wane after the initial press hysteria. He knew he couldn't stay where he was indefinitely, but if he could last the winter and into next year, when things might calm down even more, then he might make a move. He would have to find some sort of cover, though.

Danny, the gypsy boy, turned up from time to time. Billy knew that this contact was a weak point. Danny swore that he hadn't told anyone about him, least of all his dad, whom he obviously

175

didn't get on with, but even Danny knowing was a terrible risk. Even if he couldn't read the papers, something about Billy would be bound to turn up one day, and then he might put two and two together. Billy knew that the real weakness of it was that he allowed himself to imagine that, even if Danny knew, he might not betray him. He had become his only human contact and he couldn't help himself wanting to trust him.

He told Danny that he was a deserter from the army. Danny had nodded – it was common enough for those AWOL to end up on the road. The irony was that Billy had done his service. Not some easy billet, either. He'd met plenty of blokes in the Scrubs later who'd never turned up for National Service. For some of them that was their first taste of porridge. It was that that had got them off the straight and narrow in the first place. From then on they'd learned all these bad habits from being inside and never looked back. For Billy the army was part of the process too. It had taught him to kill. How to survive on the run.

Danny would go out working with his dad most days. 'Calling,' they called it. Going door to door, asking for scrap. At other times there might be odd jobs here and there. Picking potatoes or a bit of tarmac work. But when he had time Danny would often come to visit. He felt he'd never quite fit in. Half and half. Diddicoy. Not quite Romany nor gorgio. Billy, despite himself, looked forward to Danny's visits. Of course, they were a liability, but as he began to work out in his head how he might survive on the run in the long term, he realised that Danny might, after all, be invaluable to him. If he were to pass as a traveller, for instance, there were all sorts of codes and customs that would be useful to know. And Danny needed little encouragement to start holding forth. And Billy, in spite of everything else, found his voice and his strange twitching demeanour fascinating. He just had to remember that he was Joe in Danny's presence. Danny told him that he wanted to get away from his dad, that he planned to work as a 'gaff boy', working on the fairgrounds when the season started up again.

Danny also explained gypsy rituals with a clarity and precision that only someone with a certain amount of doubt about their own identity could master. He had a slight distance from it that gave him a lonely understanding that longed for an intimate mystery. Joe had the obvious gorgio ideas about Romanies and Danny tried to provoke him into bringing them up.

'You reckon we're dirty, don't you?' he'd say. 'You seen some gyppo site and there's filth everywhere, ain't there?'

Billy shrugged. He didn't want to seem rude. Danny was making some sort of point, that was clear.

'They see the site, but they never look inside the trailers. Always spotless, they are. Clean on the inside. Gorgio never understand this. They keep everything nice on the outside but inside their houses they're all dirty. They use the same water they'd use to clean themselves and do their business as they would clean their plates and eating irons. Put their own filth in their own mouths. Keep their own rubbish inside.'

Billy could vaguely understand what Danny was saying. He couldn't afford to leave anything outside his hideout that might betray his presence. He had to bury any rubbish. Cover up his own filth. But somehow the idea of keeping oneself clean inside made sense to him. Danny talked a lot about what was clean and what was not. *Moxadi*, he'd often say, meaning dirty, ritually unclean.

'Some animals, right, we reckon are moxadi. Cats, for instance. They clean themselves with their own tongue. Bring their own dirt into themselves. They can lick their own arses. Moxadi, that is. Horses, they're clean, rabbits too. But cleanest of all is the hotchi-witchi.'

'The what?'

'Hedgehog.'

Billy had heard about hedgehogs being a delicacy for gypsies.

'So you eat them, do yer?' he asked.

Danny laughed.

'Not often,' he said. 'But, like I say, they're clean. They can't groom themselves with their mouth, can they? All them spikes. And you look at a hotchi. Full of fleas in its coat. All manner of dirtiness in them spines. But that's on the outside, ain't it? That don't matter. If you're clean on the inside, that's the main thing. Ain't it?'

*

The real dread of what had happened soon caught up with me. What I had done, the cold truth about myself. The initial euphoria I had felt turned to despondency and depression. And fear, fear of the future. It could happen again if I wasn't careful. I musn't let it become a habit – I'd end up in Broadmoor.

I tried to console myself with stories of murderers more heinous than myself. The Boston Strangler, Albert deSalvo, had throttled thirteen women to death. And then there was the case of a certain Hungarian, Sylvestre Matuscka, who could only achieve full sexual satisfaction by seeing a train crash. He blew up a bridge that was carrying the Budapest–Vienna express in 1931. Such excessiveness put my little misdemeanour into perspective, didn't it? But I realised that I was reading these stories, as usual, for the salacious effect they had on me. And they did nothing to assuage my darker urges. On the contrary, rather like drinking salt water to slake one's thirst, they instead made my mouth dry with anticipation.

I had got away with it, I reasoned, and would more than likely not be detected. *Unless the killer strikes again*, the detective had said. Might he not strike again? Might I not be able to control him?

DeSalvo had been known as the 'Measuring Man' on account of his modis operandi in gaining access to the apartments of young women. He would pose as a representative for a modelling agency, with a tape measure and a clipboard, and persuade his victims to let him check their vital statistics. Initially he would merely sexually assault his prey, but he soon moved on to murder, attacking old and young alike. Given the necessity for opportunity in crime, my own MO was, by comparison, devastatingly simple. I could so easily pick up a homo somewhere, go back with them and just let myself out after I'd finished. So I really did have to resist temptation.

I resolved to keep busy, to stop drinking altogether and to

stay away from those places where homosexuals might congregate.

The Porter story had quietened down considerably. We set to work trying to buy up friends or relatives. The trick was to move quickly as soon as you found anybody who showed even the slightest inclination to sell their story. Then you'd set them up in a hotel, somewhere where the enemies couldn't get to them, and sign them up for an exclusive. Sid Franks was an old hand at this.

'They used to call me the Smash and Grab Kid,' he assured me.

We managed to buy up Trixie O'Rourke, a former stripper who had been Porter's girlfriend before he was convicted on a GBH charge in 1959. She had shopped him, apparently. We ran a good shot of her, performing at the Cabaret Club in Paddington.

I began gathering all kinds of Porter ephemera. Photos of him as a child, details of his army record, anecdotes from all manner of sources. And I began holding some of the good stuff back from the *Illustrated*. I had formed a sort of attachment to Billy. I liked the idea of possessing parts of him. He was my specimen, my subject. If I busied myself with him I could avoid any nasty distractions. And I had another plan. This could be the book I'd always dreamed of. I could do a Truman Capote job on him. It could be a way of getting away from the claustrophobic environment that I felt trapped in. Away from Grub Street, away from London. The city made me mad – the filth, the crowds of ugly humanity. It was an immoral place. Maybe I could go away somewhere quiet and desolate and write it all up.

I approached a publisher on the quiet. They seemed quite keen but were not prepared to give me an advance. Not yet, anyway.

'Of course,' they said, 'once he's been caught and it's gone to trial then we'd be ready to commission it.'

So I waited for the End. Of course, the most satisfying dénouement would be a dramatic shoot-out with the police. A properly dramatic finish to the narrative. But while I longed for a conclusion so that I could have my story, part of me wanted him to escape. For him to be free, to get away with it.

18

Two months later and Jeannie told me the news.

'I'm pregnant, Frank,' she said.

I didn't know what to say. We'd been sort of going steady but we hadn't made any plans, any promises.

'So,' I stuttered, 'um, er . . .'

'Don't look so fucking worried.'

'No. I mean, yeah, well. What are you going to do?'

'I want the baby. But that doesn't mean you . . .'

'Yeah?' I interrupted her. 'That's good. That's really good.'

'But what I mean to say is . . .'

I didn't let her finish. I grabbed hold of her and kissed her.

'So,' I said, 'things need to be sorted out.'

'What are you saying?'

'I'm saying, let's get married.'

She kind of smiled and frowned at the same time.

'What, you're going to make an honest woman of me?'

'Well, yeah. As long as you can make an honest bloke out of me.'

She sighed and shook her head.

'Look, Frank, you don't have to do this, you know.'

'No, really. I mean it. I want it. Let's do it right.'

And I did mean it. I so much wanted to do something right for a change. I tried not to pay any attention to something that nagged at the back of my mind. That it might not have been my kid she was carrying. That it might have been Dave's. I didn't want to think about that.

We had a registry office wedding. We wanted it done quickly so there was no time for a proper ceremony. Things had slowed down in the investigation but as it was I only just about managed to get a few days' leave so we could have some sort of honeymoon in Brighton. The fact was we didn't want a big do. I didn't want too many people in the job to know about it, to be honest. I mean, it wasn't exactly kosher given how me and Jeannie had first met. It could have got me into trouble. I worried about George Mooney finding out. Given his demonic ability in prying into private affairs, I knew that it was only a matter of time. I just wanted to get it done and face the consequences later.

And we were both in a hurry. I think we knew deep down that any hesitation would have killed the whole thing dead. I know that Jeannie had felt vunerable when I'd proposed to her. She felt scared of her own past. Of what might happen to her if she was on her own. I could offer her protection. And some sort of respectability. So she rushed into it without thinking too much.

It had been a secret affair up until then. Desperate. We just hoped that in time we could emerge from it into some sort of normality. Mr and Mrs Taylor. We just had a couple of witnesses. Jeannie got a girl from the hairdressing salon where she worked. I got Micky Parkes, a DC on the Flying Squad I'd been on the plot with the day Dave got murdered. I'd got to know him fairly well and felt I could trust him to keep quiet about it. Micky was a solid sort of a guy. Didn't say much, which was promising. I liked him. He wasn't my best man, though. Our best man was dead. Though it would be a long time before his ghost was put to rest. Especially with his killer still on the run. Dave was always there. Between us.

The four of us went for a drink after the ceremony. Micky went off to phone in. He was officially still on duty. When he came back there was an alert look on his face. I knew something was up.

'I've got to get off,' he said. 'There's been a sighting.'

He didn't have to explain anything more. It was obvious what that meant. Porter.

'Where?'

'Somewhere in Hertfordshire.'

'What do they reckon?' I asked.

There had been so many false sightings that a wariness had now developed about any information received. So many phone-happy civilians wanting to be national heroes and convinced that any dodgy-looking tramp was public enemy number one. I'd like to have thought that I hoped it was a hoax call and that I could go off on my honeymoon with a clear conscience. The fact was the desire to be there when we got Porter was stronger than anything I felt for Jeannie. Desire for revenge, ambition, and the plain fact that, despite all the witnessed vows I'd gone through less than an hour ago, I was married to the job.

'They're pretty certain this time, Frank,' Micky replied. 'All units are being called in.'

I think Jeannie saw it too when she caught my eye, my reaction to what Micky had said. I had to go. To be there. I tried to explain but there was nothing to say that she didn't already know. She turned away from me and bit her lip. Waking up to what she had got herself into.

*

'The yokmush,' Danny had said. 'The yokmush are coming.'

Billy was still in his sleeping bag when he heard the signal on the tripwire. He sat up and called softly for Danny to come into the hideout. He rubbed his face. It was a cold morning. Cold and damp.

'What is it?' he asked Danny.

Yokmush was a gypsy word. Yok meant eye, mush man or men. The eye men. The police. Danny explained how the caravan had been raided that morning.

'Been some thieving in the area so of course they blame us, don't they?'

It must have been all of his break-ins, thought Billy.

'So, have they arrested your dad?'

'Well, he's helping them with their inquiries. But thing is, he told them about you.'

'I thought he didn't know.'

'Well, I didn't tell him, Joe, honest. He must have seen you out and about. He told the yokmush about a stranger in the woods. They start getting all interested. Showing him photographs.'

Billy had already started to gather up some things into his rucksack. He would have to get moving again. He looked up at Danny.

'You see the photos they were showing?'

Danny nodded.

'You know who I am?'

Danny shrugged and looked away. He nodded again and turned back to Billy with a nervous smile.

'I always knew,' he said.

'But you said you didn't read the papers.'

'Yeah, but we got a telly, ain't we? I had to say I didn't know first time. But after that, well, you became a pal, like. 'Sides, it would be bad luck to turn you in. You're a hotchi-witchi. I better be going. I'll try and keep them off the scent if I can.'

*

We assembled on the outskirts of Thorley Woods. About 500 officers in all. Flying Squad and other CID, SPG and ordinary uniform units, dog handlers, the lot. It looked impressive enough at the start, but it soon dawned on us that no one really had any fucking clue what we were doing.

There was a shortage of firearms. What we did have was mostly ex-service weapons, many of which were wholly unsuited for the job. Some of them not even complete or without the correct ammunition. On top of that there was an even greater shortage of officers authorised or trained to carry guns. There were stories of briefings where guvnors were issuing firearms and when they had run out of authorised officers they would ask 'Right then, who's been in the forces?' or even 'Who wants to have a go?'

Some revolvers had holsters, others not. Some were carried in one pocket with the ammunition in the other. I saw more than one CID officer carrying a loaded and cocked pistol casually thrust into their waistband until it was pointed out that they stood a good chance of damaging a particularly delicate part of the anatomy. I'd done some weapons training. Range shooting. I didn't really have any idea of how to use a gun in the field, though. I'd drawn an ancient ex-army Webley that didn't look like it had been fired since the relief of Mafeking.

I heard one guy mutter:

'This is going to be the biggest fucking balls-up since the siege of Sidney Street.'

And so we moved off, forming up the search line, beating our way into the woods.

*

Billy heard them coming for him. A cacophony of noise. Whistles and calls, the threshing of undergrowth as they hacked away. They had no idea. No track discipline. No jungle craft. No stealth.

But he was ready. He was trained for this.

The automatic and split-second reaction to a chance encounter must continually be practised again and again under different conditions of terrain and varying circumstances.

He checked his guns.

There was confusion in their lines. He could use that against them. He could move quickly and quietly through the woods with frequent halts for observation and listening. He knew the lie of the land. They were getting closer.

Billy went to ground and waited. He would wait until they were right up close. Any distance might give them clarity. If he moved away they might spot him. But if he stayed close, with all those bodies stumbling about, they wouldn't see him. He would wait until they were right upon him, then he would

185

break cover. In the chaos he might just be able to cross their line.

*

We were bloody lucky not to have an awful accident that day. A game of toy soldiers. Cowboys and Indians. Except there were 500 cowboys and only one bloody Indian and he still managed to get away. There was confusion between the SPG and the Flying Squad. Arguments about who was supposed to be in charge of the bloody operation.

The search line was a mess. Parts of it became disconnected altogether. Some officers found themselves beating through the undergrowth only to flush out other police groups. And as the forest was more overgrown in the centre, the middle of the line moved more slowly than the flanks. This meant that the ends started to curl in. The line turned in on itself. We'd managed to surround ourselves. And one of those untrained and trigger-happy officers could so easily have ended up shooting a fellow policeman.

We found his hideout. That was something. Something to give to the press and hope that they didn't report just how much of a cock-up we'd made of it all.

The fact was we just weren't prepared for something like this. The police had never had to go through something like this before. One thing was sure. Things were going to have to change.

*

It was all over by the time I got to Thorley Woods. They had found his hideout but Porter had somehow managed to slip the net. His camp had been extaordinarily well constructed and equipped, camouflaged to blend in with its surroundings. Inside they found a home-made stove and a neatly stacked pile of firewood, a sleeping bag, two army blankets, a Primus stove and a bottle of meths, cooking utensils and mess tins, two clean shirts and some hankerchiefs all neatly folded, a store of canned food, fishing tackle, a transistor radio, a bottle of whisky and a pile of newspapers. THE

FOXHOLE OF THE FASTIDIOUS FUGITIVE was how one of the enemies subbed it. Any hopes that Porter was unable to survive on the run were dashed. A holster was recovered but no gun.

He had outwitted them. Outmanoeuvred them with animal cunning. He had sown confusion in their ranks and had somehow managed to spirit himself away. The scent had gone cold.

There were all manner of stories flying around about police incompetence. Lack of preparation, lack of equipment and firearms training. Unclear lines of command and a breakdown in communication between the Flying Squad and the Special Patrol Group. Sid Franks made me play all of this down when I wrote up the story. It was assumed that, with such a near-miss, Porter would soon be picked up somewhere in the area. But he'd got clean away.

So my book idea was on hold for a while longer. This was not the End, not yet. I felt an odd sense of being left behind. He was out there somewhere, at large, a killer on the run. My killer was still trapped inside of me.

1971

Supergrass

19

'So, is this fucking swede taking over the inquiry, then, guvnor?' I
asked Ernie Franklin as we climbed the stairs to the fourth floor of
Coco. Ernie gave me a sour look.

'Frank, Thomas Harrington is Her Majesty's fucking Inspector
of Constabulary. I don't want to catch you using the word swede
anywhere near him. Understood?'

'Yeah, sure, guvnor. But what, is he running this thing now?'

'Harrington's role is to advise the inquiry.'

'Yeah, but what does that mean?'

'Look, Frank, it says here.' Ernie read from the Home Office
statement. '"The Home Secretary, at the request of the Commisioner
of Police of the Metropolis, has agreed that in view of the wide
public interest someone independent should be associated with the
investigation of allegations recently published about the conduct of
Metropolitan Police officers."'

'"At the request of the Commisioner"? That doesn't sound
right.'

'Well, of course it isn't, Frank. The fucking Home Secretary has
set this one up himself, hasn't he? It's political, "public interest"
and all that.'

'So, he's brought a swede in to make it all look kosher?'

Ernie sighed.

'Yes, Frank. And we're to give him our full co-operation.'

Ernie didn't look well. A messy divorce and a bit of a drink problem had taken their toll. Not exactly uncommon in the job but something you'd rarely confide to a fellow officer. I suppose because it could be seen as a sign of weakness. And what could I say to Ernie? Just go through all my own failures and bloody well compound the matter. And I think, like me, he'd never quite got over the Shepherd's Bush shootings. He was still officially in charge of the case, though nothing solid had turned up for nearly five years. Mullins and Drummond had been convicted on three life sentences but Billy Porter had never been caught, and that hurt.

'This is all I fucking need, Frank,' he muttered. 'Trust my luck to be in the frame for this one.'

A couple of journalists had wired up a petty thief in South London and recorded incriminating converstions with CID officers. There was evidence of fit-ups and of receiving money in exchange for dropping charges. More damagingly, there were allegations of more widespread corruption. An internal inquiry was set up. Ernie was in the frame for this one and I was brought in to assist. We were to brief the Deputy Assistant Commisioner. It seemed straightforward, if a little messy. Discredit the journalist's evidence. Keep the lid on it. Let the silly fuckers who'd had their hands caught in the till twist in the wind but make sure it didn't spread too far.

Then a week later they brought the swede in. That's Met slang for provincial coppers. The whole thing had caused a lot of grief. A lot of bad press. It had to look like we were going through the proper motions. But Ernie didn't have much stomach for all of this. He'd always been a very straight copper. He couldn't believe that there could be such widespread corruption – it just didn't fit with the way he saw things. He was unswervingly loyal to the Met, to the Yard, to the job. What with his personal problems and now this, you got the feeling that at any moment a wheel might come off of his whole career.

I got made DI in 1969. I was part of a special team that went after Harry Starks. We got a result largely because I was able to get Tony Stavrakakis to go QE against him. I got a commendation for that. But some of the rest of my career wasn't so sweet. At the

Flying Squad certain teams were just as hookey as ever. I ended up taking the bung now and then. I'd been tainted, marked by it, so it kind of came my way. I know that makes it sound like someone was just shoving money in my back pocket without me noticing, but that was the awful thing about it. Half the time I was just turning a blind eye to whatever scam might be occurring. Passive. But as bent for it as the rest of them.

It didn't go down too well with Jeannie. I'd kind of promised her that I'd go straight. That was what we both wanted. To put the bad part of our lives behind us. But it was just too tempting to take the money – don't make a fuss, just make sure your own back's covered. So I implicated her too. I put the bad money in her account just in case anyone checked my bank statements. I reasoned that I had responsibilities, a family to support. The baby was born on 12 May 1967. A son. We called him David. Sort of an acknowledgment of something that we never talked about. That he wasn't my flesh and blood. You could tell, especially after a couple of years. The dark hair, the eyes. I recognised them, all right. But I didn't care about that. Or at least I made sure in my mind that it didn't matter. I wanted to do right by him. And the occasional bent money meant that he'd never need for anything, I told myself. And Jeannie came pretty sweet out of it too. She ended up with enough cash to set up a hairdressing salon of her own. She didn't want to become just a copper's wife, a quiet little housewife. She avoided the occasional socialising that went with the job, which suited me fine. She wanted a bit of independence, so having her own business suited her well. But she wasn't happy about where the money for it had all come from. She'd give me this look when I'd come home with a payment. She'd rarely say anything, just this resigned expression on her face and a little shrug. Like all I'd said about getting clean had been a waste of breath and we were still living off immoral earnings.

And I think that's what got to her about it. It reminded her of whoring. Doing something dirty for cash. Being ponced by someone. She wanted to be her own woman. She was happy to have her own business, but where the money had come from still rankled. She doted on the kid. A little bit too much, I thought. I felt this kind of distance from him. I couldn't help it. I tried to be a good father, but Flying Squad hours were long, weekends got fucked up by operationals. So I put in for a transfer. I wanted to go straight. It wasn't scruples so much as the nagging thought that it all might catch up with me. And I wanted to get on. I was going up, I was still sure of that. Still driven by ambition. Ambition that sometimes gave me an awful sick feeling, like vertigo. But it was all right just so long as you didn't look down. Not a fear of falling but a strange urge to jump that would occasionally give me nausea. It wasn't a fear of heights. It was a fear of depths.

So I ended up at C1. Rubber-heeling on a corruption case. That was a joke. Back with Ernie. Good old straight-down-the-line Ernie. The whole investigation had whitewash all over it from the start. And working with Ernie brought back unfinished business. The Billy Porter case. There had been periodic sightings that all proved to be false alarms. Resources and manpower on the case lessened slowly as time went on. It had been a public relations disaster for the Met, and in the end they all but gave up on it. But I couldn't. I kept my own private file. Every lead, every clue cross-checked. The memory of Dave and how I'd failed him haunted me. One day we'd catch that bastard, and I could put his ghost to rest.

I didn't like the look of Thomas Harrington. Stiff, formal, ramrod straight. A churchgoing teetotaller, by all accounts. Cold eyes behind steel-rimmed glasses. He'd been given an office in C1. All the stuff we'd collated so far on his desk. We exchanged the briefest of pleasantries, then we all sat down and he launched into it.

The allegations of corruption had come from a petty thief from Peckham, one Dennis Woods. His flat had been raided by Detective Sergeant John O'Neill and Detective Constable Ian Campbell. They had found twelve bottles of stolen whisky and on his kitchen table some electrical components and a nine-volt battery. 'A bit of jelly would go nicely with that,' O'Neill had remarked. 'And I know a man who can get some.' The implication was that they were prepared to fit Woods up with a safe-blowing kit. Woods had laughed this off, saying that he was merely repairing a transistor radio. 'We ain't joking, son,' O'Neill had retorted. 'We want some bodies, otherwise you're going away for that.' Woods was told that they wanted the names of receivers to further their investigation into a gang raiding premises in the area using skeleton keys.

Woods was duly charged with dishonestly handling the whisky. While he was in custody, waiting to appear before Tower Bridge magistrates, Detective Constable Campbell had visited him in his cell and said: 'We'll get it over today but the big bloke will want a drink.' Woods had taken this to mean paying off O'Neill and had agreed to hand over £25. This he duly did to Campbell in a pub in Camberwell the next day. He'd asked the detective constable if this was the end of it or would they still be on his back, and Campbell had answered: 'You're in the clear for now. If you get into any more trouble, give me a ring. Don't matter where. Anywhere in London I can get on the blower to someone who talks the same as me. There's a little firm in a firm, you know?' And he had given Woods his extension number at the Yard.

Then five days later Woods had been stopped on Camberwell New Road by O'Neill and a carload of plainclothes officers. 'Let me see your hands,' O'Neill had insisted, and as Woods had held them out O'Neill had pressed a sausage-shaped object in greaseproof paper into the fingers of his right hand with the words: 'There's the jelly I promised you.' Woods was told again that they wanted the names of people handling stolen goods from the duplicate key burglaries. 'Or else,' O'Neill had warned, 'it'll cost you.'

It was at this point that Woods had approached the journalists, and subsequent encounters between himself and police officers had been taped. Woods had been wired up with a radio mike and the pressmen had been plotted up in the carpark with the recording equipment. It seemed that, in lieu of information, Woods could instead pay off O'Neill and Campbell. In the Father Red Cap pub on Camberwell Green, O'Neill was recorded as saying that 'the whole business will cost you a twoer', meaning £200. Woods only had £50 on him, which he handed over, and further meetings to continue the installments were arranged. These were also taped. Also, pressure had been put on Woods to plant stolen goods at various premises so that their owners could be charged with receiving.

The 'firm in a firm' phrase had really put the cat among the pigeons. It was bad enough what O'Neill, Campbell and various other as yet unnamed officers had been up to. But the spectre of widespread hookeyness hung in the air like a bad smell. So many of us had known what had been going on and had just let it slip. Or even got tangled up in it. A lot of really good detectives had kept themselves clean. I couldn't help thinking about Dave. His straight-down-the-line approach. Ernie Franklin was an innocent, really. Something sad and naïve about him. The poor fucker probably had no idea of half of what went on. Well, he was in for a shock. The rest of us, well, we just accepted that you had to be a little bit bent for the job. It wasn't good when this became being bent for yourself, but when something like this came to the surface the best thing to do was find a few scapegoats lower down the ranks and paper over the rest of it.

But now, with this swede in on the inquiry, it was not going to be so simple. It was easy for the Met to look down on provincial coppers. Like they were a bunch of yokels or something. But Harrington wasn't stupid, that was for sure.

'Gentlemen,' he began. 'I'm aware that I'm a week behind the ball on this one. This has given the officers named in these allegations a chance to destroy evidence and cover their tracks. This means we're going to have to go over the whole background to this case in meticulous detail.'

'With respect, sir,' Ernie broke in, 'the officers involved have all strenuously denied the allegations made.'

'With respect, Detective Superintendent, until such time that the words "except police officers" are written into the statute book, I think that we can assume that they must be dealt with in the same way as other offenders.'

'Sir?'

'It seems to me that the normal conduct of a criminal inquiry – searching suspects' homes, desks and lockers – has so far been totally neglected. Instead the energy of the investigation has so far concentrated on disproving the veracity of the initial complaint.'

'Well, sir,' said Ernie, 'it is a possibility that these allegations have been at best exaggerated. After all, they are based largely on the word of a professional criminal. And the journalists concerned, rather than coming to us with their evidence in the first instance, chose instead to publish them in a deliberately sensationalist manner.'

'Documents have gone missing. Diaries, notebooks, evidence. And what has the inquiry concerned itself with so far? Taking lengthy statements from the journalists. Some of them have been held for questioning for periods of over eight hours. There have been complaints by them of harassment by this inquiry.'

Ernie shrugged.

'Well, they would say that, wouldn't they?'

Harrington sighed and leaned across his desk.

'Gentlemen, I'm acutely aware that I'm seen as an outsider. That I'm perceived as interfering in a delicate situation for the Met. But I trust that we can work together without conflicting loyalties.'

Ernie Franklin nodded cautiously. Harrington looked at us in turn.

'Well?'

'Er, yes, sir,' replied Ernie.

'Sir,' I echoed in assent.

'Right, then. Let's start with the basics. All of the detectives named were involved in an operation against South London-based gangs raiding shops and stores using duplicate keys.' He looked down at a file on his desk. 'Operation Skeleton, it was called, yes?'

He turned to me.

'Well, Detective Inspector, I suggest that is an area you might like to look at. I want you to build a complete dossier on Operation Skeleton and how it pertains to this inquiry.'

*

Five years on and Porter still evaded capture. All manner of stories as to what had happened to him began to emerge as he slowly became part of modern folk mythology. My book on him remained unwritten but my journalistic career, which had really taken off with his story, continued its strange progress.

He was free. I was trapped. We were both outsiders but at least he had got away. He was a real fugitive. I had avoided justice in a secretive and cowardly way. I hid in the streets and corridors of normality, inside. But I longed for the outside, to smell the fresh air.

And the stench of immorality around me was appalling. The Permissive Society, the Sexual Revolution – everyone was demanding their right to pleasure. Women's Liberation, Gay Liberation, it all made me feel sick. I had not given in to my terrible urges. I remained a stoic amidst all the decadence. No one would guess at the depth of my self-sacrifice.

Of course, the *Illustrated* really capitalised on all this depravity. We'd do vice every week if we could. Either that or uncovering the excesses of the permissive society – nudist colonies, wife-swapping in the suburbs. 'Any excuse for a bit of tit,' was Sid's maxim.

We could now show the whole breast in the paper. Before, Sid had operated what he called his *'National Geographic* nipple policy'. Partial nudity had to have some anthropological meaning. Up until the late sixties this had meant black flesh, a sort of Third World soft porn. But lately this had been extended.

'You know what all this sexual liberation means, don't you?' he once remarked to me. 'It means we can put white tit in the paper.'

So the breast became ubiquitous in the *Illustrated*, giving comfort to the bottle-fed masses. At the same time the paper insisted on its moral stance. There was an emerging backlash against the loose values of the Swinging Sixties, spearheaded by Lord Longford's report on the pornography trade. This was grist to Sid Franks' mill. A chance for morality through the keyhole, loudly tutting away at depravity while providing vicarious titillation to the readership.

Longford travelled to Denmark to examine first hand the effects of a more permissive approach to obscenity laws. Sid sent me off to Copenhagen to join the press pack that shadowed him, eager for copy. He'd already become 'Lord Porn', a figure of fun, a bald-pated, bespectacled, music-hall professor in an incredulous examination of the flesh pots. As part of the Danish expedition he'd visited a live sex show but had left after only a few minutes.

LORD PORN REFUSES THE WHIP, was how my copy had been subbed. *Danish débâcle in den of depravity as dirty damsel demands discipline. At sizzling Scandinavian sex show Lord Porn was confronted by a gorgeous pouting blonde who pressed a whip into the prudish peer's palm and invited him to beat her. Naturally his Lordship declined and fled . . .*

'This is fucking great,' Sid had said, looking at my piece and the smudge of a semi-clad girl that went with it. 'You know what we've got to do, don't you? The *Illustrated*'s own investigation. Our own in-depth report on pornography. An exposé on the Soho bookshop trade, something like that.'

'It's a good idea,' I agreed.

'Look,' he said, 'it's yours. I want you to mount an investigation. "We expose the blue film racket", or whatever. See if we can't set up some of the people peddling this filth. And make sure we've got plenty of examples of this depravity.'

'How big?' I asked, meaning how much could I spend on it.

'Well,' Sid replied, 'I'll have to take it to the Big Table. But I'm sure they'll be keen. We can probably throw money at this one.'

Sid came back from Tuesday's conference with a big grin on his face as he walked up to my desk.

'You got *carte blanche*, old son. Start working on it pronto. I want this to be a big one. A real coup.'

So I started to put the investigation together. The previous Christmas a light aircraft had crashed on the Belgian coast. The aeroplane had been carrying more than a thousand blue films all carefully disguised in Yuletide wrapping paper. The makers of the films were a Danish company, Hot Love. It was hard-core stuff –

sadomasochism, bestiality, the lot. And it was all *en route* to Britain. I decided to target this company and try to find out who was bringing the stuff into the country. I had a couple of reporters trawl the Soho bookshops and talk to any contacts they had. But it wasn't the retail end that I was aiming at. I wanted to get to the wholesalers.

I didn't really relish the prospect of all this muck-raking. I would be exposing myself to obscenity, most of which would merely inspire nausea, but it was the S&M stuff that I was worried about. Of course, I felt a grim fascination with it, which, I decided, I would resist. It was a test of my self-control, I reasoned, that I could stay above it all. The investigation was, after all, a chance to get on at the *Illustrated*, and work was really all I had.

The plan slowly formed itself in my head. If we could get someone to pose as a potential customer, someone who was wanting to buy in bulk, then we might be able to make contact with the people running the wholesale end of the racket. Live bait for the big fish. Some gullible businessman that the porn dealers would think they could take for a ride. A con always works best when you can make the people that you're setting up think they're the ones doing the conning. Somebody living it up in the West End and prepared to make a big wholesale order beyond the usual dealings of the small-scale filth peddlers. A convincing enough lure that could secure an introduction to whoever it was that was running the rackets. Then they could set up a business deal, a meeting at which we'd be ready for them. Tape recorders, photographs, the lot. That would be our coup. WE EXPOSE THE SOHO PORN KING or whatever. It was bound to work. But first I had to find our bait.

*

A fairground sky. The late September build-up on Woodhouse Moor. Back-End Time. The season nearly over. Silvers, pinks, purples in nimbus streaks over Buslingthorpe Ridge. The dying sun scrolling the edge of the clouds in gold. The horizon decorated like the Swirl front he'd done for the Bone Brothers. Not enough light left to get any work done today. He'd need to be up first thing tomorrow and maybe try and find a spare hand. But that gave him a bit of thinking time. The sunsets at this time of the year were always good for inspiration. He got most of his ideas from the sky.

Most of the big machines were up by now. The main rides. The Parachute and the Dive Bomber. The Dodgems and the Octopus. As Mick walked through the site the Waltzer was being set up. The stacked cars unloaded off their wagon. The ground packed and levelled as the main frame was laid out. Then the plates of painted wood, chrome and alloy were slotted into the skeleton and the whole structure was locked together.

Tomorrow they'd set up the generators. Do the layout and cable connections. Test the lamps, circuits and power systems. The final safety checks on the mechanisms and structures. Then the machines of joy would be ready to fly. The fair would come alive. A city of light. And he'd see his work the way it should be seen. Illuminated. Lit up by thousands of coloured light bulbs.

The sky was darkening now, the light diffusing into a warm red. Years of painting had taught him to see every colour in terms of pigment. There was alizarin crimson there, maybe some indigo. It all bled into the red fire of the Ghost Train. Mick smiled as the firmament brought inspiration once again. *Bang*, he thought. That was it. That's how he'd repaint the ride.

Mick was a fairground artist. He'd always been good at painting and drawing. By rights he should have gone to art school with his talent. But he'd drifted. Found himself working for Lakins before the war. Big firm, did most of the decorating for rides and sideshows. Then he went freelance. He liked the travelling life.

He had thought of settling down once. He'd had this idea of setting up a tattoo parlour. Something steady. He'd seen plenty of them during the war and he reckoned he could do better than most of them himself. When he was in Burma with the Forgotten Army he got to see some real beauties. Out East it was an art form really. The delicate oriental needlework inspired him. He spent idle hours drawing designs on any old bit of paper he could find.

So after demob he got himself a tattoo rig and rented a small shop just off Brighton seafront. But the novelty of it soon wore off. Most customers wanted the standard designs from flash sheets you could find in any parlour in the country. He missed the scope for colour and inventiveness. The sheer scale of decorating a big machine. And the movement. How you could bring flight to a ride in the way it was painted. And how the mechanism of the ride would bring the decoration to life. When you got it right it was beautiful. And he missed another kind of movement. His own.

So he shut up his shop, sold his gear and went on the road again. There seemed a purpose in travelling. Not that he quite fitted in with the fairground world. Not really a showman. Not in the circle, as it were. But he didn't mind that. It gave him a bit of distance, a perspective on his work.

The evening star had risen and now burned low in the sky. He'd start the maintenance job on the Ghost Train tomorrow. He already knew which colours he'd use. It was just a retouching job but he could do with a hand if he was to get it done in time.

He asked around and someone directed him to a bloke named Joe. This Joe wasn't a showman. He was an outsider. What circus people call a josser. With the fairground lot it's simply in the circle or out. And he certainly wasn't in. Not a showman, not part of any family. Just casual labour for the build-up. This wasn't that usual. Showmen are naturally suspicious of outsiders but Joe had obviously been around a bit. He knew the assembly order for the Waltzer. He was hanging around to see if there was any work going. A bit too old to be running about taking fares on the Dodgems like the other gaff boys, but there might be something going on the joints or the side stuff.

When Mick asked Joe if he wanted to work with him, Joe hardly said anything. He merely nodded his head and grunted something in acknowledgment. For a moment Mick thought that the man might be halfwitted but there was an intense, hunted look in his eyes that told another story.

They started work at first light, and although Joe's labours were confined to the menial it was soon pretty clear that he had a feeling for it. Mick could always tell if somebody had the eye. Joe was good company. He didn't say much but he listened as Mick explained the designs and techniques. The man seemed to come alive as he laid on paint with the enthusiasm of an apprentice. He seemed to know something about painting. In a brief exchange on the subject Joe let slip that he learned a bit when he'd 'been inside', then suddenly drew in on himself again, obviously regretting the admission. In the now embarrassing silence Mick muttered something about not caring about another man's past.

'It's all right,' he remembered saying. 'You've paid your debt, haven't you?'

By the end of the day Mick had let Joe do a couple of the grinning skulls around the hell-mouth while he finished the marbling on the pillars. They worked in virtual silence, just an occasional word or gesture. They understood each other.

The generators started up and the monstrous engines were powered into life. A charivari of pop music echoed across the site, punctuated by the hiss and clatter of the machines. Lamplight constellations outlined the shape and play of the rides and brought out their vibrant hues and markings. An artificial landscape that reeled with mad delight. A baroque mechanism of light, colour, form and motion. Industrial pleasure. An electrified arcadia. The modern engines spinning in pure imitation of ancient ritual. Timeless festival only children can fully understand.

Sparks flew up the poles of the Dodgems to crackle against the wire ceiling above. Mick and Joe walked through the fair in the quiet contentment of a good day's work. Joe had a go on the rifle range. He weighed the .22 air rifle in his hands, cradling it thoughtfully, then broke it at its barrel and lined up his five lead slugs on the counter. Each shot found its target with a dull crack. The man on the stall indicated the prizes. Soft toys of fuzz and kapok. Lurid plastic troll-like dolls with bright hair and idiot eyes. Brittle china dogs and figurines. Joe chose one of those and held it up. Mick smiled and caught that strange stare of his. Close and yet absent at the same time. Joe made a vague gesture with the cheap ornament. It took Mick a while to realise that he was offering it to him.

20

Operation Skeleton had begun in 1968. There had been a series of burglaries of shops and warehouses in London and the Home Counties with no sign of forced entry. The gang responsible had an obvious modus operandi, the use of duplicate or skeleton keys. Information gathered indicated that those responsible for the robberies were a gang of criminals based in South London. So an operation was set up to break the so-called Skeleton Gang working out of C9 Department – the Metropolitan and Provincial Police Crime Branch – based at Coco. O'Neill and Campbell were both part of the squad, and records showed that they had been very active in various investigations. O'Neill had been responsible for over twenty arrests and had received at least ten commendations for catching thieves. However, it appeared that almost all of the charges brought thanks to his activities were for receiving and handling stolen goods from the Skeleton jobs. Only one man was charged and convicted for an actual robbery and he was on record as saying that he had been wrongly arrested, having merely been in the vicinity of a clothes shop that had been turned over. A crime in which none of the stolen property had been recovered.

Also, there seemed to be a strange pattern to the Skeleton gang's activity. There would be a wave of robberies that would subside after a period of about six months. In this time a certain amount of knocked-off goods would be recovered and fences arrested while the actual gang seemed to be taking a well-earned rest. The operation itself would apparently wind down during this period. Then the gang would start busying itself again in a short but concentrated burst, and the detectives involved in the case would also go into action, again raiding a series of premises where a partial quantity of bent property would be recovered and a few minor-league receivers busted.

Dennis Woods, O'Neill and Campbell insisted, was an important informer for Operation Skeleton. Far from paying them off, they alleged, he had instead received money from the Information Fund for squealing on his associates. Having been exposed as a grass, they reasoned, he was covering his tracks and attempting to protect himself from retribution by crying 'foul'.

So far, so bad. The whole thing reeked of hookeyness. I'd come across this sort of thing so many times by now. An operation appearing to get results, taking a few mug villains off the pavement for a bit while it was lining its own pockets. If the inquiry could confine itself to this one operation, hopefully to the officers already named in the journalist's tapes, all well and good. Damage limitation, that was what it was all about. That was what everyone at the Yard was hoping for. With Harrington breathing down our collective neck it wasn't going to be easy, but he was still only involved in an 'advisory capacity' (which could mean fuck-all if we played our cards right). If need be, the whole of Operation Skeleton would have to be sacrificed, cut off at the knees. The important thing was to make sure the swede didn't start prying farther afield. This 'firm in a firm' equation was making everybody jumpy.

Ernie Franklin wasn't having such an easy time. He was having to work closely with Harrington and that was taking its toll. They were going over the press allegations together and interviewing Woods to compile their own statement of what had occurred. He was up close to all the bad stuff and it was doing him in. Ernie was old-school in that he couldn't stomach the sort of behaviour that was being described every day as he went over the evidence with Harrington. But he was also old-school in that he was fiercely loyal to the Met. He was being pulled apart by it. It didn't help that Harrington was a cold fish, to say the least. Ernie felt himself being judged daily by this upright and sober swede. His disintegrating private life and heavy drinking didn't help. We went for a swift one at the end of the first week of the inquiry. I hoped that it could be recreational but he was still absorbed by it all.

'This is diabolical, Frank,' he said to me after his fourth double Scotch.

'I know, guvnor,' I replied, unable to change the subject.

'I just can't believe the stuff I'm hearing. Can you?'

I could, of course, but I couldn't tell him that. His hand started to weave a little as it went for the glass.

'You know, Frank . . .' His voice was beginning to slur. 'It makes me feel . . .' He winced, his face screwing up in front of me. 'Dirty. It really does. I feel . . .'

There was another pause as he struggled for a word.

'Tainted,' he declared finally. 'It does, you know. It makes me feel tainted.'

'Look, guvnor,' I reasoned, 'maybe you should get off home.'

He gave a hollow, pitiful laugh.

'Home?' He laughed again. 'I ain't got a home, son. She chucked me out. You know that? Fucking threw me out on the street. I'm back to kipping in a section house like a fucking woodentop on probation.'

He slurped the dregs of his glass, sucking at the spirit's vapour.

'Fucking diabolical.'

*

Alan Khalid was a good-looking man in his mid-thirties. Half-caste, with black hair and a hawklike nose. I hadn't really thought of the angle before meeting him but it suddenly made sense: that the 'businessman' looking for hard-core pornography in large quantities should be an Arab. It would be a good cover for setting up a deal, and Alan Khalid would clearly be able to play the part of the gullible Levantine.

Alan was a freelance journalist but he could easily have been an actor. There was something mischievous about his demeanour. Vain and flirtatious, he always smiled a little bit too readily. He was convincingly shifty, perhaps a little too much so. But he was ideal for the part. My only other concern was that he might be just a little bit light skinned.

'Don't worry,' he assured me. 'I'll go on the sunbed.'

When I pitched my idea to him he was very keen and set to work on developing his seedy Arab persona. We decided that he would be from the Lebanon, keen to purchase bulk orders of blue films. He kitted himself out with a Savile Row suit and plenty of gold jewellery. He grew a little goatee and developed the appropriate speech patterns for his dirty Beirut businessman. I was worried that he might be getting a bit carried away. He tried sporting a keffiyeh but I told him that was a bit too much.

We set him up with a very swish apartment in Mayfair and he started doing the rounds of the bookshops in Soho.

Julian had really fallen on his feet with Teddy Thursby. The old lord had successfully sued *Private Eye* in 1970 over allegations that he had been connected with the gangster Harry Starks. He'd come away with £20,000 and Julian had latched himself on to him, ostensibly to help him write his memoirs.

As he sponged off the ancient peer, Julian began to cultivate an awful kind of assumed sophistication that was quite disgusting. He went all High Church, under Teddy's influence, all smells and bells and sanctimonious ritual. I'm sure he hardly believed in any of it. He indulged himself in the sins of the flesh and desired some kind of spiritual redemption. It really was horribly hypocritical. And I felt increasingly that he was looking down his nose at me, the grubby gutter-press journalist.

I had arranged a meeting with Teddy Thursby through Julian. I was keen to get any inside information that Thursby might have about Lord Longford. We met in the French House on Dean Street.

'Frank Longford?' Teddy said when I enquired about him. 'Decent enough chap, a ghastly puritan, though. Socialist and Roman. Awful combination. Why do you want to know?'

'Well, I'm doing this piece about the porn inquiry.'

'Ah, yes, of course. Another moral crusade for the illustrious *Illustrated*.'

Teddy and Julian exchanged a smile. They were laughing at me.

'Well, actually, Teddy,' I said, somewhat indignantly, 'we're doing our own inquiry.'

'Really?' he said, leaning forward. 'What are you going to do?'

I found myself telling him of my plan. I was quite proud of it. Teddy listened intently and gave a deep chuckle when I had gone through the basic details.

'Oh yes,' he muttered. 'An Arab, very good. Well, I can tell you something about Longford. Jules, get us another round of drinks, there's a good fellow.'

Julian stood up and waited.

'Oh, for fuck's sake,' complained Thursby. 'I gave you some money already.'

'I'll get these,' I insisted, and handed a note to Julian.

'Useless fucker,' Teddy muttered. 'He's pocketed half the advances for this book and he still wants more. Hardly seen any work yet either.'

'You were saying . . .'

'What?'

'Longford. Something about Longford.'

'Yes, well.' Teddy lowered his voice and leaned towards me. 'Here's a funny thing. He's visiting Myra Hindley in jail. Can you believe that? Myra fucking Hindley.'

'Really?'

'Yes. He's got her to rejoin the faith apparently. Thinks he can save her soul. He's absolutely mad.'

Sid would love that, I thought. LORD PORN VISITS EVIL MYRA, something like that. Julian returned with the drinks.

'Here he is,' Teddy announced in mock solemnity. 'My faithful amanuensis.'

Julian gave a tight little smile.

'Well,' he said, 'I'm more like his confessor, really. Isn't that right, Teddy?' He turned to me. 'It would make your hair stand up on end, some of the events in our noble lord's life. You see, Teddy's been one for absolute discretion all these years but he's afraid that once he croaks it'll all come out. Aren't you, Teddy?'

'That's quite enough, you little shit.'

'That's why he wants me to help him paper over a few cracks in the old reputation.'

'I said, that's enough,' Thursby insisted, and we changed the subject. Teddy started bitching about Ted Heath.

'There's a bloody war going on. The unions trying to bring the country to its knees. The Blasted Heath's got no stomach for a fight. Well, some of my friends have other plans.'

*

The end of the season was the busiest time for Mick. All the showmen would be in winter quarters doing repair work. And it was then that he got most of the orders for the repainting of old machines and designing the decoration for any new ones. He rented a disused aircraft hangar in Lincolnshire. The showmen would arrive and lay out the parts of the machine that they wanted retouching. If it was a new job, a ride he'd not worked on before, he'd get them to set it up. He'd have to see how it moved before he could even start. Then he'd go through his designs with the showman. His repertoire, he called it. He'd always have new ideas to try out as well. They usually trusted his judgment but Mick liked it best if they came to the final choice themselves. Showmen could often be vague about decoration and would say: 'You decide, it's your job,' something like that. Quite often the wife of the owner would have a better idea of how things should look and he'd talk it out with them.

He did his business word of mouth during the season. He'd visit all the main fairs and see what was wanted for the next, as well as doing the odd bit of on-site work. His past jobs were always the advertisement for future contracts. Not that there was ever much paperwork. It was all mostly done on trust. A spit on the palm and

210

a handshake. It was best to be around a build-up when a new or repainted ride was being put together and other showmen would be around to appraise the decoration. 'Who's machine is that?' someone once asked of a Dodgems that Mick had painted with four-foot-high letters spelling the name of the ride's owner on it. Mick was about to point to the name when he suddenly realised that the man obviously couldn't read. Fairly common among the showmen. Many of them couldn't read their own names on the rides they owned.

There was a lot of work over the winter and he sometimes brought in extra help. When things got really busy he'd have to subcontract work out to other painters. But he didn't like doing that. He relished the feeling of being on his own when the boards and the panelling of a ride were laid out on the floor of the hangar ready for fresh paint. He would walk around them figuring out ideas. The designs and the drawings, the colours and illuminations. But as he worked through a job he'd sense an oncoming loneliness. As a ride neared its completion he'd feel an awful sorrow. An emptiness as his work would inevitably cease being his own. His work for which he had no other term than the raw, intimate, painfully embarrassing word: art. His art was dying out just as he would. He had no particular desire to pass on his trade, his craft, but at times there was a silent urge to share the strange feelings that he had about what he did. He'd been on his own far too long. Through the winter months he'd find himself talking in a low, urgent tone as he paced around, laying on paint. Trying to explain it somehow, though the words that came out hardly made sense to him.

When Joe had asked him, after they had finished the Ghost Train job, if there was any more work to be had, Mick had been cautious. He'd stalled him all the time the fair was on Woodhouse Moor. Joe had got work on the Penny Arcade. Mick had stayed around to see what future jobs there were to be had. Then, when the fair was over and all packed up – pull-out time, as they call it – Mick went over and spoke with Joe. He'd been thinking it over. He was getting on, he'd reasoned to himself, and he needed a hand to get all the work done these days. He hated it when he had to farm out work. Joe had some sort of knack. A bit of an eye for it. And he wasn't too old to be taught a few tricks. He'd give him a month's trial and see how things went.

21

Stamford Bridge. Chelsea v. West Ham. Needle match. The North Stand and the Shed End warming up their voices. Call and response. Tribal. *Zigger! Oi! Zagger! Oi!* A seething echo around the ground. Like a Zeppelin-field *sieg heil. Zigger-ʒagger-ʒigger-ʒagger! Oi! Oi! Oi!* West Ham strikes up with 'I'm Forever Blowing Bubbles'. Substitute *fortune's always hiding* with *Chelsea's always running.* Taunting. The Tannoy crackles into life. 'Blue is the Colour'. Chelsea's FA Cup anthem from last year. The Shed and the North Stand sing along, dirgelike. Slightly embarrassed at such a crap song. Christmas-carol trite. *Blue is the colour! football is the game! we're all together! and Chelsea is our name.* Greeting-card poetry. The Chelsea mob breaks into a guttural chant at the end with relief.

Tannoy crackles again. Bass line throbbing into a double slam. Repeated, then vibrato organ picks up on the offbeat. Chicka-chicka-chicka rhythm guitar riff holds the space between the bass and the melody. Rock steady. Organ grinding into a mad calliope. The Harry J All Stars' 'The Liquidator' fills the stadium. A roar goes up on both sides. The skinheads' overture. Instrumental. Every terrace's soundtrack. A single tremulous note hits the rhythm. One-drop four-four time. The fans on both sides pick up the beat. Four claps and a two-click chant. *Chel-sea!* and *West-Ham!* vie for supremacy. Boot Boy choreography. Ox-blood or cherry-red Astronauts with Dr Martens' patented Air-Cushioned Sole. White Boy Reggae. Carried along by the instinctive blue-beat pulse, the whole of the

Shed is moon-stomping. Boneheads, number one clipper shorn, some with the shaved-in parting. Buttoned-down collars. The suedeheads growing out the crop, smoothies in crombies and Sta-Prest. Some with longer hair, feather cut. Blue-and-white scarves tied at the wrist, forming banners with each finger-pointed salute. Tattoos displayed. Mum & Dad. CFC. Chelsea lion rampant. Scrolled hearts. CUT HERE dotted lines. Borstal spots. On the faces. Tattooed tears.

Everyone's really geared up as the song comes to an end. The teams are coming on to the pitch. Chopper Harris leading the Blues out to a huge roar. Then there's a commotion at the back of the Shed End. A large group of West Ham fans are pouring down the terraces in combat formation, chanting. Chelsea, taken by surprise, are in retreat, scattering. A gap opens up on the Shed in front of the advancing hordes. West Ham baying triumphantly. They are taking the Shed End. Suddenly a lone figure moves into the breach. Tall and distinctive in a white boiler suit and *Clockwork Orange* bowler hat. 'Don't run, Chelsea!' he shouts, rallying his comrades from their rout. Suddenly, emboldened by this reckless rearguard action, Chelsea counter-attacks. Both sides engage, boots and fists flying.

Then the police waded in and everything changed. The tribes came together against a common enemy. Something in the air. Somebody starting a chant. A song of hatred. Something that has been taken up on terraces across the land. No one was sure where it had come from, which ground, which end, but every gang of hooligans knew it by heart. A malevolent anthem sung with mutinous fervour.

It was my idea to go to the football. I just thought it would be good to have a bit of time off with Ernie that didn't involve heavy drinking. Ernie was spending far too much time in 'The Tank', the bar at Coco. Not having a proper home to go to didn't help. But his boozing was beginning to draw comments, which, given the usual intake of your average Met officer, was saying something. As it was he brought a hip flask, but with Ernie's alcohol intake it was probably just as well he had something to stave off the DTs. He studied the programme. A bit of banter about the game. Chelsea on good form, Osgood a bit temperamental, that sort of thing. An inevitable drift in the conversation towards the inquiry. I didn't mind, as long as we could be relaxed about it. I wanted to talk, off the record, away from Harrington, about Operation Skeleton and my thoughts on how we could seal it off there, not let the whole thing spread. And in a gentle way, to get Ernie to be part of the cover-up. He unscrewed his flask, took a glug of Scotch, handed it to me.

'The thing is, Ernie,' I said, 'it all started going wrong when you got these students and hippies arrested for troublemaking at demos or picked up by the Drugs Squad. Then you'd have these middle-class leftie cunts banged up with your career villain. What happens? They start infecting them with all this civil liberties shit. And before long you've got these guys, you've known they've been at it, they know you know, but instead of putting their hands up they're fannying on about their rights.'

'Yeah, well.' Ernie sighed. 'It's a different world, Frank.'

'And now we've got Harrington and the Home Office breathing down our necks.'

'Well,' he said with a shrug, 'the swede ain't all bad, you know.'

'Really?' I replied with a little wince from the neat whisky at the back of my throat.

'Yeah, well, maybe the Met does need to clean up its act a bit.'

'Yeah, but we can do that ourselves, can't we?'

'Can we, Frank? Can we?'

I didn't like the way this was going.

'It would be good for public relations,' Ernie went on. 'A lot of people have lost confidence in the Old Bill, you know.'

'Yeah, a lot of troublemakers stirring things up. Lefties, career criminals, bent briefs. Gutter journalists noseying about for a good story.'

'I ain't so sure, Frank.'

This was not good. Ernie could suddenly become a loose cannon in this whole thing. Wreaking havoc in the Yard. Suddenly there was a big fuss at the Shed End. Fighting had broken out on the terraces. This was the way football was going. Hooligans spoiling it for everyone. A phalanx of woodentops waded in, putting it about a bit lively with their truncheons, cutting a wedge between the ranks of rival fans. A few bodies were grabbed and hauled out. A tall bloke in a white boiler suit and bowler hat was being frogmarched away by a couple of uniforms.

'Look at that silly cunt,' I remarked to Ernie.

Another officer moved in to give him a couple of punches as he put up a struggle. Boos, whistles and catcalls from the crowd. A song started up. I couldn't make out what they were singing at first. Something to the tune of 'London Bridge Is Falling Down'.

Then the chant was repeated through all the parts of the Shed End. It spread quickly, like a drop of ink in water. Both sides were singing together. It united them. The police were unable to keep the fans apart now. They joined together and started to push back the uniforms as one army. The song echoed around the stadium now. A war cry. I could make out what the bastards were singing.

> *Billy Porter is our friend,*
> *Is our friend, is our friend.*
> *Billy Porter is our friend,*
> *He Kills Coppers!*

At the end of each refrain the combined mob broke into cheers and laughter. The woodentops were driven to the back of the Shed now. They brought on dogs to hold the crowd at bay.

I looked at Ernie. Pale faced, taking nervous little sips from the flask.

'You hear what those cunts are singing?' I asked him.

'Yeah, yeah,' he muttered. 'Just a bunch of hooligans.'

'They fucking hate us, Ernie. How come they hate us so much?'

'Take it easy, Frank.'

But I was fuming. I turned to him.

'Look,' I said, 'I've had enough of this. Let's get the fuck out of here.'

So we ended up getting pissed in a local boozer after all. I took Ernie back to the section house. He wasn't in very good shape. And I was late. I'd told Jeannie I'd be home hours ago. We were only supposed to be going to the match, after all.

On the way home that song was haunting me. I mean, you get used to abuse. It's part of the job. Being called the filth and stuff like that. 'All Coppers Are Bastards' and so on. But that song, that was fucking evil. Barbaric. This bloody inquiry was supposed to be 'in the public interest', but what did it matter if the public could hate us so much? What was the point of being to rights if that's what they thought of you anyway? And it was personal. *Billy Porter is our friend.* Dave's killer had become some sort of hero. Nothing made sense any more.

I got back and Jeannie was watching *Come Dancing* on the telly.

'Where the hell have you been?' she demanded.

'Sorry, love,' I told her. 'A bit of business.'

I leaned over to kiss her on the check. She sniffed at me and pulled away.

'You've been drinking.'

'Yeah.' I shrugged. 'A couple after we booked off. I'll just go up and see David.'

She sighed.

'Well, don't wake him up. I've just got him to bed.'

I crept into his room like an intruder. I left the door open a little so I could look at him by the light from the landing. His little face was squashed up against the pillow. He looked so calm and innocent lying there. Little David. He looked so much like him. I felt a sad loneliness well up inside of me. Like I didn't belong. I gave him a beery-breathed kiss on his forehead. *Poor little fucker doesn't know what he's in for*, I thought.

I went back downstairs. I felt all these emotions choked up in the back of my throat. I wanted to talk to Jeannie. About how I felt. I just didn't know how.

'Jeannie,' I said as I came back into the lounge. 'Look, I'm sorry.'

'Don't bother,' she replied, walking past me. 'I'm going to bed.'

I went to the sideboard and poured myself another drink and sat brooding at the telly. The judges were holding up numbers. I had another drink. And then another. *Match of the Day* came on. I switched off the set and collapsed on to the settee.

*

A blond-haired youth opened the door to me when I went around to Alan Khalid's flat. He had milky-blue eyes that rolled back and forth in their sockets. A nervous little snigger. *Heh-heh, heh-heh.*

'Yeah?' he breathed languidly, letting his mouth hang open, the staccato giggle coming again from the back of his throat.

Heh-heh, heh-heh. The deranged laugh seemed to insist upon complicity in its furtiveness. He licked his lips and gave an idiot smile. He looked like a degenerate cherub.

'Where's Alan?' I demanded.

'Alan!' he shouted, swinging slightly on the half-open door.

I pushed past him. The flat was a mess. Clothes and empty bottles on the floor, magazines scattered about with the remains of their shrink-wrapping, little piles of shed skin. Alan came into view, walking out of the kitchen with a glass in his hand. He was wearing a silk dressing gown.

'Tony, effendi,' he declared in his exaggerated Arab accent. 'Have a drink.'

He handed me the glass.

'What the hell is going on?'

'Just getting into character,' he said, reverting to his usual voice.

'I can see that.'

My concerns about Alan Khalid getting carried away with his role as the decadent Arab seemed well founded. There was a dark-haired woman sitting on the leather sofa in the middle of the room. Behind her there was a film projector on a stack of books piled up on a side table. A screen had been set up in front of the sofa. She looked up at me as I walked in. She had eyes as near black as her hair, pupils wide and empty, like pitted olives.

'Who are your friends?' I asked.

'This is Magda,' he replied, gesturing vaguely. 'And this is Ralph.'

He sounded drunk. Ralph gave a coy shrug and a *heh-heh* in acknowledgment.

'And I suppose they're expenses, are they?'

'Well, you want me to be convincing, don't you? I've had to entertain some of my new-found business associates, after all. I want to put on a bit of a show for them.'

'Well, maybe this is going a little bit too far.'

'Oh, don't worry, old boy,' he insisted. 'The *Illustrated* is getting its money's worth. You can be sure of that. You won't believe some of the filth I've managed to get my hands on. Ralph, get one of the films for our friend here.'

Heh-heh.

'Which one?'

'Oh, I don't know,' Khalid mused. 'The one with the animals.'

Ralph busied himself looking through a collection of Super-8 films on the sideboard. I took a sip from the glass in my hand without thinking. It was sickly bittersweet.

'Come and have a look at this,' Alan said, walking around to the sofa. 'Budge up, Magda.'

'Never mind this,' I said, standing above them. 'I need to know what contacts you've made.'

Khalid sank into the soft leather. Both he and the woman looked up at me with a calm impatience that made me feel ill at ease. Ralph threaded a film through the projector.

'Don't worry,' Alan said. 'I've been busy. I'll tell you all about it. But first . . .'

He patted the cushion beside him.

'Sit down. Watch.'

Ralph dimmed the lights and switched on the projector. The machine clattered into life. A white square shifted about on the screen. Credits came up. *Beauty and the Beasts.*

I really didn't want to watch. I gulped down my drink, nervously. Alan refilled it. I shouldn't be drinking, I thought to myself.

'So?' I pressed him.

Alan Khalid sighed.

'Well, I've been around the bookshops and let it be known that I'm a serious customer. I've asked this Danish company you mentioned, Hot Love, if there is a London agent that deals with their stuff, but I've found it doesn't quite work like that.'

On the screen a buxom redhead was lasciviously stroking a German shepherd.

'What do you mean?'

'Well, the way the thing is organised. Wholesale and retail, they seem to be completely different operations. Oh, look at that!'

The woman in the film was crouching obscenely in front of the dog. The animal jumped up on her, tottering on its hind legs like a badly trained circus act. *Heh-heh, heh-heh*, came the hoarse voice behind me.

'Oh, Christ,' groaned Magda. 'Do we have to see this again?'

'What do you mean, different operations?' I asked, trying to ignore the spectacle.

'Well,' Khalid went on, 'the wholesale side has the greater risk. It entails smuggling the stuff in and selling it fairly cheap. But on the retail side the mark-up is phonenenal. It's better organised because there are bigger returns. It's a matter of keeping the shops legit but selling the really hard-core stuff out the back or under the counter. And I've managed to get some really hard-core stuff, as you can see.'

The German shepherd was now humping away with a bewildered look on its lolling face. The woman mimed open-mouthed ecstasy. A sudden jump cut and a new image flickered up. The woman was kissing a pig's snout.

'So,' Khalid went on, 'the really big operators are the guys running the retail end. What we want to do is set up a deal with them.'

'And who are they?'

'Well, they're pretty elusive, as you can imagine. But I think I've tracked down one of the biggest of them.'

The camera pulled out to reveal the two creatures on all fours facing each other. The screen washed out for a second, gorged with grotesque pink flesh. I drained my glass again.

'And who's that?' I asked, catching my breath.

'Fat Wally,' he said, looking down at my empty glass. 'Magda, get us some more drinks, will you, poppet.'

Magda sighed and sullenly heaved herself off the sofa.

'And Ralph, take this tiresome rubbish off. Let's have a look at that other film.'

'Which one?'

'Oh, you know,' Khalid urged softly. 'The nasty one.'

Heh-heh, complied Ralph as he stopped the film and rewound it. Magda came through with two glasses that she handed to us. The celluloid clattered out of the projector and the screen held a white square while he changed the film. I took a sip from the glass. Some horrible cocktail. My head swam a little. Maybe the drink was spiked with something.

'This you must see,' Alan Khalid insisted as the machine whirred and the next film was fed through the gate.

'Who's Fat Wally?' I asked.

'Walter Peters. It seems he runs a whole chain of shops with different frontmen.'

The image on the screen was even more jerky and unclear than in the last feature. Black and white this time rather than gaudy colour. Badly lit with a grainy quality. My temples throbbed as the camera focused on a supplicant figure. A woman – it was only just possible to make out the form – kneeling with her hands behind her back. A man walked into shot. Ralph came around from behind the projector and sat on the floor between us.

'What the hell is this?' I asked.

Heh-heh.

'It's called a snuff movie,' Alan Khalid said. 'It's supposed to be a film of someone being murdered. I'm sure it's all faked. But it's the hard-core stuff you want, isn't it?'

There was a close-up of the woman. Naked breasts heaving with quickened breathing. Eyes looking up, wide with fear.

'So, you've met this Fat Wally, then?' I asked.

'No. He likes to stay in the background. I've talked to one of his frontmen, a bloke called Ian Hesper. I've managed to convince him that I'm a serious customer but that I want to meet the main man.'

The man on the screen looped a thin leather strap around the woman's neck. He twisted it with one hand and groped at her with the other. Squeezing her breast, tugging at the nipple.

'I thought if we we got a meeting with Fat Wally, that could be the set-up, couldn't it?'

Both hands were on the ligature now, pulling it tighter and tighter. Her mouth open wide in a silent scream. Eyes bulging, tongue lolling out. Her face darkening, swelling slightly with the blood rush. A sense of constriction in my own throat, a choking feeling as I swallowed. Thoughts rushing through my head – desires, dreams, memories, feelings I worked so hard at repressing. The face on the screen blurring, losing focus, losing definition. Fantasy and reality flickering. His hand on her throat. My hand trembling.

'Tony?'

'*Heh-heh.* He's enjoying this one.'

The camera pans out. The man lets go of one end of the strap and it snakes free of her neck as she slumps to the floor. Close-up of her face, eyes wide, mouth slightly ajar, still. The reel finished, the end of the film fluttering in the projector like a trapped bird. A white square on the screen.

'Well?' Alan asked.

I rubbed my face.

'Yeah, sure,' I agreed. 'That sounds like a good idea. You set up a meeting and we can be waiting for them.'

I stood up. It was time to be going.

'Well, I better be off,' I said.

'Stay and have another drink,'

'Yeah, *heh-heh*. You were just beginning to enjoy yourself.'

I had to get out. My head was spinning. I walked to the door and Alan saw me out.

'I'll be in touch,' I said.

I wandered about Mayfair. I needed some air, needed to calm my head down. I felt sickened by the disgusting films I'd been exposed to, frightened by what the snuff movie had stirred up inside of me. *I'm sure it's all faked*, Alan Khalid had said. What was real? My head was spinning, I was drunk. I needed to sober up, get control. Get a grip.

I found myself in Shepherd Market. There were a couple of sad-looking whores soliciting. It's a nasty, rotten world, I thought, oozing with corruption. All my pent-up feelings screaming for release. The killer inside me taking over, a killer on the loose.

I found myself walking towards one of the tarts. She smiled as she saw me approach, shameless, a fleck of lipstick on her teeth.

'Looking for business, love?' she asked.

In her flat, red light bulb throbbing in my head. She runs through what's on offer, what it costs. The room grainy and out of focus like eight-millimetre celluloid. Yes, that's it, I thought. All faked, just a film, just a dream. None of it real.

I looped my belt around her neck. It's all over soon. Show's over. The film fluttering in the projector like a trapped bird. The End.

*

It was the tattoo that nagged away in Mick's mind. He'd got used to Joe being elusive or even downright deceptive about his own past. But why did he have to go and lie about a thing like that? It had already started to fade but it was a lovely piece of work. He'd caught sight of it on Joe's upper arm in odd moments. A tiger that curled around his shoulder in yellow and black. Round-eyed with a snarling grin. Like it was ready to strike. One day, when Joe was changing his shirt in his wagon, he caught Mick staring at it. He turned slightly away.

'Nice tattoo,' Mick had said.

'Yeah,' Joe grunted, picking up the clean shirt. 'I guess.'

'Let's have a look at it.'

Joe frowned and quickly displayed it for Mick to see. He started to put his shirt on.

'Hang on,' Mick insisted. 'Let's see it properly.'

Joe sighed and let Mick examine it. His torso tensed as Mick came close. The tiger hunched up a little, as if endowed with a musculature of its own.

'Nice,' said Mick.

Joe glared at him.

'Seen enough, have we?' he demanded with an indignant hint in his voice.

'Yeah,' Mick replied, withdrawing slightly. 'Sure.'

Joe hastily pulled on the shirt and started to button it up.

'I mean,' he went on, 'we don't want to be eyeing each other up too much, do we? Two blokes on their own in the middle of nowhere. People might talk.'

Mick smiled. Joe broke into a nervous laugh.

'Looks like a Jap piece,' said Mick.

'What?'

'The tattoo. Looks Japanese. Or Thai. Where you get it done?'

'Paddington,' Joe replied quickly.

Are you sure? Mick felt like saying, but that would have seemed such a stupid question. But it was an old tattoo and Mick was pretty certain that it hadn't been done in a London parlour back whenever. Even now, there were very few places you'd get work as finely done as that. His mind whirred with possibilities of a hidden narrative Joe might be holding back. That amount of fading would mean it had been done in the fifties some time. Maybe Joe had done National Service in Korea. Got it done on leave to Seoul or Tokyo. Or Hong Kong, maybe. He didn't want to pry and felt a little guilty about trying to expose Joe's past, even though it was all going on in his head. You had to trust a bloke you were working so closely with. But why did he have to go and lie about a thing like that?

Mick tried not to dwell upon it. Everyone has secrets. And there was work to be done. Joe had the knack. He knew that now. He had a good drawing hand and was beginning to learn about colours. Mick found a pleasure in imparting his craft. It was the work that was important. It would live on.

Someone brought in a wagon one day for repainting. They wanted it done just the same. The background was kind of a buff colour. Mick didn't have an exact match so they had to think of what colours to mix to get the right shade. He called Joe over.

'Take a long look at it,' he said. 'The thing is to try to see what colours are in there. What do you reckon?'

Joe frowned.

'Well, it's sort of ochre, ain't it?'

'Yeah, but what's in it?'

'I don't know, Mick. How can you tell?'

'By looking. Long and hard. It takes experience. Have a go. That's how you learn. Have a look.'

Joe gave Mick a puzzled smile.

'Go on,' Mick insisted. 'Have a look.'

Joe turned to look at the wagon. He squinted at it.

'Look, Mick, I don't know,' he said.

'Take your time.'

They stood there for almost half an hour, peering at it. Joe tried to see what was bound up in the surface of the paint. He couldn't really understand what Mick was on about at first, and after what seemed like an age was ready to give up. Then suddenly something happened. He spotted something.

'Yeah,' he said tentatively. 'Well . . .'

'Go on,' Mick encouraged.

'Raw sienna,' he declared with a little chuckle.

Mick nodded.

'Yeah. What else?'

'I don't know. Orange. Maybe . . . oh, I don't know.'

'A lot of it's guesswork, Joe. You're searching for something hidden. You have a look, then you try it out. But you have to be able to see it. You know what I mean?'

Joe looked at Mick then looked back at the wagon. For a second something made sense. He grinned. If he could have given tongue to all that flooded through his head at that moment he would have talked for hours.

'Yeah,' was all he said.

Mick encouraged Joe to work on his own designs. He came up with an idea for the decoration of a shooting range that they did that winter. It was a small job and Mick let him have his head. Wild West motifs, gunslingers and cacti with a huge six-shooter as the central illustration.

Joe could appear absent a lot of the time. He'd mumble to himself. Bits of songs and catches. Nursery rhymes. Like he was pretending to be simple. Sometimes when Mick called his name he wouldn't respond at first and Mick would have to repeat it.

Mick had figured for a long time that Joe was not his real name.

Sometimes, when they had been talking and a pause descended between them, Joe would frown and look at him, opening his mouth slightly as if he were about to utter something. It was then that Mick thought he might tell him his secret. But Joe's mouth would just tremble for a moment and then close into a dead smile. Mick always felt these moments pass with a sense of relief. He really didn't want to know.

Joe had a battered old Bible that he kept in his wagon. 'It's all in here, you know,' he once said, looking up from it. 'Sex, violence, the lot.'

They were clearing up after their last winter job. It was only three weeks off Valentine's Day when the fairground season starts. Mick saw Joe staring at a scrap of newspaper. Folding it up and stashing it in his overalls. Joe looked up but Mick had already turned away deliberately. Joe's secretive nature made him anxious not to appear over-curious. He'd thought of offering Joe some sort of partnership. He wanted him to feel that he could trust him. They had worked so well together. That was the important thing.

22

Monday morning and the Deputy Assistant Commissioner called me into his office.

'Just a quick word, Frank,' he said.

I felt a bit edgy. Maybe something had come up. Something with my name on it. The longer this inquiry went on the more uneasy everybody felt. I mean, everybody who had something to hide, that is. And it was beginning to get to me.

'Take a seat, Frank. I won't take up too much of your time.'

'What's this about, sir?'

'How are things going with the inquiry?'

'Well . . .'

I didn't know what to say.

'We all know what a difficult job it is,' the DAC went on. 'It can put an awful lot of pressure on officers involved.'

'I'm fine, sir.'

'It's not you that we're worried about, Frank.'

'No?'

'No. It's Ernie. I mean, Detective Chief Superintendent Franklin.'

'Sir?'

'Well, he's been under a lot of pressure recently. Marriage breaking up, drinking a little bit too much. You know he's been to see a shrink?'

'Really?'

'Yeah, his nerves are shot to pieces. The thing is, Frank, this is off the record, but keep an eye on him. It's a very delicate situation and we can't afford to let things get out of hand. And Franklin's been acting a bit odd lately. We're worried that he might be backing the wrong horse, if you know what I mean.'

Getting too close to the swede, he meant. I nodded. The DAC smiled.

'Just give us the nod if anything gets too lairy. We can deal with Harrington. He's only on the case in an advisory capacity, after all. But let us know about Ernie. If it all gets too much for him, well, we might have to replace him.'

'What did the DAC want?' Ernie asked me later.

I mumbled something about some paperwork that needed sorting concerning my secondment to the inquiry. Ernie had come up with another lead. Some villain called Tommy Hills had been picked up for a blag on a ladies' outfitters in Dartford. They'd got away with a whole load of schmutter, about £2,000 worth. No sign of a forced entry, so the MO made it a classic Skeleton job. The gang had been disturbed as their van had been loaded up. The van had managed to drive off in time but without one of their number, this face Tommy Hills. He was none too pleased about being left behind and he didn't take much persuading by Kent CID to start naming names. But they'd got more than they'd bargained for when he began coughing about certain arrangements with Met officers. Detective Sergeant O'Neill's name came up, and one of the Kent officers was bright enough (and, presumably, untainted enough) to get in touch with the inquiry. Still in custody, Tommy Hills had been brought up to Wandsworth prison. Ernie and I drove down to the Hate Factory to interview him.

'I'm worried about the security of the inquiry,' he told me on the way down there.

'What do you mean, guvnor?'

'Well, we're right in the middle of the Yard. Any cunt can wander in and have a sneak at the files. Or nosey about the typing pool.'

He was right. Curiosity about how the investigation was going was rampant. Certain faces very jittery about it. One DI from C9 came up to me one morning and said: 'If any of my snouts' names come up, you will let me know, won't you?' And I was happy enough to oblige. Cracks needed papering over, that was for sure. I was on the lookout for anything that might even vaguely implicate me. But Ernie, of course, didn't see it that way.

'And you know the Action Book's gone missing,' he went on.

This was a record where entries were made instructing investigating officers on their next task. It had been mislaid. These things happen.

'I think,' Ernie went on, 'we need to move the whole inquiry.'

'What?'

'Yeah. Get it out of Coco altogether. I've talked to Harrington about it. I reckon over the water to Tintagel House.'

'Aren't you being a bit paranoid, guvnor?' I asked.

Well, this obviously hit a nerve. Maybe this shrink business had got to him.

'No, Frank,' he fumed, 'I am not paranoid! I've been twenty-three years in the job and I never realised what hookeyness goes on. I've been a bloody fool. But I am not fucking paranoid! All right?'

'Yes, guvnor.'

He was right. If anything I was the paranoid one.

This Tommy Hills character was a sly one. Obviously used to doing deals. Knowing when to cough and when to clam up. We went through the statement he'd made to Kent CID and then got to talking about his relationship to DS O'Neill. Ernie did the talking.

'Yeah, well,' Hills began. 'I was working on his patch and he tried to fit me up for receiving.'

'So what happened?' asked Ernie.

'Well, he said to me: "We can do something about this."'

'And what did he mean by that?'

'Well, it was bodies or money, know what I mean? I wasn't so kean on squealing so I opted for payment. A "licence fee", he called it.'

'And how much was this "licence fee"?'

'He wanted two hundred, I knocked him down to a hundred and fifty. He agreed to that, but made it clear that this would be topped up from time to time. It cost me a bluey every time I come across him.'

'A bluey?'

'Yeah, a fiver. Whenever we met he'd pocket that.' Hills gave a mean little smile. 'I reckon he was saving me up for a rainy day.'

'Hills, these are serious allegations. We'll need dates, times, places.'

Hills smiled again.

'Listen, darling, I ain't even started. There's been much more going on than the Old Bill turning a blind eye to villains letting themselves into premises with a bunch of twirls. I could tell you stuff that would really get you sharpening your pencils. But I want certain assurances.'

'What the fuck do you mean, assurances?' I broke in.

Ernie held up his hand.

'Frank,' he chided. 'Let him talk. What assurances?'

'Well, look, I can tell you the whole lot. All the duplicate key jobs and how officers were paid off. But more besides. Stuff that would make your hair curl. But I want something in return.'

'I'm sure the courts will look favourably upon your co-operation,' Ernie assured him.

'Yeah, but I'm putting myself on the line here. If I do this, I ain't just a grass. I'll be a bloody supergrass.'

'As I said,' Ernie went on, 'if what you tell us can be verified, it will certainly mitigate against any charges against you.'

'Yeah, but that ain't good enough. I don't want to end up even doing a couple of months' porridge. I'd be a marked man. On Rule Forty-three with all the nonces. Having to watch my back all the time. Fuck that.'

'So, what do you want?'

'Full immunity.'

I laughed out loud. I turned to Ernie, expecting at least a smile on his face. He looked deadpan.

'Well . . .' he began.

'You can't be serious,' I said.

'I'm dead serious. If you want me to go QE then that's the deal. And I want proper protection and all.'

'Well . . .' Ernie said again. I glared at him but he ignored me. 'I'll have to take this to my superiors, of course.'

Hills nodded. We stood up to go.

'In the meantime,' concluded Ernie, 'I suggest you get yourself a brief.'

On the way out I quizzed Ernie about all of this.

'You aren't going to take that toerag's word for anything, are you, guvnor?'

'Well, it will all have to be properly investigated.'

'But that full immunity bullshit. I mean, he's taking the piss, isn't he?'

'I don't know, Frank. It could turn out to be the key to the whole inquiry. I'm going to talk to Harrington about it.'

'Shouldn't you go to the DAC, guvnor?'

'Not necessarily, Frank. It's all very sensitive. And if we are going to do a deal, well, Harrington can take it straight to the Home Secretary.'

This wasn't good. It wasn't good at all. This whole inquiry was getting out of hand. Ernie just wouldn't see that we had to keep the lid on it. The DAC was not going to like him going over the Yard's head to Harrington. But I had to let certain people know about this little supergrass. Hills' comment that *I could tell you stuff that would really get you sharpening your pencils* was unnerving. Maybe he was just bluffing, pretending to be bigger and better connected than he really was. But I wasn't prepared to take the risk. The firm within the firm would have to know.

Ideally I would have gone to Vic Sayles. But Vic had quit the force in 1969. Medical retirement. He was dying of lung cancer. So I didn't really have any choice. I had to see George Mooney.

I arranged a meet at the Premier Club. He was the best person to see about all this. Basically there're two types of corrupt persons. Your meat-eater and your grass-eater. A meat-eater is active in pursuing opportunities for personal gain, a grass-eater simply accepts the earners that come his way by chance. And by Christ was Mooney a meat-eater. He was bloody carnivorous. The money the Dirty Squad was taking in bungs was astronomical. It kind of created a whole economy of police corruption, sucking in people all over the Met. It was like a bloody feeding frenzy. I was, of course, more of a grass-eater. One of the grazing beasts. Bovine, docile. But I was worried that something somewhere might implicate me. I was concerned for my precious career. I just couldn't afford to let anything get in the way of that. And although I despised Mooney I knew he was the only person who could make sure that this thing wouldn't spread. I knew it was wrong going to him, but I didn't give a fuck any more.

I could see his evil little mind go to work as I walked over to his table. I knew he must already have been busying himself with attempts to undermine the investigation.

'Ah, Frank,' he announced. 'I understand you have some knowledge to impart.'

'Well, you know what it's about.'

'Hm, yes. This *inquiry*.' He pronounced the word with distaste. 'Outsiders snooping around in our affairs. I trust you realise the need to keep certain things secret.'

'Yeah, well.'

'Then we understand each other at last. Darkness is for those without.' He leaned towards me across the table. 'Enlighten me.'

I told him all about Hills' veiled allegations and Ernie Franklin's intention of following them up.

'And you say that he's willing to go straight to the swede on this one? Well, the DAC isn't going to like that.'

'No, I don't think he is. He's already had a word about how he doesn't like the way Ernie's been playing it.'

'Really?'

Mooney's little eyes lit up.

'Yeah, he's said as much, that they have been thinking of bringing someone else in.'

'I see.' He nodded thoughtfully. 'Well, Franklin isn't on the square. But the DAC is.'

*

I checked up on Walter Peters. Fat Wally. He ran the Stardust Erotic Revue in Soho, one of the more up-market strip clubs, very popular with Japanese tourists. The club was entirely legitimate – its performances carefully avoided showing anything that went beyond what was permissible under the obscenity laws. There was nothing that could directly link Peters with the bookshop trade, but it was rumoured that he controlled a number of premises through various frontmen. In the meantime Fat Wally had cultivated his image as a successful businessman. He had bought a seventeenth-century mansion in Surrey and had a swimming pool built in the grounds. There were stories of lavish parties where Peters entertained local dignitaries who'd often, quite unknowingly, find themselves rubbing shoulders with some of London's most dangerous criminals with whom Fat Wally was also keen to ingratiate himself. He had even joined the local Round Table and had appeared as Santa Claus in their Christmas charity drive.

He was an ideal subject for an expose. 'The Blue Film Boss', his corpulent form revealed by one of Alf Isaacs' snatch shots. We'd get a picture of his mansion too, maybe an aerial photograph showing the swimming pool so that the punters could see where all the dirty money had been going. Some examples of the filth he was peddling as well. It would be a big spread, a main feature on the centre pages perhaps.

There wasn't much else coming through the crime desk that week. Kevin, my junior reporter had a story for me. A prostitute had been found strangled in her flat.

'I thought this one might stand up,' he said. 'You know, the sex angle.'

I took the copy off him. I had tried to forget about what I had done, repress it, but here it was in black and white. The memory of it was like a dream, or rather, a horrible nightmare. Print made it real. A story. But it was like someone else's story, someone else who did these terrible things, someone who lived inside of me. Banner headlines throbbed in my head SEX MURDERER, EVIL BEAST. I felt like screaming. I felt like laughing out loud.

'Tony?'

I was in a trance.

'Yeah?'

'What do you think?'

I had to snap out of it. I felt a drop of sweat go cold on my neck. I musn't panic, I thought, musn't lose control.

'Yeah, sure,' I said, handing the story back to him. 'And see if you can get a picture.'

He turned and started to walk off. It was all right. Everything was all right.

'Oh, and Kevin,' I called after him. 'I need you to check up on Fat Wally.'

'Who?'

I showed him the stuff we had so far.

'Dig the dirt. Check to see if he's got any criminal convictions. Dodgy associates. Stuff like that.'

I then went to meet with Alan Khalid and we went through the set-up.

Alan had contacted Ian Hesper and ordered 4,000 hard-core Scandinavian films for which he was willing to pay £20,000. Hesper was to deliver the merchandise in batchs of 500, handed over at a motorway service station on the M4 in return for cash payments of £2,500. Khalid was to inspect a sample of each consignment before delivery. So a meeting was set up at the Mayfair flat. Hesper was to bring one of the films and, more importantly, Walter Peters, who was to confirm the contract in person.

Alan and Magda were in the flat with the projector and screen set up. Khalid was wired up with a microphone so that the conversation could be recorded. The sound man, Alf Isaacs and myself were hidden in the bedroom. At the right moment Alf would go in and get a snatch of Fat Wally. We were hoping that we could get a picture of him while the film was rolling. It would be a good picture, the porn king with blurred images of nakedness and obscenity in the background.

The whole piece was falling into place. It could kick off a campaign that could last for weeks. I'd even got Kenny Forbes, who did the 'A Doctor Writes' column, to do a little piece on the psychological effects of pornography.

The doorbell rang. I closed the bedroom door.

'Are you picking it up?' I asked the sound recordist.

He looked up and nodded. Suddenly there was commotion in the next room, voices raised. The sound man jumped a little and slipped his headphones from his ears. I looked at Alf.

'Come on,' I said, and we went through.

Four men had come into the flat. There was Hesper with a heavy-looking minder standing next to him in the classic hands clasped in front of the bollocks pose. There was a photographer taking pictures, and a little fellow in horn-rimmed spectacles who was loudly introducing himself as 'a solicitor, acting on behalf of Mr Hesper'.

The photographer was taking pictures of all of us in turn. This really threw Alf Isaacs. He was holding his own camera up in front of his face, trying to hide behind it, going 'Oi, cut that out, will you?', his huge frame all hunched up as if in pain. The little solicitor continued his prepared speech.

'My client has good reason to believe that he is being blackmailed by persons in the employ of the *Sunday Illustrated* who have attempted to unlawfully entrap him for the purposes of discrediting his good name with scurrilous allegations that he is dealing in illegally obscene material. We will be issuing a writ to this effect, gentlemen, and we have approached the *News of the World* with our own story on this unwarranted harassment.'

And with that the group of them turned on their heels and walked out. We were stunned, of course. How had we been rumbled? I spent

the rest of the evening going through every move that Alan Khalid
had made, but we still couldn't work it out.

Sid Franks was furious when I reported back to him the next
day. I spent the whole morning in the 'bollocking room'. Pausing
only to take the occasional gulp from the cloudy glass of bicarb on
his desk, he berated me.

'You know how much this fucking farce has cost us? What the
fuck has this cunt Khalid been up to? He must have fucked up
really badly for them to find out what we were doing. How did
they know?'

'That's what I've been trying to work out, Sid.'

'Well, it doesn't look like you've been very discreet, does it?
What about the Arab? Could it have been him that blew the
gaff?'

'I don't know, Sid.'

Could it have been Alan? He'd certainly been extravagant in the
way he'd conducted himself. Maybe he had been paid off by Hesper
and Peters.

'I'm still going through the expenses that cunt has been claiming.
It's outrageous.'

'I'm sorry, Sid. I really don't know what went wrong.'

'Well, that's all very well. I've got to go to the Big Table
and explain all of this. Heads are going to fucking roll, that's
for sure.'

'So,' I ventured cautiously, 'what do you want me to do with
the piece?'

'Do with it? You can shove it up your arse. The whole thing's
spiked. It's going to be a complete embarrassment.'

He took a swig of bicarbonate and spluttered.

'And you! You can forget about investigative journalism for a
bit, old son. You can make yourself useful with something a little
bit more within your capabilities. Madame Kismet's in St Thomas's
having her varicose veins done. You can do the fucking horoscope
this week. And believe me, whatever your star sign is it ain't
looking rosy.'

*

He shouldn't have gone into Joe's wagon. He should have waited for Joe to get back from his morning stroll. It was a bright frosty morning. Crystals of ice clustered on dry stalks of cow parsley. Jewelled spider's webs were strung amidst the undergrowth like little chandeliers. Joe had borrowed a can of three-in-one oil the day before and Mick needed it. He was packing away his tools and he wanted to make sure that they didn't get rusty in storage.

He wandered into the caravan, careful not to disturb anything. The oilcan was on the side table next to something wrapped in cloth. Something Joe had been oiling. It was when he reached over to the oilcan that he noticed the crumpled slip of newspaper on Joe's unmade bed. He knew that he should just take the can and go but he found himself picking up the paper. He had a premonition of something bad in the smudged letters before he read them. He wished he could just leave it all be. *This will spoil everything*, he found himself thinking, and yet he went on with it despite his better judgment.

FIVE YEARS ON AND COP KILLER STILL AT LARGE, read the headline. There was a police file photograph with the caption: *Billy Porter, the ruthless murderer of three unarmed policemen*. It was Joe. Take away the beard and the straggly hair and it was Joe all right. Or rather, it was not Joe. It never had been.

Mick reached for the wrapped-up object with even greater dread. He unwound the cloth, felt the curved butt of the German automatic in his palm. Freshly lubricated. It was a Luger, he knew that much.

Then everything happened very quickly. Joe was at the door, looking in.

'What you doing in here?' he demanded.

Mick turned, the gun in his hand.

'Give me that,' Joe insisted.

Mick felt horribly betrayed. He hadn't wanted to know. He had thought that they could just get on with it all with no thoughts of the past. He had wanted company, someone to work with. Someone who would really care about the work. Someone to share the tradition of it. Nothing else mattered. He had been prepared to turn a blind eye to all of it. But now Joe had spoiled everything. He had let Mick find out about what he had done. He had implicated him. He'd even kept the gun, for Christ's sake.

'I just came for the oil,' said Mick.

He wanted Joe to know that he hadn't been snooping about. That he was innocent of that. *If only you had covered your tracks better none of this would've happened.* All of his life he had wanted to get away from the evils of the mundane world. That was why he'd travelled. Lived on the outside of things. The childlike pleasure of decorating the machines of joy. Amusement Arcadia. It was kitsch, and cheap, but for him there had been no greater calling in life. He'd sought refuge in innocent pleasure. And yet here and now the badness had entered into it like a serpent in the garden, a mechanism of death held in a trembling hand.

'Give me the gun, Mick,' Joe said flatly, moving towards him.

'You,' Mick spluttered. 'You.'

Joe made a grab for the pistol. There was a struggle, an awful little dance as they both held on to the deadly little thing between them. They wrestled into a kind of embrace, staring at each other. Eyes wide, teeth clenched.

Then the gun went off with a muffled retort. The clinch broke and one of them fell to the floor. It all happened so quickly. A body slumped on the floor of the trailer. A rasping sound in the back of the throat and then stillness. The oilcan had been knocked over in the fracas and as blood seeped out over the floor of the caravan strange rainbow patterns diffused on its surface.

He had killed him. His mind reeled. For a second he forgot who he was. He had to think quickly. Get his story straight and decide what was to be done. It was a stupid bloody accident; it could have been either of them that stopped the bullet. But he had killed him. He threw the gun down and rubbed at his face, trying to make sense of it all. He had killed Joe. Yes, that was it. Joe was dead. And Mick would have to move on. He would have to get away from all of this and find a new life.

He dragged the body out to the field behind the hangar. He got a shovel and buried the corpse deep. He knew what he would do now. He would destroy every trace there was of Joe. No one would miss him, after all. He was an outsider. No one in the circle knew him. He was only familiar through being with Mick. So Mick would have to be careful. Suspicion would fall upon him. It would be best if he distanced himself from the fairground circuit. He had the truck and the other wagon. He would do a repaint job on his vehicles and move away from the work he was known for. The fairground jobs were in decline, after all. Mick had been fooling himself that there was any real future in it.

He gathered together all of Joe's things and put them in the wagon. He emptied a jerrycan of petrol all over the caravan. It washed away some of the brown stain of clotted blood on the floor. He lit a match and watched it blaze for a while like a beacon in the night. Then he drove off with the other wagon hitched to the truck into the darkness. He'd gone nearly fifty miles when he realised he'd made one simple little mistake. He'd left the gun behind.

23

Ernie was in an agitated state when he called me into his office.

'Something's turned up. After all this fucking time,' he told me, almost out of breath.

'What is it, guvnor?' I asked, trying to read the look on his face, wondering if he'd twigged what I was up to. 'Something about the inquiry?'

'No, Frank. This is something else.'

He sat down and caught his breath.

'A couple of days ago in this field in Lincolnshire there's this caravan fire by a disused aircraft hangar. A couple of local bobbies check it out and they find this.'

He picked up a plastic bag on his desk. There was a charred and rusted metal object in it. It was a pistol. A Luger.

'You know what this could mean, don't you?'

Of course I did. Billy Porter. One of the murder weapons, maybe. After all this time: a lead.

'So, what do we do about it?' I asked Ernie.

'Well. Forensics have got to check this with the bullets and the cartridge cases found at the crime scene. But I reckon we should make a little trip to the place they found it.'

'But what about the inquiry, guv?'

'Sod that. This takes precedence. Come on. I'll sort a driver out.'

So we motored up to Lincolnshire. It was a relief to be getting out of London for a bit. Away from the Met and all the badness. I'm not a big fan of the coutryside but it felt good to be getting a bit of fresh air. And it felt right to be engaged in proper police work instead of rubber-heeling. There was a buzz inside as we speeded out of London: we were going after Porter again. I felt bad about stitching Ernie up on the inquiry. As we hit the open road I had such a real sense of escape from it all I even toyed with the idea of coming clean. But that wouldn't be a good idea, I reasoned. Not yet. We reached the place that had been marked out on the map. A couple of patrol officers met up with us and took us to the scene.

There wasn't much left of the caravan. A charred shape in the field. A shadow left behind. Me and Ernie circled it a couple of times but there was nothing to see except the burned out shell of the trailer. There was a disused aircraft hangar about fifty yards from it. Ernie nodded towards it.

'Let's have a look in there,' he said.

One of the local officers slid the heavy door open and we went inside. A bird fluttered up towards the light from a hole in the ceiling. The building was empty. There were shapes and coloured patterns stencilled on the cement floor. Splattered paint abruptly framed by blocks of dull concrete. Outlines of large objects that had been laid out on the floor.

'This place was used by a fairground painter,' one of the officers explained.

'What?' Ernie asked.

'You know. Fairground rides. They painted them here.'

'And do we know who this artist is?'

'Well, the farmer who owns the land says it's a bloke called Mick.'

'And where is this Mick now?'

'He doesn't know. Said that he had an arrangement with him every winter. Nothing in writing. He reckons he'll be travelling around on the fairground circuit.'

'Right,' said Ernie. 'Well, that's where we need to look, isn't it?'

As we were walking out of the hangar I noticed something caught beneath the sliding door. It was a crumpled-up piece of paper. I unfolded it carefully. It was a drawing. Coloured pencils described intricate patterns and scrollwork.

'Let's have a word with this farmer, then,' Ernie told one of the local officers.

We got a description of this Mick bloke. It didn't match up to Porter at all.

'Was anyone else with him?' I asked.

'I don't think so,' the farmer replied. 'I didn't see him leave. He did a runner. He left a right bloody mess behind with that trailer. That was a bit bloody strange, wasn't it? Burning that caravan. And he didn't pay me. He was usually so reliable. That's the last bloody time I'm renting out to him.'

'Well, let us know if he's in contact again,' said Ernie, writing down his number at the Yard.

And with that we drove back to London.

'What do you reckon, guvnor?' I asked.

'Well, we've got to wait for the forensics report. If that comes up positive then we're on to something.'

Ernie looked enthusiastic for the first time in weeks.

'We need to check on the fairground world. It ain't going to be straightforward tracking this Mick down. That lot are always on the move.'

It was dark when we got back to the city. A yellow sickly glow above it from the streetlights. Ernie sighed heavily.

'Well,' he said, 'we've still got this bloody inquiry on our hands.'

I nodded grimly but thought: if the lab turns up something definite this could be our way out of it for good.

*

TAURUS: With Jupiter in conjunction with your ruling planet Mars there are opportunities in the workplace and possibilities of travel ... Doing the astrological column was a horribly tedious punishment.

And the thought that thousands of our halfwitted readership would imagine it to be arcane wisdom wasn't any consolation. I was keeping my head down. 'I want that column done properly, Meehan!' Sid Franks had insisted. I was hoping that when he had calmed down a bit I could approach him with the Lord Longford visiting Myra Hindley story and maybe get back in his good books. But for the time being I was *persona non grata* in the *Illustrated* office.

The threatened writ from Ian Hesper never materialised and I had it on fairly good authority from an acquaintance on the *News of the World* that they weren't planning to run a story about our débâcle. I'd quizzed Alan Khalid thoroughly about what could have gone wrong, but he assured me that he had no idea how we had been exposed. He was quite irate that the *Illustrated* weren't honouring all of his expenses.

I looked up to see Kevin hovering over me.

'What do you want?' I demanded tetchily.

'I found some stuff on Walter Peters,' he replied.

'Well, it's a bit fucking late for that now, isn't it?'

'Well, excuse me for breathing,' he mumbled, and started to walk away.

I was venting my spleen on him simply because he was a junior. All the other staff men had been avoiding me like the plague. I couldn't afford to alienate everybody on the paper the way things were.

'Kevin,' I called after him, as gently as I could muster. 'I'm sorry. I'm just not in the best of moods. What did you find?'

'Well,' he said, turning back, 'criminal convictions: bound over to keep the peace for house-breaking at fifteen. He went to Banstead Approved School a year later for taking away a car without the owner's consent. Then borstal for theft. And then a year in Brixton for receiving a lorry-load of stolen sweets. That was all in the fifties. He's been clean since then but he has been involved in running strip clubs and pornographic bookshops for the last ten years or so. And there are rumoured connections with some major villains. He was running a blue-films racket with one of the Richardson gang, George

Cornell – you know, the one that Ronnie Kray shot. And of course there's the Harry Starks connection.'

'Harry Starks?'

'Yeah,' Kevin retorted, as if this was common knowledge. 'Well, you know, the Stardust. That was Starks' club. Wally Peters took it over when Starks was put away.'

'Right,' I said. 'Well, thanks, Kevin. Sorry about losing my rag.'

'Oh,' he added, 'and I got that photo.'

'What photo?'

'The murdered prostitute.'

He handed me a smudge of this tart. A police file photograph, no doubt. A heavily made-up face looking resentfully out at eternity, an accusing stare, so much paint and powder. I should have felt guilt, remorse, but I didn't. I didn't really feel anything at all except a brief shiver of panic when I put the photo down and saw my thumbprint on it. As if that could somehow implicate me. What forensic evidence had I left behind? I really had to be careful.

'Yeah.' I nodded at Kevin. 'That ought to do it. But I'm not exactly running the crime desk this week. You'll have to take it to Sid.'

'Right.'

'Do you read your horoscope, Kevin?' I asked him.

'Nah,' he replied. 'Can't be bothered.'

'Oh well,' I said, looking back at my unfinished column. 'Thanks anyway.'

Pisces, I thought, flicking through a little guide to the zodiac. What does Pisces mean? Harry Starks, I thought. Fat Wally and Mad Harry. What were their star signs, their planetary conjunctions? Starks. Something clicked – THE PEER AND THE GANGSTER *Private Eye* allegations. Lord Thursby linked with Mr Starks, disproved in a court of law. A heavy libel settlement, but the gossip was that Teddy had only just got away with it. Teddy, Harry, Wally. Their orbits aligned. My mind spun for a second with cosmic influences. For a moment I could almost believe in this astrological nonsense. Then my thoughts came back down to earth with a bump. Harry, Teddy, Wally. Wally, Harry, Teddy. No, Teddy in the middle. Teddy, Wally. Wally, Teddy. I'd told Thursby about the investigation at that meeting in the French House.

I got up from my desk and took the jacket off the back of my chair. Sid Franks was walking down past all the newsroom desks.

'Where the fuck do you think you're going, Meehan?' he demanded.

'I've got a story,' I said, pushing past him.

'Now wait a fucking minute!' he called after me.

24

I was doing a bit of homework on fairs and fairground operators when Ernie came in with the ballistics report. He didn't look well pleased.

'Well?' I asked him.

'Well nothing, Frank. The tests on the gun were inconclusive.'

'What do they bloody mean, "inconclusive"?'

'The gun was too badly rusted and damaged by the fire for them to be able to be definite, one way or another. It's the same calibre as the cartridges recovered from the van and from Scrubs Lane but that doesn't exactly narrow things down.'

'So what do we do now?'

'Well, it might have escaped your notice but we do have another job on. It took some explaining to Harrington us just disappearing like that.'

'How did the swede take it?'

'Well, he did have the hump a bit. But I think I've established a good working relationship with him. And he's in a good mood. There's been some movement on our resident informer Tommy Hills.'

'Our little supergrass.'

'Yes indeed. It seems that Harrington has the authority to offer the full immunity he wants. If he can come up with the goods, that is. This could be the breakthrough in the inquiry.'

'Assuming Mr Hills isn't just telling a lot of porkies.'

'Well, obviously his testimony will have to be verified. But we can start the ball rolling. I want you to go over to Wandsworth and get a preliminary statement from him.'

'Don't you want to come, guvnor?'

'No, I can't. I've got the DAC coming to see me this afternoon.'

I knew what this might mean and I felt pretty bad about it. But then, I reasoned, if Ernie was taken off the inquiry he could get to work on the Porter investigation. And I could request a transfer to work alongside him. Everything could turn out for the best after all. It was a bastard that the gun test had turned up inconclusive but if Ernie was keen on following it up anyway and maybe getting the case reopened properly then everyone would be happy. The Skeleton Inquiry would all be nicely sewn up and we could get back to some proper detective work.

I got a driver and went down to Wandsworth. Tommy boy didn't look half as clever as he did on his last appointment at the Hate Factory. He was as white as a sheet. I chucked him a packet of Dunhill fags and he tore at the cellophane clumsily. His hand was shaking as he lit a cigarette.

'So, Tommy,' I said. 'Looks like you're going to get what you want.'

'What?' he muttered, drawing heavily on his fag.

'Your immunity from prosecution, of course.'

'Well, I'm not sure about all of this.'

'What?'

'I want to withdraw my allegations.'

'You what?'

'You heard.'

'I don't believe this. Just the other day you were ready to tell us a nice long story. What's the matter?'

'Well . . .' He sighed out a long stream of smoke. 'Things have changed, haven't they.'

'What's that supposed to mean? You got cold feet or something?'

'Yeah. Something like that.'

'Has someone in here got at you?'

Tommy Hills laughed and shook his head.

'What's so bloody funny?'

'Look, I ain't saying nothing. OK?'

'Are you not happy with the protection you've been offered in here?'

Hills laughed again.

'I ain't worried about anyone in here,' he said. 'It's out there I've got to watch it. From your lot.'

A look of fear on his face. I knew what it meant. Mooney had got to him.

'That's a serious allegation, Hills. Would you be prepared to make a statement to that effect?'

'Look, I don't want my card marked. It's more than I'm worth. Too much fucking grief.'

'You sure?'

'Fucking right I'm sure. I want to go back to my cell.'

So that was that. I got back to Coco sooner than I expected. I went to Ernie's office to give him the bad news. Outside the door I heard raised voices. The Deputy Assistant Commissioner.

'It's a matter of loyalty, Franklin.'

'Loyalty? Loyalty to who exactly, sir?'

'To your superior officers.'

'Well, maybe there's a higher loyalty than that, sir.'

'Don't get clever with me, Franklin. You think you're involved in some sort of moral crusade? You're just bloody incompetent. Going to Harrington to clear some sort of deal with a supposed witness? You should have cleared things like that through your line of command. You should have been briefing me instead of passing everything on to the swede.'

'I'm sorry, sir.'

'Sorry? I should fucking think so too. Do you realise how much damage you've done? Harrington is on the inquiry in an advisory capacity. The responsibility for the investigation rests with the Met.'

'I'm sorry, sir, I just did what I thought was best.'

'Well, you've been playing for the wrong side for too long, Ernie. We're taking you off the inquiry.'

'Sir,' Ernie croaked, barely audible, broken.

'And what's this I hear about you interrupting your work here to go on some wild-goose chase in the countryside?'

'That was pertaining to the Porter case, sir. I'm still nominally in charge of it.'

'But I've heard that this gun they found doesn't even match with the cartridge cases found at the murder scene.'

'The tests were inconclusive, sir.'

'And on the basis of that you go off, taking another officer with you, leaving a major investigation in the lurch? Without consulting me?'

'I'm sorry, sir.'

'Look, to be honest, we haven't been exactly confident of your operational abilities of late. Your personal problems are interfering with your judgment, if you ask me. Ernie, you're just not fit psychologically. I suggest you take some time off. You know, sick leave.'

*

Julian came to the door when I went around to Teddy's flat in Eaton Square.

'Tony,' he announced with forced bonhomie. 'To what do we owe the pleasure?'

'I want to see Thursby.'

'You'd better come in, then.'

Thursby was reclining on a sofa in the drawing room. He was wearing some sort of kaftan. There were piles of papers all over the room.

'Ah, Tony,' he said as I walked in.

'Teddy and I were just going through Tangiers,' Julian explained.

'Marvellous place. Just after the war. All sorts of types. The International Zone and all that.'

'Shall I get us all a drink?' Julian asked.

'Isn't it a little early?' muttered Thursby. 'What the hell.' He shuffled through some papers on his lap. 'Jules, remind me

to find those letters from Brian Howard. They're here somewhere.'

'Gin and tonic all right?' Julian asked me.

'Sure,' I replied.

'So, dear boy. How's Grub Street?'

'Not so good, actually.'

'Oh, I am sorry to hear that. What's wrong?'

'Well, Teddy, I was going to ask you about that.'

Julian came through with the drinks, frowning at me.

'What on earth's the matter, Tony?' he asked, handing me a
glass.

'I think you both know what the fucking matter is,' I said
tersely.

'Now, dear boy, let's not be tiresome. I'm sorry that I had to spoil
your little investigation. I'm sure you had the noblest intentions in
your moral crusade.'

He grinned. His liverish mouth parted to reveal discoloured
incisors.

'I just couldn't afford for things to get too close to home,' he
went on. 'I am sorry if I've got you into trouble. I did give you
that tidbit about Frank Longford. I'm sure that I could come up
with some other gossip for you if you want.'

'I'm sure what you could tell me about yourself would be far
more interesting.'

Thursby sighed.

'But then it wouldn't be gossip, would it?' he said. 'Gossip is
about other people, not oneself.'

'I could do an exposé on you, you know.'

He chuckled softly.

'Oh, I don't think so. The boys from Greek Street tried that and
it cost them. No, you'll not get me. I've got some very high-placed
friends, most of them with something to hide. I know enough about
Reggie Maudling to bring the house down. Then there's Lord
Goodman. And MI5. No, you wouldn't stand a fucking chance. I
shouldn't think that Sid Franks would be too keen to run a story

on me. You see I've always maintained a good relationship with the yellow press. It's been very useful. Your little campaign has already cost them enough now, hasn't it? And that Arab boy you used. I mean, oh dear, we've got plenty on him.'

'You're a fucking fraud, Thursby.'

Thursby sighed again.

'What is real and what is phoney? Hm? We've all got something to hide. Julian tells me that you're not all you appear to be.'

I shot a glance at Jules. He shrugged vaguely.

'We really should keep up appearances, you know. Surely you understand that. There's been far too much criticism of the institutions of state. Stupid inquiries into the police force drummed up by subversive troublemakers. Trots running the unions and trying to bring the country to its knees. Now more than ever we need to maintain public morale.'

He stared into his glass.

'Get us another drink, Jules. Tony?'

'No,' I said. 'I'm fine, thanks.'

Julian went out to the kitchen.

'You realise how much that queen is costing me. He's a bloody parasite. Maybe I should employ you to help with the memoirs. I'm sure you're not as extravagant. And more, shall we say, discreet.'

Julian came back and handed Teddy a refilled glass.

'Oh well,' he said, lifting it. 'Cheers.'

So that was that. There wasn't anything that I could do. Not yet, at least.

25

I went for a drink with Ernie at the Tank after that dressing-down he'd got from the DAC. I felt guilty about the way things had turned out. He'd only done what he'd thought was best and he'd been treated like shit. Squeezed between the Yard brass who wanted the whole thing smoothed over and the firm of bent coppers who wanted to cover their tracks. He'd been far too innocent, of course. If he'd known beforehand some of the things that had been going on he might have been forewarned. He would have been able to conduct the inquiry with more caution. As it was the whole thing ruined him. And it was my fault as much as anyone's.

'What are you going to do, guvnor?' I asked him.

I was hoping that he'd try to get back to following up these leads on the Porter case. They were pretty tenuous but it was something to be going on with. We could work on it together. I could get away from all the shit I'd found myself up to the neck in. Maybe it would help Ernie get back to form too.

'I tell you what I'm going to do, Frank. I'm taking early retirement. I've already talked about it with my doctor. I'll get a full pension and everything. Fuck them.'

'You sure?'

I wasn't expecting this. My heart sank.

'Yeah. Twenty-three fucking years' service. For what? Well, I'm better off out of it if this is the way the force is going.'

I wanted to say something. Something about how at least he'd tried to do the right thing. But it would be hypocritical coming from me.

'What about the Porter thing?'

'Oh, Frank,' he sighed. 'I'm tired. I'm tired of it all.'

'But you can't give up on that.'

'Can't I?'

He caught my eye. I was staring at him fiercely.

'Look, Frank, I know you lost a friend. We all lost something from that. But maybe we ain't going to catch the bastard. Even if the gun was the same one, that bloke's description doesn't fit. Five years on and nothing. Maybe Porter's dead. Maybe he topped himself or something. Look, we'll pass it all on to whoever gets assigned the Porter case. I'm out of it.'

There wasn't much else to say. But I didn't want to leave Ernie on his own. So we sat there drinking until the place closed.

Ernie's replacement on the inquiry was, of course, Detective Superintendent George Mooney. Seconded from the Obscene Publications Squad, he'd obviously managed to manoeuvre himself into the job. There was a horribly perverted sense of logic to it all. The Yard brass were happy and the firm within the firm was safe. I didn't particularly relish the prospect of working so closely with Mooney but I had to live with that.

And he played it all very cutely, you had to give him that. Instead of trying to stall the inquiry as you might expect he appeared to be full of zeal and enthusiasm. But the apparent energy he was putting into the investigation generated more heat than light. The swiftness with which he brought forward charges relating to the initial allegations against the two officers involved in Operation Skeleton ensured that there would be no time for suspicions of wider corruption to be properly unearthed. This, in turn, undermined Harrington, whose more careful and methodical approach was made to seem almost incompetent. The swede became increasingly marginalised and Mooney did little to disguise his contempt for the provincial officer. I'll never forget one evening when he and Harrington were walking out to the carpark together. Mooney drove a brand-new Jensen Interceptor, a really flash motor. Harrington had an Austin 1800. Mooney sniffed at the swede's car as he passed it, turned to him and said with a sneer:

'Is that the best you can do?'

Detective Sergeant John O'Neill and Detective Constable Ian Campbell were both charged with perverting the course of justice. Other Operation Skeleton officers faced disciplinaries. Convenient scapegoats had been found and the whole thing seemed nicely sewn up. Or so we thought.

Which is more than can be said for the Porter case. Eventually a senior detective was assigned to it but there seemed to be a general reluctance for anyone to take it up. It had bad luck written all over it. It represented failure. There had been so many false leads and wrong sightings over the years that nobody wanted to act upon anything unless it was definite. Another cock-up would just mean more bad press for the Met on a case that they'd failed to clear up. I knew some officers that were superstitious about even mentioning it, like it was tempting fate or something. For me it was more of a personal curse, like part of me was damned by it. I passed on what me and Ernie had on the gun and the caravan. I hadn't had time to follow any of it up so it didn't amount to much. I kept the drawing I'd found on the hangar floor. I don't know why.

All that was left to do on the Skeleton inquiry was to see through the committal proceedings on O'Neill and Campbell. Mooney had yet again taken the initiative on this. Harrington was hamstrung. His recommendations for reforming the Met were politely acknowledged and completely ignored. Soon he'd be packed up and gone. Few people at the Yard would be sad to see the back of him.

Then one afternoon Mooney came into my office. He looked ashen.

'Frank,' he said, 'I need a word.'

'What is it?'

'Not here,' he muttered, his little eyes darting to and fro. 'Meet me after work. At the Premier.'

'I can't.'

'Why not?'

'I'm baby-sitting tonight.'

Mooney laughed out loud at that.

'Oh, sweet fucking Jesus,' he declared.

But it was true. I'd promised I'd look after David that evening. Jeannie wanted to visit a friend in hospital.

'I'm sorry but that's it.'

'Well, this is important, Taylor,' he hissed. 'A fucking wheel's coming off if we're not careful. The whole lot of us could be going down. Yourself included. If we don't do something sharpish there could be two new lodges on the Isle of Wight.'

He was making reference to the two high-security prisons there: Albany and Parkhurst. I didn't know what he could mean specifically but it sounded bloody serious.

'Look, I've said enough here,' he went on. 'We need to meet somewhere private. Can't you get out of your parental duties?'

I sighed. I didn't want to let Jeannie down.

'It ain't going to be easy,' I said.

Mooney grinned.

'Then why don't I come around to your gaff?' he suggested softly. 'That'll be nice and cosy.'

I really didn't want that bastard in my house but I didn't really have any choice in the matter. David was a bit overexcited that night and it was hard to get him settled and ready for bed. We were watching *The Virginian* together when the doorbell rang. I let Mooney in. He was carrying a holdall.

I fixed him a drink as he sat down in an armchair and beamed at David.

'Here's the little soldier,' he said.

David went all shy. Then he pointed at a Stetsoned figure on the screen.

'Cowboy,' he said.

'Yes,' said Mooney. 'That's right, son. Cowboy.'

I handed him a glass and sat down on the settee.

'So what's all this about, George?'

'It's O'Neill. The cunt.' He coughed, looking sidelong at David. 'Sorry. I mean, he says he won't just duck his nut for the Skeleton thing. Says he isn't going to go away when everyone else is off the hook. He's threatening to name names.'

'Shit. I mean . . .'

David laughed.

'Rude word, Daddy!'

'Yeah, sorry about that,' I said.

'He's agreed to do a runner.'

'Right.'

'But he wants paying off, of course.'

Mooney held up the bag.

'Five grand. He's going to skip the country in the next couple of days.'

'Well, that's sorted, then.'

'Thing is, Taylor, we need someone to carry the bag. He doesn't trust me. Can't think why.'

'Oh, Christ.'

'I'm afraid so. You're going to have to be the goby on this one.'

He handed me a scrap of paper with the time and address of a meet. I heard a key turn in the front door. *Shit*, I thought.

'Mummy!' David called out, and went to meet her in the hall.

'Ah,' Mooney announced jovially, 'the dear lady wife.'

He patted the holdall and muttered:

'There's a little bit extra in here. Your commission.'

Jeannie came through into the lounge with David in her arms. Mooney stood up as she entered. I cleared my throat, nervously. She froze as she saw him. David wriggled free from her and went to sit on the settee.

'Jeannie,' I said, 'this is George. We're working together.'

Mooney's peephole eyes narrowed in on her. She was spooked.

'Oh,' he said softly. 'We've met before, haven't we?'

The past flooded back into her face. Fear in her eyes.

'I'll see myself out,' said Mooney.

And he was gone.

'What the fuck was he doing in our house?'

'Jeannie . . .'

'He's the one that Attilio was paying off. He's the one that . . .'

She flinched from saying any more. Her face creased up at the hateful knowledge of it. Then she caught sight of the bag.

'And what's this?' she demanded, bending down to grab at it.

I made a move for it myself. She pulled at the zip. I'd got hold of one of the handles. Bundles of cash tumbled out on to the carpet.

'You bastard,' she spat at me. 'You lied to me.'

'Jeannie, look . . .'

She picked up a wad of cash and threw it at me.

'Bringing bad money into the house. All this time. Saying that you'd gone straight. You bloody liar.'

'Yeah, well, look around, Jeannie. We've done all right out of all of this. You should remember that.'

'Don't try and justify it like that. Like you were doing it for us. Don't you dare.'

'But it's true. I've provided for you. And more. I've made sure that David has never wanted for anything. Even though . . .'

Jeannie's flintlike eyes went wide at this.

'Yeah?' she taunted. 'Go on.'

I felt a horrible sinking feeling in my stomach.

'Please, Jeannie,' I begged. 'Don't.'

'Don't what? Don't say it, even though we both know it's true?'

'Please.'

'Well, I'll say it, then. He's not yours. And you know what? I'm glad he's not yours. I wouldn't want to raise a kid that might turn out like you.'

There was an awful silence. We just looked at each other. I didn't know what to say. There wasn't anything to be said. David was watching us intently. You'd think with the row going on he'd react in some way. But he just looked on like it was a scene on the telly.

'Right,' I declared finally, and started to pick up the cash and put it back in the bag. I walked out of the lounge. I had a meeting to keep.

*

Behold, thou hast driven me out this day from the face of the Earth; and from thy face shall I be hid; and I shall be a fugitive and a vagabond in the Earth.

Lines of flight. Juggernauts that thundered along the motorways. The A roads and the B roads. The circle. Turning and returning. He felt he was forever falling. In an orbit of perpetual descent. Never coming to rest. Always moving on.

He had all the money they'd made during the winter and that kept him going for a while. He made sure he avoided the fairground circuit. If the gun was found people would be asking questions among the showmen, so it was best he kept well out of the way of that world. He would miss it, but then he'd never really been part of it. Never really in the Circle.

And it was easy enough to do in practice. It was then that he realised that traditional travellers don't really move. They cling to a fixed pattern. And merely oscillate within it. He could always make sure that he wouldn't run into any of that crowd since their sense of time and place was so fixed and predictable. Dates and locations of every build-up or pull-away predestined and constant. The litany of sites, King's Lynn Mart, St Giles, the Goose Fair, immovable feasts, townships that were forever being built and taken apart, that would always exist at a particular time and place.

In his mind it was harder. He went through a vertiginous delirium. Delineation. He lost track. Once, on Scotch Corner, where the A1 meets the A66, he had to pull up on a lay-by. He didn't know which way he was supposed to be going. He had no memory of how and why he had got there and which road he was supposed to take. He wasn't even quite sure who he was. Was he Mick? Maybe, for safety's sake, he should call himself something else. Become someone else. Was he someone else? It took him a while to clear the confusion in his head. *Maybe we're always on the verge of becoming someone else*, he reasoned against the awful madness of it. Sometimes he imagined that he was already dead. Riding the Ghost Train. It was then that he had to remind himself that it was Mick that had killed Joe. He had to remember that, though the terrible truth of it all would remain hidden.

And he wandered with scarcely any purpose other than being on the run. Without the nomad's sense of territory he drifted. He didn't really belong anywhere. But then he was not a traveller. He was a fugitive. As time passed he felt ludicrously charmed that he had not been caught. But maybe this was his curse.

Whosoever slayeth Cain, vengeance shall be taken on him seven-fold.

The loneliness seemed unbearable. And yet he bore it. He often thought of the other man, of their quiet comradeship. The awful guilt of what he had done. *My punishment is greater than I can bear*. But it had been Joe's fault. He had been so careless. And now Joe no longer existed.

Circumstance. Fate billets you where it wants and demobs you without warning. Orders you around the exercise yard of life. The sky wheeled above his head. The great emptiness of the firmament. The dim cinders of night like waning fireworks, burning out and falling to the ground. A road map of stars, junctions and conurbations. Mighty lonesome. Like an old and echoing country-and-western song. *Yippy-ay-oh, yippy-ay-ay. Ghost Riders in the sky.*

He found bits of painting work here and there. And the truck was good for picking up scrap metal. And he came across the new travellers. They were young and strange. Long-haired with brightly coloured vehicles. He was suspicious of them at first but they were friendly towards him. They thought he was authentic. Gypsy blood and all that. Silly fuckers. They were mostly middle-class drop-outs that hardly knew any better. Most real travellers held them in contempt. But he started to hang around with them. They were good cover and they treated him with respect. They didn't ask too many questions.

1985

Embrace the Base

26

There was trouble every Saturday night on the Hardcastle estate. It would always start in the local pub, the Queen's Head, just before closing time. Fights would break out. The landlord would call the police. Before they could respond, the pub and the flat above it would be set on fire. The affray would then spread to the estate. Six hundred people would gather and build barricades across its main entrances. Armoured vehicles would be sent in to break them down and units of police in riot gear would follow to try to take back the territory.

Sometimes the police would gain control of the situation by midnight. At other times resources would be misallocated or overstretched and they would be beaten back by the mob. On a good night they would be able to clear the area well enough for fire crews to ensure that there was no significant damage to the estate. On a bad night the whole place would be burning and the police would come under such a concentrated hail of missiles and petrol bombs that they would be lucky to come out of it in one piece.

Every Saturday night it was the same. The Hardcastle estate seemed to have no other purpose than to stage endlessly repeated dramas of public disorder. It was what it was designed for. Its labyrinth of forecourts, low-rise walkways and access balconies, blind alleys of fear and danger. Its high-rise vantage points a silhouette of menace. Its whole architecture was a solid fortress of deprivation, resentment and unrest.

I knew the Hardcastle estate quite well. So did most of the other senior officers that morning. We'd all heard of it, at least. Every force in the country had it as part of their training resources. A table-top map of its layout. A box full of wooden police vans and little wooden crowds with numbers of rioters printed on them. A set of counters with codes indicating units of the local constabulary. Four wooden police dogs, each labelled DOG.

I was part of a training seminar. In a real room with four other real officers. There was a facilitator and next to him a VDU screen that would periodically flash up information as to how events were unfolding. A room full of high-ranking uniforms. I was the only CID officer there. The only one from the Met. And the only one in plain clothes. We were to take turns in being in command of the situation. In the simulation it was early evening on the estate and trouble was brewing. The officer whose turn it was to make decisions, a superintendent from Cambridgeshire Constabulary, had spotted a problem. The eleven to seven o'clock day relief was just about to come off duty. He wanted to keep them working on overtime. The facilitator nodded and said that he was sure that the Assistant Chief Constable would support the decision, given the circumstances.

There were nods around the group as well. Overtime. It was what had kept the woodentops going all through the miners' strike. There had even been some disappointment when the strike finished and the extra hours' cash bonanza was over. The Met lads, the 'white-shirts', hadn't exactly been on their best behaviour on their tours of duty in the pit villages. We'd got a bad reputation for steaming in and asking questions later. No surprise really when you start billeting coppers in TA barracks. And the whole thing had a knock-on effect back home. Battle fatigue. All the community policing approach went up in smoke after a couple of weeks up North. Your average copper was liable to want to go out and crack a few heads on his first normal relief back on his own patch. There was a strange mix of euphoria and disillusionment.

We got called 'Thatcher's Boot Boys' so often that we started to believe it ourselves.

And there was an easiness about some of the stuff that went on. Roadblocks stopping people from going into Nottinghamshire. Turning people back merely on suspicion that they might be flying pickets. That was a bit hookey, not exactly legal really. The state going bent for the job. It was political, and a lot of the lads weren't happy about it. But then coppers always seem a bit confused when it comes to things like that. I've never really been able to understand these things myself. I knew one officer who'd always be dropping some change into these collection buckets for miners' support groups that seemed to be on every street corner during the strike. I'm damn sure that although half of him was feeling a bit guilty about what the families had to go through all those months with no money, the other half was wanting to keep the strike going and all that overtime money rolling in.

The computer simulation kept churning out problems for us to solve. Fights had broken out in the Queen's Head. A hardware store on the other side of the estate had been broken into, a large quantity of paraffin had been seized. The next officer who had taken his turn in making decisions had withdrawn all remaining foot patrols so that they could be mobilised into Police Support Units. The Assistant Chief Constable had been requested to contact neighbouring forces to get reinforcements under the agreed system of mutual aid. The pub was now on fire. Barricades were going up on the Hardcastle estate. Mobile units were being issued with riot gear, or rather 'protective equipment'.

Now all the talk was of 'bridgeheads', 'pincer movements' and 'flanking manoeuvres'. I hadn't joined the force for all this. I'd wanted to catch villains. This was more like being in the army. Being plainclothes meant that I'd managed to avoid all of this public order stuff, but it was still depressing. Like we'd become paramilitary.

The PSU units are plotted up in their vans now. They need authorisation to start deploying 'protective equipment'. 'Riot gear' was a phrase that we weren't supposed to use. There's a brief discussion about how the appearance of being, well, 'tooled up' in this way will affect the mood of the crowd. The scene in the simulation is at the stage of 'sporadic disorder'. It's agreed that it's time for the mobile units to respond appropriately to this scenario and the game moves on.

It was my turn now. I had to try and articulate what CID input would be in this situation.

'I'd investigate the burglary of the hardware store,' I began. 'Get some idea of the amount of flammable materials stolen and find out if there had been thefts of milk bottles or other containers in the area.'

There were nods from around the group.

'I'd also have the events of the previous evening reviewed to see if there was a pattern or whether it was just a spontaneous thing. I see CID involvement here as being the gathering of intelligence in order to prevent the situation happening again. I'd set up an incident room to process information and debrief officers so that we can provide a proper system of intelligence for the officer in charge.'

'Anything else?' the facilitator asked.

'Yeah,' I went on. 'I'd make sure that there were a couple of officers in a forward position maintaining surveillance of all that was happening. I'd want a constant stream of information supplied to the command post.'

The rest of the group looked at least a bit impressed.

'Very good, Mr Taylor,' the facilitator commented, and we continued with the exercise.

By now the table-top map was so crowded with wooden vans and yellow incident flashes that it was hard to see the outline of the estate beneath them. In the central forecourt was a single crowd block with the number 600 on it.

The officer now taking his turn in the exercise was a superintendent who'd seen service on Merseyside. A veteran of Toxteth 1981. The year when all the inner cities seemed to go up in flames.

District Support Units had arrived by now and he was requesting ACPO approval to use bulldozers to break down the barricades and send in snatch squads of short-shield serials. For all the talk of 'controlled dispersal' and 'containment formations', the scene now had the appearance of medieval siege warfare. Ancient imperial infantry tactics. The legions against the barbarians. He talked of the importance of making sure that the crowd didn't get control of the high ground on the estate.

Police had gained control of the Hardcastle estate by two o'clock on Sunday morning. The crowd was finally dispersed and some of the serials that had been on duty since seven the previous morning could start to stand down. A few District Support Units stayed on the scene to protect fire-fighters, who were damping down the last of the fires from petrol bombs. The facilitator congratulated us and said it was time for lunch. As we filed out he started to clear the wooden counters off the board and put them back into their respective boxes. Ready for the next time.

After the Skeleton Inquiry I went back to Flying Squad for a spell. In 1972 Robert Mark was appointed Commissioner for the Met and all hell broke loose. He actually set about implementing reforms that people had been fannying on about for years. He set up an independent unit, A10, to tackle corruption. CID would no longer be able to get away with investigating itself. Uniform branch finally got the upper hand and the power that the plainclothes department had had over the Yard was broken for good. And A10 didn't fuck about. Heads began to roll in the Drugs Squad, the Flying Squad, the Dirty Squad. I managed to get away with it. With each highly publicised corruption case I was always worried that my number might come up. But it didn't. And I got made up to Detective Chief Inspector in 1975.

George Mooney got away with it too. He took early retirement in 1973. Went to live in Spain in a nice little villa he bought with all that bent money. But he got his comeuppance in the end. He was shot dead by Harry Starks in 1979.

In 1976 Robert Mark inflicted his most humiliating reform on the Department. A new interchange policy that meant that no CID officer could expect much promotion unless they went back to uniform for a spell. Plainclothes really resented that and some said it was the end of the career detective. But I just got on with it. It felt strange being back in the blue serge.

I ended up teaching at Bramshill for a while. All those little Rapid Promotion Scheme and graduate intake faces looking up at me. Clever little bastards. Just like I had been. I was put on a training course myself. Run by the Management Services Department. We were supposed to be looking at the 'distribution of functions and responsibilities within the Metropolitan Police'. Issues of 'man management', stuff like that. We were now supposed to call ourselves the Police Service rather than the Police Force. That stuck in the throat a bit. There was a whole new set of jargon. Recommendations, restructuring. I was bored rigid.

But it paid off. Eventually I got back to the Yard made up to Detective Superintendent. C11. Criminal Intelligence. And five years later a post came up in this new team they were putting together to work with the National Reporting Centre. The Central Intelligence Unit, it was called. It meant promotion up to Detective Chief Super. I got sent on this public order seminar and I was to report the next day.

So everything was going well on the job front. I'd come through the shit smelling of roses. At the highest operational rank for CID and still only in my early forties. I was a fucking high-flier.

My personal life wasn't so sweet. A cold and loveless marriage with Jeannie. I always hoped that we could work it out somehow. But any feeling that we had had for each other seemed to have been poisoned, corrupted. Oh, it was amicable enough. No rows or anything like that. Just a sort of bitter silence. We lived our own lives. She had the salon and her own set of friends. I had my career, my precious ambition. We only stayed together for David's sake. We played the respectable couple.

We never told him that I wasn't his real father. I always felt deep down that we should have. But I didn't do anything about it. As the years passed he grew more distant from me. I kind of thought Jeannie might tell him but she didn't. I think she was scared that he might find out about her past. She still doted on him. And he was a real mummy's boy. A bit soft. He went into this teenage rebellious phase. Wearing lairy clothes and sulking about in his bedroom. I felt that he began to resent me. Saw me as some kind of authority figure, I guess. Though I never felt that I had any authority where he was concerned. I felt helpless, left out. At least he didn't get into any real trouble. He did well at school. He was doing his A-levels. But he got all of these stupid political ideas in his head. Clearly having a copper for an old man wasn't very cool. Probably called me a 'fascist pig' behind my back. He rarely said anything to my face, though. Just gave me the silent treatment.

And he got to look so much like his real father. It really spooked me sometimes. I'd catch him looking moodily at me and I'd see Dave's eyes staring out at me. My conscience. Just like the old days.

*

MURDER MONTHLY. *Free binder with first issue. Collect and keep to build an extensive dossier of the most horrific homicides in history. Each edition a fascinating study of the ultimate crime.* Such was the pinnacle of my journalistic career. To be editor of such an esteemed organ. To be honest, I was lucky to get the job. All my years on the *Sunday Illustrated* had taken their toll, a decline in the ability to write that comes with years of hack work. My meagre talent wrote itself off slowly into virtual aphasia, having endlessly manipulated a familiar set of clichés into incoherence. I continued to have a dim desire to write something substantial one day, but as time went on this became more distant and less probable. I had for a long time occasionally confided to others in the Grub Street racket, usually after a lengthy drinking session when one's sense of self-esteem shrivels just as the tongue loosens, that I was still 'working on a book'. This was forever curtailed one evening in the Three Feathers when a red-faced colleague had turned on me rather bitchily with the riposte 'Yes, neither am I'.

But fate took me out of Fleet Street, just as Fleet Street itself was moving on. The *Illustrated* was moving into new premises in Docklands. Fully computerised and deregulated. The unions were shafted. There was an angry picket line outside the new high-security headquarters, violent clashes with the police and the private-contract lorries going in and out. I took early retirement as there was a fairly good offer on the table. Natural wastage. They were glad to be rid of me as I had long since become merely part of an inventory of unwanted fixtures and fittings. And I was well out of it. I heard from fellow hacks who'd made the transition, complete with computer training and a shiny new job description, that it was pretty soulless. Huddled over their screens like cloistered monks. Hardly ever going out to find a story, scarce opportunities to spend time in the pub. And they felt under siege. The scenes outside the gate could get pretty ugly, and it was hard not to feel the anger of it all. Sid Franks would have loved to have seen all the Fathers of Chapel he'd fought with over the years get it in the neck but he'd died of a heart attack in 1981.

And I was glad to be out of it. My career had never fully recovered from the porn inquiry fiasco. I'd struggled to keep my head above water, to be honest, struggled to stop myself from sinking into the horror. I hadn't given in to my urges since that last time, I'd controlled myself, but it had meant that I'd needed to take things quietly. My mind calmed down as I got older. I entered the Middle Ages with a sense of relief that maybe the Dark Ages were over.

And *Murder Monthly* was an ideal place for me. I had been headhunted for the job – I'd done some freelance work on a similar publication years ago and my name must have come up when they were stealing ideas. It was a pretty failsafe formula for the anorak psychos. Along with the occult, UFOs, conspiracy theory, stuff on the war that had a slight obsessiveness about the

As they encircled the airbase, pennants and flowers were hung on the wire. There were a few arrests as some people attempted to cut the fence with bolt-cutters. The protesters went limp as they were apprehended. This was to be a peaceful demonstration.

Mick was there with the Peace Convoy. These were the new travellers he'd fallen in with. Hippies, drop-outs. They didn't use caravans. They converted trucks, coaches or ambulances into moving homes or lived in teepees or benders. At first he didn't have much to do with them. Weirdos, he thought. But he slowly began to realise that he was safe among them. They were mostly harmless enough. And they seemed to like him, took him for an authentic traveller. He never put them right on that one. He pretended he was from an old showman family, that he had real gypsy blood in him. He could talk the talk. And he found work. Painting their vehicles. They would ask for all kinds of lairy designs on their lorries and buses.

He'd met Janis at Glastonbury. He'd got a job painting the sets for a travelling theatre group. They were into circus skills and sideshow spectacle. They appreciated his ability to paint traditional showman designs. It made a change from the usual psychedelic stuff that people wanted. Janis was part of the troupe. He was working outdoors on a backdrop when he first saw her. She was practising juggling with a tall, lanky man. They were passing six clubs between them in a rhythmic ellipse. When they took a break she came over to look at his work. *Wow*, she had said, *it's so real*. She was, he guessed, in her early thirties. She had long hennaed hair and a nose-ring. Her face was ruddy and weathered from the travelling life.

She was living in a converted Post Office van. Multicoloured with a window installed in its side.

'I'm bored with how it looks,' she had said. 'Will you paint it for me?'

He had shrugged and nodded. They had shared a chillum of sensimillia that evening. Its sharp tang burned against the back of his throat. He felt the prickling rush of it surge up from his

275

calf muscles into his weary head. She'd encouraged him to talk of the fairground life. The showman routine he'd repeated so often he almost believed it himself.

'Wow,' she had said as she exhaled a stream of blue from deep in her lungs. 'I suppose a showman is like a shaman.'

'Yeah,' he'd replied with a grin, not knowing what the hell she was on about.

They had slept together that night in her creaking van. It had been so long since he had had sex with anyone. He felt the deep warmth of it afterwards flood through his tired body. They curled up together and he trembled slowly into a warm and intimate night.

They ended up travelling together. They got a coach and converted it. He did the painting and the coachwork, she did the mechanics. She didn't ask too many questions, which was good. He didn't do too much talking. He had plenty of tales he had picked up over the years on the road to keep her happy. She spoke a lot more and he'd listen patiently. It was nonsense, mostly. About the Goddess and spirituality. And Peace. She'd always be banging on about Peace.

Luckily it was largely a women's thing. She'd go off to join groups of feminists in peace camps pitched outside missile bases across the country. It would give him time to himself which he needed. He'd become so used to it.

But this time they went on a demo together. He felt a bit edgy as a phalanx of police came into view lined up by the main gate of the base. He'd spent so much time avoiding trouble of any kind.

The staccato of the helicopters above was deafening. Memories hovered over his head. Searching for landing zones in his consciousness. The perimeter fence was littered with banners and flowers, all kinds of mementos entwined into the chain link. Military police stood silently on the other side. The 'modplods', the peace people called them. Beyond were huge concrete bunkers and missile silos.

It's all about identity, someone had once said in some political discussion that he had struggled to keep up with. He offered no opinions but that thought flooded into his dulled mind. Identity. That's what it's all about. If only they knew. But he kept his thoughts to himself. He was an outcast, after all.

And walking past all the half-sodden detritus choking the weldmesh fencing like colourful weed, he had a sudden and strange thought. Looking at the dull faces of the modplods on patrol he felt something jar inside. Vague memories of when he was a young man. He had more of an affinity with the people on the other side of the fence than those that he marched with.

Peter was with a group of Class War anarchists that had come to the demo intent on causing trouble. IF YOU WANT PEACE, their paper declared, PREPARE FOR WAR! *If you think building chapels, planting seeds, and putting balloons on fences can stop nuclear weapons . . . then you're a fucking idiot. If you want to join in some effective action instead of holding hands, saying prayers, and other middle-class wank-offs then join the Class War mobs.*

Bright red spiky hair crowned his face. Shock-headed Peter with locks like flame. Each filament a spire or minaret calling out for angry justice. The pacifists were the enemy. Class War had already had some success that day. They had pelted Joan Ruddock, the chair of CND, with mud as she had tried to talk to the press. Now, if they could kick off a bit of trouble with the police then trudging all afternoon through the rain would be worth it.

A crowd had gathered near the wire where a couple of women had tried to cut the fence and had been arrested. Police reinforcements arrived and were trying to cordon the area off. Peter and the other Class War anarchists joined the mob that began to line up against the hastily formed police ranks. There were other militant protesters among the throng. Trots, Peter observed with disdain. SWP, RCP, RCG. Leftie wankers, thought Pete, but at least they weren't averse to a bit of a scrap.

Official CND demo stewards tried desperately to keep the peace as the pushing and shoving began. 'Remember, this is a peaceful protest,' one of them said. 'Fuck off!' Peter spat out at him.

'Fucking great,' one officer muttered gloomily to another as their serial filed into position. 'Rent-a-Mob's arrived.'

The part of the march that Mick and Janis were in had reached this point. The mob jostled against the police lines and the main part of the crowd became sucked into its heaving mass. A ululating whoop rose up. Protesters oscillating their palms in front of their mouths like childhood Red Indians. A chant went up. NO CRUISE! NO CRUISE! A few missiles sailed over into the uniformed ranks.

The police retaliated. A snatch squad stormed into the crowd and cleared a path with swinging truncheons. They dragged someone back into their lines.

I've got to get out of here, Mick thought. Janis was shouting something beside him. He tried to get her attention. The crowd was surging forward, pushing him towards the police ranks.

A huge lump of mud struck a policeman in the face. Peter laughed manically. He felt the adrenaline rush through him. He grabbed a placard from someone next to him and hoisted it over the heads in front of him. It fell short, into the mud. A senior police officer was addressing them with a loudhailer, telling them to disperse and continue on the march. More CND stewards had arrived and were trying to move people on. Peter and the rest of the Class War mob started barracking them, but the crowd did start to dissipate a little.

Peter started up a song. This'll wind them up, he thought. He was sick of all these hippy chants and peace-loving dirges he'd heard all day. Hymns, for fuck sake. Embrace the Base. Give the state a big hug and everything will be all right. There's the enemy. The Old Bill. Right in front of us.

'Billy Porter is our friend,' he began, a little haltingly. Self-conscious. If you started shouting something and no one joined in it could be embarrassing. But it was taken up as a group song by other anarchists around him.

Is our friend, is our friend,
Billy Porter is our friend,
He Kills Coppers!

There was laughter and then the refrain began again a little louder. Peter moved forward to the front of the mob.

Mick was walking away from the trouble with Janis when he heard it. At first it didn't register. Then the second time he heard the name. Recognised it. He hadn't heard that name in years. He turned back, transfixed.

Some of the officers in the line bristled at the taunt. They'd heard it first on the terraces; now it had been adopted by the Rent-a-Mob lot at political demos. The 'outside agitators' that had been described by senior officers in briefings. The crowd was thinning out now and the group of chanting anarchists became more visible.

'That's the cunt!' shouted one of the coppers, pointing at Peter, whose shock of hair stood out among the others, many of whom had covered their heads with the hoods of their track-suit tops.

'He's the fucking ringleader!'

A group of police broke ranks and advanced on the anarchists.

Mick stood listening, dumbfounded. Janis tugged at his sleeve but he ignored her. Billy Porter. They were shouting that name at the police. He suddenly felt vunerable. It was calling to him. Calling him back. He should try and stop them, he thought. Try and stop them calling out that name. It could give the game away. In a confused kind of panic, he started to walk towards the spiky-haired man who was leading the song. It was partly fear but also a strange desire to make contact. Billy Porter was their friend. What could that mean?

The Class War mob began to scatter as the police advanced. They no longer had the cover of the rest of the march which was now moving on. Peter lost his footing in the mud. He slipped and fell on to one knee. He managed to pick himself up but the uniformed officers were already upon him.

It was then that a stranger's hand caught hold of his and tried to pull him to safety.

'Mick!' Janis called out.

But he paid her no heed. For a moment he forgot that name and thought only of another's: Billy Porter.

27

I was teamed up with a guy called Derek Barnes at the Central Intelligence Unit. The Unit was set up to work alongside the National Reporting Centre which dealt with organising mutual aid during the miners' strike. Barnes was a smooth type, well spoken. Graduate intake, I guessed.

'What are your theories on public order, Frank?'

I shrugged.

'Well,' I said, 'to tell you the truth I don't really have any.'

Barnes smiled indulgently.

'Gut feelings?'

'I dunno. In my day it was just crowd control. You know, link arms and push.'

He gave a dry little laugh.

'Well,' he said, 'we all know things have changed since then. You don't mind if I give my overview?'

'No, fire away.'

'Well, I was on the original Community Disorder Tactical Options Inter-Force Working Group.'

'Bit of a mouthful,' I retorted quietly.

'Yes, quite. Anyway, it was set up at the end of 1981. All those inner-city riots. We had to do a complete rethink. So we got some experts in from a force off the mainland. Who do you think they might be?'

'The RUC?' I suggested.

'No, actually not. A lot of people would have thought so. No, it was never made public but it was the Royal Hong Kong Police that we got most of our new tactics from.'

'Really?'

'Oh yes. You see, there's a lot to be learned from our colonial forces. A long experience of dealing with the sharp end of public order. The natives are always restless.'

He grinned coldly.

'And the Hong Kong boys,' he went on, 'well, they had the blueprint for keeping the peace when it all gets out of order. It's funny, you know. All that time with the Empire, thinking that we were exporting some sort of civilisation out to the colonies, and in the end we import colonial policing back to the mother country. I guess that's why it was never made public.'

'Yeah,' I agreed, not quite sure what he was getting at. 'Makes you think.'

'But it paid off. You see, we had to have a systematic training blueprint. If one force was to reinforce another we had to make sure that they were working along the same lines. The mutual aid system depends on it.'

'Of course,' I said, not wanting to appear stupid.

'And with the miners' strike, all of this really came into its own. Remember Orgreave?'

A big scrap with a load of miners picketing a coke depot in Rotherham. I'd seen it all on the telly. I nodded.

'That was the first proper unveiling of colonial police tactics on the mainland. A show of force by long-shield officers. Dispersal and incapacitation by short-shield units. The use of horses to create fear among the crowd. It was a set piece designed to show what we could do. From the point of view of strategy and tactics it was damn near perfect. It was almost Napoleonic.'

'Yeah, well,' I said with a shrug, 'but was it policing?'

Barnes broke into a broad smile, like I'd got his point.

'Exactly!' he hissed sharply. 'That's the dilemma. If we keep entering the fray like we're in a state of siege we can so easily give the enemies of the state, the Enemy Within, as the great leader insists, we can give them a sense of justification in stirring up trouble. Can't we?'

'Well,' I said, 'I wouldn't know. I'm just a detective.'

'But that's just the sort of input we need, isn't it?'

'I guess. We need to have the right information.'

Barnes nodded.

'And intelligence. One feeds the other. Information is our raw data. If from that we can identify trends, patterns and tension indicators that affect operational bearing on deployment and resources, then we have not just information, but intelligence. Intelligence, Frank.'

I thought he was having a go now. Bandying about intelligence like I was stupid or something.

'Look,' I said, 'I'm just a detective. As I said.'

'Yes,' he concurred. 'I've seen your record. Very impressive.'

'I'm a thief-taker. Or at least,' I went on, almost apologetic, thinking about some of the hookeyness in the past, 'that's what I like to think I am.'

'But these are transferable skills, are they not?'

'Are they?'

'I think so, yes. During the strike the need to introduce a greater degree of co-ordination between forces in receiving, assessing and disseminating information and intelligence relative to the dispute was recognised. That's why this unit was set up. Officers have been selected with an ability for handling information and for having analytical skills. Experienced officers, like you, who can collate information and pass on the relevant intelligence, processed and disseminated through to force command and control.'

'But the strike's over.'

The miners had gone back in March. Without a deal. Trudging back to the pitheads with brass bands and ancient union banners. Like funeral processions.

'Yes, well, the Unit doesn't exactly have permanent status. It's an *ad hoc* thing like the National Reporting Centre. But our job is

283

to see if we can develop a compatible system of information and intelligence for dealing with all types of disorder.'

'Can't Special Branch do that?'

Barnes pursed his lips.

'Ah, well, Special Branch, bless them. They do tend to be rather busy doing MI5's dirty work for them. And often they report directly to them and keep us in the dark. No, what we are looking at here is an intelligence unit that feeds in directly to operational structures pertaining to mutual aid.'

'A column of mutual aid and support,' I blurted out, remembering how Mooney had described the masons all those years ago.

'Sorry?' asked Barnes with a frown.

'Nothing.'

Jeannie got me to tell her about the new job that evening. I knew something was up. She never took much of an interest in my work.

'Well, I'm glad it's going well,' she said. 'Look, Frank . . .'

She coughed. I looked her in the face and waited.

'We've got to talk.'

'I thought that's what we were doing,' I said.

'No, I mean . . . This isn't going to be easy.'

'Then you better just say it.'

'All right.'

She coughed again.

'I want a divorce, Frank.'

I sighed.

'Right,' I said.

'I'm sorry, but it's for the best.'

'Yeah?'

'Look, don't pretend it's not.'

'Any particular reason you've sprung this on me?'

'What do you mean?'

'You seeing someone else?'

'No.'

284

'Then why? I mean, why now?'

'Well, it might have escaped your notice but David will be leaving home soon. Going to university.'

'So?'

'Well, there's really not much point us staying together, is there? We can go our own ways. Start new lives.'

'This is what you want?'

'Yes, it is. If we could wait a bit. I don't want us to be going through this yet with David having his exams coming up.'

'Christ, you really have worked it all out, haven't you?'

'And it would be nice if we could stay on friendly terms.'

'Well, how bloody civilised. A nice friendly divorce.'

'Please, Frank. Don't make a scene.'

'How do you think this makes me feel? After all this time? Eh?'

But there wasn't much else to say without shouting so I went out for a walk and tried to calm down. It was a warm clear evening. Everything looked at peace in our little middle-class suburb. She was right, of course. Poor cow had had to put up with me all this time for the sake of the kid. I wondered if she'd ever had any real feelings for me. I had for her. Still did. I felt so empty and lonely. What was the bloody point? I thought.

*

Thursby had been going through a long decline. His wife had finally divorced him in 1977 and he'd had to sell his country pile, Hartwell Lodge. 'She wants a settlement before he drinks it all away,' Julian had told me. And Julian had certainly been helping Teddy along in that direction.

Of course, I'd never quite forgiven him for spoiling the porn exposé back in 1971. But I bore my grudge in private. He'd been a useful source for bits of gossip here and there over the years.

I hadn't been very close to Julian for a long time. Once witty and flamboyant, he'd become one of the Soho bores, that pack of would-be writers or artists or hangers-on that drank themselves stupid and imagined that they were being bohemian. And the booze really started to bring the poison out of him. He was always best avoided after six o'clock. It was a bit of a shock to hear that he'd croaked. I had a vague sense of grief, a sort of general unsettling feeling about mortality. A feeling that was only intensified by setting eyes on Thursby.

He looked dreadful as he came to the door. His face had gone from flabby affability to a drawn, gaunt death-mask. His skin was mottled with liver spots and had a jaundiced tinge. He let me in and hobbled around his untidy flat to get us both a gin and tonic.

'Well, the bastard beat me to it,' he said, handing me a glass. 'It's not fair. I feel a bit cheated, to tell you the truth. You know, at seventy-five euthanasia should be voluntary. At eighty-five it should be compulsory.'

'What happened?'

'His fucking liver gave out, of course. All those years drinking himself to death on my account. I mean on my account, quite literally. He always took advantage of our financial arrangement. They took him into the Westminster Hospital but there was nothing they could do. But do you know what he had the audacity to do?'

'What?'

'On the admissions form he had the cheek to put me down as next of kin. That was the last dirty trick he played on me. So when he croaked I had to go and identify the body, didn't I? They pulled back the sheet and there she was with a stupid expression on her face. "Oh yes," I said. "That's him, all right." It's funny, you know. In death he had this funny look on his face. He looked shocked. I thought, "You've got nothing to be surprised about, Jules." And I tell you, that's the first time I saw that queen with her mouth shut.'

Thursby stumbled over to get the gin bottle and refilled our glasses.

'So I supposed he expected that I was going to pick up the bill for him in death as in life. Imagined that I'd pay for some ritual mass in St Margaret's or something. He wanted absolution for all his beastliness, I guess. We all do, I suppose. Wanted a proper send-off, that's for sure.'

'So are you going to arrange it?'

Thursby chuckled hoarsely.

'Heavens, no,' he declared.

He sniffed and the light caught a triumphant glint in his eye.

'We're burning him at Golders Green tomorrow,' he said.

He leaned forward and looked at me imploringly.

'You will come, now, won't you?'

Julian's send-off was a depressing affair. A handful of his drinking friends turned up at the crematorium. A strange-looking creature in a black silk dress and a veiled hat sat at the back. At first it was assumed that she was a transvestite, but it turned out she was a maiden aunt from Eastbourne. Teddy said a few words and managed to sound convincingly moved by the occasion. There was a rich sob to his voice as he intoned some solemn words about one called before his time. Then he pressed the button, the curtains opened and the coffin trundled mechanically into the furnace.

There was a wake in the the French House. Thursby plonked the urn unceremoniously on the bar.

'I don't know what the hell I'm supposed to do with this,' he declared.

Some queen suggested that we should scatter his remains over the parade ground at Chelsea Barracks. Teddy had slumped down in a chair in sudden melancholia.

'Oh, why does death have to be so bloody?' he groaned.

I'd had quite enough of all this. I made my excuses and turned to leave. Thursby tugged at my sleeve.

'Come and see me,' he said, looking up plaintively. 'At my flat. I've got something to show you.'

*

Mick sat staring at the cell wall. *This is bad*, he thought. In all his time on the run he'd tried to be careful. *Stay out of trouble*, that had been his watchword. At the merest smell of it he'd be off. He'd covered his tracks well over the years. And here he was banged up over a stupid demonstration. He'd only gone on it to please Janis. How could he have been so fucking stupid after all this time? It was that song. That was it.

They'd charged him with obstruction. He'd been fingerprinted and photographed. This could be the end of it now. It could all come out. No more running. All of that had been an illusion of freedom. This was real. The cell. This was now. The past had only existed as a prelude to this. This was where he belonged. This was where he had always been headed. He tried not to give in to an awful sense of relief. A desire to give himself up.

Maybe he should kill himself. That would be a way out. They hadn't taken his belt away. He could hang himself. He looked around the cell to see if there was some way of attaching the belt to something.

Then the door banged open and somebody was pushed inside. It was the spiky-haired kid he had tried to pull away from the police.

'Wait a minute,' he had said as he'd tugged at him. 'Wait.'

Then he'd been grabbed himself by a couple of the uniformed squad and had been dragged off and taken into custody.

Mick came out of his suicidal reverie and looked up at the young man. The cell door banged shut. Peter smiled down at him. *Maybe he can help me*, Mick thought. He didn't know how, he just felt a strange pang of hope.

Peter looked at his cellmate. He had long greying hair and a beard. But this guy wasn't a hippie, he thought. He looked like a real traveller, not like those stupid crusties with their 'alternative' lifestyles. Middle-class drop-outs and lunched-out hash-heads. This bloke looked like he'd really lived it. There was something familiar about his eyes as well, but he couldn't quite place it.

'Thanks for trying to pull me out of there,' he said.

'Yeah.' Mick shrugged. 'Sure.'

'Pete,' said the man, and held out his hand.

They shook hands.

'Mick.'

'Thanks, Mick. I owe you one.'

Peter sat next to him on the bunk. Mick didn't know what to say. A childish tune was going through his head. A nursery rhyme. He turned to Peter. His spiky hair gave his face a startled look, thought Mick, as if he were in a permanent state of shock.

Still the song went through his head. The tune of it. What was the tune? 'Oranges and Lemons'? He hummed to himself. *When will you pay me say the bells of Old Bailey?* Peter frowned at him as he lullabyed softly, trying to murmur out the melody. *Here comes the candle to light you to bed, here comes the chopper to chop off your head.* No, that wasn't it. But something about London. 'London's Burning'? No. 'London Bridge Is Falling Down'. That was it.

'That song,' Mick said.

'What?'

He dah-dahed it quietly. Wary of the naming words. Peter joined in in a whisper.

'. . . is our friend, is our friend. Billy Porter is our friend. He kills coppers!'

Peter hissed the last line and chuckled softly.

'You know who Billy Porter was, don't you?'

Mick shrugged. *I don't know*, he thought. Act like I don't know.

'He killed three of the filth back in 1966. Geoff Hurst wasn't the only one who scored a hat-trick that year.'

'Don't like the Old Bill much, do you?'

'They're the enemy,' Peter replied flatly.

'I thought you lot were into peace and all that.'

'No. Not peace. War.'

'What?'

'The class war.'

'Oh, yeah,' said Mick. 'That.'

Politics again. He'd never understand it. But this bloke was different from the Peace Convoy lot he'd got to know. All that stuff that Janis went on about. About men being to blame for everything and stuff like that. Going back to nature. Dropping out. He'd just felt he'd been falling slowly all of these years. No, this was different. They were angry. The hippies he'd known were anti-police, that was for sure. They called them 'Babylon' and stupid names like that. But this lot, they wanted them dead. Billy Porter was their friend. Maybe he could make sense of that.

Friend. But. Friend. There was grief in the word. He remembered when he had been a fairground painter. He'd had a friend. Then. A friend he had murdered. Now he had been caught. It might all come out and he would have to face the truth. But he didn't understand it. What was the truth, after all? *Billy Porter is our friend*. They seemed so certain of that. They knew something that he didn't. Maybe it could explain what had happened.

The cell door opened and they were taken out to the charge room. He could scarcely make out what the custody officer was saying. He felt a dull, calm sense of one condemned. It was all over. Then the words that the officer was saying began to come together. They were being released with a caution. He was supposed to give an address and Peter suggested that he give them his. He owed him one, as he said.

A couple of friends of Peter's had been waiting for him at the station. Mick felt drained. An empty sense of relief that seemed like disappointment. He wanted it all to end now. He'd had enough of running. Janis was nowhere to be seen. Maybe she didn't know where he was.

'You want a lift, mate?' Peter asked.

He should wait for her, he thought. But he needed to get away.

'Where you going?' he asked.

'London.'

Mick grinned. *London Bridge is falling down*. Yeah, that's where he'd go. That's where he'd settle all of this.

The Class War Transit van dropped them off on an urban clearway just south of Vauxhall Bridge. 'You can crash at our place, if you want,' Peter had said. He meant a squat that he and another occupant of the van, Johnny, were living in near by.

A whole square of houses had been taken over by squatters. The area had been earmarked for demolition in the late seventies to make way for a new school. The existing tenants had been rehoused and the properties were boarded up. But then the plans for the school were postponed indefinitely and the education authority was left with over a hundred empty homes on its hands. Squatters started to move in at the beginning of the eighties and within five years the whole neighbourhood, save for a smattering of the original occupants who had refused to move, had been taken over by them.

They walked through the square. The half-derelict houses had been renovated in a haphazard way. Windows fixed with what was at hand, plumbing improvised, front doors painted garishly in a bricolage of occupation. There were graffiti on the walls: NO CRUISE, MEAT IS MURDER, STOP THE CITY, EAT THE RICH − strange apocalyptic warnings. One graffito announced: BEWARE OF MONSTER No. 15. Mick had heard about the squats in the city. Janis had gone to stay in one a few times. Many of the Peace Convoy seemed to use them as winter quarters. Mick had always declined. He had wanted to avoid the cities up until now. And staying on-site all year round had helped to establish his reputation as a real traveller.

'Here we are,' Peter announced.

They had arrived at a house with a black front door with a huge circled A on it. An old ambulance with a tarpaulin covering it was parked outside. There was someone underneath it. A pair of legs protruded from it and was moving crablike along the tarmac. Peter banged on the side of the vehicle.

'All right Mutt?' he called.

A metal tool clanged to the floor and a figure emerged from beneath the engine. It was short and stocky and wore tattered overalls, tongues sticking out of unlaced and scuffed boots. His hair was cropped short at the front with long, matted dreadlocks hanging down the back. He was covered in oil and grease.

'Uh?' he grunted, looking up at them from the gutter, squinting against the light.

291

'Meet Muttley,' Peter said with a grin. 'He's our liberated animal.'

Muttley smiled, showing a gap in his front teeth.

'Go to the shops, Johnny,' Peter told his friend. 'I'll get the tea on.'

They went upstairs to the kitchen. They was a huge stack of unwashed utensils in the sink. The table was littered with pamphlets and papers. There was a black flag hanging on the wall. Beneath was a clipping from *Class War*. It was a photograph of a policeman with blood running down his face. HOSPITALISED COPPER, it read. BACK BY POPULAR DEMAND. BRIXTON PC BASIL BASTARD BASHED ON THE BONCE BY A BOULDER IN THE BLOODY BATTLE OF THE BARRIER BLOCK. Next to it was a smudged and long-neglected rota.

Johnny returned with the groceries, cradled to his chest. A box of tea bags, two tins of baked beans and a packet of digestive biscuits. He dropped them on to the table. Peter picked up the tea and broke open the cellophane on the packet. Muttley grabbed the biscuits and groaned.

'What's the matter?' asked Johnny.

Muttley pointed the digestives accusingly at Johnny.

'The ingredients,' he said. 'Read the ingredients.'

Johnny took the packet from him and looked at the tiny writing on its side.

'What?' he said.

'Just read the fucking ingredients.'

'Leave it out, Muttley,' Peter commented as he poured water from the kettle.

'Wheat flour,' Johnny began falteringly. 'Vegetable oil and, um, hydrogenated vegetable oil and . . .'

He stopped for a second.

'Go on.' Muttley insisted.

'Muttley.' Peter groaned.

'Animal fat,' said Johnny finally.

'Yeah, animal fat. I told you digestives were no good.'

'There can't be that much of it in them,' said Peter.

'That ain't the fucking point, is it? I thought we agreed that this was a vegan household. Fucking animal biscuits.'

Johnny put the digestives on the table. Mick stared at them. He was starving, but he thought it best not to make a grab for them as he was tempted to. He would have to go along with all of these strange rules and rituals. He would have to try and fit in. Until he was ready to make his move. Peter handed him a cup of tea. It was made with soya milk. He took a sip. It had a powdery texture to it, like sawdust in his mouth.

Muttley made a veggie stew later. They sat around the kitchen table with a bottle of cider and a couple of spliffs. Peter held forth with exaggerated stories of rebellion and complaints that 'peaceful demos were a waste of fucking time'. He talked of the need for direct action.

'We should do something really spectacular, you know?' he said, looking around the room.

Peter seemed very much the boss of the group. Muttley would argue with some of his comments but Johnny seemed in constant deference. Occasionally Mick would be asked his opinion at various stages of the rambling discussion, and he'd nod or shrug. All he could think about was where he was going to sleep that night. As it got late Peter said that he 'could have Frank's room' and Johnny led him to a chaotically untidy bedroom.

28

I didn't really know what to do after Jeannie asked for the divorce, so I threw myself into work, as per usual. Plenty of overtime to be had. I could half convince myself that it was an important job. It was easy to feel clever at the Central Intelligence Unit. A sense that we were looking on things from some higher ground, getting some sort of view of it all. We had the use of PNC2, the Police National Computer, and we were given privileged access to classified documents. The ACPO Public Order Manual was restricted to Assistant Chief Constable rank and above, but I got to have a peek at it – well, Section Three on intelligence-gathering, that is. It gave my ego a bit of a boost, that I was somehow in the know, that I was trusted by the higher-ups and on my way up there myself. The manual defined three areas of intelligence: 'live' – that of immediate concern to effective planning of operations; 'strategic' – long-range stuff of little immediate operational value; and 'counter-intelligence' – used to respond to or neutralise anti-police propaganda or rumours. All three ingredients would combine to form a 'total intelligence product', like some advertising slogan. A miracle cure.

It was just the sort of jargon that Barnes thrived on. He was always turning practice into theory. He was the new generation of copper. Happiest when he was staring at a computer screen. He was OK to work with, I suppose. He could be a patronising bastard but he was always civil. The first time we went for a drink together and he ordered a Perrier water, well, I knew he'd never be a bundle of laughs.

We would identify trends, patterns affecting operational bearing on deployment and resources, identify individuals engaged in crime who crossed force boundaries. There was much talk of 'tension indicators', of being able to spot flash-points that could lead to unrest and disorder. We were constantly on the lookout for the Enemy Within. The local troublemakers or the outside agitators. But when the inner cities went up again in the autumn, in Handsworth, Brixton and Tottenham, we missed the one factor that had sparked off the riots in all of those areas: police action itself. We had become the Enemy too. Sent into the ghettoes like the occupying force of a foreign power.

But before that, at the beginning of the summer, we just thought that we had all the angles covered. We weren't going to be caught out like back in '81. And the government owed us. We'd won the miners' strike for them, for Christ's sake, and it was up to them to back us up. But it was that summer that something else happened which brought everything back and to a head.

It was the first big job for the Unit post the miners' dispute. This year the annual Stonehenge Festival was to be banned. It was a hippie carnival that coincided with the summer solstice and had always been a bit of a public order nightmare. There were fears of damage to the the ancient site, apparently, and access to the the stones was to be dramatically curtailed. English Heritage, who were responsible for the site, and the National Trust, who owned the thousand or so acres that surrounded it, secured 'precautionary injunctions' against certain named persons, forbidding them from trespassing on the property. Wiltshire County Council had closed certain roads around Stonehenge, using the Road Traffic Regulation Act that had been passed only the previous year and allowed such action if there was a 'danger to the public'. On top of this, the Wiltshire Constabulary had been setting up roadblocks on other routes and were warning travellers not to proceed and threatening to arrest them for obstruction if they tried to. As with the flying pickets trying to travel into Nottinghamshire during the miners' strike, they would be in breach of the peace, they claimed. It all looked pretty tight.

Our job was to provide information and intelligence as the travellers, the Peace Convoy as it became known, were crossing force boundaries. A large part of the convoy had come straight from Cambridgeshire, where they had been involved in a large demo against cruise missiles in Molesworth. We had to try and collate all that was known about this ragtag band, in particular to identify the 'certain persons' named in the injunctions. It was hard to build up any clear patterns about their behaviour. Their moving lifestyle didn't help. There were rumours that among this supposed peace-loving gang was a hard core of armed troublemakers. But there was no structured leadership or organisation. There were links with CND and the Peace Camps but nothing official. They didn't really shape up as enemies of the state as far as I was concerned. Barnes went into this whole analysis of the 'counterculture', something he'd picked up from university, no doubt. But there was something about them being travellers which struck a chord with me. I didn't know what it was, but it was as if I were looking for some other sort of evidence. By the end of May the convoy had crossed the border into Wiltshire.

There was all sorts of literature, pamphlets and newsletters, but none of it made any sense. Pure hippy mumbo-jumbo, most of it. There was a simple bright orange flier that merely stated: STONEHENGE *85* FREE FESTIVAL STARTS JUNE 1ST MIDSUMMER EVE 23RD A303 WILTS BE THERE OR BE SQUARE. I started looking for clues elsewhere.

There was a big stack of surveillance photographs of the convoy *en route* that I went through. All these brightly painted vehicles. Trucks and double-decker buses, coaches and vans. There were slogans daubed on the sides of some of them. PEACE CONVOY, FIGHT TRUTH DECAY, MYSTERY TOUR, STONEHENGE – GO FOR IT! And there were all these strange symbols. Rainbows and peace signs, suns and circled As, weird Indian writing. I was looking for patterns, connections. All these hippie designs started to swirl around my head. There was something that I couldn't quite figure out that was in the back of my mind. The answer to something. For a moment I even thought that I was having some kind of fucking mystical experience. Then it hit me. I found it. One of the vehicles, a converted coach, had been more delicately decorated. Older-looking. I looked closely at the photograph. It was a beautifully crafted paint job with a more traditional design than the others. It looked like a fairground wagon. I'd seen it before. I felt a brief shudder inside. Someone walking on my grave. Someone walking on Dave's grave.

I put the photograph in my briefcase. I made some sort of excuse and left work early. When I got home, David was mooching about the house.

'Shouldn't you be at school?'

'I'm revising,' he replied indignantly. 'I've got my second English paper tomorrow. A-levels. Remember?'

I put my hands up.

'OK, OK.'

He gave me his habitually resentful stare. There was something odd about his eyes. Eyeliner, it looked like.

'Are you wearing make-up?'

'Yeah. So?'

'Oh, for Christ's sake.'

He grinned and I immediately regretted reacting in that way. It was just the effect he was after. I went into the spare room. I dug out my Billy Porter file and shuffled through it. There it was, the drawing I'd found on the floor of the disused aircraft hangar all those years ago. I got the photo out of my case and compared them. It was the same bloody design. I stared at it. The pattern. I didn't know what it meant. But it was a clue, a lead. Something else had slipped out of the file. It was a newspaper clipping. Police file photographs of the three officers murdered on Scrubs Lane in 1966. Dave's face staring out from oblivion at me.

I went downstairs and phoned the Yard. I found out that the

297

Peace Convoy was being herded into the Savernake Forest as a containment measure. Harsh music coming from David's bedroom. I called up to him. He came out on to the upstairs landing.

'What?' he called back.

'Can you come down a minute, please.'

He sighed heavily and clumped down the stairs.

'Yeah?'

'Look, I've got to follow up a job. Can you tell your mother I might not be back tonight?'

'Sure.'

He turned to go back up to his room.

'David?'

'What is it now?'

'Look, I know that we don't always get on but I wish ...' I shrugged, not sure of what I might say next. 'You don't hate me, do you?'

He blushed. Now I was embarrassing him. His face was so full of life. I loved him so much but I could never find the way to show it. Dave was still alive. In him. I was the one that was dead.

'Dad,' he moaned.

'Look, I know we don't talk much but there's something I have to tell you. Something you have a right to know.'

I should be the one to tell him, I thought.

'What are you talking about?'

'I'm not your father,' I blurted out. 'Not your real father.'

'What?'

His face creased with incredulity.

'Let me explain.'

'No!' he exploded. 'I don't want to hear this! I do not want to hear this!'

'David ...'

'You bastard!' he shouted at my face, and ran up the stairs.

I went out and got into the car. I felt numb. It was done. It was all over. I tried to concentrate on the matter in hand. I was after Dave's killer again. That would keep me going when I wanted to give up altogether. As I pulled out of our close I thought there was rain falling. As I reached across to turn on the windscreen wipers I realised it was tears in my eyes.

*

Thursby staggered about his flat in a stained dressing gown. The drawing room was cluttered with piles of papers, scattered books, empty bottles and glasses, discarded clothes and crusted plates. Teddy backed into a side table and it crashed to the floor.

'Bugger,' he muttered, and continued to rummage around.

'Ah,' he said finally. 'Here it is. Yes. And this.'

He had gathered up a box file and a bundle of notes tied together. He brought them over, cleared the sofa of its detritus with one sweep of his hand, and we sat down together. He held up what he had recovered and offered it to me.

'I want you to have a look at this.'

'What is it?' I asked, taking it from him rather gingerly.

'It's the book me and Jules were working on,' he replied. 'My memoirs.'

'Why are you giving them to me?'

'I need someone to finish the work. It's nearly all there. It just needs writing up.'

'I'm not so sure, Teddy,' I said.

He patted the back of my hand.

'Have a look. That's all I'm asking,' he implored.

'Why me?'

Teddy coughed.

'Well, I need someone I can trust,' he said. 'To be discreet. You've always understood the importance of discretion, Tony. I admire that. And I know you've always had literary aspirations.'

'Well, I don't know about that.'

'Don't deny it. Here's your chance. I know you've always wanted to write a book. It'll be worth your while. Julian drank all the advance away but I'm sure that we can, you know, renegotiate a contract with the publishers. I only ask . . .'

He looked about the room furtively.

'I only ask that you, you know, put a little gloss on my reputation. That's all I want now. I'll be dead soon. I want to be remembered for the good things. I don't mind a bit of colour, you know, my "flamboyant" lifestyle and all that. But some things are better left unsaid. You know what I mean, don't you?'

I knew exactly what he meant. He feared the truth about his own life as much as the extinction of it. He was terrified of all his indiscretions being made public when he was dead and unable to sue for libel. An authorised biography might preserve his precious reputation. We'll see about that, I thought to myself.

And I was quite flattered to be asked. It was a chance to write a book after all. I took all the papers home with me and spent the night looking through them. There was some sort of manuscript but it was all a bit threadbare. Sparse chapter outlines. Childhood, youth at Lancing College, Oxford in the twenties, the Bright Young Things. Plenty of anecdotes about Evelyn Waugh, Harold Acton and Brian Howard. Stories of wild parties and gossip about sybaritic goings-on all dealt with in a thoroughly discreet manner. Entry into politics: member for Hartwell-juxta-Mare, the rising young star of the Tory Party. Opposition to appeasement and sticking by Churchill during his Wilderness Years highlighted. Marriage to Ruth Cholmondely-Parker in 1935. The childlessness of the union delicately commented upon, the lovelessness of it omitted. Cabinet office and the high point of his political career was rather crassly juxtaposed with the Abdication Crisis and 'war clouds looming over Europe'. Then the scandal of not declaring a business interest to the Commons was dealt with as 'a gross misunderstanding that nevertheless, for the sake of my honour and that of the government, left me with no option but to resign my post'. The subsequent 'freezing out' by Churchill, who he had stuck by earlier, was described, alluding to a sense of hurt and bitterness felt by Thursby. Postwar he becomes the flamboyant backbencher with periodic iconoclastic outpourings from the sidelines. Radio and television appearances. Newspaper columns for the *News of the*

World and the *Sunday Illustrated*. The life peerage in 1964. Harsh criticism of Edward Heath's leadership and his disastrous fall from power in 1974. The victorious libel suit against *Private Eye* over allegations of connections with the gangster Harry Starks – 'the worst kind of scandal-mongering from that notorious muck-raking rag'. The last part was all glorious twilight in honourable decline. Thursby's thoughts on politics and statehood, his pious belief in High Church principles. Huge praise for Margaret Thatcher: 'at last, the Tory Party and the nation have a leader who has the courage of her convictions'. An almost fetishised thrill at her unequivocal self-belief and iron will. Last thoughts and reflections, sage-like warnings about the future.

It was an appalling exercise in self-deception. Vacuously empty, a closet without the skeleton. Of course, I could quite understand Teddy's desire to cover everything up. I almost pitied him for it. But I wanted the real story. And, by Christ, I was going to get it.

*

Johnny was a painter of sorts. He was into graffiti. 'Paint-bombing', he called it. He felt a calling to decorate and add text to any bare wall or empty hoarding he came across. He explained it to Mick when he was showing him some of his work on an underpass near by.

'It gives it meaning,' he said.

'What?' asked Mick.

'You know, everything.' He gestured vaguely at the bleak urban clearway. 'It's like subtitles.'

Mick looked around and smiled. Johnny was right, it was all like some foreign film. But there was only one way he could make sense of it all.

There was another sort of graffiti that Mick noticed. More elaborate, decorative. Not slogans but simple naming, using different aerosols that airbrushed depth and intricate designs around complex lettering. Multicoloured calligraphy that reminded Mick of the fairgrounds.

'That's hip-hop,' Johnny explained.

301

And Mick got some work through Johnny. Painting and decorating. When the foreman saw how handy Mick was with a paintbrush he offered him more work after the job was finished. Johnny just couldn't work quickly enough, but he didn't seem to mind when Mick was asked to work on a bigger contract instead of him.

He worked on a warehouse in Docklands that was being converted into loft apartments. It was cash in hand, no questions asked. Piece-work. Laying on paint. Not the elaborate decoration that he was used to doing. It was methodical, just laying it on. Blocking it out. There was something calming about it as he went to work with a roller. Covering space. Painting out everything. Making the past a blank surface.

And he found he could earn quite a lot. He worked long hours and started to save up cash. He would need this. Soon he would have enough to get what he required.

He'd get back to the squat late in the evening. It was always in a state of chaos. He spent half the night cleaning up the kitchen. The fading rota on the wall that listed names and household duties didn't look like it had been attended to for months. He added his name to it and ticked one of the boxes.

Nothing was said about whether he could stay or not so he took action himself. He cleaned out an unused room that was full of junk and redecorated it.

Peter always talked about action. He was always occupied with something or other. Meetings, demos, distributing leaflets and newspapers, holding forth about whatever issue was current. Swearing loudly at the television news. Full of a sense of injustice. But despite all of his talk of 'activism' he seemed passive. As if all his actions were a minor distraction from some big event.

'One day,' he'd mutter darkly. 'One day, we'll fucking show them.'

There was a big demonstration outside the new premises of the *Sunday Illustrated* in Docklands. Mick went along with them. It was quite close to where he worked. Peter joined a group of young men who covered their faces and busied themselves hurling missiles at the police lines. Police in riot gear retaliated, but the stone-throwers were behind the main ranks of the protesters and were able to get away. *They're just bloody hooligans, really*, Mick thought. And they'd sing that song again. The Billy Porter song. It sent a shiver down his spine.

Mick would go drinking after work. It helped him to relax after long hours painting. But he was looking for something as well. The whole of the area was being tarted up for big business, but there were still plenty of pubs around where he could find what he wanted. He was cautious. He knew from experience the look of a man that might have what he needed. Or might know someone who did. But he had to be careful in how he made his approach. Someone fencing bent gear. Or drugs. It all seemed to be drugs these days. He bought some speed off a guy in a pub on East Ferry Road because he seemed a likely prospect and he wanted to gain his trust. The speed helped him work the long shifts he'd taken on as well.

There was a meeting in the café on the corner of the square. It was squatted too. It served up cheap veggie food, a gloomy candlelit place. The meeting was about the future of the square. There was a big split between those that wanted just to be squatters and those that thought they should organise themselves into a housing co-op and apply to the Housing Corporation for funding. Peter was, of course, loudly in favour of the former view. Anything else was 'selling out'. Mick realised that all these people were against so many things. Against the state, the police, the rich. Against animal testing, whaling, nuclear weapons, pollution. Against capitalism, Thatcher, Reagan. Against racism, imperialism, fascism, sexism, heterosexism. But, above all, they were against each other. They were always squabbling among themselves. Always arguing about the best course of action but never getting around to doing anything. Mick knew what he had to do. There was no argument about it in his head. He had no choice.

In one of Peter's pamphlets he found a picture of the police file photograph of Billy Porter. The one they had used on the wanted posters. Crudely reproduced into a xeroxed icon. BILLY PORTER, read the rubric, WORKING-CLASS HERO. Mick folded it up and shoved it in his pocket.

He lay on his bed in the evening. Muttley was practising juggling in the room above. Three faded tennis balls made spasmodic ellipses around a bare-bulb sun. Mick heard a soft triple thudding on the ceiling as Muttley lost control of his little solar system. The loneliness of planets, out of orbit, falling from their spheres. It would be soon now, he thought.

29

Operation Daybreak ended in bloody mayhem. In over twenty-five years in the job I'd never seen anything quite so diabolical, and I've seen my share of fuck-ups, that's for sure. The behaviour of the Wiltshire Old Bill and whatever other mutual-aid Police Support Units waded in that day was fucking appalling. If I'd stopped to think about what I had witnessed with my own eyes in England's green and pleasant fucking land I don't know what I'd have done. But the fact was I had one thought and one thought only: I had to find the owner of that coach I had seen in the photograph.

What with the bank-holiday traffic and the roadblocks that the Wiltshire Constabulary had set up I didn't get to the Savernake Forest until nightfall. I could see the Peace Convoy campfires glowing against the brow of a hill. There were police vans everywhere. A helicopter strafed the woods with its searchlight, turning the trees into ghostly white negatives. I parked up on a lay-by and tried to get some sleep.

Just before noon the next day the convoy set off south on the A338 with dozens of reinforced police vans full of riot police in pursuit. The police helicopter clattered above. I started up the motor and gave chase. Soon enough the caravan of brightly coloured hippie vehicles and tooled-up police Transits came to a halt. I got out of my car and made my way to where the convoy was on foot, flashing my warrant card at any woodentop that tried to get in my way.

There was a police roadblock up ahead at a junction with the

A303. Some of the convoy vehicles then moved on to this road to get away, only to find another roadblock farther down. It was a trap. I pushed my way through the first roadblock, warrant card held high.

'What the fuck's going on?' I asked the nearest officer.

'We got some unfinished business to deal with,' he replied with a West Country drawl.

By the time I'd passed the line of police vans leading to the convoy it had already kicked off. I heard shouting and jeering. Whole serials of officers in riot gear making low battle cries, drumming truncheons against shields. It was bloody ugly. There was something like evil in the air.

There was the sound of breaking glass as the Wiltshire Constabulary had decided that the best way to enforce High Court injunctions was to smash the windscreens of as many of the travellers' vehicles as they could get to. Riot sticks were jammed into radiators that hissed mournfully as they were broken. Scruffy-looking hippies who hardly looked like dangerous enemies of the state were being dragged out of their vehicles and bludgeoned. I saw one policeman hit a woman who had been shrilly remonstrating with him with a truncheon. As she fell to the ground I noticed she was pregnant. Fucking swedes, I thought. What the fuck do they think they're doing? But, as I said, I had only one priority on my mind at the time: to find that fucking coach.

As I got near to the front of the convoy, the first few buses and vans suddenly started up and turned off the road, crashing through a hedge and a wooden fence into an adjacent field that was planted with beans.

In the hours that followed tragedy and farce seemed inseparable. As the helicopter buzzed overhead, police vans gave chase as what remained of the convoy made circuits of the bean field. It looked absurdly comical at a distance, like some dreadful stock car race, then when it came around close again you could see the ugly maliciousness of it all. At times the convoy vehicles turned to aim themselves at the pursuing riot vans, then veered off, sowing confusion in the police ranks.

Convoy vehicles that had not been completely trashed were commandeered by the Wiltshire force and were being used as battering rams against their quarry. They had some success with this, but when they were used up there was a stalemate. All the PSU vans and riot police regrouped. This was endgame, you could feel it. The helicopter came clattering in low. Its loudspeaker made a metallic announcement:

'Those who wish to leave without trouble should drop their weapons and walk out!'

A few men and women, children and dogs slowly emerged from the battered vehicles. Then hundreds of riot police waded into what remained. It was then that I caught sight of the coach. A whole serial of riot cops boiling into it, pulling out a woman by her hair. There was an orgy of destruction as police smashed up all the vehicles that remained on the bean field. This 'counterculture' Barnes had gone on about was being beaten into submission.

The sun was coming down over the bloody aftermath. A hot summer's day nearly over, the golden hues of the early evening light illuminating what might have been a quaint rural scene. Except that it framed a grotesque tableau of chaos. A churned-up field littered with debris, the remaining travellers being frogmarched away, lines of police trooping back to their vans, visors up, some with helmets removed. A nervous buzz of post-conflict euphoria. Some were smiling, joking and laughing.

'That'll teach the fucking hedge monkeys a lesson,' I heard one officer say.

Others looked shellshocked, battle-fatigued. Wide-eyed at what they had seen, what they had done.

Over 500 arrests were made. Some of the convoy's dogs were destroyed on police orders. It was dark before I managed to track down where the woman who had been in the coach was being held. I had to pull rank and talk to the Assistant Chief Constable to get access to her. He was reluctant at first but when I told him, in confidence, what it was about he complied. Her name was Janis Green. A WPC brought her into the interview room. She looked dazed and disorientated. She had a split lip and a yellowing bruise under one eye.

'Janis?' I asked softly.

She nodded slowly.

'Do you want to sit down?'

She shrugged and scraped the chair out from under the table and slumped in it sullenly. I tried to catch her eye but she turned her head at an angle from my line of vision.

'I'm Detective Chief Superintendent Frank Taylor.'

She looked sidelong at me.

'I want to see a solicitor,' she muttered.

'Look, Janis, this isn't about what you've been charged with. I can get you released, straight away. I just need to ask a few questions.'

'I'm not saying anything until I see a solicitor.'

I sighed.

'Look, if you co-operate with me they'll drop the charges.'

'We weren't doing anything wrong.'

'Well, that's up to the courts to decide, isn't it?'

She scowled.

'Why do you hate us?' she asked.

I couldn't answer that one.

'Look, you won't have to go through any more hassle if you just answer a few questions.'

Janis shrugged.

'Lovely paintwork on your coach,' I went on, casually, like I was making polite conversation or something.

She turned and frowned, looking directly at me for the first time.

'What the fuck has that got to do with anything?'

'Just saying, your coach . . .'

'My coach? My bloody coach? It isn't just a coach, you know. It's my home. It was. You lot . . .' Her voice caught in a sob. 'You fucking destroyed it.'

She was crying now. But at least she was coming out of the

shock. Now she might open up. I took out a packet of fags and offered her one. She took it in a trembling hand and I lit it for her. She wiped her battered face and took a deep drag at it.

'Who painted it?'

She looked up, puzzled.

'Was it someone called Mick?'

There was a flash of recognition in her eyes that she couldn't hide.

'What's it to you?'

'I need to find him.'

She took another sharp pull on the cigarette and looked about the room anxiously.

'Just tell me where he is and you can go.'

She chewed at her bloodied lip thoughtfully.

'I don't know,' she replied. 'He got arrested.'

'What, here?'

She shook her head.

'No, not here. A while back. At Molesworth.'

*

Thursby's door was opened by a fortyish queen with blond flecks in his hair and a sunbed tan. He kept the chain on, his pinched, leathery face peering out at me.

'Yes?' he hissed.

'I've come to see Teddy.'

'He's not well. Confined to bed.'

'I'm sure he'll want to see me.'

'Whom shall I say is calling?' he asked, petulantly.

I gave him my name. He let me into the hallway.

'Stay there. He's really not up to having visitors, you know.'

The queen trotted upstairs. I could hear his whining voice and Thursby's, deeper and insistent.

'Wait here,' he said when he returned, walking out into the kitchen.

He came back with a tray. There was a cup of tea on it and a bowl of what looked like gruel.

'Take that up to him.'

'What on earth is this?' I asked, taking the tray.

'Complan. He needs feeding up. Don't let him have any drink, mind. I know he's hidden a bottle somewhere. I've got to get off. I can't spend all day looking after his lordship.'

He took a coat off the peg in the hallway and put it on.

'Tell him I'll be back tomorrow,' he said as he went to the door. 'No booze, mind. Doctor's orders.'

I climbed the stairs and, balancing the tray in one hand, knocked softly on the door.

'Come,' groaned Thursby from inside.

I walked in and put the tray on his bedside table. Thursby was propped up in bed with a pile of pillows. He looked ghastly.

'Tony,' he said, with a deathly rictus of a smile. 'How kind of you to visit. I'm sorry about Derek. He can be a bit tetchy. Can't get the staff, you know.'

He picked up the tray and sniffed at it disdainfully.

'Oh, sweet Jesus, will you look at this slop.'

He put it back on the side table.

'Maybe you should eat something,' I suggested.

'No appetite, dear boy. No bloody appetite left. Tell you what I need.'

He smiled again, baring a row of discoloured teeth protruding from receding, puttylike gums.

'I need a drink.'

He breathed the word lovingly.

'Are you sure? Derek said . . .'

'Oh, never mind her,' he snapped. 'I've secreted a bottle of brandy in the cupboard under the stairs. Just for medicinal purposes, you understand. Go and get it and a couple of glasses. Then we can talk.'

I did what he said and poured both of us a large glass. Thursby took a sip.

'Ahh!' he exhaled. 'Almost makes me feel alive. So, my boy, have you looked at the work?'

'Yes,' I replied cautiously, taking a sip myself.

'And what do you think? You'll do it, won't you?'

'Well, I've looked through it all and I can't help thinking that there's something missing.'

Thursby gave a rich low chuckle. His loose and flabby jowls quivered slightly.

'Well, of course, dear boy. There have been some, shall we say, necessary omissions. But you surely understand the need for discretion.'

'Yes, but if I'm going to write all of this up I need to know the whole story. I'd like you to take me into your confidence. You can trust me.'

Thursby's yellowy eyes emitted a faint sparkle.

'Yes,' he said. 'Of course. I mean, that was the deal with Julian. I showed him everything. I need to unburden my soul, Tony. I'd like to let you know it all, I really would. You know, despite the split with Rome, the Anglican Church never got rid of the sacrament of auricular confession. But as with confession I require sanctity. Promise me that. That you'll write the book as planned. Then you can know all the rest.'

I took another mouthful of brandy and thought for a second.

'You say you showed Julian everything.'

'Oh yes.'

'What do you mean, "showed"?'

'The diaries, of course.'

'You kept diaries?'

'Oh yes. Quite comprehensive. You see, they are the source material. The arrangement with Julian was that we would use them as a basis for the book and then . . .'

Thursby shrugged and drained his glass. He let out a fumed sigh.

'And then?'

'And then we'd destroy them.'

Diaries. Teddy Thursby had kept diaries. The thought of it ran through my head as I poured him another brandy. My mind reeled at what they might contain. All that knowledge, an incomparable source of scandal. And Teddy wanted them destroyed and in their stead some tepid form of memoir as his testimony. Christ, that would be like the burning of the library at Alexandria.

Teddy was droning on about something. His rheumy eyes peered up at me. He noticed my distraction.

'Are you paying attention, Tony?' he asked.

'Sorry,' I replied with a slight shake of the head. 'What were you saying?'

'Oh,' he groaned. 'Nothing much. Just how Winston was such a cunt to me. Gave me the cold shoulder after I got into hot water over not declaring a business interest to the House. Not much of a scandal, really. I wasn't that naughty, after all. I mean, look at it now. All these fucking grammar school oiks in the lobby now, their snouts in Ian Greer's trough. Renting themselves out to Arab businessmen. It's a bloody gravy train. My meagre sins rather pale into insignificance.'

'I want the diaries, Teddy,' I suddenly blurted out.

Thursby gave a start. One of his pillows slipped and fell to the side of the bed.

'What?' he spluttered. There was a fearful look on his sallow face.

'I mean,' I went on, softening my tone, 'I want to have a look at them.'

He eyed me suspiciously. I refilled his glass and took another shot myself.

'I can trust you, Tony, can't I?'

He looked up imploringly. He was utterly helpless.

'Of course you can, Teddy. We'll work on the book together. I'll do a proper job of it. Not like Julian.'

'No,' he muttered. 'That useless little shit.'

He drained his glass and held it up for more brandy. I raised the bottle by its neck.

'We appear to have finished this one off, Teddy.'

Thursby gave a little childlike moan.

'I could go and get us another,' I suggested.

His eyes lit up.

'Oh, goody!'

'And while I'm up I could dig out those diaries of yours. Just to have a little look at them. You know, size up the weight of the material we'll be working from.'

He nodded. I took the keys to the flat and went out into the night to find the nearest off-licence. I was quite drunk and glad of the evening air to clear my head of the fetid atmosphere of Thursby's room. I went through it in my mind: how to gain access to his journals. I could contrive to become his literary executor, gain possession of them that way. Then, when he croaked, they'd be mine. There would be all sorts of procedures, paperwork and such. It all seemed unduly complicated. There must be an easier way.

I came back with the brandy rolled up in paper. Teddy raised himself from semi-slumber as I entered. I unwrapped the bottle and held it up like a trophy. Thursby's sunken face beamed into half-life.

'Let's have another snifter,' he wheezed. 'Just a tincture.'

He held up his glass expectantly.

'Uh-uh,' I teased playfully. 'First things first.'

'Oh yes,' he groaned, his visage sunken once more. 'Well, if we must. But remember our agreement.'

'Of course,' I said, filling both our glasses and holding mine up for a toast. 'To the great work,' I proposed, and we clinked receptacles.

'They're in a tin box under the bed,' he instructed.

I put my glass on the side table and crouched down to rummage underneath him. It was filthy down there – scraps of old newspaper and soiled crockery. My hands found the box and I slid it out. I tried the lid. It was jammed.

'I can't open it,' I said tetchily.

'Well, it's locked, of course,' he replied indignantly. 'I'll get the key.'

He fumbled in the side table drawer and handed it over. I turned the lock and opened the treasure chest. There was a pile of bound books inside.

'They're all here?'

'Well . . .' He shrugged. 'A few entries here and there might be missing. Some of the more *outré* stuff that I've already been through with Julian. You know what he was like. Always sniffing around for filth.'

'Well, there's plenty left to be going on with. It'll be quite a job.'

'Oh yes,' he said. 'But let's leave it for now.'

'Of course,' I said, slamming the metal box shut and relocking it. I put the key on the bedside table. 'Another drink?'

'Rather.'

I was getting drunker. I felt a familiar darkness descend on my mind. Teddy was holding forth again. Giving his opinions on the current state of things.

'Ah!' he breathed. I caught a whiff of alcohol and decay. 'The blessed Margaret. She's got a stomach for a fight. Took the fucking miners on and saw them off. Not like the blasted Heath. He was fucking useless. Never had the nerve. She showed them. A real leader.'

I stood above him, looking down at his atrophied form. I could so easily put him out of his misery. He was dying for it anyway. What had he said? *At seventy-five euthanasia should be voluntary, at eighty-five it should be compulsory.* Compulsory. Dying for it. The blackness was beginning to take hold.

'That it had to be' – he sniffed with apparent distaste – 'a woman.'

I looked at the folds of skin in his neck which shuddered like a wattle as he spoke. Revulsion sobered me. Compulsion was tempered by a sense of necessity. I didn't want to touch that rotting flesh, the rank corruption of it. I would take little pleasure in dispatching him. It would not be like the other times. I was in control now, I would be taking a life again but this time I had a logical motive.

'But what a woman, eh? What did that Frenchman say? The mouth of Monroe, the eyes of Caligula, what? Heh, heh.'

He grinned, baring his yellow teeth. I picked up the pillow that had slipped to the side of the bed and plumped it up. He caught my intent stare.

'What?' he said with a mirthless smile.

'Let me make you comfortable,' I suggested.

'No,' he managed to utter.

But I move quickly. *Yes.* I smothered him with the soiled pillow. *Yes.* I held it hard against his face. He put up a bit of a struggle. His left arm reached out blindly to the key on the table and it tinkled to the floor, but he gave in to the dreadful softness of the pillow. Taking a life. I'd got away with it before. This time I was clear-headed about the whole thing. It wasn't even revenge. Well, maybe a bit. But I was doing him a favour, after all. The hand went limp with the rest of him. I released the pressure and there was an awful groan of expiration.

I retrieved the key and claimed what was mine. His diaries. I was taking a life, all right.

*

Mick worked three days and nights on the trot. The speed kept him going, though he managed to grab a couple of hours' kip here and there. And there was a shower in one of the completed flats that he could use. The gaffer didn't mind. The quicker the work got done the better it was for him. And Mick was a good worker. Didn't say much, mind. But, boy, was he a grafter. He obviously really needed the cash.

Work, work, work. It had been a means in itself for so long. It had fed the restlessness. As the travelling had done all those years. On the run. Now it was a means to an end. A higher purpose. The End. Billy Porter is our friend.

He came back to the squat at the weekend. His heart sank as he wandered into the kitchen. It was a bloody mess as usual. He went to his room and dumped his bag on the bed. He took out something wrapped up in cloth and hid it under a loose floorboard.

Peter, Johnny and Muttley were all sat around the television in the front room. There was a row of beer cans on the wooden pallet on the floor that they used as a coffee table. Mick wanted to say something about the state of the house but they all seemed so intent on the screen. Engrossed in the images that flickered with blue light from the telly.

'Fucking bastards!' Peter was commenting loudly. 'Fucking fascist pigs!'

It was the evening news, and a droning voiceover was accompanied by images of riot police moving in on a line of brightly coloured vans and buses parked by a field.

'Mick,' Johnny called to him as he noticed him enter, 'come and have a look at this. It's your lot, isn't it?'

Mick sat on the edge of the sagging sofa and peered into the television. He couldn't work out at first what he was looking at, then, slowly, it began to take shape. He recognised some of the vehicles. It was the convoy.

'The pigs are on the fucking rampage,' said Peter. 'Just because they wanted to get to Stonehenge. It's a fucking fascist state.'

It all looked so unreal. Mick thought he could see Janis amidst the confusion. But he couldn't be sure. He felt he might be imagining the whole thing.

'Fucking hell, mate,' said Muttley, patting him on the arm.

They all seemed to be looking at him. Like they expected some comment from him. Like he was supposed to say something to contribute to the endless complaining that went on. But he wasn't going to say anything. He wouldn't waste his breath. He was going to do something.

He suddenly felt a wave of confusing feelings wash over him. Guilt about Janis. Relief that he had avoided her fate. A sense of purpose seemed to emerge from the madness of it all. Of things falling. Falling into place.

On the screen they could see the windscreen of a truck being smashed by police truncheons. There was something apocalyptic about it. Something that made Mick feel all the more certain of what he was to do.

'That is fucking outrageous!' Peter shouted.

They had no bloody idea. They would sit around all day and moan on and on. They would never do anything. They were lazy. Peter was always going on about the working classes but he seemed not to have done a day's work in his life. They all signed on. Did a few silly little scams that they thought were so clever. Housing benefit fraud. A bit of shoplifting. Turned the electricity meter upside down to fiddle it. Gas-meter bandits. Less than that. They thought they were Enemies of the State. They couldn't even keep the house tidy. They were useless. It was up to him. He would have to end it all. Bring things to some sort of conclusion. Not wait for some imagined day of reckoning.

He got up and started to walk silently from the room. Johnny looked up at him.

'Are you all right, Mick?'

He stopped for a second and nodded.

'Yeah,' he said. 'I'm all right.'

He was all right. Everything was going to be all right. He'd got what he needed. After weeks of searching around dodgy pubs he'd found it and had earned enough cash to get it. He would make sense of it all at last.

30

I wasn't officially part of the operational team that was to go in that morning but I wanted to be there. I had to be there. By rights it should have been my arrest. I'd done all the work. Gone and checked with Cambridgeshire. They still had Mick's fingerprints.

'We really should have destroyed these,' the swede arresting officer had said.

Thank Christ they hadn't. They also still had a record of the address of the guy he'd been released with. I'd done a match with the dabs. It was him, for fuck's sake. Him. And he was mine.

Or should have been. Of course, it all had to go by the book. Procedure. The Flying Squad team assigned to it knew me and could hardly refuse me tagging along. I could identify the suspect, after all. And I could pull rank.

The address was in this whole block of squats. Weird rows of houses like some sort of hippy township. We were plotted up for an early morning dig-out. Two Flying Squad cars, one at the front and one covering the back, and a C11 surveillance vehicle. Those in the team with pink cards had drawn firearms, but there was an Armed Response Unit on call as well in an unmarked van. A gunship, they called it. D11, all tooled up and raring to go. Most of them veterans of the Spaghetti House or Balcombe Street. Some of them ex-SPG. I hoped it wouldn't come to that. I wanted him taken quietly and cleanly.

*

The telephone jolted me into consciousness like an electric shock. I'd slept soundly that night. I'd come home in the early hours and hidden my booty and then gone to bed and dropped off easily, calm in the knowledge of what I had done for once. The bell rang again.

I kept a bowl of water and a flannel by my bed. It was an old trick I'd learned when I'd been a reporter. That way you could wipe your face and clear your head before you picked up the receiver. So no matter how sleepy or drunk or hung over you were you wouldn't make the mistake of having a semiconscious conversation and missing out on some crucial bit of information. It had been quite a while since I'd worked on the paper and might be expecting a call in the middle of the night, but old habits die hard. And I was glad of it. This might be important. I might well have to get my story straight first time. I let the phone ring a couple more times and pressed the cold flannel against my face. The night's brandy had taken its toll but my mind was shaping up. I imagined, of course, that Teddy's body might already have been discovered. So I went through my alibi. It was very simple. Yes, I had been there, I'd left at eleven (this gave me enough leeway with the time of death). No, he didn't look too good but he had a friend coming around the next morning. It would look like natural causes anyway, but one cannot be too sure. I took a breath and picked up the receiver.

'Yes?'

'Tony?'

'Yes?'

'It's Kevin.'

Kevin had been my junior on the crime desk years ago. He was now a senior correspondent on the *Illustrated*. For a second I thought that the press might already have heard about Thursby's death. But it was something else. He had got a tip-off on another story and he wanted my help. I looked at the clock. It was five-thirty. I sighed and dabbed my forehead with the damp cloth.

'All right,' I said.

319

He gave me an address and I agreed to meet him there in an hour.

*

He went to the bathroom and shaved off his beard. He swept back his hair from his face. He used some hair gel he found to comb it into the style he had had all those years ago. He looked into the cracked and stained mirror. He was himself again. He was ready now.

He went to his room and lifted the loose floorboard in his bedroom. He carefully took out the wrapped object. He slowly unwound the oil-stained cloth. He rotated the cylinder of the revolver slowly. It clicked gently, satisfying. It was good to have a gun in his hands again. It had been such a long time.

All those years ago on that crisp winter morning when he'd left his wagon to go for a stroll. He'd come back to find Mick holding up the pistol accusingly. He hadn't meant to kill Mick. It was an accident. But he had meant to kill Joe. With Mick gone he could become him. Take his identity, use his driving licence. Joe was just someone he'd hastily put together. So he got rid of him.

Being Mick was risky. He'd had to avoid the fairground circuit and anyone who might have known him. But the hippy travellers were a different world and they were easily taken in by him.

He felt a sudden grief for Mick now that he was finally dead. It had been a good disguise to become the man he had killed. Now Mick was gone for ever. Joe was gone. He was Billy again.

The grief surged through him. Friend. Mick had been his friend. But Billy Porter is our friend. Their friend. He pulled out the cylinder and loaded the gun. This was his friend. His only friend. He felt the weight of it in his hand. He looked down the barrel. The sun was coming up. He was ready.

He went into the upstairs front room and, parting a badly tacked-up curtain, looked out of the window. There was a car in the square. They had come at last. He shoved the revolver into his waistband and went to Peter's room.

Peter felt someone tapping the end of his bed. *What the fuck?*

he thought. He blinked out from under the covers. A thin beam of light chinked into the room. Dust motes danced in its pale stream. Someone was in his room.

'Who's that?' he murmured.

'It's me,' came the reply.

Mick, he thought. Mad Mick, as they'd begun to call him behind his back. What the fuck did he want?

'What is it?'

'Come on.' The voice was urgent. 'Get up.'

'What?'

'House meeting.'

'For fuck's sake.'

The curtain was being drawn open. The low dawn light fingered the room. Peter rubbed his face. Mick looked different. Beard gone and hair slicked back. A manic look on his face.

'Come on. They're coming.'

'Mick . . .'

The new face stared down at him.

'I ain't Mick,' it said, and moved in close to his. 'Don't you recognise me?'

'Stop fucking about.'

'Come on. I'm your friend.'

The new face broke into a grin and gave a low chuckle.

'Mick!' Peter shouted. 'You fucking loony!'

'I told you,' the face insisted sternly. 'I ain't Mick.'

Peter felt a quiver of fear at the eyes that stared down at him.

'Who . . .' he stammered. 'Who are you?'

The face laughed again.

'Oh, you know who I am. I'm your friend.'

There had always been something familiar about him. Something he could never quite place. There had always been something different about him. He wasn't just some ageing crustie. What was it? He who had been Mick fumbled in his pocket and pulled out a piece of paper.

'This,' he said. 'Might jog your memory.'

He unfolded it and handed it to him. Peter squinted at it in the gloom of the morning. It was a picture of Billy Porter. WORKING-CLASS HERO. He looked up at the face. Fuck, he thought. Twenty years of ageing but the features were undeniable. It was Billy Porter. He was Billy Porter.

'Jesus,' he muttered.

'Yeah.' Billy nodded. 'Something like that.'

Peter sat up in bed breathing hard. Billy had got something else from his pockets. A gun. He held it up in front of Peter's face.

'Now come on,' he said. 'Get your clothes on. I've got something to show you.'

Peter tried to wrap himself up in his bedclothes and hide but Billy was pointing the revolver at him now.

'Come on,' Billy said. 'Up we come.'

He pulled on his jeans and put on a T-shirt. Billy nodded towards the door and Peter followed him out to the front room. Billy beckoned him to the the window.

'Look,' Billy whispered harshly, holding up the pistol to the vertical, cocking its hammer.

Peter looked out and saw two groups of men getting out of cars and making their way towards the house.

*

I watched as they made for the door. I was supposed to stay in the car but I couldn't resist getting out to get a better look. This should have been my arrest, for Christ's sake. I closed the door behind me and started to walk up to the house myself.

Suddenly a shot rang out and everyone dived for cover as it ricocheted, a report echoing around the square. Crouched figures started to scuttle away from the house. I kept moving forward. I didn't give a fuck for my own safety. I wanted to be in on it.

*

Kevin's tip-off had been that the police now knew the whereabouts of Billy Porter and an arrest was about to be made. It was a real coup for Kevin, something he could sell freelance as well as run for the *Illustrated*. The thing was he didn't have time to research all of the back story and he knew that I was the best source of knowledge for that.

I met him on the corner of this square in Vauxhall. He had a photographer with him. Not like the snatch men of old. These guys had huge lenses on their cameras. Like rocket launchers. They could get a clear picture from miles away.

We watched as a group of plainclothes officers approached the house. The photographer was firing away and moving about to get the best angle. I had a horrible empty-stomached hangover. But I was glad to be there. There was a sort of bleary-eyed sense to it. This could be the end of the whole affair. We heard the shot and the confusion that followed.

'Did you get that? Did you get that?' Kevin was panting at the photographer as we all crouched for cover instinctively.

There was a hiatus as the explosion receded. A brief silence and calm, as if the bullet had sucked everything into a vacuum for a moment. Then someone in the house started singing.

*

Peter stared at the shattered glass of the window through the thin blue haze of smoke from the discharged revolver. He gave a short nervous giggle.

'Fucking hell.'

'This is now,' Billy announced. 'No more waiting.'

'Steady on.'

'This is happening now.' He held up the gun. 'This is this.'

'Take it easy, Mick.'

'The name ain't Mick, is it?'

'No, I mean . . .'

'It's Billy. Billy what?'

'Billy Porter.'

'And what is Billy Porter?'

'Sorry?'

'I said what is Billy Porter?'

Billy was almost shouting.

'What?'

'You know,' he insisted, cocking the hammer of the gun and holding it against Peter's head.

'I don't. Oh, please, I'm sorry. I don't know.'

'You know,' Billy repeated, in a soft voice now.

'Please.'

'The song. You know the song, don't you? Sing it.'

'Billy Porter,' Peter croaked.

'That's it.'

'Is our friend.'

'Go on.'

'Is our friend, is our friend.'

'Louder. Come on, sing out, boy.'

Johnny slept through the whole thing. Muttley heard the commotion and scrambled out of bed. He pulled on a pair of trousers and went down to the front door.

*

The D11 gunship started up and moved towards the house. Immediate Action Drill. The three-man team checked their weapons as the van screeched to a halt. Flak-jacketed, bristling with equipment, they bundled out and took positions for rapid entry. It was their operation now. The suits had fucked up badly. It was up to them to finish it.

Muttley stumbled out of the front door and found himself surrounded by crouching uniformed figures, their weapons aimed at him.

'On the floor! Now!' they shouted at him.

He hit the deck.

*

I was up close to the house now. The D11 team were standing over a prone figure. The door to the house was swinging open.

I rushed inside. I could hear the singing coming from the upstairs front room. I tiptoed up the stairs.

'Come on!' came another voice. 'Come and get me, you fuckers!'

It suddenly came to me that this was what he wanted. It was a very public suicide attempt. But I wasn't going to let him have that. Those trigger-happy bastards from D11 would be only too ready to oblige. Christ, we'd got tooled up over the years. Porter himself had been part of that. I'd seen it all. And I was tired of it. Tired. It struck me then that maybe I wanted it all over for myself too. All over. Jeannie, the only woman I'd ever loved. David — I owed him for his father. My best mate. My buck. I wasn't even armed. But I was ready. I felt an exhilarating sense of recklessness.

I walked into the room. There was a spiky-haired boy on his hands and knees. Billy Porter stood over him with a pistol against his temple. He looked up as I entered. His eyes glared at me.

'Hello, Billy,' I said.

I felt calm. Prepared.

'Get back!' he spat out at me. 'Get back or I'll kill this fucker.'

'Please,' groaned the boy.

He wasn't singing any more.

'Why don't you kill me, Billy? Like you killed the others. Like you killed Dave.'

'I'm warning you. Stay back.'

'What's the matter, Billy? Lost your bottle?'

Now. I never felt so alive. So close to death. Everything had led up to this moment. This was now. It all suddenly fell into place. Made sense. Another breath and it would all be over. I put my palms up and edged forward.

'Come on, Billy,' I said. 'It's over.'

'It ain't over. It ain't fucking over.'

There was an awful pain in his eyes. A pain I shared. All the years falling away. We'd both had enough.

'Come on, Billy. Let's go home, eh?'

He closed his eyes for a second and nodded. He brought up the pistol and aimed it at my face. I closed my eyes and waited for the shot. Someone was thundering up the stairs behind me. I felt a blow against my back as someone pushed past me. There was a shot. I thought: this is it. This is the end. As I recovered my balance I saw Billy Porter hurled to the floor by the force of a bullet from the gun of one of the D11 officers who had stormed into the room. He was standing over Porter now. The boy was snivelling at his feet, his nose against his boots. Sobbing in gratitude.

'It's all right, son,' he said, patting the spiky head. 'It's all right.'

*

The photographer got some good shots of the body-bag being carried out of the squat. Kevin was really animated. He'd got a good story. That's what it was all about. I knew the excitement of that, to be there on the scene and to have something really explosive to file. Front-page stuff. And I'd be able to help him with the background to the whole case. I'd seen it all through. It was Kevin's story, but it was my book. I could do it now. I had all the material. I had the End. It wouldn't take long and it could be rushed into print while the public interest in it was still fresh.

A killer brought to book. All the details pieced together for consumption. And the moral of it all? Well, there didn't seem any moral certainties left. Porter's story hardly had the power to shock any more. Later that year a policeman was hacked to death in a riot on a Tottenham housing estate. Violence escalating, police tactics becoming more brutal. Society seemed in a war of attrition with itself.

As for Thursby's diaries, well, they were another matter. I had to be careful with them; after all, I wasn't exactly their legitimate owner. But they were mine by right of possession and I would guard them jealously. They were a source, a word-hoard of scandal and gossip that I would be able to draw from. I had taken a life, admissions and revelations that could eclipse my own desire for confession. My own misdeeds hidden for ever. The writer, telling all, revealing nothing. I had the power of revenge for all those years of fruitless muck-raking. All the details, the reputations laid bare, the secrets I could use. And I would use them. I wasn't sure how yet. But I would think of something.